CATHERINE DUNBAR

FALSE IMAGES

"English historian Dunbar, who won the Mary Elgin award for her debut book, has now written a first mystery, a romantic thriller that probes the undercurrents of family relationships, in the captivation, if slightly breathless, tradition of Mary Higgins Clark.... Dunbar's facile style and intricate plotting, as well as her haunting images of English family life and its secrets, will enthrall readers."

—*Publishers Weekly*

FALSE IMAGES

CATHERINE DUNBAR

ibooks
new york
www.ibooks.net

DISTRIBUTED BY SIMON & SCHUSTER, INC.

For Fay and Owen
With Love

A Publication of ibooks, inc.

Copyright © 2000 by Catherine Dunbar

Introduction copyright © 2004 Barbara Peters

An ibooks, inc. Book

ibooks, inc.
24 West 25th Street
New York, NY 10010

The ibooks World Wide Web Site Address is:
http://www.ibooks.net

The Poisoned Pen Press World Wide Web Site Address is:
http://www.poisonedpenpress.com

ISBN 0-7434-7976-9
First ibooks, inc. printing January 2004
10 9 8 7 6 5 4 3 2 1

Printed in the U.S.A.

FALSE IMAGES
An Introduction by Barbara Peters

A lifelong fan of British mysteries as well as a major importer of English titles for The Poisoned Pen Bookstore, I am rarely surprised by some overlooked gem. *False Images* by Catherine Dunbar is certainly an exception. While the author has written several historical sagas, as the Brits say, and won the Mary Elgin Award for her debut in that field, her first mystery snuck by me until it appeared on my desk as a submission for publication.

This is all the more shocking since it is a truly excellent book embracing most of my favorite things: an intelligent heroine with an interesting profession (restoring art), difficult family dynamics (difficult, not *weird* which is so often the case today in this age of intense psychodrama), a dashing lover, a killer with a rational agenda (okay, he's a nut, but at least you can understand *why* he's bent on exacting revenge), and heapings of suspense.

False Images takes place in London, but—did I mention the lovely country house? And of course, in a high stakes art world, the money?

Leone Fleming leads a quiet life by choice, sharing space with her friend Philippa, whose increasingly chic gallery off the north end of the Portobello Road attracts the great and the good. Leone spends most of her leisure time with her father, the distinguished and high-profile judge Sir Richard Fleming. Ever since the night her mother said goodbye so calmly and then vanished forever, Leone has wanted to protect Sir

Richard from further hurt. In fact, so close is her tie to her father that it once split her off from her lover, Jack, a man not about to settle for second place.

But now, Jack is back. That sends out one little ripple. And Leone has a new commission, the cleaning of a charming portrait executed in 1742 by Walter Devis. It's come from Whitcombs, a reliable house. Why then the fury of Piers Carlton, son of the painting's owner, at her work? It makes huge waves. Then comes a shocking murder.

Dunbar controls her plot nicely, creating a clear sense of menace as she intelligently twists the action of her romantic thriller. And her characterizations are beautifully vivid. *Publishers Weekly* in its glowing review ends, "Dunbar's facile style and intricate plotting, as well as her haunting images of English family life and its secrets, will enthrall readers." Its sister publication, *Library Journal*, sums up: "Art history and art galleries mix with mischief, as Leone sorts out the bad guys and her feelings toward an ex-lover. Excellent plotting and detail, scary manipulations by the villains, and swiftly paced prose have made this a hot item in Britain. Highly recommended."

I couldn't have said it better myself. I'm delighted that this hit for Poisoned Pen Press in 2000 will gain a much wider audience through its ibooks publication.

The mystery I now have to solve is, where is a second suspense novel from Dunbar?

Enjoy.

—Barbara Peters
Senior Editor
Poisoned Pen Press
January 2004

Acknowledgments

I should like to thank all those people who so gener-
ously gave of their time to assist with background
material for this book and in particular: Dr Diane
Waller, Chair Elect of the Federal Arts Therapists
Board, CPSM, for her help on art psychotherapy; D.S.
Darren Curtis for his advice on police procedure and
Philippa Abrahams and Christopher Wellby for
sharing with me the art of picture conservation.

—Catherine Dunbar

Prologue

The room was filled with the scent of lilies. The sweet, heavy smell was so pungent it tickled her nostrils, making her want to sneeze. She wouldn't, of course, couldn't, for to do so would give away her hiding place. Even in her dream Leone could feel her heart beat just that little bit faster at the thought of discovery.

Carefully she eased her position. From across the shadowed hallway she could hear her mother playing the Steinway in the drawing-room beyond, her light fingers skilfully gliding over the notes. She loved that sound. Loved sitting here, hidden behind the thick curtains of the bay window, the summer sun beating through the window-panes across her back, listening to the notes as they rose and fell, carrying her with them. It was far more exciting than being stuck with Kitty, her nursemaid, at the top of the house.

Leone drew her knees closer to her chest, hugging them more tightly. In her sleep she stirred, a faint knot of apprehension catching at her.

She knew what was about to happen—knew because she'd had this dream so many times before.

The music had stopped. She could hear the sound of her mother's high stiletto heels crossing the hallway, hear the whisper of her dress against her silk stockings.

Then she felt the cool rush of air as the curtain was swept back and her mother was standing before her, laughing softly. 'So this is your secret hiding-place, is it, little bear?'

Every detail of her mother's face was clear to Leone at that moment: the high cheekbones and slightly aquiline nose, her wide, dark-flecked green eyes, every carefully brushed strand of copper-red hair. Everything was so clear and intensified.

'Don't worry, your hiding place is safe with me,' her mother whispered, bending down to kiss her. 'Be good while I'm away and do what Kitty tells you, won't you? And I'll be back for supper, in time to tuck you in.'

Her mother turned then and clipped her way across the wooden floor of the hall, pulling the front door open. It was windy outside. The skirt of her blue dress, reaching to mid-calf, swirled about her legs in the breeze.

'Love you, little bear.'

Now was the moment. Now. Leone stood up. She tried to call out but, though she opened her mouth, no words came. It was as if the air were pressing down about her, too thick, too heavy.

Why couldn't she call out after her mother? Why couldn't she warn her? On that fateful day, not knowing what lay ahead, she hadn't been able to stop her mother from leaving, either.

This time might be different. She could change everything.

She started to run then—out through the open door and down the stone path. Her breath was coming in short, sharp gasps. Even now, she could feel her sandalled feet pounding against the hard stone slabs warmed by the summer's sun, could feel the wooden gate rough beneath her hands as she frantically tried to push it open.

'Please…' She was sobbing now as she fumbled with the stiff catch. But even as she pushed open the gate and stepped out on to the pavement, she knew she was too late.

The car had gone. The car which would take her mother to her death.

In the past this was always where Leone would awaken, whimpering and gasping for breath. But tonight it was different. The dream continued. Tonight she was walking back up the path towards the house and, in the way that time shifts in dreams, it was much later now, colder. The house was in shadow, the front door tightly closed.

She came up the steps, lifting her hand to the door, then hesitated. Something was wrong. The hair on the back of her neck prickled. She shuddered as she withdrew her hand.

What was it that made her so afraid? Was it simply the knowledge that, now her mother had gone, inside the house she would be greeted only by a ghastly all-consuming emptiness? Or was it something more?

She stretched out her hand again. She must force herself to find out, to go in. But as she reached out, her fingers felt as if they were pressing against a great weight. It was as if her mind were fighting against her body, struggling to prevent her from opening that door. Protecting her from what lay within. Panic settled in her stomach, like a deep cold cavern. She felt suddenly afraid, aware of unseen dangers closing in on her.

She awoke with a jolt then, gasping for air, damp with perspiration. Her fingers clutched the bedcovers, the muscles of her shoulders tensed as tight as any prize-fighter's. It was always like this after the dreams; the tension, the half-fear of the memories stored away inside.

Slowly, she forced herself to sit up, breathing deeply to steady herself. Then she climbed out of bed and went across to the bathroom to splash her face. The water was ice-cold; the shock of it made her shiver. She hung for a moment over the basin, eyes closed, then slowly she straightened and dried herself off. In the mirror she could see her reflection. She was very like her mother in looks; the same green eyes and high cheekbones, the same nose. Only her hair was different; wheat blonde and fine, not thick and full like her mother's Pre-Raphaelite curls.

She walked into her sitting room and settled herself on the small two-seater sofa. She felt calmer now.

Leone wondered what had made the dream return—she hadn't had it for over a year now. And why had it changed tonight? Was it simply that a missing piece of the past, a childhood memory, hitherto buried so deep, was trying to emerge, or was it, rather, a portent of the future? She didn't know.

But she was certain of one thing. The dream would come again. And when it did, she would have to have the courage to open that door and find out what lay beyond.

Chapter One

'Sir Richard? Would you like to come through now?'

Richard Fleming put down his paper and followed the mini-skirted assistant through the double glass doors. The 'On Air' studio light was flashing at the far end of the corridor. Richard glanced at his watch. Ten minutes before his programme slot. Plenty of time.

He walked into the hospitality room—or hostility room, as it was irreverently referred to at the radio station. It was small and quite without charm, with low black sofas crammed tightly against its cream-coloured walls. Not exactly the sort of place to raise your spirits, thought Richard wryly, taking in his unglamorous surroundings.

Yet for all that he preferred radio interviews. The handful of live television debates he'd done hadn't really been a success. He didn't have the looks for it, for one, and these days Joe Public had definite ideas of what was wanted. Besides, he was too impatient to put up with all the intricate games of television. Radio was infinitely more subtle, relying on brains rather than gloss for success. Much much more to his liking.

He sat down, placing his black calf briefcase carefully by his feet. Know your strengths, his father had once told him, and your enemy's weaknesses. And though that advice had been directed towards felling the school bully in the playground, it was a maxim to which Richard still clung.

His strengths—his native wit, his sharp incisive mind, his terrier-like determination—he'd put to good use. He'd clawed his way up through the legal system, and now had the satisfaction of knowing that as a highcourt judge—with every likelihood of making the Appeal Courts—he had gone as far as he'd dared hope.

As for his enemy's weaknesses? He had always known those. Instinctively.

'Sir Richard?' Sarah, the elfin-like producer of the John Brodie *News and Views* programme put her blonde, short-cropped head round the door. 'Shouldn't be too long now. John's just tying up the last interview. Can I get you something while you wait? A coffee, perhaps?'

'Just a glass of water for the interview, thank you.'

'Of course. Evian do?'

'Perfectly.'

Sarah smiled. She liked Sir Richard. A bit formidable, but he always did the job he was called in to do. And that voice. She could still remember the first time she'd heard him speak on radio about a year ago on *Question Time*. He was so persuasive. She'd almost found herself nodding in agreement, even though he was expounding the merits of bringing back capital punishment, a notion which went against her every liberal instinct. He had a reputation for showing offenders about as much compassion as Attila the Hun, but she'd always found him unfailingly polite. Not like some of the egotistical bores who came in, prancing around as if they were God's gift and treating them all like dirt.

'Right then, I'll leave you in peace for the moment, shall I?' she suggested, seeing him lift his black briefcase on to the magazine-covered table in front of him. 'John should be ready in about five minutes. I'll call you then.'

'That'll be fine. Thank you.'

Richard watched Sarah's tall, slender frame disappearing purposefully down the corridor and then turned his attention back to his briefcase. He clicked open the catches and delved beneath the mountain of papers, drawing out the six pages of notes his clerk had carefully typed out for him for this afternoon's debate on the government's role in determining prison sentencing. As he began to scan through them, one headline in particular caught his attention: 'The Catherston Murder Trial'.

He paused, his square-tipped fingers tightening around the edges of the papers. He'd been the presiding judge on that case and remembered it well; it was a particularly gruesome affair.

Joan Catherston had murdered her husband, stabbing him to death with a nine-inch kitchen knife, puncturing his body twenty-eight times. She had claimed self-defence, citing her husband's abusive behaviour, but he hadn't been convinced. There was too much that didn't fit. Her history of jealous rages when she'd discovered his affairs, for one.

When he'd sentenced her to life in prison, though, women's groups had been outraged.

Richard had been unmoved. He was not afraid of unpopularity. If a judge were to perform properly there could be no room for sentiment.

Now with all the discussions about sentencing being aired, the women's rights groups again were in full cry.

Richard, however, stood by his decision. As he so often told his daughter, Leone, it wasn't always possible to balance Justice and Mercy perfectly. And when it came down to it, if he had to settle for one, it would be Justice every time.

Leone might be impressed by Portia's speech in *The Merchant of Venice* but in his view, the qualities of mercy were greatly exaggerated.

He pushed a hand through his thin grey hair and then leaned forward to return the notes to his briefcase, closing the lid with a snap.

He'd have to be careful not to voice his opinions too vigorously on such matters tonight, though. The studio audience was a fragile, sentimental crowd and he wanted to win the debate, after all.

Winning was important to Richard. It always had been.

~

While her father was plotting his line of attack, Leone Fleming was standing by the huge north-facing window looking out across the Portobello rooftops, her thin arms wrapped around her as if in defence against the irritants of the past twenty-four hours. It had been a day of minor catastrophes.

It was late afternoon, the last of the wintry grey light filtering across the polished oak floor of the gallery. Too late now to try to sort out the last, and definitely the most complicated problem of the day.

Behind her, propped on an easel under the skylight, rested the source of her exasperation: a small painting, an engaging family portrait of the Wallace family, by the eighteenth-century British painter Arthur Devis.

At first glance the task had seemed straightforward. Certainly when Whitcombs Gallery had sent it in the previous day to be restored for one of their forthcoming exhibitions, she had thought it would be a fairly quick, routine job. The four photographs she'd taken of the picture—two of the front of the canvas, two of the back, one set with and the other without the frame—hadn't revealed anything untoward when she had developed them that morning in the tiny darkroom at the back of the studio.

But as soon as she had begun to test an edge of the portrait for the first phase of restoration, taking her cotton swab stick dipped in isopropyl alcohol and gently removing the old layer of varnish, she had sensed something was wrong. It wasn't just the tell-tale signs of changing colour on the swabs she'd used—an ominous darkening showing the removal of more than just varnish—but something more, something instinctive.

Her seven years of restoring works of art had given her a sixth sense about irregularities in paintings: a line here, a background there, a face looking awkwardly modern in an old-style portrait.

Mostly it was just over-zealousness on the part of previous restorers, would-be artists who couldn't resist repainting and re-touching this, removing and rearranging that, often horribly oblivious of, and quite insensitive to, the painter's original conception. Even the Mona Lisa, it was said, had not escaped and had lost her eyebrows in days gone by to an over-enthusiastic restorer.

Sometimes, however, it was something more than a careless sleight-of-hand. Leone had seen her share of forgeries.

She regarded the Devis painting solemnly from a distance for a moment, her green eyes narrowing slightly as she took in its every detail, then threaded her way past a haphazard collection of frames and partly restored canvases until she stood in front of it.

It was a charming enough piece. The Wallace family were gathered together in an elegant drawing-room and the interior, typical of Devis's early style, showed carefully measured proportions and exquisitely handled detail. Sir George was portrayed leaning against a small table, his globe and telescopes to hand. His wife, resplendent in a blue gown, was seated on a high-backed chair beside him, her youngest child on her knee. With the eldest boy, flute in hand, standing in mannered pose behind his father, and his two young siblings kneeling to the right of their mother, intent on building a house of cards, it was a scene evoking marital contentment worthy of a Richardson novel.

Leone took a step back and thrust her hands into the pockets of her beige linen jacket. The charming naivety of the portrait, the obvious use of lay figures, was so distinctive of Devis's style it couldn't be a forgery, surely? Besides, when she'd rung Whitcombs Gallery that afternoon to check on the picture's provenance, her contact had insisted that this was a well-documented piece. It had been executed in 1742, and had stayed within the Wallace family ever since.

Yet there were hints of other brushstrokes, she was sure of that. It could of course, have been Devis himself painting over his own picture. That was common enough. Goya, for instance, had painted the portrait of Dona Isabel de Porcel directly over a completed male portrait and the dark curve of the man's eyebrow could still be seen on Isabel's chin. But Leone wasn't entirely convinced that was the case here.

She rapidly catalogued the stylistic elements she knew she should expect from Devis, and those that seemed incongruous. Was there one homogeneous style or evidence of more than one hand?

She stretched out and pulled over the mounted microscope, and was about to change the lens to a more powerful x35 to examine the painting more carefully, when the telephone started to ring.

It was Philippa, one of her closest friends and partner in the gallery which they had set up together two years before. Ringing, by the sound of it, from a very crowded and lively wine bar.

'Leone! I'm glad I caught you.' Her voice was bubbly, she was obviously enjoying herself. But then Phil usually did. 'I was afraid you might have left hours ago.'

'No, still here, for my sins.'

'Listen, I'm in deep shit.' Philippa raised her voice as the buzz of high octane chatter rose in the background. 'I need an address and number from the diary on my desk. I've an appointment first thing tomorrow with a new artist and for the life of me I can't remember where his studio is. And I ought to ring and confirm, I suppose…'

Leone smiled. Phil was notoriously chaotic. It was part of her charm. 'Hold on and I'll go and check for you.' She put down the phone on the table and then picked it up again. 'It may take a while,' she warned.

That was the understatement of the year. Deciphering the hieroglyphics on the pharaohs' tombs would be a lesser task than sorting through Phil's disorganised jumble.

Leone switched on the lights to the gallery below and went downstairs. Phil's hideously cluttered desk was at the back of the room, piled high with the usual assortment of papers. But this evening, by very good fortune—or had Janie, the receptionist, finally been brave enough to make an attempt at tidying up?—the diary was on the top of the pile.

She picked it up and flicked through to the relevant page. There it was: Steve Ross—29 Arcadia Road, followed by a scribbled note to the effect that the artist had been recommended by Larry Kutz. Praise indeed.

By the time Leone had returned to the phone the background noise of the wine bar seemed to have increased by several decibels.

She had to shout the address and phone number down the line to Phil.

'Got it. Thanks.' Leone could imagine Phil writing down the instructions on some stray wine-list. She hoped to heaven she remembered to take it with her when she left.

'No problem.'

'Listen, what are you up to now?' asked Phil. Leone heard her break off to whisper, 'Well, if you insist Paul, but this must *definitely* be my last.' Then: 'I mean, if you're finished at the studio, why don't you join us? There's a crowd of us going on to the Pharmacy later on.'

Leone hesitated. 'I can't. I've promised to have supper with Father tonight.'

'Ah.' Phil knew better than to suggest Leone break such an arrangement. Evenings with her father was sacrosanct. 'Well, tell him from me that I thought his interview this afternoon was terrific.'

Leone groaned. She'd missed it. With all the confusion of the picture she'd failed to tune in. And he was bound to ask her opinion of it this evening.

'You didn't forget?'

"Fraid so.'

'Oh, lord.' There was a brief pause. 'Well, never mind, he need never know. Just tell him you particularly liked his jibe at the MP about not mixing penal policy with party politics.'

Leone laughed. Phil was a dab hand at the art of bluffing. She'd always had that capacity, even as a diminutive eleven-year-old when Leone had first met her at boarding school.

'So you're sure you won't come? Matt's here you know. Been asking after you.'

'Has he?' Leone was secretly flattered. Matt was a friend of Paul, Phil's latest man of the moment. A hunk, no less. She'd met him briefly at a party she'd been to with Phil the weekend before.

'Put in a good word for me, will you? And for God's sake, be *subtle.*'

'What? So you don't want me telling him you fancy him like mad, then?'

'Phil!' Leone wouldn't put it past her to do such a heinous thing.

Phil laughed. 'Don't worry, Leone. Trust me. I have it under control. I shall prise him out of Kate's clutches, immediately. You're missing a treat, though. Sure you won't come?'

'Positive.' She was secretly tempted, though. She adored her father but he could be heavy going and the Pharmacy was always fun. Phil's boisterous crowd were sometimes a little hard to take *en masse* but tonight their ebullience would have been a good foil to her mood. And there'd be the added bonus of Matt Renshaw, too. 'Look, must get a move on,' she said quickly, before she allowed Phil to lead her astray. 'See you tomorrow then. Have a great evening.'

'I shall. I'll be in latish…'

'Fine. And if I'm not here then I'll be at the Courtauld. I think I may have to have the portrait x-rayed.'

'Sounds like a problem looming.'

'I hope not.' It had started to rain. Leone could hear the droplets beating against the skylight. 'I'll know more tomorrow.'

'Right. Listen, have to go.' A man's voice sounded in the background, muffled and not a little slurred. It was Paul, Leone supposed, telling her to get a move on. 'Thanks for the address.'

'Any time.'

Leone put down the receiver and went across to close the window. It was now dark outside, the sky a brownish purple. A few smudged stars showed between the clouds.

In the street below people were scurrying home, side-stepping the puddles, heads down against the driving rain. A discarded white plastic bag was fluttering across the pavement, in and out of the light and dark.

Leone moved back across the room and switched off the extractor fan—she was always careful to have it on when she was working with solvents, she got blinding headaches if she didn't—then started down the stairs to the gallery.

Her coat was hanging on the stand, but the umbrella was missing. Phil, no doubt, had pinched it earlier that afternoon and, no doubt, would leave it in the wine bar.

She turned on the alarm, switched off the lights, and then made a hasty exit. The alarm, always temperamental, flickered ominously for a moment, then settled to a steady red glow. Outside, in the shelter of the doorway, Leone slipped on her blessedly thick, woollen coat.

The rain seemed to be easing. If she were lucky she would get home before the next downpour.

She started to walk briskly up the hill towards Notting Hill Gate.

⌒

He sat in darkness listening to the rain. He preferred the dark. It helped him concentrate his thoughts. He needed that. He needed to think what to do about Leone Fleming. And he had to do something, that much was clear. What he'd just heard made it imperative.

He flexed his fingers carefully, leaning back until his head touched the cold grey wall behind him. He sat without moving, the different textures of the night slowly filtrating the room.

This needed careful planning. His mind turned over all the possibilities and probabilities: he wanted his retribution to be slow and sweet. No one screwed up his life and got away with it. No one.

After a while he lifted his head and smiled. Oh, but it was a perfect plan. He was going to enjoy this. He was going to enjoy this very much.

Chapter Two

'My God, you're drenched.'

'Am a bit.' Leone shook out her coat, which now bore more resemblance to a bedraggled mammoth than anything a designer would lay claim to. The heavens had opened with a vengeance just as she'd turned into Ladbroke Grove and she'd cursed herself for deciding to leave the car at home that morning.

'Don't say you walked *all* the way from the gallery in this?' her father asked, laying aside his newspaper.

'It's not so very far.'

'How odd you are sometimes, Leone.'

Leone had to smile. Her father still on occasion treated her like a child. She was twenty-eight years old, for heaven's sake.

'Actually,' she said, hoping that her voice carried conviction, 'there's something invigorating about walking in the rain.' She shook out the last raindrops from her long hair and walked through from the hallway into the light, elegant drawing-room. It was a spacious room, expensively papered in dark green, with high ceilings and long sash windows at either end. A fire was blazing in the hearth, flames licking at the iron throat of the grate. 'So how was your day?' She crossed over and perched herself on the arm of his chair. 'I thought the interview was terribly good. Were you pleased with it?' She couldn't admit to having missed it.

He took a sip of whisky, obviously gratified. 'Thought I handled that slippery MP rather well, I must say. I'm all for stiffer punishments but the government's policy of putting sentencing back into the hands of the politician is definitely to be discouraged. As I said on the programme, it simply doesn't make sense for people who have neither seen nor heard the victims or witnesses, nor even listened to the arguments at the trial, to be responsible for determining the actual time served. Sheer nonsense, I say. Discretion should remain with the judiciary.' He looked across at her, his eyes sharp and alert. 'Anyway,' he went on, taking another sip of his drink, 'I won the vote at the end of the programme, I'm glad to say. Despite all that badgering by those women's groups. Damned nuisance, they are. Won't ever admit they've got their facts wrong.'

For a man in his position her father was still a remarkable chauvinist, thought Leone. He had little time for female lawyers. Yet, paradoxically, he'd been devastated when she wouldn't follow in his footsteps and read for the bar. She'd never expected such passion from him on the subject. Perhaps, since she was his only child, his ambitions for her had overcome his prejudices. On the other hand maybe it was because he had so little regard for what he called the 'wishy-washy' art subjects at which she had excelled at school.

She glanced at him now, sitting in the deep rose-coloured armchair, head tilted slightly back as if deep in thought. He seemed particularly tired this evening; his fleshy cheeks had hardly a hint of colour and he looked far older than his sixty years. It worried her to see him so exhausted, especially since his recent operation.

She moved across the hearth and sat down in the chair opposite him. She was still chilled from her walk in the rain and she leaned forward slightly to hold out her hands to the fire. As she did so, he opened his eyes and smiled at her. He had never been a strikingly handsome man—his features were far too coarse and irregular for that—but when he smiled his eyes, a deep, vital blue, gave him an almost mesmerising vibrancy.

When Leone had been away from home at boarding school, it was that intensity of colour that she remembered. That and his voice: beautiful, deep, persuasive. And even as a child she had seen how both could easily be capable of swaying a jury. The power of presentation: far more potent than truth.

Her father had finished his whisky. She stood up, stretching out her hand for his empty glass.

'Would you like another one?'

'That would be kind.'

She went over to the corner drinks cabinet and drew out a bottle of Laphroaig, pouring one for her father and one for herself. Then she came back to the fireplace.

'So…' Her father took the glass from her. 'Did you have a successful day?'

'Not bad. I've finished the vast maritime piece at last.'

'The van de Velde?'

She nodded.

'And were you pleased with it?'

'Pretty much so. The tears mended well.' The result of wild goings-on at a teenage party. She'd been appalled when the owners had told her. Obviously it wasn't only in the fantasy world of *Yellow Pages* advertisements that such ravages took place.

'You'll be glad of the space cleared, I should think. You must have been awfully cramped.'

'Not really. Masses of room.' She waited. It was usually at this point that her father made some unflattering comment about the gallery. He hadn't liked the idea of her taking it on with Phil, not least because its position off the north end of Portobello Road put her right in the middle of the North Kensington estates. He was forever trying to persuade her to move to somewhere he considered more suitable.

Leone, however, loved that part of Ladbroke Grove with its small Portuguese community, their delicatessens, coffee houses and restaurants. She certainly wasn't about to move. The house they'd converted suited them well, whatever her father might think, with Phil's gallery occupying the enlarged ground floor and Leone's restoration business on the floor above. Besides, Phil had strong ideas of where she wanted her gallery to be and, despite Richard's insistence, Knightsbridge did not appeal.

Leone leaned back in her chair. She adored her father and they were very close, but he could be incredibly dogmatic and dominating. After her mother died her father had become overly protective of her. Now, because he'd been used to running both of their lives for so long, he was reluctant to relinquish his hold. Phil called him a bit of a control freak, but that wasn't it really. He just cared for her. A little too much, sometimes perhaps. She tried to be firm with him, to ignore his meddling, but sometimes it was easier just to go with the flow and agree with him.

But for all his faults, he'd been a wonderful father. All through her childhood he'd put her first, managing to juggle his career and private affairs so as to allow himself time to spend with her. He'd been a steadfast rock throughout her life. But sometimes she wished he'd let her have some room to manoeuvre. She wasn't six years old any more, and she was more than capable of running her own life. Try to tell *him* that though, Leone thought to herself.

She took a sip of whisky, the rich peaty taste lingering on her tastebuds. She could feel herself beginning to relax at last, the tension in her fingers easing against the icy coolness of her glass.

In the kitchen at the back of the house Fernanda, her father's Portuguese housekeeper, was humming softly as she finished the final preparations for their supper. Leone loved that faintly mournful sound. How often as a teenager had she sat on the high wooden stool in that cosy kitchen and watched Fernanda work?

It was all so familiar. So easy. Perhaps that was why she had felt slightly apprehensive about moving back here. She had the uncomfortable sense of the Sirens beckoning.

Yet when her father had his heart by-pass operation last summer and Leone had, quite simply, needed to be on hand for him, it seemed the obvious solution. There was the basement flat, entirely separate from the main house, enticingly vacant. What could have been more convenient? It meant giving up the flat in

Shepherd's Bush she'd rented for the past two years, but it seemed a small price to pay for her own peace of mind. She told herself it was only a short-term move, just until her father felt fully recovered. But she was conscious of the repercussions of such a decision. She didn't want to feel she was moving backwards at a time in her life when she ought to have been moving forward. Jack, she knew, would never have approved. But then, Jack had never approved of anything where her father was concerned.

'What was that?' She was aware that her father was speaking. 'Sorry, I was miles away.'

'I was asking if you'd remembered to book your car in for a service tomorrow.'

'Oh, lord.' She had, but she'd have to cancel it if she were going to take the Devis in for Rupert to have a look at. 'Slight change of plans,' Leone replied. 'I've got to take a picture across to the Courtauld in the morning. There's something I want them to x-ray for me.'

'Oh?' He straightened slightly. She could sense his interest. 'Some sort of problem?'

She settled back and told him about the discrepancies in the Devis portrait.

Her father pulled a cigarette from the packet on the table beside him and lit it. He leaned back, exhaling slowly. 'And what did Whitcombs have to say when you told them? Shouldn't imagine they were too pleased.'

'They weren't. They need it for their exhibition. They were absolutely adamant I must be mistaken,' she told him, 'but I'll have to speak to them again tomorrow. I'll need their consent to take the portrait to the Courtauld.' Especially since she was hoping that they would pay for the x-rays.

'And who did you say was the artist?' her father enquired.

'Arthur Devis.'

'Can't say I've even heard of the fellow.'

'I'm not surprised. He's not particularly well known. I thought I might raid your library after supper to see what else I could dig up about him. There's a rather good book in there on British portrait painters. I remember looking at it for some background on John Hamilton Mortimer.' She put down her empty glass and glanced across at her father.

He was staring down at the fire. The art books had mostly belonged to her mother. By tacit agreement, they seldom spoke of her. Even now, it was painful to him. She knew they must have loved each other very much. She remembered those first awful weeks after her mother's death when he'd seemed near breaking-point. She'd heard him pacing his room night after night. He'd ceased to eat, becoming progressively more silent and reclusive. If his widowed sister, Mary, hadn't taken them both in hand, she dreaded to think what might have happened. She'd been almost afraid of him in those days, fearful of what he might do.

She poured herself another whisky. 'Well, I'll have a nose around after supper, if that's all right with you.'

'Do that, yes.'

Leone studied her father. There was a constrained tightness to him tonight that troubled her; an all-consuming weariness. She wasn't sure what had brought on his present mood.

A difficult case? No, she didn't think it was that. And it couldn't have been the interview. That had gone famously, by all accounts.

Later, during dinner, she tried to find out what was worrying him, but he was a true Grand Master at evading questions, side-tracking the conversation on to his forthcoming trip to Bordeaux. Wine, and claret in particular, was one of her father's great loves. Many an evening he'd tried to instruct Leone on the merits of the different vineyards, on the quality of the various wines, on their colour, limpidity and viscosity. It was important to him that she should know how they were made, how they looked and tasted. Leone herself would have been more than content with a cheap bottle of Australian Chardonnay but, experienced in the art of humouring him, she was politic enough to keep this to herself.

After dinner she left him savouring the last of the Château d'Issan and went up to the library. It was on the first floor overlooking their own small garden and the communal garden beyond. Her father did most of his work when he was home in the library and his huge mahogany desk dominated the room. Leone pushed open the door breathing in the familiar smell of cigars, leather and old books.

There were over two thousand books in here. Her father was an avid collector, his particular passion being medieval history. If he hadn't read for the bar, he always said, he would have pursued his love of the Middle Ages, presumably becoming a crusty old professor in one of the universities. She wondered how it would have suited him to give out lectures rather than penal sentences.

Leone flicked on the lights. The art books were kept predominantly on the right-hand side—a pristine collection, not like her own battlescarred and well-used hoard—and were stacked across three shelves, stretching from floor to ceiling.

She found the books she was looking for and spread them out on the desk. There were only a few references to Devis, not all of them complimentary, but it was enough to give her a clearer impression of the man and his methods. She made a few cursory notes, returned the books to their shelves and then went back downstairs to the drawing-room.

The only sound in the room was the loud metallic click of the clock on the mantelpiece. Her father was reading and Fernanda had long since left to catch her bus home.

He put down his paper and looked up as Leone sat down opposite him. 'Successful?'

'Pretty much so, yes.' At least she wouldn't seem completely uninformed when she spoke to Whitcombs the next morning. 'Gives me a bit of ammunition, anyway.'

'Quite right. A good healthy piece of out-manoeuvring never went amiss.'

She smiled. Her father could never resist stressing the importance of stratagems. 'I think I ought to be going, actually.'

'Must you?'

She nodded. 'It's almost eleven. And I should store these notes on Devis on to the computer before I go to bed.'

'Then leave you must.' Richard still had some papers to look through himself before he retired.

He stood up and followed her out into the hallway. It had stopped raining now, and as she opened the door Leone could see the wide steps gleaming like oiled skin under the pale light from the street lamp.

'Don't forget Thursday, will you?' he reminded her. He'd invited her to a drinks party at his Inn.

'I won't. But I've got to go to Jibby Beane's first.' Jibby was a wonderfully weird, inspired art dealer who'd started work out of a tiny flat in Gloucester Terrace.

'I'd appreciate your support, you know.' There was a rawness to his voice which made her look up at him.

'What about Margot?' She was one of her father's more persistent widowed devotees. 'Won't she be there?'

'No.'

From his abrupt reply, Leone guessed Margot must have fallen from grace. Presumably she'd committed the cardinal sin and mentioned marriage, foolish woman. Her father was adamant about not marrying again. Leone guessed he didn't want the emotional risk of losing someone he cared for a second time. Sometimes, however, she wished he'd take the plunge. He always said he didn't need anyone in his life except her. As a child that knowledge had given her great comfort. Only later had she realised it could be a curse as well as a blessing.

She looked up, seeing the despondent look in her father's eyes. He was playing for sympathy, she knew. His speciality, long since perfected, was to make her feel guilty, yet there was a seam of honesty in his act. His loneliness was real.

'I'll be there, don't worry,' she said, taking her coat from out of the hall cupboard. She didn't want to let him down. 'I'll leave Jibby's early.'

'Are you sure?' Now he was certain of her support he could afford to be generous. 'I wouldn't want to spoil your evening.'

'You won't. Jibby's is always impossibly packed out on her opening nights so it's probably wiser to leave early anyway.' That much was true. Sometimes her flat was so full the crowd spilled down the stairs and into the street.

Her father stood there, hands plunged deep into his pockets. 'Well, if you're certain.' He looked relieved. 'I'll see you at Lincoln's Inn at seven.'

'Thursday, then.' She touched his arm gently, willing herself not to remark on how tired he looked. 'Thanks for supper.'

She let herself in to the cosiness of her small flat, and settling herself down at the walnut secretaire got out her laptop and started to edit the Devis notes. But it was no good. Half-way through she stopped. She couldn't push the image of her father's tense, grey face from her mind.

Something was troubling him, she could sense it.

Richard sat at his desk in the library, looking out over the balcony. Moonlight flooded the garden square, bathing the damp trees in a ghostly white sheen.

He drew in a deep breath. He couldn't concentrate on his workload tonight. He leant forward, resting one elbow on his knee, and pinched the bridge of his nose between his thumb and forefinger. He was feeling extremely tired, that was all.

Yet he knew it was more than that. His gaze flickered over the morocco-edged blotter, past the pile of neatly stacked legal papers to the stark white envelope propped up in the letter rack.

The letter had been waiting for him when he'd got back from the radio station that evening. It was from Ted Barnes, an old acquaintance formerly of the Metropolitan Crime Squad.

Richard stretched over the desk and picked up the envelope, drawing out the thin sheet of paper and unfolding it methodically. He adjusted the anglepoise, squinting at the cramped black handwriting.

Ted Barnes was simple and to the point. He was writing to warn Richard that Vic Morenzo, a gangland heavyweight whom

Richard had helped to send to prison fifteen years before, was about to be released from Parkhurst.

'He's still as mad as hell at being put away,' Ted wrote, 'and swearing he'll get even with those responsible. He's still a powerful man in the jungle out there and I think we should take this one seriously.'

Outside the wind was rising, brushing against the trees and pulling at the last of the autumn leaves. Their dark shapes shimmered, reflected in the lamplight from the window.

Richard pushed back his chair and stood up. He'd received threats before now, it was one of the hazards of his profession. But this was different. He remembered Morenzo had screamed abuse at him from the dock after sentencing, threatening to get him and his family. And it seemed that, unlike most of his fellow criminals, Morenzo hadn't forgotten his threat. Even after fifteen years.

It set him apart.

Richard read the letter through again, then folded it into its creases and put it back in the envelope.

He couldn't pretend he wasn't concerned. Not for himself— he wasn't about to let some little thug intimidate him—but he had Leone to think about. Morenzo's threats had included his family as well and he recalled only too clearly what this animal was capable of.

He sank down into the leather chair and lit a cigarette. He could still visualise those autopsy photographs of Tommy Brice. Brice had worked on a bank job with Morenzo and had shown the ill-judgement to turn informer when the police had arrested him. The day after Morenzo had been brought in for questioning Brice's mutilated body had been found by workmen near Whitechapel. They hadn't been able to eat for a day.

Nothing was ever proven against Morenzo but it was generally acknowledged that he'd ordered Brice's execution. Morenzo, it seemed, was not a man who forgave easily.

Richard raised his right hand to his temple and pressed his fingers against it for a moment, staring down at the envelope on the desk before him. He knew he'd be foolish to ignore the warning.

Ted Barnes was sensible and practical. Not one to over-react.

And if he spoke of dangers, Richard knew they were there.

Chapter Three

'Well, what do you think?'

Leone stood in the reception of the Courtauld Institute peering over the shoulder of her old tutor, Rupert Huntingdon, as he removed the last layers of bubble wrapping that covered the Devis portrait. She'd spent three years training under his guidance at the Courtauld and he was, in her opinion, one of the best. Leone always enjoyed watching him work.

Rupert tilted the painting this way and that under the light, scrutinising the brushstrokes and the craquelure which etched the painting's surface.

'Well?' she prompted again.

He ignored her quizzing. He didn't even glance up at her. Instead he turned the picture round and removed a small section of brown paper tape which covered the tacking edge.

'The canvas seems in keeping,' Leone volunteered. Dating was based on stitches per inch, and this particular canvas seemed to match the pattern for Devis's era.

'It could be cut down from a larger canvas of that time, of course.' Sandy lashes blinked behind Rupert's thick-rimmed glasses.

'Then you think it might be a fake?'

'Suspicious, certainly.' Rupert was, as ever, cautious to the end. 'But if it's a fake, it's a clever one.' He straightened, then drew out a white handkerchief from his jacket pocket and proceeded to polish his spectacles. 'You say it's well documented?'

She told him the details.

'Curiouser and curiouser.' He glanced back at the figures in the picture. 'Well, leave it with me and I'll take it through to the lab and see what they can come up with. Can you busy yourself until twelve, say?' The test plates would take at least two hours to process.

'Easily.' Covent Garden with its myriad shops and galleries was only a short walk away.

'Perfect.' Already Rupert was gathering up the picture. 'I'll see you at midday, then.'

Leone walked out past the black wrought-iron gates of the Institute and crossed The Strand, heading north. Covent Garden market was bustling with people. She hadn't expected it to be so busy at this time of year. It was a weekday and the tourist season was officially over, but people were milling everywhere, and even the jugglers and entertainers were still performing on their regular patches at either end of the high-domed piazza.

She loved the atmosphere here, more intimate than Paris's Pompidou Centre, though no less lively. Less than twenty years ago the place had been a thriving wholesale fruit and flower market catering for the whole of London, though little evidence of that remained.

Leone passed by the white columns of Inigo Jones's seventeenth century church and headed off to the outer perimeter of the market. She nosed her way unhurriedly around the packed stalls, stopping for a coffee at Leonardo's, then went on to visit one of her favourite galleries on Floral Street. It was quarter past twelve by the time she finally set off back towards the Institute.

The x-rays were already waiting for her in Rupert's office.

As she entered he took the prints out of the buff-coloured envelope and spread them out on his desk for her.

'I think, my dear, you have a problem,' was all he said.

She glanced down. She didn't need him to say anything more.

She could see precisely what he meant.

‿

'All rise,' bellowed the court usher, and a muffled shuffling of heavy winter shoes followed as everyone got to their feet.

Richard Fleming waited until the court was upstanding, bowed, and then made his way through to his chambers behind the courtroom.

It was the second day of a murder trial and it was becoming increasingly evident that the prosecution had insufficient evidence with which to convict the teenage suspect. It was going to be a bloody waste of time, he thought angrily. The defence had taken apart the prosecution so-called star witness that morning.

He removed his wig and had just placed it on the back of a chair when the internal telephone started to ring. It was the clerk.

'Detective Chief Inspector Barnes here to see you, sir. Shall I bring him along?'

'Give me a couple of minutes, will you, Hawkins?'

Richard took off his judicial robes and hung them on the back of the door. Then he slipped on his jacket, patting the right-hand pocket to check his cigarettes were in place as he did so. He was trying to cut back, but he had a feeling that today's meeting with Ted was not the right moment to start.

There was a light tap at the door.

'Hello, Ted.' Richard warmly shook hands with the small, square-shouldered man who was shown in. 'Good of you to call round.'

'Least I could do. I was on my way to the West End anyway.'

'Well, it's appreciated.'

Ted liked that about Richard Fleming. Always made a point of acknowledging favours, however small.

He sat down, giving a quick glance round the room. It was similar to that of the other judges, full of dark panelled wood, sombre leather and a smattering of respectable prints.

'So,' Richard looked across the desk at him, 'would you like a drink, or are you officially on duty?'

'Have you a whisky?'

'Of course.'

'A small one then. Drop of water.'

Richard took a bottle of J & B out of the corner cupboard and poured out two whiskies, adding a splash of water to each from the jug his clerk had left on a tray for him. He handed one of the glasses to Ted, then sat down opposite him.

'Have you made any progress since our chat this morning?' he asked.

Ted nodded. 'I have, yes.'

Richard wasn't surprised. Ted was the quietly efficient type. 'And does the Governor still concur with your view that Morenzo may pose a danger?'

'He does, I'm afraid. But since he hasn't actually made his threats publicly, we can't charge him. Simpler if he did. But he's far too clever for that.'

'And what about my query about police protection?'

'For Leone?'

'Yes.'

Ted curved his plump hands around the heavy cut-glass tumbler. 'I've drawn a blank there, I'm afraid. They don't consider her to be at risk.'

'But in the court that day Morenzo threatened my whole family,' Richard protested.

'I know, Richard. But Morenzo's a vindictive little bugger. He also threatened several other people; the two Crime Squad detectives who were responsible for bringing him in, Judge de Lisle…The department has to take a certain line.'

'Which is?' Richard's expression was stiff and controlled. He could guess what was coming.

'That we'll offer limited protection to the key figures involved and cover the rest by putting a tail on Morenzo himself.'

'And do you think that will be adequate?'

'It's the best we can do, Richard. You know that police resources are stretched to the limit.'

There was a brief silence. Richard delved inside his jacket and drew out his packet of cigarettes. Ted was sensitive when it came to criticism of the police force and he had no wish to antagonise him.

'So, how are Marian and the boys?' he asked, deeming it wise to change the subject. He clicked open his lighter and settled back against the soft leather chair, watching the smoke spiralling up from his cigarette. 'Didn't you say Malcolm had just started at Newcastle?'

Ted's expression eased. He put down his empty whisky glass. 'Both boys are at university now,' he said, pride flooding his face. 'Derek's in his final year at York.'

It hardly seemed possible. The last photograph Richard had seen of them they'd been two young boys scrapping on the lawn. 'You must miss them.'

'Marian does. But she's recently joined this ecclesiastical needlework group. Goes on courses all over England. She's even doing something at Westminster Abbey next month.'

'Is she?' Richard found it hard to come to terms with the image of burly Marian, ex-Crime Squad herself, settling down to do delicate needlepoint. Yet he wasn't about to mock. He knew how insidious boredom could be. How destructive.

He sat back, nursing his whisky glass in his hand, listening vaguely as Ted chatted on.

Theirs was an odd affiliation. Their paths had first crossed when they'd both attended the same local school in north London, though Richard had soon left to go to the nearby private school. They hadn't been friends then and Richard would probably never have given tubby little Ted Barnes another thought, but for the fact that one of his first cases as a fresh-faced barrister had been to defend a young policeman accused of planting evidence on a drug dealer.

Richard had never doubted Ted's innocence and pleaded so eloquently in his defence that the jury had gone against all expectations and unanimously returned a not-guilty verdict.

Ted never forgot the help Richard had given him. He'd been able to repay him over the years with a few favours.

Richard was too much of a snob to embrace actual friendship with Ted, and Ted was too realistic to expect it. But they respected each other. And Richard knew loyalty when he saw it. He valued it.

He leaned forward to stub out his cigarette. Ted was asking after Leone.

He gave a quick nod. 'She's in wonderful form, thanks.'

'Any serious boyfriend on the scene, yet?'

'Too busy getting her business off the ground,' Richard said tightly, trying not to wince. Ted was always asking if Leone had any fellow in tow.

He sat back, folding his arms across his chest. He couldn't pretend he wasn't secretly relieved that Leone was uninvolved at the moment. Her fling with that wretched fellow a few years back had been an utter disaster. He could have told her Jack Thursley wasn't the man for her. She'd been too blind to see what he was up to. All the while trying to turn Leone against him, her own father, for God's sake.

But Thursley had been forced to turn tail in the end, hadn't he? Met his match. Though Richard wasn't sure what might have happened if he hadn't been rushed to hospital with that heart attack. Would Leone had left with Jack for Hong Kong? Possibly. And it would have been the biggest mistake of her life. He could see it, even if she, blinded by so-called love, couldn't. As it was, when she'd come to see him in intensive care, he'd begged her to stay, shamelessly falling back on emotive words like duty and sacrifice. And when she'd wavered, Thursley had acted just as Richard had known he would. Too proud to plead, too angry to reason, he'd given her an ultimatum and then simply packed up his bags and left.

Leone had been upset, of course, but it had been for the best. Jack Thursley couldn't have made her happy. And by the grace of God, he'd been able to see him off.

Richard allowed himself a smile. *Know your enemy's weaknesses.* It worked every time.

He gave his glass a quick swirl then took a sip of whisky. Ted was asking after Leone's business.

'Going extremely well, thanks,' he said.

'Last time we spoke she was about to jet off to New York to restore something there for one of its museums, wasn't she?'

'The Metropolitan,' Richard agreed with a nod. 'She often seems to be in demand out there.' Although Richard hadn't wanted Leone to start up on her own, he was gratified by her success. 'She's built up a very good reputation.'

'Talented girl.'

'Yes, she is.'

Richard eased his bulk forward in his chair, his thoughts curving back to his daughter and Morenzo's threats. Despite Ted's assurance that Morenzo would be tailed, he still felt vaguely apprehensive. 'Listen Ted, about Leone. Should I warn her about this Morenzo business?' He hadn't intended to, but he wondered, given the circumstances, whether it might not be expedient.

'Leave well alone,' Ted insisted. 'The less she worries about it, the better. Morenzo's going to be watched day and night, after all.'

'If you're sure?'

'Certain.'

If it looked as if things were escalating, Ted knew they could easily provide Leone with a personal-attack alarm. The sort used mainly in domestic violence cases, with panic buttons linked directly to the police. But he was pretty certain it wouldn't come to that.

There was a soft knock at the door. It was the usher.

'Sorry to disturb you, sir. Counsel would like to speak to you in private before you return to court.'

'Tell them I'll be free in about ten minutes,' Richard told him. Counsel, he assumed, was about to start bargaining. He wasn't surprised.

'I won't keep you any longer, Richard,' Ted said, pushing back his chair and standing up. 'But before I go, there is something else I wanted to warn you about.'

'Concerning Morenzo?'

Ted nodded. 'I heard from the Governor this morning that they're releasing him earlier than expected. Some nonsense about the press. That's one of the reasons I called round.'

'I see.' Something about Ted's awkwardness put Richard on alert. The seed of concern that had been sown took root deep down inside him. 'So when exactly do you expect him to be released?'

Ted cleared his throat, shifting a little uncomfortably.

'He's due out from Parkhurst this afternoon. At about two o'clock.'

There was an awkward silence.

Richard was careful to show no emotion. He stood up to show Ted out. 'Thank you. It was good of you to let me know.'

After Ted had left Richard glanced at his watch.

It was almost two o'clock now. At this very minute Morenzo was probably walking out through the prison gates.

And that meant he would be up in London by late afternoon.

Chapter Four

'Am I glad to see you. It's been like a madhouse here all morning.'

'Sorry, I got delayed,' said Leone, struggling into the gallery with the Devis picture. 'Dreadful jam at Scotch House Corner.'

She glanced apologetically at Janie, the receptionist, and then did a swift doubletake. Janie's dark chestnut hair of yesterday was now a brilliant peroxide blonde.

Leone was used by now to Janie's spur-of-the-moment image changes. At first she'd been shocked by them but now she secretly admired her. It showed a strong streak of non-conformity.

Noticing her reaction, Janie ran a hand through her short-cropped fuzz, and grinned.

'What do you think? I did it last night.'

'Suits you,' said Leone. 'But I thought you swore you'd never go blonde again after the last fiasco.'

'Oh, that was Majorca,' said Janie, matter-of-factly. 'The bloody swimming pool.' The chlorine in the water had made her hair turn green. She said she'd felt like a mouldy tennis ball bobbing around in the hotel pool all week. 'Thought I'd try again, though.'

'So, does Ronnie approve?' asked Leone. Ronnie was Janie's boyfriend. Tall, lean, black and very beautiful.

'Says it makes me look like Madonna.'

'Ah.' Leone assumed Ronnie meant that as a compliment.

She went through to the back of the gallery to hang up her coat. 'Phil not back yet?'

'No. So either her new artist fella is absolutely brilliant and she couldn't bear to tear herself away, or he was so bleeding awful she's had to stop off at a pub to get over the shock!'

Janie was nothing if not candid.

'She could have gone on to another client, you know,' suggested Leone.

Janie smiled. 'Not a chance.' They both knew Phil was not that organised.

The telephone started to ring. Janie grimaced. 'It's been like this all morning.'

A second later she was covering the mouthpiece. 'It's Whitcombs. It's the third time they've rung today.'

'I'll take it upstairs.'

'Right. And these are your other messages,' she said, handing Leone a scribbled list. 'There's a proper little pest that's been on your tail all morning about some painting. Right aggressive so-and-so, he is. Piers Carlton.'

'Carlton?' Leone frowned. The name meant nothing to her. She'd have to sort it out later.

She went upstairs to her studio and picked up the extension. It was Iain McAllister, the owner of Whitcombs. No mere manager, then. It had gone to the highest level.

'I gather there's been some sort of misunderstanding about the Devis picture,' he began in tones so honeyed that she could almost hear them dripping down the receiver. 'You do realise that there can be no question about it not being the genuine article. The painting has been with the family for over two hundred and fifty years.'

'I do appreciate that, Mr McAllister.' Leone knew to tread carefully. Galleries could be unbelievably neurotic when there was a hint of scandal in the air and Whitcombs had always had a very sound reputation.

'As you can imagine, Lady Carlton is terribly upset by even the merest suggestion that something might be amiss. She's a direct descendant of Sir George Wallace and the painting is of great personal and sentimental value to her.'

'I do understand.'

Leone's mind raced. Lady Carlton, he'd said. So no doubt the belligerent Piers who'd so irritated Janie that morning was either the son or the husband. And he was probably on the war path.

'You are aware that the portrait has been documented down through the generations?'

'Yes, I am,' admitted Leone. 'But I have to point out, Mr McAllister, that there are discrepancies. The results of the x-rays carried out by the Courtauld show definite signs of another picture underneath the Devis portrait.'

That silenced him.

'The Courtauld are suggesting they carry out a pigment analysis,' she went on. 'That should clarify matters once and for all—if you think Lady Carlton would agree, that is.'

'I'm sure she'd agree,' McAllister asserted quickly.

'Then presumably you don't wish the picture to be returned at this stage?'

There was the merest pause. 'Well, obviously I can't confirm that without speaking to Lady Carlton first.' McAllister's response was carefully modulated.

'It seems the sensible solution though, doesn't it?' Leone felt like a nanny trying to coax her recalcitrant charge to take his medicine.

'I'll get back to you as soon as possible,' said McAllister. 'End of day, latest.'

Leone put down the receiver. McAllister, though cautious, had hardly appeared the devious sort. Perhaps, after all, there was a perfectly innocent explanation for the inconsistencies.

In the meantime, she might just do some background research into the Carlton family. Forewarned was forearmed, as her father frequently reminded her.

~

Philippa Hope-Brown leapt off the No. 52 bus in Ladbroke Grove and cut through the crowded backstreets towards the gallery.

She felt strong and clear-headed, the elation of the morning reflected in her quick, light steps. She knew, with steely certainty, that today she had uncovered an amazing talent.

When she'd arrived at Steve Ross's studio that morning it had all seemed so unpromising. He'd opened the door to her, a fair-haired man with neat features and a clear, pale skin, and his manner had been so quiet, so colourless, that she'd been tempted there and then to make her excuses and run.

But she'd stayed, thank God. Some instinct had prevailed.

The canvases had been stacked round the studio, every one of them turned to face the wall, the morning light slanting across their bland, mono-toned backs. They'd chatted briefly, and then he'd walked over to the deepest stack and, like a magician producing a series of aces from an empty hand, had slowly begun to turn the canvases outwards, one by one.

She'd been totally unprepared for the sheer vibrant energy of his paintings. The absolute pleasure of that moment had been so acute, it made her tingle even to recall it. The pictures had power and intensity, yes, but there were subtle layers of interpretation in the colour, shape and form.

Steve Ross had used the dramatic colours of Van Gogh with the black outline of Gauguin to brilliant effect. Colour, distorted form, altered perspectives pushed against the senses. Looking at the paintings, Phil had immediately thought of the work of Munch, the pressure of feelings forcing the bounds of the visible in the same almost dreamlike way.

She'd watched with growing excitement as he'd moved on to another stack and begun to turn each picture slowly towards her, carefully, like the delicate unfurling of the petals of a flower.

It was an extraordinary sensation to inspect them, knowing they were exactly the type of pictures she'd been looking for ever since she'd opened the gallery. Bold, intelligent pictures that challenged every sense and emotion.

When he'd finished with the last collection, he had turned towards her and moved across the room to her side. There was an intimacy to his movement which she understood. By showing her the pictures, he had revealed himself. He stood there, so close that she could see the granulation of colour in his yellow-brown eyes. Fox eyes, alert against dangers. And looking at his face, she knew that his passivity was only a veneer. He was a man of intense passion and emotion.

They'd talked for hours, Phil carefully drawing him out. She'd told him about the gallery, about her concepts and aims. She'd even chatted to him about Leone and her side of the gallery. And then they'd discussed his future projects and ideas.

That had been most intriguing. So often Phil had found that painters didn't have the strength to flourish once they'd left art school. Flowers without water. But here was someone whose style was evolving all the time; from the early simplistic, almost child-like style which brought to mind those ingenuous Ken Kiff paintings, to the more complicated, colourful Ayres-like canvases which he'd only just finished that year.

She'd asked him why he had never held an exhibition before and he'd explained quite without guile she was sure, that he'd been searching for just the right person to take him on, someone he could trust. She'd felt quite humble that she should have been the one he'd chosen. Though outwardly bursting with confidence, Phil was still sometimes wracked with doubts as to her own abilities, and she found Steve's faith in her oddly touching.

Now, as she made her way towards Portobello, her pretty oval face glowed with pleasure as she recalled his words. She strode out, long-legged and lean, her dark brown eyes bright and alive with optimism.

Steve Ross was going to change her life. She could feel it.

~~

'Mr Carlton, threatening me will make no difference. I'm simply not in a position to release the picture to you without authorisation from either your mother or from Whitcombs Gallery.'

Leone glanced up as the gallery door swung open and saw with relief that Phil had arrived at last. She'd need Phil's bolstering good spirits after this wretched conversation. No, delete conversation, that implied some sort of civility; this could only be described as a one-sided vitriolic diatribe.

'I'm sorry, Mr Carlton. As I've said, I'll be only too happy to oblige once you've obtained authorisation from Whitcombs. I suggest you ring them direct. In the meantime, I really have nothing further to say to you.'

'Jesus! Who on earth was that?' Phil asked her as she slammed down the telephone.

'Some aggressive little twit called Piers bloody Carlton.'

'Piers Carlton? Oh, lord, not him!'

'You know him?' She wasn't entirely surprised. Phil, being the social animal she was, seemed to know just about everyone.

'Yes, unfortunately.' Phil gave a small grimace and crossed the gallery to her desk, which Leone had commandeered for the moment, settling herself down on its edge amongst the clutter. 'He's an appalling piece of work. Made the mistake of accepting a lift from him once after a gallery opening. Tried to pin me down in his wretched Porsche, the little creep. All clammy hands and slimy tongue. Disgusting.'

'Sounds it.'

'Had to knee him to get out. Quite indignant he was. Called me a frigid bitch.' Phil cast Leone a wicked smile. They both knew she was neither. 'He's unscrupulous, too. He was an absolute pig to Zara Kotinsky on the opening night of her first exhibition. Don't you remember my telling you about it?'

'Can't say I do.' Phil was always recounting tales about her contemporaries at art college.

'Oh? Well, Zara had just put together this cracking exhibition and had even managed to attract some influential bigwigs to the preview, when who should waltz into the gallery but the art lover from hell.'

'Piers Carlton, I presume?'

Phil nodded. 'It was way before the official time of the preview, but it was Zara's first show and she was keen to let in anyone who showed a smidgen of interest. So in he comes and proceeds to buy four of her best paintings.'

'That doesn't sound too awful to me.'

'Wait. So he hands over his cheque and then what do you suppose he does?'

Leone smiled. Phil knew how to string out a good story. 'Can't imagine.'

'Starts taking the pictures down off the wall. Says he needs them immediately.'

'What? Before the show is finished?'

'Before the show has even started! Well, I know some Japanese buyers do exactly that now, but then it was unheard of, and you can imagine what a state Zara was in. Her four best works about to disappear out of the gallery before the critics had even caught a glimpse of them.'

'I'm beginning to remember the story now. That was Piers Carlton, was it?'

Phil nodded. 'He was utterly implacable. Zara said she would have stood a better chance mud-wrestling a crocodile than persuading Piers to change his mind. Luckily, her old art tutor arrived in the nick of time. Managed to talk some sense into Piers. Told him that if he took the paintings away before the exhibition opened, he would detrimentally affect his own investment, as the critics would hardly be likely to rave about blank spaces on walls. Piers finally agreed to leave them in the gallery. But it spoilt the evening for poor Zara.'

'I'm not surprised.'

'So be warned. Piers Carlton is quite without scruples. He's a vindictive so-and-so, who'll stop at nothing until he gets what he wants.'

Leone put down her pen and tore off the top page of Phil's notepad. Her scribbling had been so violent during her conversation with Piers Carlton it had indented several layers of paper below. She hadn't realised how angry he'd made her.

'Henry Gorrell told me much the same thing when I spoke to him today,' she admitted. 'Said Carlton had a reputation as a Rottweiler of the first order in the City. Told me to watch out for him.'

'So why are you dealing with him?' asked Phil, twisting round to pick up a folder from her desk.

'I'm not, actually,' Leone said. 'I'm restoring a picture for his mother.'

'Which he wants sent back rather badly, I gather?'

'Extremely badly, yes. Swearing to commit all sorts of blue murder. Claims that I've caused his mother untold anguish. She's eighty and an invalid and the shock of my accusations has made her suffer a relapse, apparently.' Leone's voice was sharp. She didn't believe that last allegation for a moment.

Phil leaned over and touched her shoulder. 'You all right?'

Leone nodded.

'Do you know what I'd do? Just pack up the picture and send it back,' Phil said. 'It simply isn't worth the aggro.'

'But I can't do that,' Leone reminded her. 'It's Whitcombs who've instructed me, not Piers Carlton, remember?'

'So it is.' Phil smiled. 'Correct to the last, I see.'

Leone knew she was teasing, but there was a core of truth to her words.

She knew she was always wary, so fastidious. Unlike Phil, whose relaxed and easy-going attitude seemed to bring instant rewards, Leone could never allow herself to let go. Jack had been the only one of her boyfriends to succeed in lifting the portcullis across her carefully guarded emotions.

She was aware it stemmed from her mother's death, of course. Ever since that time she'd kept her feelings on a tight chain, afraid to let them loose. Even as a child she'd been careful to hide her thoughts and her grief, conscious of upsetting her father. Knowing too, that if she let go, along with the grief would come an overwhelming sense of guilt.

How could she explain that to her father? She'd been the last person to see her mother alive and somehow she knew she should have been able to prevent her from going to her death.

She thought of the dream again. Perhaps there was nothing more sinister behind that door than the dark shadow of her own emotions. Maybe that was all she had to face and acknowledge.

There was a rustling beside her. Phil had shifted from the desk and was slipping the black and white checked jacket off her shoulders. Leone saw her bend forward, the long, lean line of her back curving slightly as she murmured something to Janie.

Leone suddenly noticed how animated her friend looked.

'Never asked how the morning went,' she said. 'Sorry. How was it all?'

Phil spun round. 'Breathtaking. Brilliant.' Her almond-shaped brown eyes were alight with unsuppressed pleasure. 'Honestly, Leone, this man is seriously talented.'

'And he wants you to represent him?'

Phil laughed. 'Oh ye of little faith! Of course he does.' Her confidence was so acute, so physical, it gave her an almost sensual glow.

Leone had seen these signs before. She hoped to heaven Phil wasn't falling for the artist as well. Her past affairs with her protégés had not been without mishap. But then caution had never been Phil's way.

'Listen, it all fits so perfectly,' Phil was saying. 'Liz Cunningham is dragging her feet. There's absolutely no way she'll have her work ready for the exhibition next month. I can take the pressure off her, postpone her show until January, and put on Steve Ross's work instead.'

'Could you put it all together in time?'

'Of course. His studio is bursting with suitable stuff.'

Janie slipped past them, clutching a coffee cup. 'Yes, please,' Phil called out after her.

The telephone started to ring.

'I'll get it,' shouted Leone. The chances of Janie breaking off her coffee-making ritual to answer it were fairly remote.

'Philippa Hope-Brown's gallery,' she said, flicking the switchboard button.

'Leone?'

A man's voice, muffled, distorted. Not one she recognised.

'Yes?'

'It is Leone, isn't it? *Sweet, sweet* Leone.'

The voice was low and husky; so creepy it made her skin go cold.

She tensed. 'Who is this?' she asked sharply.

There was silence.

'What do you want?'

His breathing became more pronounced. 'You'll find out, Leone.' There was a short, abrasive laugh. 'You'll find out soon enough.'

She heard a sharp click and the telephone went dead.

Her heart started to hammer wildly. She stood there, unable to move for the moment, leaning heavily against Janie's desk.

'Are you all right?'

She hadn't heard Phil come up behind her. Her hands were shaking as she slowly lowered the receiver.

'Yes, just some weirdo…' She fought back a shudder.

But he'd known her name. That was what frightened her. Recovering herself, she quickly punched in the 1471 number, hoping to track down where the caller had dialled from. But he'd put a block on the operator's trace. This was no off-the-cuff call. It had been carefully planned.

She took a deep breath, trying to regain some sense of rationality, some semblance of calm. Who would want to scare her? It didn't make sense. Who would have reason to make such a malicious prank call?

The answer was obvious, of course. Piers Carlton. Trying to put the wind up her. Using bullying tactics, that was all. *The bastard*. Like hell she'd return the picture to him now. She wasn't about to let herself be intimidated, she told herself fiercely.

She should have sensed then that the Eumenides were gathering.

Chapter Five

Vic Morenzo stared moodily down at the glass of beer on the polished table in front of him. It was supposed to be one of the great pleasures of getting out of prison: to be able to taste a proper pint of English best brew in your local pub. But it hadn't been like that. It had been a total let-down, if the truth be known.

He glanced across at the bar. His younger brother, Tony, was leaning across the narrow wooden counter busily chatting up the dark-haired barmaid whose little black dress was so tight it looked as if she'd been shoehorned into it.

He was supposed to be ordering the food, not trying to get her knickers off. Jesus! He'd had better service in prison, he thought bitterly. There at least they'd shown him some respect. He'd been known as someone to stay clear of and no one would have made him wait around like this.

Vic pushed his hands through his grey-flecked hair. At least Tony and the boys had arranged a little show for him tonight at the club. Best stripper this side of Mayfair, so Tony said. Right little goer. He gave a grim smile. Now *that* was the other thing he was looking forward to again.

The girl at the bar let out a simpering laugh and glanced his way. He winked at her, a bit of a come-on look, but the vermilion-lipped smile she gave him was so forced he lifted his eyes and returned her look with one of such chilling hardness it made her flinch and look away.

That was the thing about Vic. With his undistinguished features and average build he appeared little more than an innocuous middle-aged punter to the casual observer. Until his eyes slapped you with fear.

Vic pulled out a packet of cigarettes, a wave of resentment washing over him. That was the trouble. He wasn't in his thirties like Tony any more. He was nearly forty-five, for God's sake. He'd kept in shape in prison—he thought he looked fitter than Tony, in truth—but his brother now had the swagger and the confidence which had once been his and Vic knew that the barmaid's jaded reaction matched that of the two big-breasted girls on the waterfront this afternoon.

Past his prime, that's what those pouting, moist lips seemed to tell him. He snapped open his lighter, drawing heavily on his cigarette.

All those lost years. All the best years.

He was going to make the motherfuckers pay. All of them.

He glanced down to Tony's mobile which lay on the table in front of him. If his brother didn't come back sharpish he'd start to make a few more phone calls. There were things he had to do.

He adjusted his position, leaning his head back against the wood panelling. He liked to have an overall view of the place. That way he knew when someone noticed him, could tell the instant he was pinpointed. It paid to keep alert. That was something Tony hadn't learned yet. Tony wouldn't have spotted that police tail for instance.

Behind him, out beyond the mullioned windows, the traffic of Whitechapel rumbled on. That at least hadn't changed. About all that hadn't, though. This whole area had been well and truly tarted up since he'd been put away. Only a few pockets of the old life were left behind.

His old mum must have hated it, thought Vic. He'd offered to move her in the good old days when he'd been in the money, but she had turned him down flat. Well, she would, wouldn't she? He could understand that. She'd wanted to stay with her friends. Been through too much with them. The Blitz and all that.

But it had killed her in the end, staying here. The tenement flat had been damp and he could still remember his anger at watching his mum struggling up six flights of evil-smelling stairs with her shopping and washing, just because a gang of bored little seven-year-olds had destroyed the lifts again.

She wouldn't have died if he'd been here. He knew that. He'd have been at hand to help her. Tony had tried, but right in the middle of Vic's sentence he'd been sent down himself for six months, and besides, he just didn't notice the little things, did he? Tony wouldn't think to check his mother's fridge to make sure she had food for the week, nor see if the heating was high enough in her flat. Tony was like that, a little careless of others. You couldn't blame him. Look at him now, still chatting up that stupid bitch of a barmaid. He hadn't even ordered the food yet. Typical of Tony, that.

Vic leaned forward and stubbed out his cigarette. No, it wasn't Tony's fault his mum hadn't survived that last cold winter. The blame lay with those who'd helped to put him away. That silver-tongued barrister for one. The judge would never have given him such a hefty sentence if that piss-faced barrister hadn't banged on about Vic being a danger to society. Load of crap, that. And the barrister knew it.

Make an example of him, he'd urged.

Just because the Bill had lost face. As if it were his fault they hadn't the brains to discover where he'd hidden the last bit of money.

Biggest armed robbery since the bullion raid at Heathrow, it had been. Vic was still proud of helping to organise that. And if it hadn't been for Brice and that other weasel informer they'd have got clean away with it. The press had called it the 'Most Daring Raid of the Decade'. Well, no point going with the small fry, was there? But it had cost him.

He stared sullenly down at his beer. He was only just beginning to realise how much.

When he was nicked he'd been about to hit the big time. He'd already acquired the gloss of money and sophistication: smart girls, fast cars. He'd got the boys' respect. He'd had power. His own little businesses were booming. In fact the whole bloody world had been at his fingertips.

Look at him now. Jesus, it was enough to make a grown man weep. But he wasn't beaten yet. He'd get it all back. The boys would rally round. He'd kept his mouth shut, after all, and there was his share of the money they'd stashed away to come. Set him up nicely that would. Money meant power and Vic knew that's what counted. Power. Getting ahead, running things. And he'd regain what status he'd lost if it was the last thing he did.

In the meantime, though, he'd make the bastards who'd brought about his downfall pay. He knew how to hurt that barrister, just as he knew where to hurt each and every one of those fuckers who'd sent him down. He'd had fifteen years to find out their Achilles' heels. Fifteen long bloody years. They'd live to regret the day they'd crossed him. He'd tread carefully, though. The police were just waiting for him to make one false move. He wasn't a fool. He knew the way they worked. The police would haul him in the first moment he stepped out of line. Well, he could wait. Softly, softly…

He pushed his drink away and picked up Tony's phone. A few more calls then he'd have to try and lose that police tail. He had some urgent unfinished business to attend to before the boys' welcome-home party tonight.

He smiled. An eye for an eye. He liked that.

~

'Hello, I wasn't expecting you.'

'I know.' Leone put down her bag on the hall table. 'Fernanda dropped a note through my letterbox to say she'd taken in a package for me this morning. Have you seen it?'

'Have you looked in the hall cupboard?'

'No.' She should have thought of that. It was one of Fernanda's favourite hiding places. 'Thanks.'

Her father put down the book he was reading. It was the one on French medieval churches she'd given him for his birthday.

'Have you time for a drink, or must you dash?'

She glanced at her watch. It was just after six.

'I've time for a quick one,' she said. She wasn't due out until eight. 'But I absolutely must have a long hot soak before I venture out tonight. I positively reek of cleaning solvents.'

'In my day all the nice girls smelt of Chanel No. 5.'

'And they all went to little Swiss finishing schools. I know,' she laughed. She went over and made herself a spritzer. 'I wonder what's happened to all those schools. Do you suppose *anyone* sends their daughter to such antediluvian establishments any more?'

'I'm certain they do. Not every father thinks the LSE or a degree in industrial engineering is the answer, you know.'

'How positively prehistoric you can be sometimes,' she teased.

'What nonsense. I let you read chemistry.'

'Instead of law, I know.'

She'd had a terrible fight over it with him. But even then she'd known she wanted to do picture conservation and that to be accepted into somewhere as hallowed as the Courtauld Institute—where they only took on five students a year—she'd need a decent first class degree and a good working knowledge of chemistry.

It was one of the few times she'd gone against his wishes and it was only Aunt Mary's timely intervention on her behalf which had finally clinched it.

She came and sat down opposite her father, stretching her slim stockinged legs out towards the fire.

'You're still stuck in the Middle Ages when it comes to women. You do know that, don't you?'

Her father contrived to look hurt. 'As it happens, it's a fallacy that women in medieval times were so oppressed,' he said. 'When their husbands went off to the Crusades, the running of the estates was left to them entirely. They were given great responsibilities.'

'And when their husbands returned they were banished back to their ivory towers again. Women of today wouldn't stand for it.'

She saw his lips tighten.

'Women of today want their so-called freedom and they don't care what they destroy to get it,' he said tetchily, with that touch of steel he could bring to his voice. 'What they totally ignore is the debris that's churned up in their wake as they power towards their goals. Wait till we see the effects of *en masse* single parenting. Two parents aren't necessary, they say. Well, I could show them. We see the evidence in the courts every day. But every time someone tries to point out the facts—and they are facts—it causes a political storm. Do you know by what percentage crime in the under-fourteen age group has grown over the last five years?'

She had a feeling that if she didn't stop him now, he'd be on to unemployed youth, given half a chance. As ever, facts and figures to prove his point.

'Daddy, stop! You're sounding depressingly like a prosecuting counsel again, you know.'

'What nonsense! You see, even my own daughter has a built-in barrier against unbiased criticism of her own kind.'

'Unbiased? I like that!' But she was amused. Like most barristers her father couldn't resist a chance of verbal sparring. The mental hop-skip-jump of it all. She wasn't even sure if he truly believed everything he said. Possibly he did. He was appallingly opinionated about social issues; the result of living in his own masculine empire.

On the other hand, even when his sister, Mary, had lived with them when her mother had first died, she seemed to remember that he was just as out of touch and dogmatic in his views. Perhaps he'd always been that way. Mary had once said that her father's idea of a compromise was to do things his way and for no one to argue about it. He hadn't changed much.

She saw that he'd picked up his book again and was fingering the edge of the pages. He'd nearly finished it, judging by the marker. There was a new one out by the same author, something on medieval villages, which had had a very good review. She'd have to remember to order it for him for Christmas.

Leone turned the glass round in her hand. It was the love of medieval history and culture which had brought him together with her mother. He'd gone to explore Winchester Cathedral, and her mother had been there viewing the brasses. She was an art student at St Martin's, and this had been part of her finals project. They'd glanced at each other across the rows of dark wooden pews and in the still silence of the church, beneath the glass window depicting the martyrdom of St Stephen, had fallen instantly for each other.

At least that was what Aunt Mary had told her. Aunt Mary, though, was an incurable romantic. Leone found it hard to imagine her father suffering a *coup de foudre*.

She finished the last of her drink.

'I suppose I ought to be going.'

'Where are you off to?'

'A party at Josie and Andrew's,' Leone replied. Andrew was Phil's older brother. They had been friends for years. Leone was godmother to his latest offspring, a dynamic blond two-year-old, who already seemed to be following in his father's footsteps in the charm stakes.

'How's his cabinet-making business doing?'

'Pretty well, considering.'

The present economic climate didn't help. But Andrew produced objects of such exquisite workmanship that there was always a steady line of patrons beating a path to his door. Just as well with a wife and two children to feed. 'One day you ought to come to see his workshop, you know. You'd be impressed.'

'One day I shall.' Her father glanced down at the book in his hand.

She knew he wouldn't, though. Venturing down to the darkest streets of Brixton was not his scene. He played safe. But she couldn't blame him. So did she. Her mother's death had marked them both in its way.

She put down her glass and went over to kiss him good night.

She wouldn't let herself think how different things might have been.

～

He watched as she moved across the softly lit drawing-room to kiss her father good night. A pretty thing—light and vulnerable, like the voice he'd heard that afternoon.

From where he stood he could see them quite clearly. He watched her touch her father's cheek tenderly with her hand, her straight blonde hair falling across her face as she bent over to embrace him.

He drew back a little, the murky shadows of the garden moving and twisting about him like Salome's veil.

Soon would be the time to act.

He stayed low and started backing away through the darkness towards the unsecured side gate.

He could wait.

Chapter Six

'Goodness, you're in early.'

Leone took off her coat and hung it up on the stand, casting Phil an impressed look. Phil was hardly ever in before ten o'clock and here she was, already at her desk punching catalogue notes into her computer.

Phil took a sip of coffee and returned the cup to its precarious position amongst the jumble on her desk.

'Steve Ross rang last night,' she said by way of explanation. 'He's very keen on my suggestion of doing this exhibition next month. It's a terrific idea, of course, but it'll mean a terribly tight schedule.'

'Can you manage it?'

'It'll be tough, but hey…' She gave a bright smile and an expressive shrug.

Leone walked over to Phil's desk. A pile of photographs was scattered across the papers on top. 'Is this his work?'

'Yes. Brilliant, isn't he?'

Leone picked up the prints and glanced at the top one. It was of an enormous canvas showing what looked like a pond, a lily and a frog in bright crimsons, pinks, greens and black. The brushstrokes were wild and dramatic but remained distinct, the colours still clear despite the depth of impasto.

'Mm. Very bold.' His paintings, with their unfettered energy, reminded her a little of the work by the Dutch painter, Karel Appel.

Phil laughed. 'You should see your face.'

'What do you mean?'

'It's so obvious you don't much like it.'

'Nonsense. Actually, I think it works surprisingly well.' She started to flick through the rest of the prints. His style changed, becoming more abstract, but still with the bold hard-edged blocks of colour. Not exactly to her taste, but his use of imagery, patterns and colour was remarkably effective.

'Your appreciation of art stopped with the Impressionists. That's your trouble,' said Phil.

'And yours started with the Cubists. That's yours,' retorted Leone amicably.

'You make me sound like a champion of the "cutting edge" brigade,' said Phil. 'Honestly, Leone, I'm considered rather tame by most of the other contemporary galleries. Look at Jay Jopling at the White Cube…' Jay had been responsible for promoting Damien Hirst and his pickled sheep exhibit which had caused a stir a few years back. 'I'm conventional in comparison.' She gestured at the current exhibits on show. 'See, not an installation in sight.'

'Actually I think you've managed the perfect balance,' said Leone. 'You've got a loyal following. And you've had plenty of successes. Look at Liz Cunningham. She's had three exhibitions now and every time they've been a complete sell-out.'

Phil grinned. 'And I think Steve Ross will prove an even bigger hit.'

'You're very excited about him, aren't you?'

'Very. And I know I'm right. I rang some clients in Amsterdam this morning and they were champing at the bit to see his work.'

Leone smiled. 'Then you'd better get organising.'

Phil glanced back at her screen. 'I'm trying to. Really I am,' She moved the cursor a couple of points and then looked up again. 'There's a fax for you, by the way.'

'Is there? Who from?'

'Howard Steinberg. Something about your trip to New York. You didn't tell me you were going out there.'

'It's only for five days. And yes, I did.' She put the photographs back on Phil's desk. 'Do you want another coffee?'

'That would be great. Can't let the old caffeine level fall.'

Leone took Phil's mug and went through to the back kitchen. It was a small room, opening out on to the parking area at the back of the gallery. There was a sink and an antiquated cooker, which Phil used to heat up exotic creations for her opening nights. Ronnie was always promising to trade it in for a newer model 'down the market' but as yet nothing had come of it.

Leone took the jar of Nescafé out of the cupboard and switched on the kettle.

'Do you want milk?' she called out.

'Please. And a sugar. Feel in need of sustenance this morning.'

'Oh?' An ominous sign. 'So how was your evening with Paul?' she asked tentatively.

'All right.'

There was a distant lack of enthusiasm in her voice.

'Only all right?'

'He's getting rather tedious if the truth be known. I've really more or less decided to stop seeing him.'

'Ah.' Phil tired of her boyfriends easily—three months was the record. She was too restless for long-term commitment. Mind you, she didn't always choose prudently. Paul, for instance, though undeniably handsome, had the sort of well-groomed looks which were so often found in the City boardrooms, where a sleek appearance merely disguised less attractive behaviour. Great fun, he might be, but he was also egotistical and vain, and far too interested in talking about his Ferrari and smart flat in Chelsea Harbour.

The kettle was boiling. Leone spooned the coffee into the mugs and poured in the water.

'We have nothing in common really. And then last night we had this bloody awful row.'

'About what?'

'Art, if you can believe it.'

Leone could. Phil had some very strong opinions on the subject.

'He asked me if I was stuck on a desert island, which one picture would I want to take with me.'

'And what did you say?'

'It wasn't what I said that caused the problem.' Phil's head appeared round the door. She'd obviously tired of drawing up a suitable list of guests to invite to Steve Ross's exhibition. 'It was his choice.'

'Which was?'

'The *Mona Lisa*.' Phil leaned up against the door frame and rolled her eyes heavenwards. 'I mean how hackneyed can you get? But that wasn't the worse of it. I asked him why he'd chosen it.'

'And?'

'No raving about the poetry of Leonardo's lines. Oh no—I could have almost forgiven him that. No, he chose it, he tells me, because it's one of the most expensive paintings in the world and it wouldn't lose its market value while he's stuck on this desert island. God! Can you believe it? I mean, I knew he was a dealer in the City but I thought he had some sort of soul.'

Leone smiled. The thought of Paul and a soul was an interesting one. 'Obviously not.'

She handed Phil her mug. Her friend's life was full of minor dramas; in fact she thrived on them.

They stood for a moment in silence, sipping their coffee. They were very similar in looks, both tall and slim, with high cheekbones and long straight blonde hair though the differences in their characters showed in their faces. Phil's was open and sensual, Leone's more reflective, the bones more finely sculptured.

Phil started back to her desk. 'By the way,' she said casually, 'Mum's asked me to tell you that if you can spare a few days over Christmas, she'd be delighted for you to come down to Cornwall with us. Very insistent, she was.'

'How kind of her.' Leone followed Phil out of the kitchen.

'Kindness doesn't come into it. She says she's relying on you to keep the peace.'

'In your family? Impossible.' Leone laughed.

She loved Phil's noisy and exuberant family. Like Phil, they were an easy-going and friendly crowd, rather like a pack of outrageously undisciplined dogs. Utterly charming, but exhausting *en masse*. How Phil's mother, Alison, coped with them all, Leone never knew, but despite having five children of her own she'd always found time for Leone. Right from the very beginning Alison had spoiled her, remembering her birthday, taking her on holidays, having her to stay for weekends, even encouraging her to pursue her interest in art—something Leone's father had studiously failed to do.

It was Alison who had bought Leone her first box of watercolours and had taken her and Phil on short painting expeditions during their holidays. Leone had shown talent from the start. Her mother had also been a talented artist—a fact borne out by a small assortment of sketches and watercolours which Aunt Mary had given to Leone shortly after her mother's death.

The collection was mostly of recent paintings of the Suffolk countryside and Leone's favourite now hung in pride of place in her sitting-room. It was a charmingly executed watercolour of an old mill set by a dark expansive lake. A hasty study, done swiftly—judging by the moody leaden sky—because a storm was imminent.

Leone loved it, not only for its simplicity, but because of the images beyond.

She could imagine her mother as she rushed to finish it before the rain came torrenting down, see her hastily packing her brushes and paints and little green canvas stool, see her pause briefly to pull the top of her lightweight jacket up over her head as she ran for shelter under the branches of the towering oak tree depicted in the corner of the sketch.

Leone felt a sense of intimacy whenever she looked at the painting, as if she could stretch out and touch her mother. And even now, when she herself painted, she had a sense of closeness with her mother, a correlation with things past.

'So I'll let Mum know you'll try to make it then, shall I?' Phil's voice came from next door. Leone could hear the low purr of the computer.

'Yes, do. I'd better check with Daddy first, though. I'm not sure what his plans are, yet.'

Phil treated this remark with well-practised tolerance. 'Fine. There's no hurry. Anyway, if you give him a bit of warning he might like to organise a trip to Bordeaux again.' She knew he'd done that one year and that it had been a great success. 'Or what about staying with your Aunt Mary for a few days?'

Leone shook her head. 'Remember, they had that blazing row a few years back. Things are still a bit sticky between them.' To this day she wasn't exactly sure what that had been about.

'I thought they'd patched things up.'

'Not really, no. You know what families can be like.'

'Well, he might like to try pastures new?' Phil suggested.

'He might.' Leone thought it doubtful. Her father was impossibly set in his ways.

She saw Phil had stopped typing and was looking at her in that speculative way of hers.

'I know what you're thinking,' she said defensively. 'But it isn't that easy. I feel responsible for him. Especially since his heart attack.'

'I know you do. It's understandable.'

'And I don't always let him have his way.'

Phil didn't comment.

'I don't,' she insisted. 'I do stand up to him when it matters.'

'Not always, you know,' Phil replied.

Brown eyes met green. Leone knew what she was thinking about. Jack. How her father's disapproval of him had finally led to the ending of their affair.

She walked over to the fax machine and began to tear off the printed sheets.

'Andrew told me Jack's coming over to London on Monday for the week to tie up some deal on a painting,' Phil said, her voice studiously casual. 'Did you know that?'

Leone concentrated on the sheets in front of her.

'No. Andrew didn't say anything to me,' she said.

She wasn't entirely surprised, though. Andrew was still very cautious on the subject of Jack. They'd been close friends from their Oxford days and Andrew had been the one responsible for bringing Jack and Leone together. In those days she'd been in her first year at the Courtauld mastering the technique of gesso, and had been sharing a flat with Phil and two other art students in Fulham. She'd met Jack at a party at Andrew's flat and they'd hit it off instantly. Six months later they'd moved in together. Perhaps that had been part of the problem. Her father hadn't really had any time to adjust since everything moved so fast.

Phil put down her coffee mug. 'Perhaps I shouldn't have said anything either,' she said.

'Don't be silly,' Leone insisted. 'It was all over years ago. Anyway, Jack's married now.'

'Engaged.'

'Well, engaged, married. Same thing.' He'd found someone else at any rate. It didn't surprise her. Jack wasn't one to hang about feeling sorry for himself.

Phil sat back with folded arms. 'It's just I didn't want you to go bumping into him unexpectedly. Thought you'd be frightfully miffed if you found out I'd known and hadn't told you.' She had never been comfortable with deceit.

'Probably would have been,' admitted Leone. 'But there's little chance of my encountering him, is there? I'll be in New York, remember?'

'So you will.' Phil concentrated on her coffee. She'd a soft spot for Jack. He was bright and intelligent and sexy enough to turn a bloody nun on. They'd made a good-looking couple, Phil thought: Jack with his distinguished dark looks and Leone with her slender, aquiline features and that glorious honey-blonde hair. Still, Leone seemed fairly adamant it was all over, so Phil wasn't about to rake over old ground.

Leone picked up a pen from Janie's desk and busied herself making a few cursory notes across Howard Steinberg's fax. She wasn't sure what she felt about Jack Thursley's visit. It had been almost four years since they'd split up and Jack had moved out of their flat and gone to Hong Kong. She hadn't seen him in all that time. Life had moved on. She'd had plenty of other boy-friends since—one of them quite serious—but she hadn't felt ready to commit herself to any of them. Instead she'd thrown herself into work and now had a thriving business. But Jack would see beyond that success and might ask difficult questions about happiness and emotional fulfilment.

So it would be easier not to see him. It made it all less com-plicated. No questions, no recriminations. Leone had no wish to risk losing the thin shreds of her own composure.

Besides, if she saw Jack again, what was there to say that hadn't been said four years ago? Nothing had changed.

No, wiser by far not to meet. New York offered a timely escape.

She picked up the telephone and, ignoring Phil's censuring look, asked for details of flights to JFK.

～

Piers Carlton sat in front of his trading screen, watching intently as the columns of numbers flickered and changed. Taking risks was part of his life and he would have laughed if he'd known of Leone's aversion to them. He positively thrived on that feeling of walking along a knife's edge. The markets he dealt in were driven by fear and greed. And he understood both.

About him the trading floor was bursting with its usual com-motion. The noise was deafening. Two hundred or so traders and their accomplices sat crammed tightly desk against desk, crowded into their tiny space like sheep being hauled off to slaughter.

There was nothing personal in the room. No photographs or plants, just the odd signpost to indicate an individual position. A porno mag, the *Racing Post*, a flag. There was no room for any-thing more sentimental. Nor would the traders wish for it. Bond calculators were jammed against phone handsets and computers' screens, desk space at as big a premium as land spots in Tokyo.

Piers Carlton's computer screen flickered on the desk in front of him, casting a ghastly green pall over his angular face. It made him look unearthly, like a vampire trapped in sunlight. All the traders looked the same. Pallid, gaunt faces that never saw enough natural daylight.

The traders weren't complaining though. They didn't come to the City for their health. They came to make money.

Piers picked up his handset and executed a quick trade, closing out a position at a modest profit. He scribbled out a trade ticket, dispatched it, and then he settled back at the screen again, like Cerberus at his gates.

The dollar/DM exchange rate was moving his way. On a tip-off Piers had traded on them heavily yesterday afternoon. They were now nudging up a few pfennig more.

He felt the adrenaline pumping. He was about to make a killing.

The temptation to sell now and take his profit crept in but he wanted to hang in there as long as possible. He was sure the price would life a few points more.

'Call for you, Piers. Line One.'

Piers grabbed the phone and jammed it under his ear, tilting his head to hold it in position.

'Piers?' The voice was tentative, unsure.

'Mother? Where the hell have you been? I've been trying to get hold of you all morning.'

His mother's voice, slightly hesitant, came back down the line. 'I was out. Margaret drove me over to Whitcombs.'

'You went to see them? For God's sake, why? All I asked you to do was to ring them and demand that they get the Devis picture sent back. You have managed to do that, haven't you?'

There was an ominous silence. He could almost hear her vacillating down the phone. He pushed a hand through his sleek black hair, his thin mouth hardening.

'Mother? You have got them to phone that Fleming girl, haven't you?'

'Darling…'

She hadn't. God, she was pathetic. He knew what was coming. But he didn't want explanations or excuses.

'Mother, I can't believe you can be so moronic. Don't you understand? We need to sell that picture. You know as well as I do our financial position. Just get it back.'

He slammed the phone down and swung round in his chair, his gaze flicking across the screen in front of him. He wasn't certain his mother did fully understand the extent of their debts. It had begun with those bloody Lloyds liabilities. He wasn't sure what on earth had persuaded him to underwrite so heavily in those syndicates. Greed? Probably. It had seemed such a sure-fire thing at the time. A quick, easy way to make money. They were still trying to pick up the pieces of their shattered lives.

He knew they were luckier than many, though. Hatherington Hall had a reputation for being full of pictures which any self-respecting collector would be eager to own. That had always been his lifeline: that he'd be able to sell the paintings if his back were really against the wall.

He'd known it would all have to be done discreetly of course. There were plenty of illegal fences who could move dodgy pictures but he thought he could do one better than that. He had a semi-respectable dealer friend who was willing to help out—for a generous fee, of course. The lucky thing was Piers still had letters pertaining to the paintings' histories—some even commissioning the pictures from the painters themselves—a great bonus when trying to sell a suspect painting. A picture's provenance was all important. And his father had at least been sensible enough to sell discreetly—and as long as Piers and his fleet-footed dealer friend chose carefully, preferably to someone not too high-up the scholarly ladder—their little confidence trick should go undetected. Besides, he could always claim ignorance of his father's dealings, couldn't he? Say he'd sold in good faith, unaware of what his father had done years before? At least he could have done so before all this had come to light.

His mother sending in the Devis picture to Whitcombs threatened to destroy all his plans. What on earth had possessed her to do such a thing? Of course, she hadn't known, as he had done, that the Devis was a fake. Nor, thankfully, did she realise that half of the paintings at Hatherington were also of dubious origin.

His father had kept those facts to himself.

He'd only confessed the truth to Piers on his deathbed. Divulged his guilty secret about how he'd quietly sold off a dozen or so of their best known pictures and had copies of them made to keep the truth from the family.

'Gambling debts, m'boy,' he'd rasped to Piers, 'only way to bail myself out, don't you know. Your mother doesn't suspect a thing. Keep it that way, will you?'

With his dying breath he'd passed on the shame of his secret. And the secret would have stayed hidden but for Lloyds. You couldn't go dropping a cool million and expect to come out unscathed.

All was not yet lost, however. As long as Piers could get the Devis picture back before anyone suspected that it was a forgery, no one would start questioning the Hatherington collection. He could sell one or two quietly to a few carefully selected, gullible, private buyers via his art-dealer friend and all would be well again.

So it all depended on getting the Devis picture back.

The green flickering figures on the screen in front of him began to dance. The DM moved a few more ticks then wavered. Piers hit the phone like a cobra striking.

In two minutes flat he'd sold out. The position was cut, the profit made. Quick and ruthless, that's the way he liked it. He leaned back, stretching his long arms up over his head. Some days it just worked like magic.

As he started to scribble out the trade ticket, his thoughts went back to the picture. His mother was going to be pretty useless about getting it back, he could sense that.

It was up to him, then. *Carpe diem.* He'd known it all along.

And he wasn't about to let that Fleming girl destroy all his carefully laid plans.

～

New York in winter had a charm of its own. Leone loved those crisp, blue-skied mornings and as the yellow cab made its way along Fifth Avenue she felt her spirits rise.

She'd been here for just over a week now and had almost completed two pictures for Steinberg. A third she'd have to take back to London. It was in a far worse state than Steinberg had suggested and the tear and severe flaking might prove a problem unless a new lining was applied to the original canvas as extra support. It was a potentially tricky process—one of the few areas where British restorers surpassed their American counterparts—and would need specialist treatment. Leone had already contacted an expert she knew, a friend from her days at the Courtauld, and he'd agreed to restore the picture for Steinberg provided Leone could bring it back with her when she flew home. Leone would be laden but it couldn't be helped. Long ago she'd learned that there was no such thing as travelling light in the art world.

The cab pulled to a halt and Leone stepped out on to the SoHo sidewalk. It was almost midday and already the gallery-owners in their smart Agnès B suits, their immaculately made-up faces hidden behind Ray-Bans, were on their way to take swift salad lunches. A few artists, drawn by the winter sunshine, were sitting out on the metal steps of their industrial loft spaces, clutching mugs of coffee and gazing out across the roof tops.

This part of New York, with its nineteenth century cast-iron buildings and cobbled streets, had always appealed to Leone. It had once been full of factories and warehouses and was known as Hell's Hundred Acres because of numerous fires that had occurred, but then the artists had moved in, drawn by the huge, cheap loft spaces. Many of them, in their turn, had now moved on—as had some of the galleries who believed the grass might be greener in Chelsea—but the area was now in the middle of a mini-renaissance and was still the nerve centre of the international art market. At weekends it was usually packed with tourists and sightseers, but now it was quiet, with only a handful of trendy shop and gallery owners hurrying purposefully through the streets.

Leone glanced at her watch. She had agreed to be back in mid-town by two o'clock. Howard Steinberg wanted her to look at a picture he was hoping to buy in an auction. That gave her just over an hour to call in on the string of galleries she had promised Phil she would try to visit.

Leone pushed her way through the narrow tangle of streets, past the Chinese sweatshops and primal-scream workshops in adjoining lofts. Downtown New York was a hodgepodge of neighbourhoods, its very incongruities giving this part of the city peculiar energy and creative spark. Ahead of her, across Canal Street, lay ever-expanding Chinatown, and to the east Little Italy. Cross a street or two and the nations changed, instantly, effortlessly. Puerto Ricans and Jews, Italians and Chinese, invisible frontiers all around her, shifting, changing. Old worlds tussling with the new.

It was impossible not to feel the energy, the sheer vitality of the place. Leone pushed her hair back from her glowing face, feeling the fresh breath of wind stirring up from the river. She was glad she had made the decision to come to New York. She hadn't realised just how much the imbroglio surrounding the Devis picture had started to weigh her down. Away from it all, she could rise above Carlton's threats and view everything more rationally. She felt calmer, much more in control. New York always revivified her and this time, especially, she'd needed the sense of freedom this city gave her.

It wasn't just the Carlton tangle which had depressed her, she saw that now. She wasn't sure why but, just lately, she'd felt that the comfortably insulated world she lived in had become airless and unaccountably disturbing. She needed time to sit down and reevaluate things. Leone was keenly aware that her life was in a state of free-fall—her private life anyway.

So, time for a re-think perhaps. These past few days had made her see how intertwined her life had become with her father's of late. It had happened so slowly, so covertly, over the past year or so, she'd been unaware until this trip of how dependent he'd become on her. More so than ever. She adored him, but she saw it was time to claim her own life back. She'd have to be tougher, more ruthless. She wasn't sure whether she could be. It was easy to make rational decisions here away from any emotional pressures, but it would be difficult back in England with her father playing for her sympathy. He knew how to make her feel disloyal, how to send her on a guilt trip for leaving him alone.

Leone hunched her shoulders against the cold. The wind was getting up. She made her way to the last gallery she'd promised to visit for Phil and then hailed a cab to take her back to Steinberg's apartment. She felt generally pleased with her success, having had a positive reaction to Steve Ross's work from all the galleries she'd called in at. Phil would be delighted.

'So, mission accomplished?' Howard Steinberg greeted her warmly as he opened the heavy mahogany door of his penthouse apartment to her. 'And successful, I trust?' Success was important to Steinberg in any shape or form.

'I think so, yes.' Leone followed him into the huge, high ceilinged reception room with its panoramic outlook across New York's skyline. As always, it was a view which took her breath away. 'Even Leo Castelli's showed some interest.'

'Well then, this Steve Ross must be good.' Steinberg looked suitably impressed. 'If I were a contemporary art man I might even be tempted myself.' He spread his frail, wrinkled hands in a small gesture and smiled. 'But you know my partiality…'

She did indeed. Old masterpieces. Very expensive ones at that. Steinberg was really very conservative in his taste and rarely took risks. But she could understand that. He'd come over to New York in the late 1930s, the son of a German Jew with hardly two cents to rub together, and even though he now owned a multi-million dollar publishing company, he was still cautious when investing his resources.

Not that he was tight with his money. Unlike many of the super-rich, Howard Steinberg was unfailingly generous to those whom he liked and trusted. If someone worked hard for him, he would reward them lavishly as Leone knew only too well. Steinberg and his wife spoiled her hopelessly whenever she came to New York.

'So, where are we off to?' she asked. 'Christie's?'

Steinberg smiled and nodded. 'Park Avenue.' He put a cigar into his mouth. He looked more like a wizened George Burns than ever. 'There's a small nineteenth-century landscape I want you to look at for me. It's covered with varnish, thick as a rabbi's beard. What is it hiding, I want to know…'

'A multitude of sins, probably.'

Steinberg took a puff on his cigar. 'That's for you to tell me.'

It was a game. Leone knew he didn't really need her advice. He was as astute and keen-eyed as a hawk, despite his advancing years.

They came out into the panelled hallway and rang for the elevator. Steinberg pulled his cashmere scarf more tightly around his neck.

'So, Leone, tell me. If I acquire this picture can I count on you to restore it for me?'

'You know you can.'

'It will mean rearranging your schedule and delaying your flight back to London for a few days or so. Could you manage that, do you think? It's an imposition, I know that.'

Foolishly, she hadn't realised that he'd want her to restore it immediately. She should have guessed. With Steinberg everything was immediate.

She hesitated, thinking of the heavy workload awaiting her in London. Then she thought of an extra few idyllic days at the Pierre Hotel, away from all the responsibilities and turmoil. A few more days in which to fit in the Met and Broadway, to catch up with old friends. She might even be able to do some serious shopping. She'd seen a fabulous dress in Bergdorf's.

Expensive—as in Third World Debt—but what the hell. She didn't treat herself that often.

'With a bit of reorganising I think I *just* might be able to swing it,' she said.

'Good.' The lift had arrived. Steinberg took her arm and ushered her in past the uniformed porter. 'I have to confess I was relying on you to say that,' he said. 'But let's wait and see anyway. The picture may not be all that I suspect it to be.'

Leone looked up at him. One look at his smile told her it would be. Steinberg was seldom wrong.

⌒

Leone woke up and stared blindly into the grey dawn light. She didn't know what had awakened her. A second later, she heard the telephone ring, the sound bursting across the silence of the hotel room like the blast of a bugle.

She forced herself fully awake and fumbled blindly for the receiver. 'Hello?'

'Leone? It's Phil. Sorry to ring at this hour…'

'Phil?'

She was awake at once. She reached for the lamp and switched it on, blinking in the sudden brightness. The bedside clock said 5:55 a.m.

'Listen, Leone, I don't want to alarm you, but there's been a burglary at the gallery.'

'What?'

'A burglary at the gallery,' Phil repeated. 'I'm here at the moment. The police wanted me to check with you to find out what was up in your studio. I'm afraid I wasn't quite sure. I know you'd cleared most of the paintings, but what was left?'

Leone sat up to clear her thoughts. 'Not many, actually.' She took a deep breath. 'Let me see. There was a Nicholas Matthew Condy, one small landscape, school of Claude Lorraine, a Victorian portrait of a girl and a dog…'

'The two from Morgans?'

'I'd finished those. I delivered them back to Hazlitts late on Saturday.'

'And the Devis, did you send that back?' She could almost hear the underlying panic in Phil's voice. 'It's not in the safe any more, you know.'

There was the merest pause. 'I took the Devis to my father's,' Leone told her. 'I thought it wiser.'

'Thank God for that.'

Leone reached over and took a sip of water from the glass on the bedside table. Her mind was beginning to get into full gear. 'So do you know yet if anything was taken?'

'Well, if the Devis is safe and the two from Hazlitts were returned, then it looks as if we were lucky. You must think me an idiot for bothering you. It's just when we saw the Devis wasn't there…'

'Janie knew I'd taken it home…'

'Well, unfortunately I haven't been able to get hold of Janie yet. She must be at some all-night rave with Ronnie. So you can imagine when I opened the safe and found the Devis missing I thought that sod Carlton had somehow managed to pinch it.'

'Actually that's why I removed it. I thought he might come and make a fearful fuss about it. Bully Janie into letting him take it. If it wasn't at the gallery then there was nothing he could do about it.'

'Well, he obviously thought it *was* still at the gallery, didn't he?'

'You don't actually think he was responsible for the break-in, do you?'

'Stands to reason.' Phil's voice sounded insistent. 'I've no proof, of course. The police say whoever broke in wore gloves, so probably no chance of fingerprints, but the place was turned upside down and yet nothing was taken, not even the cash-box. That's no ordinary burglar, is it? They were obviously looking for something they didn't find. And to me, it positively reeks of Carlton. We both know how unscrupulous he is. I've told the police to go and look him up.'

Leone could envisage Piers Carlton's fury at such an intrusion. 'He'll be thrilled to bits by that,' she said.

'I know,' Phil gloated. She felt no sympathy for the man at all.

'When the police arrive everyone will think he's been done for insider trading or fraud. Should cause a few rumours to rocket through the market. Serve him right.'

Leone remembered Carlton's threats to her. 'Does, rather,' she agreed. 'By the way, have the results come back from the Courtauld yet?'

'No. Not that I've seen anyway. Do you want me to chase them up for you?'

'Don't worry. I'll do it myself on Monday.'

'You're back this weekend then?'

'Should be all finished here by Saturday. Probably catch the night plane back on Sunday.'

'Great. Listen, did you have time to pop into Leo Castelli's with those photos of Steve's works?'

'I did, yes. And they were very interested. O'Donnel said he'd ring you. I went to one or two others who seemed very interested as well.'

'Fantastic.'

'I'll admit it, Phil; Steve Ross may not be my cup of tea, but there seems to be a very positive reaction to his work over here.'

'Didn't I tell you?'

'You did.'

'And I should have everything set up by the twentieth for the exhibition. The whole thing seems to be slotting into place.'

'Brilliant.'

'Listen, I'd better dash.' Leone could hear murmurings in the background. The police were obviously still there. 'Glad the Devis picture is safely tucked away.'

'So am I. Let me know if the police get any leads, won't you?'

'Sure,' said Phil. 'And I'll get Banhams round to change the lock on the back door and get the alarm checked over.'

'Would you? Sorry to leave you to do everything. I know you're frantic.'

'No problem.'

'See you Monday, then.'

Leone put down the receiver.

She wondered if she should ring her father and warn him about the Devis picture, then decided against it. There was no need to worry him. Carlton didn't know where she lived, after all, and her father's safe made Fort Knox look like a piggy-bank.

She glanced at her watch. It was just after six o'clock. There was no point trying to get back to sleep now.

She climbed out of bed and padded across to the window. Her room overlooked Central Park. The leafless trees looked grey-black in the dawn light. It had been raining and a solitary jogger in red all-weather gear was slowly pounding down the glistening path, a dot of colour in the gloom. Like the obligatory splash of red in an Impressionist painting, she thought idly, turning back from the window.

Leone walked cross to the bathroom and started to run a shower. Phil's telephone call had unnerved her a little. Carlton was a troublemaker. She wondered if she shouldn't have followed Phil's advice, ignored Whitcombs' directive and sent the Devis picture back.

It would have been simpler, certainly.

Outside she heard the familiar wail of a siren as a police car sped along Fifth Avenue. She slipped her nightie off over her head and stepped under the shower.

And as she stood there, savouring the piping hot water streaming down over her body, she thought of Piers Carlton breaking into the gallery.

It hadn't frightened her off. It had only made her more determined than ever not to be beaten by him.

Chapter Seven

Vic Morenzo gulped down his drink. The Blue Angel Club was just picking up. A group of stray punters were downing their drinks in the bar area, while a few of the girls arranged themselves decoratively across the sumptuous velvet seats.

Tony had done well with this place, Vic had to admit. He looked around him. The air was tinged with the smell of cigarette smoke and cheap perfume, but apart from that it had a touch of class about it. It looked plush, stylish. The girls looked good, too. You had to be careful these days—Aids and all that. But this lot looked highclass.

He had to hand it to Tony. The club was in better shape than when he'd been running it. Mind you, fifteen years ago, all you had to have was a string of half-way decent strippers and no one gave a damn about the surroundings. Now, people were more fussy.

He glanced over to the floorshow. There was a different stripper every twenty minutes or so. Different shape, different colour, different style. Sometimes a couple dancing together, sometimes a pair of girls. That last always went down well. Always got the punters sitting up.

At the moment a stunning black girl was dancing semi-naked to the strains of 'Pretty Woman'. A Naomi Campbell look-alike, all arrogance and legs. She was stretching her long arms high over her head, jiggling her small pointed breasts.

He watched as she bent almost double, her long corkscrew hair brushing the floor. She swayed backwards and forwards, her legs spread apart, her taut black buttocks glistening sexily in the spotlights. Jesus! What an arse.

He watched as she hooked her fingers into her lacy white panties, running them provocatively along the top and sides; then she slowly began to ease the panties down her legs, standing with her back to the audience, head turned over her shoulder.

Vic caught his breath. She really was a stunner. He would have to get himself some of that tonight.

First, though, he had business to attend to.

He stood up and made his way past the line of girls, the so-called meat seats, and out into the foyer. He gave a quick nod to Mona, the 'head girl'. It always paid to acknowledge her. She might have had the face of a wizened monkey, and God only knew how she managed to squeeze those huge pendulous breasts of hers into that lurex top, but she ran the girls.

Upstairs in the offices, Tony and Gary had their heads down over the books. Tony lifted his head and gave Vic a small salute as he came in.

'Doing all right then, bruv?' he asked, smiling. He had remarkably even teeth, giving him a sharp, predatory look that even his charm couldn't quite manage to disguise.

'Like the black girl downstairs,' said Vic, thrusting his hands into the pockets of his suit jacket.

'Denise? Yeah, right little mover, ain't she?' He nodded in the direction of his drinks bar. 'Help yourself, Vic. Won't be a mo.' He turned his attention back to Gary, pushing a hand quickly through his dark, short-cropped hair.

Vic poured himself a brandy and settled down in the soft leather chair. All around the walls were huge glossy pictures of girls in various stages of undress. Every one had been a stripper at the club at one time or another. One or two had even been here in his day. He remembered the red-haired Maureen—fantastic little stripper she'd been.

He glanced back at Tony, half-listening to what was being discussed. Something about the loan sharks. He felt a sharp wave of resentment that Tony wasn't bothering to bring him into the discussion. It wasn't that Tony was cutting him out, exactly, it was just that he wasn't cutting him in. As if he didn't need him or his advice any more. A new power-base had obviously been established. He'd have to deal with it. Tony was perfect for running the street business because that's what he understood, but Vic wanted the rest of it back. Tony was getting too big for his boots and if he didn't mend his ways Vic would have to put him in his place, brother or not.

Tony lit a cigarette and blew the smoke out noisily.

'So that's settled then, Gary. Can't have Frankie bragging about that in the pubs, can we? See to it.'

'He's history, Tony.'

'Good lad.'

'Right.' Gary stood up. 'Good to meet you again, Vic,' he said, stretching out his hand. Like Tony he was wearing a beautifully cut dark grey suit. It had to be Armani. Vic was very conscious that his own was of lesser quality. Big mistake. He'd have to rectify that. 'We'll be seeing more of you, I hear. Tony says you're raring to get back into the business again.'

'That's right.' A tight little smile sketched his lips. He wished to hell the little prick would just leave. He certainly had no intention of discussing his plans with him. He suspected Gary resented his return. Probably thought he'd try and elbow him out.

Dead right, he would. He'd have to have a word with Sonny about dealing with him. As far as Vic was concerned Gary was finished. And if he wouldn't go quietly then he'd have Sonny gently persuade him. Or do it himself. He'd enjoy that.

'So,' he said, as soon as Gary had gone and the door had been pulled to, 'have you got what I asked for?'

Tony flicked the ash off his cigarette. 'Yes.'

'Well?' Vic felt his anger rising. Tony was being reticent about the whole thing, controlling. He hated that.

'Listen, Vic, are you sure you know what you're doing?'

'Jesus!' Vic banged his glass down on the table. He felt his anger rip through him like a knife. Tony was acting like his keeper. 'I don't need any lectures from you, baby brother. If I want to blow the fuckers off the face of the earth, that's my business.'

'Calm down, Vic. Calm down.'

'Calm down? When those bastards have screwed up my life?' He was standing up now, leaning over the desk, jabbing his finger against Tony's chest. 'Nobody stitches me up and gets away with it, do you hear? Nobody!'

Tony pushed away Vic's hand. 'I hear you, Vic,' he said.

He was careful to hold on to his temper. Vic had always been the mercurial one, but since he'd been out of prison he seemed more volatile than ever. He'd have to watch that. Too much coke.

Vic stood for a moment looking down at his brother, then he sank slowly back into the chair.

'And what about the other business I asked about? What did you find out about that?'

For a moment Tony debated lying. But he knew it was pointless. Vic would find out the truth soon enough.

Vic waited. He was watching Tony like a hawk, sensing his indecision. 'Well?'

'You don't want to know…' Tony began.

The smile faded from Vic's face. 'Oh, but I do, Tony,' he said. His voice was quiet but lethal, like the quivering shake of the rattlesnake. 'I do.'

Tony took a deep breath and stubbed out his cigarette. It had become an obsession with Vic, this business. And obsessions could be dangerous. He had the feeling that the back-wash from this might drown them all, but he couldn't hold out on his brother because of that.

Quietly he told Vic what he wanted to know.

'Brilliant.'

'Do you think so?'

'Absolutely.'

Leone stood by Phil's desk looking at the photograph of Steve's painting Phil had chosen for the invitations.

In bright swirls of greens and reds, it was startlingly effective. Again she was aware of the sheer energy of his pieces, the unfettered way he'd covered the canvas with a series of hurriedly applied gestural marks, she was sure at times just smearing paint straight from the tubes.

She glanced up. Phil was leaning up against the edge of the desk, her right hand re-arranging the photographs on the top, first one way then the other.

Leone could sense her restless excitement.

'The exhibition's going to be a monumental success, Leone. I can feel it in my bones. I've never been so sure of anything in my life.'

There was a fierce pride to her voice which Leone hadn't heard before. She guessed it went beyond a mentor's simple belief in her protégé.

All the signs were there. She could almost see Phil's happiness radiating through her bones and lighting up her face. She hoped to heaven she wouldn't be hurt. Phil's transparent honesty made her vulnerable.

Phil looked up, sensing Leone's apprehension.

'It's all right,' she said, 'honestly. I know what I'm doing. Anyway, nothing's happened yet.'

'Yet?' Leone had to smile. Phil was the eternal optimist.

Phil started to gather the photographs together. 'This one's different, Leone.' Her voice was soft, serious. 'I think I could fall for Steve in a *big* way. He's bright, he's amusing, he's sensitive...'

'And do you think he feels the same?'

'I do, yes.'

'But he hasn't said anything?'

'He's not that sort of person. When you meet him you'll understand. He's reserved, doesn't say a lot. Better at showing his emotions with paint and canvas than with words. But I can relate to that.'

One of Phil's strengths was her ability to see beneath the layers of a person.

'He had a beastly childhood, you see. Suffered terribly. Lost both his parents when he was nine.' She glanced at Leone. 'Well, you can sympathise with that, can't you? And painting's been his salvation, really. His way of expressing himself. He says he views every painting as another step into his unconscious. And I think it's that unflinching boldness, that honesty, which comes across in his pictures. I think that's their strength.'

Phil was equating the man with his paintings, bringing them together as one. She often did this with her artists.

'Do I gather you're smitten?'

Phil laughed. 'Could say that.'

'So when do I get to meet him?'

'Soon. This week sometime. He's coming over to sort out exactly which paintings we should use for the exhibition. Wants to get a better feel of the lighting in here.'

'Sensible man.' The wrong lighting could kill a picture.

'Doesn't like to leave things to chance,' Phil admitted. 'Careful planner is our Mr Ross.'

Leone smiled. 'A man after my father's heart.'

'Precisely.' Phil moved a coffee cup and started to clear up the photographs. Underneath was an invitation. 'Oh, I forgot to tell you about this preview in Albemarle Street,' she said, handing Leone the card. 'It came while you were away. I accepted for both of us.' Some of the critics would be there and Phil would be able to prime them for Steve's exhibition. 'It should be fun. Loads of champagne and bright young things.'

'I'm still appallingly jet lagged,' Leone protested. Previews at that particular gallery never finished early. She hadn't slept at all on the night flight over having been seated next to a hyperactive, jiggling seven-year-old whose mother had sensibly positioned herself with her two older children on the other side of the aisle.

'Nonsense.' Phil's dark eyes sparkled. She was having none of it. 'The only way to beat jet lag is to keep on going. You'll never readjust your time clock otherwise.'

'Mm.'

'Anyway, I need a lift there.'

Leone laughed. That was much more to the point. 'Phil! You're hopeless.'

'I know. But will you? Please?'

'No more than half an hour?'

'Not even a second more.'

'All right, then.'

'Thanks. You're a real pal.' Phil stood up, coffee cup in hand. She went through to the kitchen and switched on the kettle. 'By the way, did you ever sort out the Courtauld and those results?'

'I rang them this morning,' Leone said, nodding as Phil held up a box of herbal tea to her. 'I had a rather odd conversation with them, actually.'

'Odd? Why?'

'Well, while I was away in New York, they received a call from Whitcombs, apparently, asking them not to proceed with the test.'

'I see. And did Whitcombs say why they were calling a halt?'

'That's what's so strange. I've spoken to Whitcombs and they have denied making the call.'

Phil made a face. 'Piers Carlton up to his tricks again, I presume.'

'Seems likely, doesn't it? Anyway, Whitcombs said they'd check with Lady Carlton to see if she was responsible for terminating the tests. She'd said nothing to them about it…'

'You know,' said Phil, carefully pouring the water into the mugs, 'the sooner you get shot of that picture, the better. It's caused nothing but trouble. After the burglary I had a good mind to send that weasel Piers Carlton the bill from Banhams for fixing the lock and alarm. Cost a fortune.'

'I noticed that.'

'Send the Devis back,' repeated Phil firmly. 'After all, it's not really our concern whether it's a fake or not. Your obligation is merely to restore it. That's all. The rest is between Lady Carlton and her conscience.'

'It's not Lady Carlton's conscience I'm worried about. It's her son's.'

'Even that's not your problem. It's not your responsibility to expose fakes, however noble-minded you think you're being.'

Leone took the cup of camomile tea Phil was holding out to her. She was right, of course.

'The trouble is,' she said, 'Lady Carlton still seems keen to discover the portrait's authenticity. And since she owns the picture, if she wants the tests carried out, I think I'll have to oblige.'

'That's a different matter, of course. But if she authorises those tests I think you'll have to be quite firm with her and tell her to keep her son off your back. Tell her you can't put up with conflicting instructions.'

Leone grinned. 'I can't. Far too exhausting.'

'Well, then.'

The phone had started to ring. Leone glanced over her shoulder at reception. Janie wasn't back from her late lunch.

'Talk of the devil. Bet it's Whitcombs.' Leone leaned over and picked up the receiver.

'Philippa Hope-Brown, please.'

As soon as she heard the voice she knew who it was. Steve Ross.

She found it rather touching that he'd used Phil's full name. There was old-fashioned respect in that. His voice was well modulated, quiet, careful; not at all like his pictures.

Leone smiled as she covered the mouthpiece.

'It's for you. Steve.' She grinned mischievously. 'Do you want to take it?'

'What a thing to ask!'

Phil seized the phone out of her hand but Leone noticed when she spoke her voice was deceptively composed.

'Hello, Steve? Yes, thank you for calling. One or two things I thought we ought to work out…'

Leone picked up her tea and made her way upstairs to the studio.

She liked the sound of Steve. Not the usual ebullient, peppy sort Phil attracted. He seemed quieter, more reflective.

Had finally Phil got it right? The thought cheered her.

She turned on the high-powered spotlight and pulled her stool closer to the easel in the centre of the studio, leaning forward slightly to examine the landscape painting positioned there.

From downstairs she could hear Phil's laughter. Perhaps, amid all the chaos surrounding the Devis picture, one thing, at least, was turning out favourably. About time, too.

With a bit of luck it might even mark a change in all their fortunes.

Three hours later, head bent under the open bonnet of her car, Leone wished she hadn't tempted Fate by presuming things were looking up. The battery had gone flat and the jump leads—which she could have sworn were in the boot of her car—were nowhere in sight.

Phil stood beside her, pulling on her gloves, looking maddeningly unperturbed by it all.

'You can't do anything now,' she reasoned. 'It's too late. We'll have to leave the car here.'

'All we need is jump leads and a willing soul,' protested Leone. It was so silly to be floored by such a simple fault.

'Well, I for one have no intention of leaping out into the traffic to wave someone down,' said Phil doggedly. 'Honestly, Leone, the car's quite safe here. Leave it. We'll catch a bus to Piccadilly. I might even treat you to a taxi.'

Leone hesitated a moment, then slammed the bonnet shut. 'Such extravagance,' she teased. Phil determinedly travelled by bus whenever she could. 'I thought you despised taxis.'

'No, I only despise their prices,' Phil corrected her. 'But tonight I'm on a high roll. I feel serendipitous. Besides, I'm freezing.'

'So am I,' admitted Leone. She pulled the collar of her woollen coat more tightly across her face. 'If we see a cab let's grab it.'

It was a fortuitous decision. Barely had they flagged down one of the few black cabs to venture down Ladbroke Grove than the rain started. There was not a bus in sight.

'A lucky escape, if you ask me,' said Leone.

'A sensible managerial decision.'

'Based purely upon your need to get to the champagne as quickly as possible.'

'What nonsense,' Phil declared. 'It's the exhibition I'm interested in.'

Leone laughed. 'That'll be the day. Anyway, it'll be too crowded to see much. Always is.'

And it was crowded. After the taxi dropped them unceremoniously on the pavement outside the gallery, Leone and Phil had to elbow their way through the bottle-neck of people at the doorway. Why was it people always congregated at such an inconvenient spot?

'Really, they ought to make it more selective,' complained Phil, as she struggled through the throng.

'If they made it more selective they probably wouldn't invite us,' Leone replied.

'Good point.' Phil plucked a glass of champagne from a silver tray being ferried past by a smart-looking waiter. 'That would never do.'

Leone glanced around her. She couldn't see many of the pictures because of the heaving masses, but the few she caught sight of already had red stickers prominently placed beside the frames.

She picked up a catalogue from a small glass and chrome table by a mirror. Three artists were on show tonight; all well-proven, solid, not too experimental, each one likely to appeal to the prosperous middle-class clientele who were gathered here.

The gallery knew its market.

'Oh, hell.'

Leone heard Phil's agitated voice and looked up from her catalogue.

'What's the matter now?'

'I *swear* I didn't know…'

'Know what?'

'That *he'd* be here…'

'Who?'

But even as she asked that question she guessed. Somehow she'd known that by retreating to New York she wouldn't avoid him.

She felt the faintest cool breath of air and sensed, even without turning, that he was standing behind her.

'Hello, Leone.'

She swivelled round, glad of the champagne in her hand. 'Hello, Jack.'

He looked just the same, a little thinner perhaps, but still with the same dark good looks. And still, judging by the tilt of his square-jawed chin, as argumentative and bolshie as ever.

'I thought you were in New York.'

'I got back this morning.'

'Ah.'

She didn't bother to say that she'd thought he'd be back in Hong Kong by now. No point. She was conscious of the strained silence between them. But what could she expect? It was never going to be easy, this first meeting after such a bitter parting. She noticed that Phil, the coward, had already slipped away into the crowd. Some support she was.

'So…' Jack was regarding her with a look she couldn't quite interpret. 'How have you been? Andrew tells me you've set up in business with Phil.'

Leone nodded. This was safe ground. 'Yes, for our sins. I'm still restoring and Phil's running a gallery on the ground floor. She's doing terribly well.'

'Not surprised. She always had a good eye. Not afraid to break new ground.'

'And you? I hear you're about to get married.' There: she'd said it. Now it was all out in the open. She glanced up at him. Not even a flicker.

'Next summer. Isabel wants to come back to England for it in June.'

Isabel obviously suffered from a typical ex-patriot's romantic view of England in flaming June, forgetting that it usually poured during Ascot, Henley and Wimbledon.

'I see. What fun.' She realised after she'd said it that it sounded patronising. She hadn't meant it that way. She hadn't meant it to be anything more than a bland, neutral comment. That was, of course, what they were reduced to now. She tried again. 'Your parents must be very pleased.'

'They are.'

'How are they, by the way?' She'd liked his parents enormously. A sprightly, handsome couple who'd been unfailingly welcoming towards her.

'Feeling their age a bit. Father's leg is playing up. It's the cold, I suppose. Never helps.' He gave a light shrug. As their only son he knew they felt his absence sorely. 'Still, they're in good spirits. Trish and her two boys keep them on their toes.' Trish was Jack's married sister. She lived close by his parents in Oxfordshire.

'Well, give them my regards, won't you?' It sounded a bit inadequate, she knew, but somehow 'love' sounded too personal now. She didn't want that.

'I will, yes.'

Leone took a sip of champagne and looked round the room. Phil was nowhere in sight. She'd probably gone down to the basement to see the rest of the exhibition.

'I suppose I ought to ask after your father,' he said.

She didn't miss the brittleness of his voice. She knew his opinion of her father. It had been the crux of the problem between them.

'He's well,' she replied brusquely.

'And as dictatorial as ever, I suppose? Still the Ghengis Khan of Kensington?'

He spoke lightly enough, as if it were a joke, but the smile he gave her didn't quite reach his eyes.

She stiffened. 'You never give up, Jack, do you?'

'Sorry.' He made a swift apologetic wave of the hand. 'Old habits die hard. I promised myself I wouldn't do that.'

'You were never much good at keeping promises.'

'Ouch.' He attempted to look contrite but his grey eyes held an amused glint to them which spoiled the effect. 'Listen, I apologise,' he said. 'Let's not quarrel.'

Someone jostled past her, nearly spilling her champagne. Leone steadied her glass quickly.

'I'm not the one quarrelling,' she said.

He gave a half smile. He was standing so close that she could see the dark smoky flecks to his grey eyes.

'Anyway, what is there to fight about? What happened was a long time ago,' he said. 'We both have other lives now.'

'Yes, we do.' She fixed her eyes on the oil painting of Venice on the wall behind him. 'And whatever went wrong was our fault, Jack, not my father's. The decision was ours.'

'Yours,' he corrected her softly.

She should have stopped the conversation there, she knew. It was heading down a dangerous path. But she couldn't stop herself. She hadn't realised until now how much pain and anger hovered just below the surface.

'You didn't give me much choice, you know,' she said quietly.

'I gave you a very definite choice, if I remember correctly.'

She looked up at him, her green eyes sharp. 'You were unfair then, Jack, and you're being unfair now. You know very well why I couldn't go to Hong Kong.'

'Couldn't leave your father, I know.' His lips tightened. 'Couldn't. Wouldn't. And it seems nothing's changed, Leone. He's still running your life, isn't he?' And she let him, he thought, because she felt responsible for him being alone. Somehow in some ludicrous, illogical way she blamed herself for her mother's death, as though she could have stopped it somehow. 'And you're still out to punish yourself. You're like Andromeda chained to her bloody rock.'

His words took her breath away. She took a step backwards, almost as if he'd slapped her.

'Just shut up, Jack, will you? You don't understand a thing. Never did.'

'I understand everything. That was always the problem.'

'The problem, Jack, was that we were always rowing. Just like now. We couldn't sit together for five minutes without you stirring things up. You were never content to let things lie. Tell me, how does Isabel cope?'

He ignored the bitchiness in her voice. 'I don't row with Isabel,' he said calmly. 'She isn't that sort.'

'And I'm not that sort with anyone else, Jack,' Leone threw back. 'I'm calm and rational and really quite nice.'

He held up his hands in a sudden gesture of subjugation. 'All right. I give in. I don't know how we got into this.' He paused uncomfortably, looked towards her, then away. 'I'm sorry, really I am. It just threw me meeting you like this.'

'It took me by surprise too, Jack.'

'Yes. Well, I never did know when to shut up. Always was a bolshie sod, wasn't I, Leone?'

He caught her eye and then laughed. He had a glorious laugh, deep and resonant. It was one of the things she'd loved about him.

She felt the tension between them ease.

Perhaps, she reflected quietly, it was only to be expected they should have argued like this. The last, necessary picking of the scabs.

'Pax,' he said. 'I apologise. Truly. And I promise to try to behave like a civilised being for the rest of the evening.'

She raised a supercilious brow. 'Can you behave like a civilised being?'

'Yes. Isabel's been training me.'

'Ah.'

He looked down at her, with a slightly quizzical look, as if searching her face for something he couldn't find.

There was a small, awkward silence. Then he said: 'Now, are you going to walk round the exhibition with me and tell me all about New York? I promise faithfully not to mention your father again.'

He was on his best behaviour. Now that the last of the blood had been let she supposed that this was how they'd be with each other should they ever meet again—scrupulously polite.

They had been friends once, friends before they became lovers. It seemed a pity that loving could destroy that. But it was almost impossible to go back.

They walked round slowly together. In between looking at the pictures Jack told her about the Chinese shipping magnate he was working for in Hong Kong. He was trying to build up a comprehensive art collection for him. Leone knew Jack would be brilliant at that. Jack had gained a first from Oxford in art history and had a catalogue in his head of every art collector and artist from Agar to Zurbaran. More to the point, he was a fakebuster of the first order and could spot a forgery a mile away.

She glanced across at him. Hong Kong suited him. He looked lean, muscular and fit. Happy, too. Much less restless than the Jack she'd known four years ago. She wondered how much of that had to do with Isabel. A lot probably. She tried to imagine what she was like, this fascinating Isabel, who had tamed and changed Jack in a way she'd never managed to during their two years together. And despite herself, she couldn't help feeling a tinge of jealousy at Isabel's success. Why hadn't she managed to make Jack happy like this?

She took a sip of champagne to steady herself. Their meeting had unsettled her more than she'd imagined. It had been too sudden. She hadn't had time to acquire any sort of protective shell. That was the trouble with life—it gave you no warnings. You really needed rearview mirrors so that you could see the rusty old bits of the past coming back up on you again in time to take avoiding action. Too late now. No escape. Jack had just landed fair and square on her bonnet.

'You all right?' He was watching her carefully. God knows what he imagined she was thinking.

'Fine.' There was a flatness to her voice, but Jack didn't seem to notice.

They walked on round the gallery together. By the time they'd finished the rounds Jack had bought a small oil painting of Bosham—Isabel had grown up close to that part of Sussex, so he'd announced—and Leone had managed to add two potential clients to her list.

She might have been able to tally a few more had she wanted to stay on but she was beginning to feel the strains of jet lag.

'I'm going, Jack,' she said, glancing at her watch. 'I'm still on New York time.'

'I think I'll do the same.' He nodded over her head at an acquaintance at the far side of the gallery. 'Listen, I'm glad we had a chance to square things between us a bit. I hated us parting so acrimoniously.'

'So did I.'

The same distant politeness. She almost preferred it when they were fighting.

'So…' He paused, a little uncertainly. 'Can I drop you somewhere? I've got the car.'

'Thanks but no. I'll jump into a taxi.'

'You're sure? It's raining pretty hard out there.'

'Positive.'

'Goodbye then, Leone.' He bent to kiss her lightly on the cheek.

'Goodbye, Jack. And, despite our earlier fracas, I do wish you well, you know.'

He smiled then. 'I do know, yes.'

By the time she'd collected her coat he'd gone. Outside the rain was coming down in sheets. She watched people diving from doorway to doorway along the streets, little groups huddling under the dripping awnings like grateful survivors of a shipwreck.

She turned up the collar of her coat and, ducking her head, emerged into the street. The wind was bitter, the sleety rain cold against her cheeks. She could see a dark blue car pulled up under a street lamp a few yards down the street, but that was all. No taxi was in sight.

She had just started to make a dash for it when a white Fiat pulled up alongside her. The passenger door swung open.

'Jump in, for heaven's sake.'

She didn't hesitate this time. She was already soaked and her legs were spattered with dirty water from the puddles. 'Thanks, Jack.'

'Think nothing of it,' he said genially. 'Where to?'

'Lansdowne Crescent.'

'Right.'

She waited, expecting him to make some barbed comment about returning to her father's fold, but he said nothing. Instead he slid the car into gear and drove off down the deserted street towards Piccadilly.

'Oh, hell.' Leone began to feel in her pockets.

'Lost something?'

'The catalogue.' She must have put it down when she'd collected her coat.

'Do you need it?'

'Do, rather. I scribbled down the numbers of those clients on the back of it. I wouldn't mind, but one of them is ex-directory.'

'Easily sorted out.'

He made a rapid right turn and then another. Leone had quite forgotten the fast, unyielding way in which he drove. More like a Parisian than a Londoner. Once or twice she had to hold her breath as he tore down the street towards another car with the blind determination of a knight in a jousting match.

'Here we are.'

She opened her eyes. Somehow they had returned to the gallery without mishap. She pushed open the door and slipped inside. It was still relatively crowded but luckily the catalogue had not been moved from where she'd left it. She ran back to the car, dodging the puddles.

'Thanks,' she said as she climbed back in beside Jack.

'No problem. All set now?'

'Yes.'

He drove off more slowly this time. Leone noticed that he kept on glancing up to the rear-view mirror.

'Anything wrong?'

'Not sure.'

He made a sudden right turn, swinging round so fast that she almost fell against him.

'What was that all about?'

'Tell you later.'

'It wasn't the police, was it? You didn't drive down a one-way street back there?'

'No, I didn't,' he retorted drily. 'I see your faith in my driving hasn't improved.'

'That's because your driving hasn't,' she commented tartly. 'I bet they make you have a chauffeur in Hong Kong.'

'They don't *make* me.'

'But you do.'

'Yes.'

They drove on in silence, under the by-pass and up into Knightsbridge.

There was a bottle-neck at the lights with Sloane Street. The torrential rain had brought the traffic to a crawl.

She saw he was still checking in his mirror.

'For heaven's sake, Jack, what is the matter? If it were the police following you they'd have pulled you over by now.'

'It isn't the police,' he said quietly. 'And it's not me they're following.'

'Well, that's a relief.'

'I think it's you.'

Jack peered through the darkness to where Leone sat, hunched against the car door. She looked deathly pale. He cursed himself for being so blunt.

'Are you all right?'

He saw her close her eyes and take a deep breath.

'Bit of a shock, that's all,' she said. 'I mean, all that business about tailing us from the gallery…'

He pushed the car into top gear and began to weave his way through the traffic. He knew this part of London well, all the little backstreets. He thought he'd a good chance of losing the blue Granada now.

'They were parked outside, I'm sure of it. They didn't follow me when I first came out of the gallery, it was only after I stopped for you that they began to shadow me. When we did that quick circle to pick up your catalogue, that's when I first suspected them.' Grey eyes met green. 'It's not a coincidence…'

He watched Leone push her hands together tightly, her thumb moving against her palm. She knew more than she was telling him.

'Someone's playing silly games,' he said gently. 'Have you any idea who, or why?'

She nodded. She looked so very vulnerable sitting there he was tempted to stop the car and take her in his arms. But he knew that would never do. At the gallery he'd been almost relieved when they'd fought, glad that they'd erected a barrier. A distance. Perhaps that was why he had unconsciously provoked her. He didn't want the memories barely submerged to start surfacing. He had a new life, and didn't want to become entangled in the old.

'So, do you want to tell me about it?' he asked.

'I think it's someone called Piers Carlton.'

He listened while she explained about the Devis portrait, about the phone call and the burglary.

'He owes a fortune. Lost a mass to Lloyds then tried to bail himself out by trying to do some clever stuff on the exchange market and became even more unstuck, apparently. At least that's what Henry Gorrell told me.'

'And he's just trying to frighten you, bully you into returning the picture?'

'I think so, yes. Well, Phil thinks the burglary was a scheme so that he could claim insurance on the Devis but, of course, that failed when he couldn't find the picture.'

'Well, you must tell the police.'

'They know about the burglary.'

'And now there's tonight's little episode.'

'There isn't an awful lot to tell them, Jack.' She pushed a strand of hair back for her face. 'That someone followed us along Piccadilly and Knightsbridge? We have no proof of it. We weren't threatened in any way. And the car—the blue Granada—that hardly sounds like Carlton's, does it? He's a Porsche man, so it's either borrowed or hired and probably impossible to trace back to him.'

'He sounds too clever for his own good, this Carlton chap.'

'He's not clever, he's just slippery as hell. And if he hadn't been so unscrupulous I'd have sent the picture back to him, no questions asked. Now I'm quite determined to prove the wretched things a fake.'

'Have a care, Leone.'

'You used to approve of fighting talk.'

'Did I?' He knew very well he had. But that had been against her father, not against a nutcase like Carlton.

He glanced in the rear-view mirror. There was no sign of the blue Granada. His series of detours had worked their trick.

Ten minutes later they drew up outside the white stuccoed house in Lansdowne Crescent.

He switched off the engine. 'Will you be all right now?'

She nodded. 'Thank you, yes.'

'Might it not be sensible to stay with your father tonight?' He loathed suggesting it, but he was still concerned.

She shook her head. 'I don't want to do that, Jack. I don't want to start to be afraid of being in my own flat.'

He could understand that. If she moved up to her father's house she might never be able to move back.

'Listen,' he said, looking straight ahead out into the darkness. 'If you want me to, I could sleep on your sofa. I've not lost the art, you know.'

She smiled, touched by his offer. She had forgotten how kind Jack could be. But the idea of his six-foot-two frame stretched out on her tiny sofa was not a restful one. 'No, it's kind of you, Jack. But there's no need. I'm fine now…'

'Really?'

'Really.'

'I'll see you in, anyway.' He didn't like to think of her returning to dark rooms and silence.

They got out of the car and went down the path to her side entrance. The rain was easing now.

He waited while Leone inserted the key and threw open the front door. She paused in the doorway. 'Thanks again, Jack.' She made no move to kiss him.

'Good night, Leone.'

He stayed until she'd closed the door and then went back to the car. He didn't drive off at once. He wanted to wait for a while, just to make sure. He sat there in the darkness, shivering slightly in the cold. In the morning, he promised himself, he'd find out what he could about that weasel Piers Carlton.

After twenty minutes, only two cars had passed him. Neither had been a blue Granada. Jack stretched, stiff with cold, and turned on his engine.

He could go home now.

At least Leone was safe for tonight.

He waited until the Fiat had pulled away from the house and then he switched on his lights and drove carefully up the curving tree-lined street towards the white house.

He knew they'd spotted him following them tonight. At first it had worried him but then he'd imagined her fear, and it had made it all the more exhilarating.

A cat-and-mouse game, that's what he was playing. Teasing her, toying with her. He hadn't expected to enjoy it so much. He glanced at the house as he drove slowly by and smiled.

But like all games, he'd have to put an end to it soon.

Chapter Eight

Leone walked past the dark stone walls of St John's Church, head dipped against the icy wind. She was late this morning. A stream of harassed looking mothers were already delivering their noisy offspring to the nursery school on the corner of the crescent.

She quickened her pace. The sharp cold air made her catch her breath. She hadn't slept well last night, but it was anger that had kept her awake, not fear. Anger at Carlton for following her, for having the nerve to try to intimidate her.

She grimaced. She could imagine him at Harrow, a vindictive fifth-former tyrannising all the new boys, making their lives hell. Well, you've misjudged your quarry this time, she thought; I'm not going to let you win.

She crossed Ladbroke Grove and turned into Stanley Gardens. She loved this part of London. In Victorian times there had been a racecourse here. But when the scheme faded, the land was turned over to speculators who'd kept the sweeping curve of the course and huge tracts of gardens, so that now each of the terraces had its own communal gardens, some as large as six acres. Six acres in the centre of London. Hardly surprising the prices of houses in the area were so high.

By the time Leone reached the gallery, both Phil and Janie were already in. Phil was sitting at her desk, encircled by files and photographs and odd bits of paper. She reminded Leone of a magpie perched in its nest surrounded by its prized clutter.

'I'm so sorry about Jack being there last night,' she said, watching Leone hang up her coat. 'I swear I didn't know he was coming.' She carefully balanced her coffee mug on the edge of her desk. 'Did you just about survive? I looked around for you at the end but you'd already left.'

'Jet lag got the better of me.'

'Well, as long as it was jet lag and not Jack. I did wonder. At one stage I glanced across the room at you both and I could almost hear the sabres rattling. It distinctly looked as if war had been declared…'

'It had. But we decided to be grown up about it and call a truce.'

'Jack grown up? My, things must have changed.' Phil grinned. She liked Jack a lot but she knew he'd given Leone a difficult time at the end. He didn't know the meaning of kid gloves. 'Oh, by the way,' she continued, 'Ronnie called in. Asked if we could sort out an evening to talk over the costumes for the carnival. He was suggesting next Thursday.'

'Sounds good to me,' said Leone.

She loved helping with the Notting Hill Carnival. They'd been assisting with it since Phil was at art college. She'd been friends with a Trinidadian girl and, along with an enthusiastic crowd from college, had been commandeered into helping design and make the outfits for one of the bands. Now it had become something of a tradition, made more pertinent because their gallery was in the carnival's heartland.

The door bell rang. Leone looked up. A middle-aged woman in a black-and-white-checked suit was standing outside, black cape tightly pulled around her, gloved hands bunched against the cold. Officially, the gallery didn't open until ten, but they seldom adhered to that.

'Another one after a Perez piece,' said Janie, pressing the buzzer to let her in.

Over the past few days there'd been a steady flow of people to see the intricate metal sculptures which Phil now had on show. The exhibition had been slow at the start but then the art critic of the *Evening Standard* had written a rhapsodic article on the young Spaniard's work, and buyers were now positively fighting over the pieces, like bargain hunters at the first day of the Harrods sale.

Phil winked at Leone then slid across the gallery to give the new arrival a brief explanatory chat about Pablo Perez and his work. She wasn't endeavouring to make a hard sale, Leone knew—all the pieces already bore red dots anyway—but when Phil took on an artist she believed in their work so completely she wanted to convince everyone of their excellence.

'Another one who'd read about us in the *Standard*,' she said, coming back to Leone after a few minutes. 'Amazing what one little piece of publicity can do. One minute there's hardly a drop of interest, now we're swamped. It isn't as if Pablo's pieces have changed at all, for heaven's sake.'

'Never underestimate the power of good publicity,' Leone said. Jack had always made a point of stressing its importance. 'After all,' he'd once told her, 'what is a squirrel but a rat with good PR?'

He had a point.

'I'll make certain Steve gets coverage to the point of satura-tion,' Phil replied, making her way back to her desk. 'Did I tell you that the *Sunday Times* colour supplement was interested in doing a piece on him?'

'No!' Leone was impressed. 'Fantastic.' Phil must have called in more than a few favours there. If she managed to expose Steve to that sort of circulation, it would be an incredible boost.

'Fast piece of footwork, that,' Phil confessed. 'Tried to tell me I was far too late for their deadline. You know how sniffy they can all be about production schedules.' She sat down and switched on her computer, logging into her catalogue notes. 'But when I told the reporter that the response to this exhibition had already surpassed Liz Cunningham's first show, he sat up and listened. They're always hoping to be the first to discover new talent.' She tossed her pen down and leant back in her chair, hands behind head. 'Trouble is, Leone, all this interest scares me rigid.'

'But why?' Leone kept her voice calm. She knew it would have cost Phil a lot to admit her own worst fears openly and bluntly. Phil liked to keep up a front of total confidence.

'Because I'm as nervous as hell I might screw it all up, that's why.'

'You won't,' Leone insisted. She had great faith in Phil's ability. Phil might give the impression of being disorganised and all over the place, but she had hard commercial sense when it came down to business and her artists.

'Think about the fantastic job you've done with Pablo's sculptures. And they were hellishly difficult to show well,' Leone went on.

She could, however, understand Phil's fear. She had so much riding on this exhibition, personally as well as professionally.

She watched Phil idly begin to move the cursor on her flickering screen. She sensed she wanted to talk over something more with her.

After a moment Phil glanced up. 'Listen, Leone, I'm seriously thinking of increasing the size of Steve's exhibition.'

Leone tried to hide her surprise. Phil liked to run a tight schedule but even for her it was cutting things terribly fine.

'Have you time?' she asked. Printers could take ages with the catalogues, especially if there were any colour illustrations involved.

'I think so, yes. I know it's last minute, but there's been such interest I don't want to lose that momentum. What do you think? Steve's produced such spectacular pieces. I just want everyone to know what he's capable of.'

'You don't want people to feel force-fed, though,' Leone warned.

'That's the very dilemma,' Phil admitted. 'And I *know* small and exclusive has always worked well before. But this time...' She gave a light shrug. 'Well, I just feel it's worth the risk.'

'Then do it,' Leone urged. She trusted Phil's instincts. 'And if you need more hanging room take over some of my space upstairs.'

'You wouldn't mind?'

'Of course not. Be my guest.'

Leone's studio on the next floor had been designed so that it could be sectioned off into two smaller areas if necessary. Phil seldom bothered to make use of it, though, preferring to keep her artists' shows more intimate.

'What if I popped up later on this morning to sort out the lighting?' Phil suggested. 'Steve's coming in then anyway. We won't get in your way.'

Leone smiled. A dreadful lie, of course. Phil and Steve would be clambering over all Leone's stuff to reach the lights and wire supports. She'd just have to get organised and move it all to safety.

Phil glanced up as Leone picked up her coffee mug and started to move off.

'By the way,' she said, 'Rupert rang this morning just before you arrived.'

'Did he?' Leone took a deep breath. The results of the pigment analysis on the Devis picture. This was what she'd been waiting for all week. 'And?'

Phil gave a quick apologetic wave of her hand.

'And nothing. You know what Rupert is like. Wouldn't so much as give me a hint. I tried quizzing, cajoling—not a whisper. All he would say was that he was out for most of the day and could you ring him just after four?'

'Right.' A stay of execution for Piers Carlton then. But the hatchet *was* coming. And she'd enjoy wielding it.

'I suppose this means we'll have Carlton out of our hair once and for all,' said Phil, grinning. She began to key in the dimensions of one of the catalogue pictures. 'What a simply blissful thought.'

'Isn't it just?'

Leone didn't mention last night's little episode with Carlton. Phil would only overreact and start jumping up and down and saying that they should call the police. But what was the point? There was nothing to go on, so what action could they take?

Besides, as Phil herself pointed out, it was all almost over now.

The phone on Phil's desk rang. It was Janie in reception.

'Phil, if you've got a moment, Mrs Buckmaster would like to discuss a possible commission.'

'I'll be right through.'

Phil glanced at Leone. As sole agent to the artists whose work she presented, she was always doubly pleased at the prospect of an additional out-of-exhibition sales.

'By the way, what are you doing for lunch?' Phil asked as she pushed back her chair and stood up.

'Working through it. I've got to finish that landscape. They need it back by Friday at the latest.' Leone was trying to catch up from her two weeks stay in New York.

'Oh?' Phil sounded disappointed. 'I'd hoped you might be able to join Steve and me at the wine bar, that's all.'

'Wouldn't I be in the way?'

'Absolutely not, silly. Anyway, Steve says he wants to meet you. Says I've done nothing but talk about you.'

'I hope you haven't.'

Phil grinned. ''Course not. But he knows we're best mates. And anyway I really want you to come. I want you to get to know him a bit.'

Leone met her gaze. I want you to like him, was what she really meant.

I hope to God I do, thought Leone. She knew she was about to step on dangerous ground. She'd always been brutally honest about Phil's men in the past. This time it might have to be different. Treading-on-glass time.

'All right,' she said. 'But can you give me 'til one? It'll give me a chance to make some headway with the picture.'

Phil looked pleased. 'Sure. One it is.'

Leone started up the stairs, coffee mug in hand. Sunlight was streaming in through the skylight. She pulled her stool over to the easel and sat down. She loved this part of restoration: to watch a picture reborn through cleaning was one of the great joys of her work.

She stretched out to the table beside her and, picking up a bottle of isopropyl poured a small amount into a glass beaker, adding a measured amount of white spirit to dilute it. Then she reached for her pair of magnifying lenses and locked them on to her head. Time to start.

Dipping her home-made cotton bud into the liquid she applied it to the top right-hand corner of the canvas, gently rolling the swab backwards and forwards on the same spot. The patch of yellow-grey sky was transformed as the dirty varnish came away. It always excited her, that acute colour change, the idea that beneath the coloured varnish lay untold possibilities.

The phone started to ring. Leone pushed back her lenses and swung round to pick up the receiver.

'Leone?'

'Yes?'

'It's Jack.'

'Oh, hello Jack.' She propped the mouthpiece against her chin. His voice sounded muffled. She could hear the blare of loudspeakers. He was obviously at some train station or other.

'I just thought I'd check to make sure everything was all right after last night.'

Leone smiled. She'd forgotten how caring Jack could be—or had she just not allowed herself to remember?

'Everything's fine,' she said.

'You didn't have any more trouble then?'

'Not even a murmur.' Another announcement blared in the background. Curiosity got the better of her. 'Jack, where on earth are you?'

'Heathrow.'

'Heathrow? Don't tell me you're about to leave for Hong Kong?'

She could hear the low reverberation of his laugh down the line.

'Not quite, no. Paris. Only for a few days. I've got some business I need to sort out over there.'

'I see.'

She picked up a pen and began to doodle on the notepad. It would have been simpler if he were leaving. Safer. She had the sense she was walking on the rim of a volcano. One false step and she would fall into its fiery depths.

There was a pause. She could picture him standing there in his long dark blue coat, small battered briefcase tucked between his feet. There'd be no other cases. Jack always knew how to travel light. She wondered if Isabel did too. Somehow she thought not. She saw her as a three-Louis-Vuitton-case girl.

'So,' Jack was saying, 'I'll ring when I get back in a few days, shall I?'

She took a deep breath. He was just being kind.

'There's no need, Jack. Really. I expect to have the results from Rupert this afternoon and then the whole wretched business will be over and done with. Carlton might think he can bully me, but he can't do a blessed thing against the Courtauld. He'll just have to accept their findings.'

'He'll wriggle like a fish on the end of a hook,' Jack said.

'I know that.'

'And he's a vindictive little so-and-so, be warned.' There was a slight pause. Leone sensed he had found out a few more things about Carlton, but he didn't elaborate. She didn't ask him to. She didn't want to give him leave to go poking around in her life any further. Questions would only encourage him.

'I can manage, Jack. I know what I'm doing.'

'I hope you do, Leone.'

'Jack, trust me. This stupid Carlton débâcle will all be over by the time you get back from Paris.'

She couldn't hear what he said next. His words were lost in the crackle of another announcement.

'What?'

'Just take care, Leone. Look got to go, they're calling last boarding on my flight. I'll ring when I get back.'

'Jack, I'm quite capable of looking after myself…'

Her protest was wasted. It was too late. He'd rung off.

She put down the phone. She wished Jack hadn't seen fit to

involve himself, she didn't want him taking control. There were enough people trying to do that, without his joining in.

Still, she thought, turning back to the picture, once she'd spoken to the Courtauld she'd soon have all the loose ends tied up. Then there'd be nothing for any of them to worry about, would there?

⌒

'Are you sure about this, Ted?'

'Quite, I'm afraid.' Ted sat at his desk, the phone cradled against his ear. Through the glass door of his office he could see a young policewoman sorting through a mound of paperwork in the next room. 'The boys did a double-check on the number plate. No doubt about it. Morenzo was observed driving past your place late last night.'

'I see.'

Richard Fleming's voice was matter-of-fact, but Ted could detect a hint of tension. He must have been half-expecting this, but the news that Morenzo had gone so far as to carry out a possible recce on his house had obviously given him a short, sharp jolt.

'How the hell did he find out where I lived?'

Ted heard the chink of glass against glass and pictured Richard replenishing his whisky.

'Money can buy anything these days.'

There was a brief silence.

'So,' Richard said after a moment, 'what's the next plan of action?'

Ted did not reply at once. Through the window he could see a squad car pulling up in the courtyard. Two young policemen climbed out. Barely out of school, they looked. He thought of the meeting he was due to have with the review board that afternoon. He knew what they were going to say. He'd seen what had happened to Evans and Smith after thirty years in the force. Jesus, he was too young to retire.

'Ted?'

Richard's voice pulled him back to the present. 'Sorry Richard?'

'Our plan of action?'

Ted cleared his throat. 'Nothing concrete, really. More of a waiting game. We can't bring Morenzo in for the moment. Nothing to book him for. With what we've got on him so far, his solicitor would be able to get him back on the streets in five minutes flat. My guess is it was nothing but show and bravado. He probably knew the boys would be there when he drove past your house and was out to taunt them, cause a bit of a stir. But we'll keep our lads on to him.'

'And do you still consider him a threat?'

Ted reached for his coffee cup. 'Let's just say, I think we should continue to give you protection.' His undercover lads had reported that Vic was still adamant he'd even the score against those responsible for sending him down, and though Vic had lost some of his power-base he was clawing it back and was still potentially dangerous. 'But who knows? With a bit of luck Vic may just decide to settle for the quiet life.'

'The quiet life? He was staking out my house, for God's sake,' Richard exclaimed.

Ted took a sip of his coffee. It was cold. Typical. 'I've a feeling last night's little episode was mostly to give us the two fingers, that's all. A display of power. Vic's into that. There've been no other incidents worth mentioning, have there?'

'No.' There'd been a few odd phone calls the previous week, where the line went dead the moment the receiver was picked up, but that was all.

'Nothing at all?'

'No.' Richard paused. Ted could hear the creak of his leather chair as he leant back in it. 'Well, there is one thing. It's probably not connected.'

'Yes?'

'Leone's gallery was broken into last week.'

'I see. Anything taken?'

'No. The police investigating the case thought the burglar must have been disturbed mid-task.'

'I'll check it out.' Ted made a note on his scratchpad. 'But to my mind, there's unlikely to be a link. Vic's the type who'd have made a point of leaving his mark. A small piece of vandalism to underline his threat, that sort of thing. More likely to be local teenagers out to pilfer some drug money.'

'My conclusion exactly.' The area was rife with petty break-ins. It was one of the reasons Richard had been against Leone setting up the gallery there. Not that she'd paid him the least bit of attention.

'Listen, Richard, there's no need for concern on this one. My boys have got it all under control,' Ted said. There was a tap at the door and Pearson's head appeared round the frame. Ted gesticulated for the young detective to wait. 'I just thought you ought to be kept up to speed with developments, that's all.' Richard was a man who liked to meet his enemies head on. Even at school he'd been like that.

'I'm grateful you did, Ted.'

'Nothing to worry about, I assure you. But it always pays to keep on the alert.'

'My view precisely.' There was the snap of a lighter and a long intake of breath as Richard lit a cigarette. 'When we're both a bit less underwater let's make a date for lunch.'

'Good idea.' It was what they always said. They seldom managed it.

⌁

Ted put down the phone and called Pearson into his room.

'Any news on Morenzo?' he asked.

'Yes, sir.'

'And?'

Pearson shifted his feet a little uneasily. 'I'm not sure you'll want to hear this, guv.'

Ted sighed. He sensed his hope that Morenzo would content himself with the quiet life was about to be blown apart.

He leant back in his chair and loosened his tie. 'Tell me the worst then, Pearson.'

⌒

Vic Morenzo watched Denise push back the sheets and slide out of the bed. She really did have an amazing arse, he thought, watching her sway across the bedroom to the bathroom. She walked everywhere naked. No scrabbling for a wrap every time she left the bed like some of the other tarts. He couldn't stand it when they made a pretence of being the shy virgin.

He stretched out and picked up a packet of cigarettes from the bedside table. Outside it was raining. He could hear its heavy splatter against the window panes. He hated that sound. It reminded him of prison.

Vic turned on his side to watch Denise walk back across the room.

'Come back to bed.'

'I've got to go to work.'

'You *are* working…'

She gave him a weak smile. She never thought much of his little jokes.

'Tony'll kill me if I don't turn up for the show.'

Tony. Always bloody Tony. It was really pissing him off. Hadn't she any idea of who had the real power here?

'I said come back to bed.'

'I can't.'

'Come *here*.' He could feel a jolt of anger rising. He was tired of this game. He was out of bed and across the room in an instant. He'd teach her to argue with him, the stupid bitch. He grabbed her by her hair and gave her a sharp, stinging slap across the cheek with the palm of his hand. 'When I tell you to do something, fucking do it, understand?' He tightened his grip on her hair, yanking her head sharply round.

'You can go to…' Denise began, then stopped.

The look in his dark eyes scared her. She'd heard rumours of what he'd done to that East European girl in a fit of temper last week. Broken her nose and sliced open her face with a knife.

The girl still wasn't working. Denise couldn't afford for that to happen to her.

He struck her a second time. 'Understand?' Then a third time, harder still.

A wave of pain washed over her, making her eyes water. She nodded, silent this time, knowing better than to resist as Vic tightened his grip on her hair and pulled her back across the room.

He flung her down on to the bed, then climbed on top of her, pinning her down. 'Get on with it then, girl.' He dug his fingers into her neck, dragging her head down between his legs. 'Make me a happy boy, then.'

She was careful not to show any hesitation. She knew him in this mood. Knew the damage he could inflict.

Too much coke, of course. It was making him violent and unpredictable. And his obsession with settling scores didn't help. He'd flown into a violent rage when she'd asked him about it, vicious little sod. Nearly taken a knife to her.

Denise mixed with all sorts in this trade and she knew a dangerous man when she saw one. If it weren't for Tony paying her a fortune for entertaining his big brother she'd be out of here in a flash. Because sooner or later he was going to snap. She knew the signs.

Just don't let me be around when it happens, she thought.

She should get out while she could, she knew, but Tony wouldn't like it.

And besides, when it came down to it, money was money after all.

Chapter Nine

'So you can imagine my reaction! It was the last thing I was expecting.'

Phil, deep into a bottle of lunchtime Chardonnay, was in one of her outrageous story-telling moods. Leone sat across the table from her listening as she regaled them with a tale about the artist whose work she'd been to see the previous evening. She was in sparkling form, obviously relieved that the lunch seemed to be going well.

'But didn't you realise when you first walked into the studio?' Leone asked. She helped herself to some more fish pâté. It was terribly good. She wasn't surprised that the wine bar was packed.

'Not really, no,' Phil admitted, taking a sip of wine. 'I noticed the studio had a peculiar aroma about it, a sort of pungent, rank whiff, but it wasn't until I saw the far wall covered with these odd patchworks of tiny animal pelts that I realised what the smell was.' She pulled a face. 'It was so macabre. I mean, I could see what the artist was trying to achieve, but it reminded me too much of a gamekeeper's booty of vermin strung up on a fence. I've always hated those. Anyway, he was most indignant when I told him I couldn't take him on, said I would regret it when he became famous. I told him I could live with that.' She grinned. 'The truth is it was the smell that put me off more than anything. I just couldn't have stood those putrid pelts in our gallery day after day. But he insisted the smell was a vital part of the whole experience.'

Leone laughed. 'Thank God you refused. I'd have moved out the moment he brought his furry friends in.' She had a feeling that the smell would have remained long after the exhibits had gone, permeating every corner.

'I suppose he was trying to emulate Jana Sterbak,' said Phil. Sterbak was a Czech-Canadian well known for her work in rubber, chocolate and meat—the most famous of her exhibits being a cocktail dress made of raw flesh which dehydrated and wrinkled with the passing of time.

'I like Sterbak. I saw her work at the Serpentine a while back.' Steve spoke with quiet conviction. 'Fascinating.'

Leone glanced up. Steve was looking across at her.

She could see why Phil had fallen for him. He had a strange, compelling quality about him. His eyes were yellow-brown and alert, and behind the mask of self-assurance was an air of vulnerability which made her wonder what adversities he'd faced—who or what was responsible for the harsh contrasts in his face.

'Sterbak's all right, I suppose,' Phil was saying. 'But her works so obviously derive from Joseph Beuys…'

'The father of us all,' Steve said. 'What artist born this side of the sixties hasn't been influenced by him in some way?'

'Are you?'

'Of course.' He smiled at her. 'When you look at my pictures, don't you feel it?'

Feel rather than see. He did that, Leone noticed: always spoke of the emotions rather than perceptions.

His fox-like eyes met Leone's. 'Phil says you paint too.'

'Only a little. Very amateurish stuff…'

'Nonsense,' broke in Phil. 'You're very good. A bit conventional, but very sound.'

Steve smiled. 'So tell me, before you start with a picture, do you begin with the idea of colour and shape or with a sense of emotion?'

'Shape and colour, I think.' Why did she say 'I think'? She could never have risked emotion. Never.

He nodded. 'Shape. Yes, I can see that.'

'And yours always begin with emotion?'

'Always.' He took a sip of wine and put the glass back on the checked tablecloth. He had beautiful hands, Leone noticed. 'When people look at my pictures I want them to ask themselves not what they see, but what they feel. I want them to experience the power of their own passions as well as my own.'

Leone thought of his huge canvases daubed with bright, tempestuous colours. Ruled by emotion, she could appreciate that. Exposing dark secrets layer by layer.

'Have you always begun your pictures like that?' she asked. 'Even when you were young?'

He stretched out and refilled their glasses. 'Didn't paint much as a child. You might say I started late.'

'He was sixteen,' put in Phil, resting her chin in her hands. She was watching him carefully across the table, attentive as a nanny with her charge.

'Sixteen?' That *was* late.

'Oh, of course when I was much younger I dabbled a bit,' he said. 'My father used to paint and I used to sketch alongside him when I was small, but when he died…' He paused, looked across at Phil as if for support, then continued: 'When both my parents died, I stopped. They were killed in a fire when I was nine, you see.'

'God, I'm so sorry…'

He gave a light, dismissive shrug.

'Anyway, I stopped.' He picked up a fork and began to draw it slowly across the tablecloth. It left ridged tramlines on the surface.

'Because of their deaths?'

'No.'

'Then why?'

'Because…' He paused, putting down the fork. Leone saw Phil touch his sleeve, encouraging him gently to go on. He cleared his throat. 'Because when they died I went to live with my mother's sister. She took me in, you see.' Leone was aware of his voice changing. His face tightened. 'Her husband didn't exactly approve of artists. Thought they were a lot of nancy boys. Used to show his disapproval if he caught me painting.'

'He *punished* you for painting?' She could hardly believe it.

'Used to take his belt to me.' He smiled. It was a thin smile. Leone sensed that the beatings had been brutal. He had not been a happy little boy.

'I'm so sorry,' she said quietly.

He gave a slight shrug and drained his glass. 'I was lucky, though. When I was sixteen I managed to get away from him and I met someone who encouraged me to take up art again. It was my salvation, really. It was my way back out from hell. It saved me from going insane…'

He looked at her. His gaze was very intense. She found it a little unnerving.

Phil squeezed Steve's arm. 'Steve says every painting is another step into his unconscious. That's what gives them their power, their vibrancy. His canvases aren't just mere *surface* excitement. The drama and realism go deeper.'

Leone could see that. No wonder she found his paintings perturbing. She thought of Dante. To journey out of hell one first had to delve deep inside oneself and confront one's own demons. Could she be as honest about her own as Steve had been? She thought not. She had to admire him for that.

A waiter approached their table bringing some more wine. She hadn't been aware of Phil ordering it. Phil was obviously intending to make an afternoon of it.

Leone glanced at her watch. 'God! It's after two thirty already.' She had to get back to finish the landscape. 'Listen, will you forgive me if I run?'

She stood up and retrieved her coat from the back of her chair.

'I'm really glad we had a chance to have lunch,' she said, stretching out her hand to Steve. 'I've enjoyed our chat. And our discussion about the Cubists. You still haven't convinced me about Pollock, though…'

'Oh, give me time and I shall.'

She laughed. 'You do know in his painting "Birth", the bent leg at the bottom of the picture was lifted from *Les Demoiselles*?'

'Of course.' All his charm was in his smile. Leone could see why Phil so susceptible to good looks, had fallen for him. 'But I don't believe that detracts from the greatness of his works. All artists borrow from each other and reinterpret, don't they? Writers, composers. Look at Mozart…' He put his head slightly on one side as if assessing her reaction to this, then shrugged. 'But I can see I have yet to convince you. Next time I shall.'

'Perhaps,' she allowed. She sensed he liked his own way.

He leaned back in his chair, arms folded across his chest. There was a slight air of challenge to his stance. Infinitesimal but there all the same. Phil had warned her he could be moody at times. Artist's temperament, she called it. It was part of the attraction, Leone suspected. Phil never liked life to be dull.

Phil leant over the table to top up Steve's glass.

'Steve and I are just going to sort out the last little details for the exhibition,' she said. 'It shouldn't take long. Tell Janie to hold the fort until I get back, will you?'

'Right. I'll leave you to it then.' Leone slipped on her coat. 'Catch you later.'

Phil gave her a quick farewell salute. Already her attention was back with Steve. They sat, heads bent close together like two plants arching towards the same ray of light. Phil had taken a little notebook from her bag as if to emphasise that it was purely business and not pleasure which had kept her behind in the restaurant. Her face, though, told a different story.

Leone swung her bag over her shoulder and stepped briskly out into the street. She wasn't quite sure what to make of her first meeting with Steve Ross. He was so different from Phil's usual boisterous, pleasure-seeking companions. Quiet, reflective, disciplined—according to Phil he jogged every morning early, without fail, to keep himself fit for the rigours of painting.

Intriguing, Phil had called him.

And Leone, easing her way past the bag-laden lunchtime shoppers, found she couldn't argue with that.

⌒

'You're sure about this, Rupert?' Leone stretched forward in her chair to rearrange the swabs on her work desk, tucking the receiver firmly under her chin.

'Absolutely.'

'The Carltons won't be too thrilled.'

'No one ever is, my dear, when they're told their precious heirloom is a worthless fake. But the pigment analysis is quite conclusive.'

'Right. Well, thank you for ringing me, Rupert. I'll pass the news on to Whitcombs.'

Leone put down the receiver. The results had come as no surprise but she still saw them as some sort of vindication. She gave a slight smile. She had him. Carlton couldn't wriggle out of this one now.

She picked up the phone to ring Whitcombs when Janie buzzed her through reception with another call.

It was Phil.

'So much for only being half an hour,' teased Leone. 'Don't tell me you're still at the wine bar.'

''Course not.' Phil sounded suitably wounded. 'I'm at Steve's. We're just on our way to his studio to sort out a few extra pictures.'

'You've definitely decided to expand the exhibition then?'

'Yes. Steve agrees it's worth taking the risk.' There was a muffled sound as Phil covered over the mouthpiece presumably to say something to Steve. 'Listen,' she continued after a moment. 'I rang to say I don't think I'll be back this afternoon.'

'Oh, yes?'

'It isn't what you think at all, you know,' Phil sounded almost prim. 'Sorting out the pictures is going to take longer than I expected.'

'Glad to hear you're taking your work so seriously.'

'I also wanted to know,' Phil went on, unperturbed, her voice purposefully business-like, 'if I could borrow your car next weekend. I've booked Art Moves to bring the first selection over next Saturday, but they can't manage the rest and Cadogan Tate can't bring them either.'

Phil gave nothing away in her voice. Leone assumed Steve must still be at her side.

'Next weekend? I can't see it being a problem,' she said. She assumed Phil would be dismantling Perez's display Friday week. They always tried to run exhibitions back-to-back so as to avoid wasting space or time. This often meant working into the early hours of the morning, busily packing up one exhibition and unloading the next without pausing for breath. And as Phil's reputation grew, the schedules were becoming tighter and tighter.

'Right then,' Phil said. 'I'll see you tomorrow.'

'Fine. I'll tell Janie.' She hesitated. All through the conversation she'd become increasingly aware of a fierce reverberating sound like a Hell's Angel revving up his motorbike in the next-door room. 'Phil, what's that awful row?'

'Steve's Burmese cat. She's sitting on my knee. Purring.'

'But you hate cats.'

'Ssh.'

Leone laughed. 'Honestly, the depths to which some people will sink to make a good impression. Have you no shame?'

'None. Listen,' there was a hint of conspiracy in her voice, 'got to go. I'll ring you later tonight when I get home.'

Leone put down the receiver and smiled. She could envisage Phil sitting there, all innocence, fussing over the unsuspecting little moggie.

But somehow she suspected that Steve Ross was far too astute to be fooled for a minute.

⌒

Piers Carlton slammed down the telephone with a furious oath and sank forward, head between hands. If only that stupid interfering bitch had sent the picture back when he'd asked her to, none of this would have happened.

He was ruined.

Unless he could think of something quickly, he was utterly and completely finished.

He sat without moving, revolving in his mind the implications of Whitcombs' phone call. No one would touch any of the pictures from Hatherington now that the Devis had been exposed as a fake. The whispers would begin. He could foresee the effects of the catastrophe slowly piling one on top of another, the gradual, painful slide into bankruptcy as he floundered to meet the loan he'd taken to offset Lloyds liabilities.

He shuddered involuntarily. It was what he had always dreaded, fought against. He could still remember as a twelve-year-old watching his father come home, staggering in blind-drunk, having lost a fortune in London at the White Elephant Club. He could recall the bitter row which had taken place, and the shattering sound of his mother's precious pair of porcelain Meissen hounds hitting the floor as his father angrily hurled them across the drawing-room. Days of silence had followed. They'd had to cancel their holiday to Italy that year. Piers remembered lying to his prep-school chums about where he was spending the summer, the shame of it. And he'd sworn there and then that he would never allow the same humiliation to befall him again.

He'd been true to his word. As soon as he'd hit the City a few years later he'd set his mind to making money. Serious money. Nothing would stand in his way as he ruthlessly began setting down the stepping stones to financial security. Now his perfect world was beginning to collapse, rot from within. If he wasn't careful he'd lose the lot. He couldn't conceive how he'd manage—without his Porsche—without his house in Chelsea. Hatherington Hall was of no use, it was hocked up to the hilt already.

And then there was Cressida. Young, beautiful and entirely mercenary. What of her? She might swear her undying love when downing the champagne amid the silk bedsheets in cosy

SW3, but she wasn't exactly the type to stand by her man. Piers had no illusions. She'd be off with the first flash Harry at the first whiff of scandal.

He slammed his fist against the desk partition in a surge of primitive anger. 'Shit!'

The computer rattled ominously as he punched the partition violently again. No one paid any attention. The other traders were used to Piers' outbursts.

Piers slowly lifted up his head and ran his hand through his hair. He had to have time to think. On the trading screen in front of him the column of figures flickered as the dollar strengthened marginally. Instinctively, he picked up his handset and cut his position. The profit was there for the taking. He should have hung in longer, he knew that, but today he hadn't the mettle for it.

He sat for a moment, watching the ever-changing numbers then slowly, deliberately leaned forward and turned off the screens. Pointless to stay on. He would only start to lose money, and he could ill-afford that. He stood up, stuffed a few papers and analysts' reports into his briefcase and made for the door. What he needed now was a drink. Several drinks.

He grabbed his dark blue cashmere coat off its peg and set out for Corney & Barrow in Broadgate.

~

The doorbell was ringing but he made no attempt to answer it. He sat in the darkness barely moving, his fingers slowly flicking the edge of the journal in his hand.

He didn't want to see anyone tonight.

He glanced down at the magazine. God knows where he'd picked it up originally. It was months old.

He ran his fingers over the flat surface of the photograph. It was slightly larger than the others on that page. God, how he hated those smiling faces. He read the caption again. 'Miss Leone Fleming and Sir Richard Fleming attending a charity dinner at the Guildhall.' Looking so bloody pleased with themselves.

He'd laughed when he'd first seen it. Now he couldn't remember what he'd found so funny about it.

He took a pair of sharp-pointed scissors and began to cut across the page.

He sliced across their bodies.

Across Leone's head.

Snip. Silly bitch.

Keep the anger under control, he told himself. His mother had always told him that when he was a child. You'll hurt someone one day if you don't master that temper of yours. She'd been right, of course.

He took a deep breath. The hatred was so strong he could almost taste the sourness of it. He had to try to contain it. How could he think carefully if his anger were so fierce it almost consumed him? And he had to think carefully. Plan his next move.

He began cutting again, the thin shards of paper falling to the ground.

Across the face.

Snip.

He found he was laughing now. He wasn't sure why. Except there was something very satisfying about cutting up someone you detested. Therapeutic, they'd probably say.

His hands were shaking now. Was it excitement or anticipation?

Do it.

Across the eyes.

Especially the eyes.

Snip. Snip. Snip.

Serve the silly bitch right.

Chapter Ten

The sound of the telephone made Leone jump. She'd been lost in her own world all morning, deep in concentration, struggling to remove a stubborn bit of varnish from the corner of the landscape. She put her swab of cotton-wool aside, pulled the phone nearer to her and picked up the receiver.

'Miss Fleming?'

The woman's voice was not one she immediately recognised. It was elderly and unmistakably upper-class, the sort that said 'gel' instead of 'girl' and would have defended the empire with its last dying breath.

'Yes?'

'This is Lady Carlton speaking. I was wondering if we might have a little chat.'

Leone held back a sigh. She'd been expecting this, ever since she'd told Whitcombs the results of the pigment analysis. She'd thought the call would be from Piers, however, rather than his mother.

'Lady Carlton, I'm not sure if I'll be able to be of much help to you,' she began.

'My dear, I'm sure you will.' There was a slight pause and the sound of a nose being briskly blown. 'I was more than a little upset by the telephone call I received from Whitcombs last night…'

'I imagine you were.'

'I still can't believe it. That Devis has been in the family for years. Passed down from generation to generation.'

'It's true, though, I'm afraid. No doubt about it.' Leone took care to emphasise this last sentence. She felt herself becoming defensive. Why should she justify her position? 'I shall send you a copy of their results, of course, but I assure you the Courtauld was quite clear in its findings.'

'I'm only too aware of that, Miss Fleming.'

There was a silence. Outside in the street below Leone could hear a car radio blaring out a Phil Collins number as someone slowed at the corner. A wisp of the song floated up through the studio's open window before the car roared off down towards Ladbroke Grove.

'The truth is,' Lady Carlton went on, 'there are several things I wish to discuss with you. I was wondering if you could come up to see us in Suffolk? Perhaps you could bring the Devis portrait with you.'

Inwardly, Leone groaned. This was just the sort of complication she'd hoped to avoid.

'I'm not certain that would be possible. I don't normally deliver pictures myself, you see,' she replied. 'I usually get a courier to deliver for me. Or clients come and pick up their pictures themselves.' She really didn't want to get involved in journeying up to Suffolk.

'I understand that, Miss Fleming. But I do wish to talk to you face-to-face about something rather important and it's difficult for me to get down to London. I'm disabled, you see. In a wheelchair.'

It was a statement without self-pity. Lady Carlton came from a generation and class who did not whinge about their difficulties.

'I'm sorry, Lady Carlton, really I am, but I'm not sure I'll have time to come up to Suffolk,' Leone said firmly. 'But as regards transporting the picture, a company called Art Moves is very efficient, I can assure you.'

'I'm sure they are,' interrupted Lady Carlton. There was a steely dignity to her tone. 'But I fear you miss my point, Miss Fleming. I would like you to come up to Hatherington. There are several things I would like you to look at for me. Other paintings. Do you understand what I'm trying to say?'

Leone understood only too well. Other paintings that might equally be frauds. She may have unearthed a hornets' nest.

'Look, to be honest I think I'd be wasting your time; I'm no expert. But I can give you the name of someone at Sotheby's…'

'I don't want someone at Sotheby's. I want you, Miss Fleming. I trust your opinion.'

For the first time during their conversation Lady Carlton's voice faltered.

Leone inwardly sighed. She did not want to be involved. She tried to block out an image of a frail Lady Carlton in her wheelchair.

'I'm afraid it's out of the question,' she said, hating herself.

'I'm sorry to hear that. I was rather relying on you, you see.' There was the merest pause. 'I know it's an imposition but I do need your advice. I should be so terribly grateful, my dear. And you will, of course, charge me your usual fees and travel expenses?'

Despite all her resolutions, Leone felt herself wavering slightly. Old-fashioned civility was so rare in these days of graceless modern aggression she felt it working on her like a soothing charm.

'It would be far more sensible for you to instruct Sotheby's,' she began. But even to her own ears the intransigence was no longer there.

'I was never one to be sensible,' Lady Carlton informed her brightly, 'I rely on instincts. And my instinct tells me that you'll be discreet and efficient.'

'I could only give you an uninformed view and it would be on an entirely unofficial basis.' Why was she relenting like this? Phil would be furious with her.

'I expect nothing more.'

'And there would be one very important proviso.'

'Yes?'

'On no account will you inform your son of my intended visit, nor of its purpose.'

'He hasn't been badgering you has he, the tiresome boy?'

'A little more than badgering…' Leone paused. 'Quite a lot more, actually.'

There was a silence. Leone got the impression that her words had not taken Lady Carlton entirely by surprise. She obviously knew of her son's uncertain temperament.

'I can promise you Piers will be told nothing of this.'

'I have your assurance on that?'

'Yes.'

'Then I'll ring you next week to fix up a mutually acceptable time for my visit.'

Leone felt she could hear the old lady letting out her breath with relief.

'Thank you, Miss Fleming. You've lifted a great weight off my mind. Thank you.'

Leone put down the receiver and leaned back in her chair, clasping her hands behind her head. Had she been a fool to give in? The trouble was, she'd always been easy prey for a sob story. One quaver of the old lady's voice and she'd succumbed like a mother with a tearful child.

Do you know what you've let yourself in for, you fool? she asked herself. What if Carlton finds out you're intending to go up to Hatherington?

She turned back to the landscape, trying to banish the thought from her mind. Apprehension stirred within her, like an armed horseman on the horizon edging nearer, but she determinedly fought it down.

All she knew was she wouldn't tell Phil of her decision. Or Jack, for that matter.

⌒

Phil stood at the top of the studio stairs watching Leone as she worked. The soft strains of Bach's double Violin Concerto drifted across the sun-flecked room, barely audible above the whirr of the extractor fan. People had their own rhythms to which they liked to work.

Monet had painted to Debussy, so they said. Steve liked Liszt.

She'd been surprised when she'd first heard the Concerto in E flat wafting through his studio. She'd expected something less flamboyant, somehow. It seemed to contradict the image she had of the quiet, reflective Steve. Yet Liszt himself was a man of contradictions: the showman and the committed artist, the virtuoso and the recluse, the hedonist and the abbé, an extrovert yearning for a life of serenity. Perhaps that was why Steve had chosen him. Contrasts created a sort of spiritual, brooding energy.

'You all right?'

Leone had stopped working and was looking at her.

'Fine. Just bored with sorting out the catalogue.' Phil came up the last step, the tips of her fingers trailing the top of the banisters.

'How was last night?'

'Actually, I tried to ring you when I got home but you weren't there.'

'Sorry about that. Matt Renshaw rang up to ask if I wanted to see that French film on at the Gate.'

Phil brightened at her news. She thought the rat would never ring. 'The divine Matt Renshaw? He rang and you didn't tell me! And was he as gorgeous as you'd thought he'd be?'

'Bit of a disappointment, really,' Leone admitted. He was too like Phil's old boyfriend, Paul. Fancied himself rotten. 'All gloss and no substance, if you know what I mean.'

Phil grinned. 'God, you're difficult to please!' she teased. 'I'd have jumped at him!' In reality, she probably wouldn't have. She'd learned her lesson with the pretentious Paul. Phil was moving towards the quieter, more reflective type. 'So,' she said, 'if Matt wasn't up to much, what was the film like? Was it the one with Emmanuelle Beart in it? Any good?'

'Fantastic. Worth catching if you can,' Leone said. She reached out for her coffee. 'So, did you manage to sort out the last of the pictures?' She obviously didn't want to talk about Matt Renshaw any more.

'Pretty much. It's a fantastic collection, you know. And you'll never guess what?' Phil paused long enough to make sure she had Leone's full attention. 'Steve's given me one of his pictures. Imagine that? A thank you for all the hard work I've been putting in for the exhibition. It's an absolute stunner. Come and have a look when you've time. It's downstairs in the back room. Even *you'll* be impressed by this one!'

She'd been quite overwhelmed when Steve had given it to her. None of her other artists had been so generous, even those who had a lot more to be grateful for than mere hard work.

'So, is it all going great guns?' Leone asked.

'The exhibition, you mean?'

'No, silly. Your relationship with Steve.'

'Oh, that. Pretty good, as it happens.' She stretched, leaning slowly back against the banisters. 'But I've decided not to rush it this time. Taking things slowly for a change.'

'That must be a first.' Leone swivelled round in her chair to face her with a grin. 'Your Steve Ross isn't gay, by any chance?'

'No! *Certainly* not! If you must know, he's wonderfully sexy. t's just…' Phil stopped. It seemed oddly out of place for her to be talking of having misgivings about going to bed with Steve. Old-fashioned principles about love and commitment had not entered the equation before.

Leone was smiling. 'He's wonderful. He's sexy. And you've got a problem?'

'There isn't a *problem* as such. I just want to be sensible, that's all.'

Phil ran the tip of her index finger slowly across the tip of Leone's desk. She could see Leone's surprise. Sensible was not an adjective she usually associated with herself, either.

'You're not sure of him, is that it?' Leone asked gently. She didn't want to probe but she sensed it wasn't just the boredom of cataloguing which had driven Phil upstairs.

'Not sure of myself, actually.'

'Ah.'

'You see…' Phil hesitated. She knew the answer, of course. She'd already trodden through the secret quarries of her mind. 'I don't want it to be just a game this time,' she said at last. 'I want to be sure. I *like* him. I like him enormously. But I'm just not certain it's love with a capital L or just plain lust.'

'That's never stopped you in the past,' Leone pointed out. 'Remember Marco. And Tristan…'

God, was she going to name them all now? Phil wondered. A roll of honour for the fallen. That was the point, of course. Leone was always cautious, looked and considered before she leapt. Phil usually just leapt. Easy, uncomplicated, it had always worked in the past.

But yesterday afternoon, something had held her back. She'd been aware of the faintest of undercurrents, of the need to tread carefully.

'Steve's different,' she said quietly. 'That's the point. He's not as emotionally robust as Marco or Tristan.' She was both wary of his vulnerability, and of her own responsibility. 'He's had such a bloody awful life, what with his parents dying and that sadistic uncle of his. I don't want to hurt him, Leone, that's the crux of it. I don't want to be the one to give him another kick in the teeth.'

'Who says you will? It might just be the real thing this time.'

Phil ran her hand slowly across the smooth, wooden grain of the desk. 'It might. The trouble is, you know what I'm like…'

Phil was too selfish, too protective of her own space, to countenance serious involvement. She'd seen her mother, motivated by the idea that children need an unselfish adult to offer guidance and shelter, to render their world safe, give up a promising career as a set designer to devote herself to the increasing demands of her family. Phil didn't want to have to make that sacrifice.

So where did it leave Steve? Phil leant forward, resting her hands against her chin. Hell, she still felt just as confused. Perhaps it would be wiser not to think about it until after the exhibition was over. She was not due to see him for the next few days anyway and it wouldn't hurt to put everything on hold for a few weeks, would it? It would give her time to get her emotions together. She knew she wasn't holding back just because she was afraid of hurting Steve. She was afraid of her own vulnerability, too. She'd never felt this way before.

She took a deep breath, glancing across at Leone. She wondered if she'd seen through her little act. Probably. Leone didn't miss much.

'Anyway, I'm not seeing him for the next couple of days,' she said. 'Too much to do organising his exhibition.' She straightened, stretching her arms high above her head. 'Which reminds me, I'd better get back to the wretched catalogue.' She was glad, for once, to be snowed under. It took her mind off Steve.

'Look, if you're really stuck, I'll give you a hand,' Leone offered.

It was a generous offer. Phil knew how tight Leone's own schedule was. 'Thanks, but I think I'll just be able to swing it,' she said. 'If I work late this evening I should make the printer's deadline tomorrow...Oh, hell!' She suddenly remembered one of her phone calls last night. 'There's a book launch I promised to go to...'

'Which one?'

'Diane Thomas's. At Leighton House. Some book on art psychotherapy. I promised faithfully I'd go.' Diane was an old friend of her mother's. 'She rang especially. Asked if I could rally round a few friends.' She looked pointedly at Leone. 'Apparently numbers are a bit thin on the ground and you know mother's too busy down in Cornwall to come up for it.'

'Don't look at me.'

'Oh, come on. You came to the last one of Harry Winter's.'

'That's why I said, don't look at me.'

'Honestly, Leone, it wasn't that bad.'

'I know these wretched self-publicity book launches. There's one glass of warm white wine, Bulgarian probably, and somebody sitting by the door with a pitifully huge pile of the author's new book so you can't escape without buying one.'

'Nonsense. It'll be fun.'

'Phil, it'll be as much fun as having your teeth extracted by a dentist with the shakes.'

'Quick drink, that's all. I can only stay a few minutes anyway. I've got to get back to finish the catalogue.'

'Ah, now it all becomes clear. You want me to drive you, don't you?'

Phil grinned. Leone knew her too well. 'Now there's a thought…'

'Honestly, you treat me like your own private chauffeuring service.'

'Can I take it that's a yes, then?'

'I've masses of work to do…'

'Perfect. So have I. A quick half an hour and then out?'

'Half an hour?'

'At the outside.'

'Just don't let me be cornered by some bearded young academic with halitosis again.'

'Oh, God!' Phil grinned, remembering what had happened to Leone last time. She was too nice, that was the trouble. Phil would have had no qualms about leaving him looking alone and pathetic in the corner. 'Don't worry, I've got a nose for these things. Diane's a sweetie and this one's going to be fun. Trust me.'

Leone's sarcastic reply was lost in the shrill peel of the phone.

Phil, watching her lift the receiver, decided it was a good moment to make her exit.

⌒

Piers Carlton drove through the tall electronic gates of the Harbour Club and parked his Porsche in the red-bricked courtyard outside.

Twice a week he came here to play tennis against a regular set of City friends, all old Harrovians or Etonians. Cressida had complained at first about the time he spent there until he'd told her precisely who his partners were and exactly what they were worth. Cressida had shut up then. Piers knew how to impress her. She'd always had that fatal weakness, that susceptibility to revere the rich and famous, the beautiful and entirely worthless.

Piers came through the reception and past the swimming pool. He could see one or two determined souls performing their mandatory lengths in the flickering blue water on the floor below. Fitness was taken seriously here. Or at least being-seen-to-be-fit.

Piers glanced at his watch as he made his way through to the changing rooms. It was ten to six. After he finished his game he would go straight to the Hope-Brown Gallery. He'd spoken to the receptionist on the telephone earlier and she'd told him the Fleming girl would be back from her evening meeting by seven. Perfect timing.

Last night, while sitting in his flat he'd realised he had to see the meddling bitch face-to-face. Confront her. It was the only way. He had to persuade her to keep her mouth shut about the Devis picture.

And at this moment in time he didn't care what it took.

~~

Leone and Phil stood at the top of the staircase at Leighton House, scanning the densely populated drawing-room in front of them.

'So much for nobody coming to this do,' remarked Phil, plucking a glass of wine from a passing waiter's tray and easing herself into the room. 'Any more and it would be like the Black Hole of Calcutta.'

'Not exactly low on numbers, is it?' Leone agreed. Phil, she saw, had conveniently disregarded the fact that her own previews were usually far more crowded than this.

She took a sip of wine. It was surprisingly drinkable. Australian. Not exactly subtle, but pleasant all the same.

'The chap in charge of Diane's books downstairs told me there are five authors collaborating on this publication, that's probably why there's a crush,' she told Phil. 'Presumably each of them panicked when they thought there weren't going to be enough guests.'

'And caught poor suckers like you and me. Typical,' said Phil.

She made a face but Leone could tell she was relaxing into the mood of the party. She'd already polished off most of her wine and was holding her glass out to a harassed-looking waitress for a refill.

'Heavens, do you see who I see?' Phil said, giving a nod in the direction of the long sash windows. 'Andrew! He didn't tell me he was coming.' She gave her brother a quick wave and they started to ease their way through the crowd towards where he was standing, deep in conversation with a small, bearded man.

'So you received the frantic late-night call too,' he grinned as they reached his side. He gave them both a kiss. 'Three-line whip and all that. I've even seen Marcus Merriman here.'

'Marcus? Goodness!' Marcus was an old flame of Diane's who had dropped out of sight several years before.

'She's really called in the cavalry this time, hasn't she?' Andrew smiled affectionately down at his sister and laid his arm gently on her shoulder. 'So how are you? Exhibition going well?'

'Brilliant. Sold out. Even getting some commissions coming in.'

'Clever you.'

Watching them together, Leone smiled. She'd always envied Phil's easy, close relationship with her brothers. When she'd been younger she'd often tried to imagine what it would have been like to be part of a large, boisterous family such as Phil's. After staying with the Hope-Browns for a week or so, returning home felt like listening to a single reed-thin voice after experiencing the full pleasure of the Grand Opera.

'Now,' Andrew turned back to her, pushing a hand through his untidy mop of brown hair, 'have you met Hugh? He's one of the coauthors of the book. Wrote the section on the role of art psychotherapy in prisons.'

They all shook hands. Hugh's grip was firm, but his hand was thin and bird-like. She hadn't immediately realised how small Hugh was, though perhaps he merely seemed it beside

Andrew's big, cuddly, teddy-bear frame. She wondered how he coped with those beefy villains in prison. Perhaps it helped not to be considered a threat in any way.

'Hugh has a theory about the significance of symbolisation,' said Andrew, enthusiastically attacking the prawn wontons being brought round. 'Now that will interest you, Phil. I seem to remember you were really hooked on art psychology at one time, weren't you?'

Leone had forgotten that. When she'd first left college, Phil had been keen to follow in Diane's footsteps. But somehow, almost without intending to, she'd slipped into selling her friends' paintings for them instead, and the art-psychology venture had faded into oblivion.

Just as well, Leone thought. Phil's happy-go-lucky character was far more suited to charming prospective clients than trying to diagnose the emotional trauma of others. She would not have had the patience to deal with dysfunctional patients.

But she was still fascinated by the subject, Leone could tell, and what had intrigued her about art psychology then still drew her now. She saw Phil turn the full force of her enthusiasm on Hugh and what he was discussing.

'Because verbalism is our primary mode of communication we're more adept at manipulating it, don't you agree? And that's why art psychotherapy works so well: because it doesn't obey the rules of language.'

Leone smiled to herself. Hugh made it all sound so highbrow. Art therapy might be complicated, but boiled down to its bare bones surely it was only a way of analysing a patient through their paintings and drawings rather than talking from a couch?

She left Phil and Hugh discussing symbolisation and the theories of Jung and turned back to Andrew who asked her how her business was going.

'Phil tells me you're awfully busy at the moment.'

'Am, rather. Goes in fits and starts though.'

'Know exactly what you mean,' agreed Andrew. His own business constantly ran on a financial knife-edge. As it happened, he'd just received a rather large order from a Japanese company. A week before that, though, he'd been wondering where his next commission would be coming from and how he could possible manage to meet that month's mortgage repayment. He hesitated a moment, as if assessing her, then asked, 'So how did you find Jack when you saw him?'

She glanced quickly up at him. She'd forgotten Phil would have told him of their meeting. Phil had about as much discretion as a tabloid gossip columnist.

'Oh, in pretty good form, actually,' she said, recovering. 'Hong Kong obviously suits him.'

'It does.' Andrew took a sip of wine. 'I think he'll miss it terribly.'

'What?' Had she heard him right?

'Hong Kong. He'll miss it when he comes home.'

'He's coming back? He didn't tell me that.' Surprise lifted her voice. She remembered Jack's sleek look of contentment, his enthusiasm for his job. 'He seemed so settled.'

'Yeah, well…' Andrew thought about being politic then decided against it. 'I think Isabel wants to come home,' he admitted quietly. 'She misses her family. Doesn't want to make Hong Kong her home.'

'Oh, I see.' Leone felt her lips tighten into a bitter line. When she'd wanted to stay in England Jack hadn't been so willing to make such compromises. Isabel's wishes were a different matter, it seemed.

'Of course, nothing's settled as yet, but the changeover in 1997 altered things a bit…'

Andrew was rattling on about the effects of the British handing over the island to the Chinese, something about whether or not Beijing government had decided to classify the art market under Foreign Affairs, but Leone was barely listening.

She was thinking about her last savage row with Jack. She remembered his angry dissection of her relationship with her father and her equally venomous condemnation of his restless ambitions. Now his ambition had suddenly proved less important, and family ties more so. It was strange how quickly perspectives changed. Jack would be able to justify it, of course. He could justify anything. Still, it was interesting he'd said nothing to her about coming home.

'And of course, there's always Singapore…'

She saw Andrew was looking at her expectantly, waiting for her to reply. 'Yes, right,' she said, hoping Andrew wouldn't realise she hadn't a clue what he was talking about, 'there's always Singapore.'

He smiled at her. Andrew was no fool.

He took her elbow. 'Come on,' he said. 'Come and say hello to Diane. You remember her, don't you?'

'Of course.' They'd met on several occasions at the Hope-Browns' house in Cornwall. Diane was a close friend of Phil's mother, Alison. They'd been at art college together in the early sixties. A golden time, according to Alison, with artists such as Hockney and Warhol; a time, she would pointedly say to Phil, when art students were actually made to draw every day.

'Hello, Andrew. Sweet of you to come. And Leone, too…'

Diane, small and sprightly, greeted them warmly. She was obviously very pleased with the launch. Several of the press had come, it seemed, and the *Telegraph* wanted to do a short piece on her to tie in with the book. 'They're particularly interested in my work with anorexics and depressives. You know, art psychology has suddenly become all the rage. Five years ago, people associated it solely with mental institutions and rarely took any notice of it; now, it's become far more accepted.'

'I think it's seen to be of great advantage to those patients resistant to conventional psychotherapy, isn't it?' asked Andrew.

'Yes, it is. Verbalisation is linear in communication,' Diane explained, getting into her stride. 'Art expression is spatial in nature. That's its advantage…'

'Diane!'

They were interrupted by a squat, square-shouldered man pushing his way into their circle. 'I've just had a peek at the book. Wonderful.' He pressed his florid face up against Diane's. 'Bringing art psychology to ordinary people, splendid idea.'

Leone saw Diane try not to wince at his words. How sanctimonious and arrogant the academic world could be sometimes, thought Leone. She saw Andrew raise his eyebrows and grin at her. Ordinary people, indeed.

She took a sip of wine. Through a fleeting gap in the crowd she caught sight of Phil who was deep in conversation with a tall, slim girl whose auburn hair was pulled sharply back from her thin, pointed face into a French plait. Phil was obviously enjoying herself. Her face was flushed and her voice was happily raised. She was showing no signs of wanting to leave.

Leone tried to attract her attention through the crowd but failed.

'You didn't fall for the one about only staying for half an hour, did you?' asked Andrew, watching her antics with faint amusement. 'Foolish child. Have you ever known Phil to leave a party in full swing?'

'She's got her catalogue to finish. Printer's deadline.'

'She'll sweet-talk her way into earning a reprieve.' Andrew knew his sister's skills.

'She already has once.'

'Typical.'

A waitress was bearing down on them, carrying her platter of spicy sausages and kebabs. Leone stretched across and skewered one.

'One more drink, then I'll have to round her up,' she said, glancing at her watch.

'What a little optimist you are,' declared Andrew, tucking into his kebab. 'You know what Phil is like at these affairs.'

'I do.' A party animal, that was Phil. Put more than two or three people in a room and the extrovert in her would take over.

'You're far too nice to her,' Andrew went on, skewering another two sausages before the waitress moved hurriedly on. 'She exploits you shamelessly.'

Leone grinned. 'Don't I know it? But I don't mind.'

She wouldn't allow Phil to do so otherwise. The truth of it was, she enjoyed being involved in Phil's schemes, loved her boundless energy and the pleasure of being sucked in by it and carried along.

But it worked both ways. She knew Phil needed her own, careful measured approach to offset her reckless one. Life often balanced itself.

Jack had never grasped that. When he'd accused her of allowing her father to manipulate her, he hadn't understood that the pattern was a mutually acceptable one that had developed between them over the years, that always there had been a careful balance of give and take. And if now she seemed to be giving her father more than his due, it was because all through her childhood he'd been the one to make sacrifices. Jack might see him as demanding but to Leone he was the devoted father who'd somehow managed to juggle his career and private affairs to allow himself time for her sake. Jack, however, had never understood that.

Leone looked round for an ashtray in which to drop her cocktail stick. When she looked up again Phil had disappeared from sight. Bad sign that. It would take the top scientists at NASA to re-route Phil now.

Ten minutes more, she promised herself, and if Phil wasn't ready she'd just have to leave without her.

With a resigned air Leone stuffed the stick into her pocket and allowed the waitress to top up her glass again.

Chapter Eleven

Ronnie stood in the freezing cold, leaning up against the door. The gallery was deserted.

'Shit!' He pressed the doorbell again.

No one was answering. He was late, of course. Janie must have got tired of waiting and gone on to her sister's already. She had never considered patience a virtue, Ronnie thought to himself.

As he peered in through the glass door he was sure he could see the dim flicker of a light at the back of the gallery. The soft shifting of shadows. Janie was more than likely in the back room making herself another of her endless cups of coffee. Answering the door would not take priority over that.

He let out an exasperated sigh and glanced down the street. It occurred to him that if he went round to the little courtyard at the rear of the gallery he could bang on the door and get Janie to let him in. Probably give her the fright of her life, but if she were imprudent enough to leave him standing out here in the freezing cold what could she expect?

Pleased with the thought he made his way down the deserted street. The gates to the courtyard were locked but he clambered over them easily enough. He'd not spent his childhood evading the heavies on his estate for nothing.

He came quietly across the paved stones. The little window at the back was heavily secured with bars. It was dark and looked as shiny as slate. He peered in. Nothing. Janie must have left for her sister's after all.

Yet he'd been sure that someone was in there.

It was then that he noticed the door. It hadn't been closed properly. He frowned, then saw the black rubbish bin standing next to it. It was full and there were several black bags thrown haphazardly against it. Janie'd been putting out the rubbish then—and left the door off the latch as she'd gone to collect the rest. Ronnie grimaced. He'd have to speak to her about that. He knew how quick some of these opportunist burglars could be. He knew, because a lot of the fellas on his estate wouldn't have passed an opportunity like this.

He moved forward silently. The door creaked slowly open under his touch. A little fright. That would teach her to be more careful next time.

He came through into the kitchen. He could hear a rustle of movement in the gallery. A low dull sound, like a zip slowly being undone. She was so close. He had only to step out of his hiding place and he could have touched her.

The sound came again. More of a rip this time. She must be tidying up the last of the rubbish. Soon she could be coming back to put out the garbage.

He could heard the soft pad of footsteps coming his way.

Now was the moment. Just step out and whisper her name. She'd probably jump out of her skin with fright and give him hell for scaring her.

He smiled, stepping confidently out of the shadow. Then stopped, his eyes widening.

This was not Janie.

He felt a wave of alarm as he took in the black hooded figure, knife in hand, before him. Jesus! That had been the sound: not rubbish being torn up, but canvases being slashed apart. A bloody madman. He hoped to God that Janie'd got away in time. He could see her leather jacket wasn't on the coat rack. He knew he had to say something, do something, to keep him at bay. This was no time for heroics. You didn't argue with knives.

'It's all right, man,' he said, lifting his hands up, palms outwards in a sign of subjugation. 'Whatever you've done here is nothing to me. I'm leaving. See…?'

Keep cool, man. Keep cool. It was like a silent mantra.

Slowly Ronnie started to back off into the kitchen space. He could sense the door behind him. Very slowly he reached his hand out towards the doorknob.

He was almost there, when the figure lunged at him. He moved so quickly Ronnie didn't know what had happened.

Ronnie felt the pain explode inside his chest. He raised his arms up desperately trying to defend himself as the knife came down again and again. He tried to keep standing, tried to will himself not to crumple. Once down he knew there would be no getting up.

The man began to laugh.

It was the laughter that frightened Ronnie more than the dark, or the shadows, or the pain. It was as if he knew how frightened he was of death.

Oh Jesus. He felt his legs beginning to crumple beneath him. He was aware of a thin line of dust along the little furrow of the skirting board in the kitchen, of the soft cream tone of the carpet.

Then his head slammed against the floor.

And there was nothing.

'So much for half an hour.'

'But it was fun, wasn't it? Go on, admit it.'

'Not bad,' Leone allowed. If she conceded more than that Phil would take it as vindication for delaying them for so long and be even more dilatory next time. It had taken the very real threat of having to walk back to the gallery to get her moving as it was.

They came down the last of the worn wooden steps and slipped past the blue-tiled Turkish room which had been Lord Leighton's pride and joy a hundred years before, then out into Melbury Walk.

'Home, James,' said Phil, opening the door of Leone's car with a grin.

She flung her copy of Diane's book on to the back seat—Leone had been quite right about not managing to escape without buying one, both of them had been cornered—and settled into the front seat. She regretted now having consumed quite so much wine. She'd wanted to keep a clear head. Cataloguing was such a meticulous business. Still, it was nothing that a couple of strong black coffees couldn't put right.

It was just starting to rain as they turned into Ladbroke Grove. The streets gleamed in a pale, reflective light.

A few minutes' later they reached the gallery and Leone pulled over into a space opposite the building.

'Janie's left the lights on,' she remarked as they climbed out of the car. It was small wonder that the bulbs kept needing to be replaced.

'It's a sort of welcome home,' said Phil, unbothered. 'She often does it when she knows we're coming back late.'

'She often does it, full stop.' Given half the chance Janie'd have the whole place looking like Blackpool's illuminated pier.

Leone pushed open the gallery door and stepped inside. As soon as she crossed the threshold she knew something was wrong. It wasn't just that the alarm had so obviously failed, it was something more.

Something about the silence which hung over the gallery was both eerie and frightening.

There was someone else in there.

She took another step forward then stopped. Papers from Phil's desk lay strewn across the floor.

'What the...?'

She heard Phil give a little cry behind her. 'The bastards! Steve's picture! Just look at what they've bloody done to it!'

Leone turned. The picture Steve had given Phil had been slashed apart, jagged strips of canvas hanging forward like flaps of skin on a carcass.

'It's ruined,' Phil whispered. 'The shits. How could they have done such a thing?'

She was almost in tears. Leone knew how much the painting had meant to her. She'd been so proud that morning when she'd shown it to Leone.

'That's it. I'm going to phone the police,' Leone said, as she touched the torn fragments of the vandalised canvas. If Piers Carlton was responsible for this, he'd gone too far this time.

She went across to Janie's desk and picked up the phone. Behind her Phil was trying to pull together the torn remains of the painting. 'The bloody Philistine!'

Leone picked up the telephone and started to punch in the emergency number.

'Leone!'

The urgency of Phil's voice made her slam down the phone and spin round. Phil was leaning heavily against the kitchen door, whitefaced and trembling.

'What is it?' she asked. 'What's wrong?'

It was then that she saw Ronnie's body crumpled on its side on the kitchen floor, the blood pooling around him like a crimson lake.

⌒

I was there all the time, Leone. You didn't guess though, did you? I was outside the gallery watching you. I was waiting for you. You didn't notice my car when you arrived though, did you? So careless, that. You were in far too big a rush to get into the gallery.

I saw you, though. And I saw your face when you found my little piece of handiwork. Did you like that, Leone? Each thrust was for you. Just you.

It's been an amusing little game, hasn't it? Exhilarating and irresistible. A little like foreplay, I suppose. A slow, teasing build-up to the climax.

And what a climax it's going to be, Leone. I can promise you that.

Chapter Twelve

'All right now?'

'Yes, thanks.' Leone gratefully took the glass of whisky her father was holding out to her. 'Still a bit shocked, though.'

'Not surprised. A nasty business.' He handed a drink to Phil and then turned back to her. 'I still blame myself. I should have taken Morenzo more seriously.'

'You're convinced he was involved then?'

'I am. And Ted Barnes agrees with me. Says the destruction of the picture is a typical hallmark of Morenzo. And then there was the assault, of course. It certainly wasn't one of the lads from the nearby estate after drug money this time, that much is obvious. Morenzo's the most likely candidate on this.'

'I suppose so.'

He glanced across at her. 'You sound doubtful. You surely don't still think your fellow Piers Carlton would be capable of such an attack, do you?'

She wasn't sure what to think any more. 'I suppose not.'

She took a gulp of whisky. The liquid scorched her throat but she felt its comfort. She needed that. She still felt very shaky.

Her father walked over to the window and pulled back the curtain an inch.

'I should have warned you about Morenzo,' he said quietly. 'Damn fool not to.'

Leone looked at the stiff line of his back.

'There's no certainty it was him,' she pointed out. She was finding it difficult to take in her father's words about Vic Morenzo. When she'd first seen the vandalised picture she'd been certain it had been Carlton. A malicious attack. Now it seemed both her father and Ted Barnes were certain he hadn't been involved. Ronnie's attack had been too vicious and frenzied for someone like Piers Carlton, Ted Barnes insisted. Perhaps he was right. But what did they actually know about Carlton when it came down to it? Did they really know to what lengths he'd be prepared to go to defend his family's honour and fortune?

She took another sip of whisky. 'Besides,' she went on, 'warning me against Vic Morenzo wouldn't have made much difference. I had Carlton to contend with, remember? Anyway, it's all out of our hands now. Didn't you say the police were on their way to pick up Morenzo for questioning?' And Carlton too. Whatever her father might say, she'd insisted on that, just to be on the safe side.

'So Ted Barnes told me, yes.' Her father turned his cigarette lighter over and over in his pocket. He didn't feel now was the moment to tell her that Ted had also pointed out that they wouldn't be able to hold him for anything much beyond thirty-six hours without formally charging him. And to do that they needed concrete evidence. Without it, Morenzo would be back on the streets again.

He stretched inside his jacket pocket and took out his slim silver cigarette case. 'I suppose our only chance is that Ronnie will be able to shed some light on who was responsible for the attack,' he said, lighting up and inhaling deeply. 'Provide a formal identification.'

'No chance of that at the moment,' Leone said.

'But he's still holding on?'

'By a thread.' Janie was at the hospital with him now.

Leone pushed her hands tightly together. She found it unbelievable that Ronnie could have suffered such a vicious attack and survived.

When she'd first seen him slumped in the kitchen, seen his

blood and the extent of his wounds, she'd been certain he was dead. But some instinct had made her check, just to be sure. She'd steeled herself and knelt down beside the blood-soaked form, gingerly placing her fingertips to the side of his neck, and had stiffened with shock when she'd felt a faint, almost indiscernible, pulse.

She shuddered at the recollection of the clamminess of his skin, at the memory of his white shirt patterned so grotesquely with blood. Leone took a sharp breath and leaned back in her chair, cradling the glass of whisky more tightly in her hand, trying to rid herself of the images.

Across the room Phil was sitting by the fire, staring down at the ribbed cuff of her blue woollen jumper, very still and silent. She'd been quiet ever since they'd found Ronnie. Phil, so vibrant and at one with life, found it difficult to deal with the peripheries of death.

Leone looked up. Her father had come to settle himself on the arm of her chair, his great bulk perching awkwardly above her.

'I think you ought to stay with me tonight.' He stretched out and covered her hand with his. He wasn't much given to physical displays of emotion but it had shaken him to the core to think of what might have happened had Morenzo found her in the gallery that evening.

'You're probably right,' agreed Leone. 'I think I'd be happier here.' The thought of sleeping, though, was far from her mind at that moment.

'And what about you, Phil?'

Phil looked up. She appeared dazed and confused. 'What?'

'I was suggesting that you and Leone stay here tonight. Simplest idea, don't you think?'

'Probably, yes.' Fatigue was in her voice. She straightened a little and took a sip of whisky. 'Andrew might come round, though.'

She'd phoned him the moment the ambulance had taken Ronnie off to St Mary's. Andrew was the brother she was closest to, the one she could always rely on to drop everything to take care of her.

She pushed her hands wearily through her hair. 'What time is it?'

'Just on ten,' said Leone, glancing at her watch. She saw Phil draw in a breath, as if steeling herself.

'That late? I've got to finish Steve's catalogue yet.'

'Phil, don't be stupid! You can't. Not tonight.'

'You're in no fit state to think about tying up catalogues, Phil,' Richard pointed out gently.

'I've got a printer's deadline to meet,' she insisted. She got to her feet. At least the catalogue notes were safe. She'd given them to Janie to proofread in the morning and knew they were still tucked safely away in one of the drawers of Janie's desk. 'Besides,' she said, 'I doubt I'd be able to sleep in any case.' Her voice sounded steadier, more resolved.

'You won't be able to get back into the gallery though,' Richard reminded her. 'Forensics won't have finished there yet.' They might not even have started. Being so late they'd more than likely simply sealed the gallery, leaving it under police guard until they could start work in the morning. 'They won't let you back until they've completed their tests.'

'Damn!' Phil ran her hands over her face with a sigh. 'I hadn't thought of that. How long will they be, do you expect?'

'I'm sure I can find out for you,' Richard said.

'If you could get hold of your disk and notes, couldn't you bring them back here?' Leone asked Phil. Even if Phil were allowed into the gallery, the thought of her trying to work there by herself made her worried. Shifting images kept racing through her mind: images of Steve's slashed picture, of Ronnie lying there, his chest ripped open. 'You could work from Daddy's computer. It's compatible with the one at the gallery. You wouldn't mind, Daddy, would you?'

'Of course not.' Richard moved across to the glass-topped table and stubbed out his cigarette. 'Listen, I'll phone Ted. See if he can cut through the red tape and allow me access to the gallery. If he can—if forensics have finished—I'll go down and pick up the disk and notes for you. I think I'd be able to persuade them to let me in.'

Leone shot her father a quick appreciative smile. She knew he didn't entirely approve of Phil's plan but for once he was keeping his own counsel.

She watched him leave the room, then turned back to Phil. At least there was some colour in her face now.

'Are you sure you'll be up to it?' she asked quietly.

'Positive.' Phil lifted her hands over her head and stretched. It was a casual gesture, reassuring in its familiarity. A sign that she was relaxing. She managed an apologetic smile. 'Sorry, I've been pathetically weedy.'

'For heaven's sake, it was a shock to us all.'

'Never was any good with blood. You remember at school when Penny Watson had her two front teeth knocked out by a hockey stick?'

'And it was you that they had to carry off the field! Of course I do.' Leone kept her voice purposefully light. It wasn't just Phil's mood she was trying to lift. It was her own. She couldn't stop thinking about Ronnie.

She stood up and went over to the window and drew back the curtain a chink. Outside the street seemed very dark, the pavements glistening like oiled silk. In the garden behind a cat yowled.

The truth was she still felt vulnerable, exposed. It didn't matter that her father had told her that the police were on the alert. Tonight's little episode had been aimed at her, that much she knew. But who could bear her such malice? Carlton or Morenzo?

She let the curtain slip back into place as she heard her father walk back into the room.

Whatever else, she didn't want him to know how much the attack had frightened her. She pushed her fingers tightly into the palms of her hands to steady herself and turned back to him with a smile.

⌒

That night she had the dream again.

The sweet scent of lilies filled the hallway as before, her mother's voice was as tender as she bent to kiss Leone farewell.

'Love you, little bear.'

Oh, if only she could just hold that moment. If only she could hold the dream just there.

But already time had swept on, already her mother had disappeared down the path. Why did her mother always hurry to her death?

That had never occurred to her before. How eagerly her mother hastened towards her fate. How quick her steps were. How light and confident.

'Wait, please wait.'

In her dream Leone was running down the stone path to the wooden gate, pushing it open. But the street was empty. The car had gone.

Too late. Always too late.

She stood for a moment, staring down the deserted street then turned back towards the house. It lay in shadow now. She came up the mossy path then slowly up the steps, one by one, until she stood before the door again.

This time there was no force holding her back. It slid open easily under her touch.

For the briefest of moments she hesitated, then stepped inside.

The hallway was deserted. From the drawing-room she could hear the mournful sound of a single note being played on the piano over and over like the sad tolling of a bell.

She crossed the hallway. The door to the drawing-room was open. She stepped inside, her eyes flicking across the room. Her father was hunched over the piano, head bowed, striking the ivory key again and again.

'She should have stopped,' he said, without looking at her. 'It would have been all right if only she'd stopped…'

His voice was embittered, accusing, as if he blamed her mother for the accident. Had it been her fault then? Leone had never been told. She wanted to know what had happened, wanted to ask, but something in her father's manner held her back. She saw the bitterness in his face. It frightened her a little. She had never seen that fierceness before.

'It was her fault,' he went on. He closed his eyes. 'I warned her. I told her...' He pushed his hands wearily across his line-etched face. She couldn't hear his next words.

'Told her what?' She tried to get him to repeat what she had missed. She knew the words were important. But he gave a little shrug and stood up.

For a moment he stood, staring at the Flemish painting on the wall above the chimney-piece. Then his gaze returned to her.

'Come here, Leone,' he said. 'I want to show you something.'

In her dream she was aware that time and place had changed, that perspectives had shifted. She was no longer a six-year-old child. Past and present seemed to flow into each other. Her father leaned towards her. His expression was perfectly calm but she sensed even before he stepped aside what she was about to see; knew because the image had been with her all evening, haunting her. She felt her stomach tighten in anticipation.

'No!'

She shrank back but he caught hold of her arm. 'You must look, Leone,' he said. His gaze didn't falter. His voice was soft, reasonable. 'You must identify the body.'

She could see the mound covered by the blanket from where she stood. She knew it was Ronnie's body.

Leone saw her father bend down over the crumpled form and slowly begin to draw back the sheet. Why was he looking at her so strangely? Then she saw the tiniest corner of a blue silk dress and knew it was not Ronnie who was lying there, but her mother.

'No! Please.' She couldn't bear that. Couldn't bear to see her mother's lifeless body. She felt the hairs bristling along the length of her arm. 'No!'

She awoke with a sickening jolt, panicky and out of breath, her whole body shaking.

The dream had been so real.

She stared into the darkness, trying to steady herself. It hadn't actually been like that, of course. She'd never seen her mother after she'd died. Her father had told her about the accident, had told her her mother had died and gone to heaven, but she hadn't seen the body. She'd seen the coffin. She remembered it being carried slowly past her as she'd stood beside her father in church, his huge, comforting hand clasped tightly around hers. She remembered the wreaths of flowers, the people in black, the tears. But most of all, she remembered the sound of the earth being sprinkled on to the coffin as it lay in the freshly dug grave.

How long was it since she'd thought of that? How strange it was that all the smallest, tiniest details were coming back to her now. Things she'd forgotten. Things she'd never even acknowledged she'd known.

It was her fault. She'd heard her father say those words that day. She knew that now. She knew she'd seen him sitting by the piano the day after her mother had died. It was all coming back to her.

Leone tucked her arms under her head, watching a shaft of moonlight spread across the wall of the bedroom.

It had been her mother's fault then, the accident. And for some reason, she hadn't allowed herself to recognise that in all these years.

She took a deep breath and slowly let it out. In through the nose, out through the mouth. She felt calmer now.

I warned her…

She adjusted the pillow and turned on to her side.

What had he warned her about? Driving too fast? Skipping the lights? Faulty brakes…?

It had started to rain again. Leone could hear the wind rising. Somewhere across the landing a window rattled in its frame.

Her mind was a maelstrom of swirling fragments of conversation, half-formed, hazy. She lay there, trying to unravel the jumble of her father's words. She recalled his face as he'd spoken them. She sensed their importance.

Why had she pushed them into the hidden depths of her mind? What had he said to her that day in the drawing-room?

She stared at the wall, trying to focus her mind, but the truth lay maddeningly just beyond her reach.

Chapter Thirteen

'Are you sure you want to be doing this?'

'Keep my mind off Ronnie. Don't want to be sitting at the hospital all day, do I? Drive me mad.'

Leone and Janie were back at the gallery. It was three o'clock in the afternoon and the police had only just left. They were set on the unenviable task of trying to tidy up the mess.

Leone crouched down and started to sort through the papers. There were still faint, almost indiscernible lines where the police had made tapings on the carpet for traces of fibres and dirt. She tried to ignore them, concentrating instead on organising the papers into some sort of orderliness, but it was hard to pretend nothing had happened here. A tense, almost tangible air of violence hung across the gallery. In the kitchen, the carpet had been ripped up and taken away, the bare floorboards left exposed were symbolic of the gallery's violation.

Leone glanced across at Janie. She was busy pushing papers back into a blue file. She looked deathly pale still, her small elfin face pinched tight. Leone had tried to make her go home several times, but she'd doggedly refused.

Leone sensed it was Janie's way of defying the demons. It was like getting back on to a horse after having been thrown off. The same courage, the same refusal to give in. That was Janie all over.

The phone started to ring. It had been going all afternoon. Bad news always travels fast.

Janie put down the file and picked up the receiver.

'Yes? No, we're perfectly all right. Yes, business as usual. Pablo's exhibition? It finishes tomorrow. Yes, that's right. Then we're showing work by Steve Ross, starting Thursday of next week.'

Her voice sounded dry, factual. Its brittle tone spoke volumes more about the fragility of her emotional state than anything she might have said.

'Another two for the exhibitions "long gone" file,' Leone said, holding out two invitations which Phil had obviously stuffed under a pile on her desk and forgotten about. They were now decidedly past their view-by dates. 'And one for next month. Current file.'

Janie took them from her mechanically. 'Current file. Fine.'

They methodically worked on. In the silence every movement, every rustle of paper, was accentuated. Eventually they were done. Leone filed the last of the papers and stood up, stretching.

'Do you want some fennel tea?' she asked Janie. She knew how much Janie liked herbal teas.

'I'll make it.' Leone noticed she made no attempt to move. Even though they'd tactfully moved the kettle and tea supplies upstairs to Leone's studio, tea-making had an inescapable association with the kitchen and the attack.

Leone glanced at Janie. She was sitting, staring down at her hands.

'Sure you're all right?'

'Got to be, haven't I? Can't have me collapsing as well as his mum.' She looked up and folded her arms tightly beneath her breasts as if protecting herself.

'He'll make it, you'll see,' Leone said. She wouldn't allow herself to think otherwise.

'His brother didn't.'

'What?'

'He was knifed, too, you know. Got into a stupid argument over a measly half-gram of coke. That's why Ronnie's mum is nearly going crazy now.'

'Janie, I'm sorry. I didn't know.'

'Why should you? It isn't something Ronnie talks about. Lenny was only fifteen, you know. Stupid fool. That's why Ronnie doesn't hold with knives. Lot of good it's done him.' She gave a tight grimace, nervously fingering the line of silver studs in her right ear. 'Jesus! What a mess.'

'He'll pull through. You have to keep believing that,' Leone said quietly.

'I know.' Janie straightened. 'And I do believe it. He's a tough little bugger. It's just when you see him lying there with all those bloody tubes hanging out of him…' Her voice caught slightly. 'Jesus, though, life sucks sometimes, doesn't it?'

'Does at the moment.'

'Anyway, this isn't getting us anywhere, is it?' Janie took a deep breath then pushed back her chair. 'Time for a cuppa, I guess.'

Leone placed the files on her desk. 'I'll come up with you. I ought to get going with the Nicholson picture.' She sensed Janie shouldn't be left alone.

They went up to her studio. Leone unlocked the door to the safe and drew out the landscape. She set it up on the easel under the skylight.

Behind her she could hear Janie going through to the washroom and filling the kettle with water. She came back into the studio and started to get the mugs out of the cupboard.

The gallery doorbell rang. Janie put down the cups and looked over the banisters.

'It's Steve Ross,' she said.

'Oh?' Leone stood up. Phil was at the printers, trying to tie up the catalogue. 'I'll go down.'

She went down the stairs. Steve Ross was standing outside, the collar of his black leather jacket turned up against the wind, hands stuffed into the pockets of his denims against the cold.

'You look freezing, come on in,' she said, unlocking the glass door.

'Phil told me what had happened to Ronnie,' he said in a low voice, stepping inside the gallery. 'I'm so sorry. How is he?'

'Holding on.'

'That's something.'

'He's not out of the woods yet, though.'

'Well, you wouldn't expect that would you? Not after an attack like that. Have the police managed to interview him yet? Got some sort of ID on the attacker?'

Leone shook her head. 'He's still on a life-support machine at the moment. One of the stab wounds pierced his lungs.'

'God! I'm sorry.'

'Rotten, isn't it? Janie's just about to go off and see him again, so we'll get another update soon. Cross fingers and all that.'

There was the sound of footsteps above them. They looked up. Janie was leaning forward, elbows resting on the wooden rails of the banisters.

'Steve, hello. Want some tea or coffee? I'm just making some,' she asked. She looked grimly determined to be cheerful.

'Thanks, I'd love some coffee.'

Steve followed Leone upstairs. 'So, the police have finished here then?'

'About an hour ago, yes.' She turned to look at him. 'You heard about your picture?'

'Phil told me, yes.'

'Such a mindless bloody thing to do. Phil was devastated.'

'I know that.' He'd told her not to worry, but she'd been mortified, feeling somehow at fault. But how could she have known what was going to happen, for God's sake?

Janie was pouring the boiling water from the kettle into the coffee mugs. 'Milk and sugar?' she asked Steve.

'Just milk, thanks.' He took the mug from her.

Janie handed Leone the Far Side mug Phil had given her for Christmas. 'Listen, I might just slip off to the hospital if that's all right,' she said.

'Of course. And for God's sake ring me if there's anything I can do to help.'

'Thanks.' Janie managed a smile. 'And I'll be in tomorrow.'

'Leave it open. Only come if you want to. I'll be here early and Phil'll be starting to pack up Pablo's exhibition.'

'I need something to take my mind off Ronnie,' Janie said. She pushed a hand slowly through her spiky hair. There was something very reassuring in that movement, like the comforting feel of stroking a pet. 'Say I come in about lunch-time?'

'That'd be a great help.'

'Right. I'll be off then. I'll switch the phones through.'

'Thanks.'

Leone watched Janie go downstairs. Her small face was drawn with the effort of hiding her emotions. She wished Phil had been here to jolly them all along. Phil always knew how to lighten the mood.

She glanced across at Steve. He was sitting on the tall stool by the stairs, feet crossed at the ankles. He was staring down into the gallery below. She could see the muscles in his jawline working. She couldn't tell what he was thinking but guessed he was as affected by the tense atmosphere as much as she was.

He looked up, saw her watching him. He didn't seem embarrassed.

'Look, don't let me hold you up,' he said. 'You keep on working, don't mind me.' He took a sip of coffee. 'That is, if you don't object to my just sitting here.'

'No problem.' Leone smiled. She was in truth rather glad of his company now that Janie had gone.

Steve stood up. 'What exactly are you doing?' he asked.

'Retouching.'

'I see. And would it be a cardinal sin to ask if I could stand behind you and observe?'

Leone laughed. 'Feel free.'

At the Courtauld Institute Rupert, her tutor, had sat directly behind her for hours scrutinising her work and giving her advice. She'd found it disconcerting at first, having that sensation of someone watching over her, of invading her space, but now she barely noticed.

'So, this is the creative part,' said Steve, watching her carefully apply the paint to a tiny corner of the landscape.

'It's not truly creative at all,' Leone admitted, wiping her brush on a clean piece of cloth. 'That's the trouble. You constantly have to fight the temptation to interpret the painting in your own way and just try to remember exactly what the original artist was trying to achieve.'

Steve grinned. 'How very restrictive. Wouldn't suit me at all. Don't you find it frustrating, keeping your imagination on a tight rein like that?'

'Sometimes. I just have to remind myself that this is *conserving* and that I have to keep my *creating* for when I dabble in watercolours in my spare time.'

'So you dabble in watercolours, do you?' His voice was teasing.

The soft pale transparency of that medium didn't appeal to Steve at all, she knew. He worked in oils. He liked to use small brushstrokes of vibrant contrasting colours side by side to make the canvas shimmer and gleam. Red against green, purple tussling with yellow, orange with blue. Colours designed to make each other more vivid. More powerful.

His eyes left hers moving to the line of brushes and containers by the sink. 'I shouldn't mock,' he said after a moment. 'My father loved watercolours: that was his medium.'

She glanced up at him. Phil said he didn't usually talk about his family.

'Was he any good?'

'I thought so. But he never made the big time. You know, usual story.' Steve's lips tightened slightly. He made light of it now, but he knew that lack of success had depressed his father. 'He had to work as an art teacher to keep the money coming in,' he went on. 'To be honest I think he'd have been quite happy living hand to mouth and just painting, but mother wouldn't have any of it. She never understood how he was willing to forego the luxuries of life just to be able to paint. It must have been rather hard on her. I suppose it's either part of you or it isn't. And if it isn't you can't understand how someone else can be so passionately consumed by it. Father was forever disappearing off to paint. He'd forget everything. Time, appointments…'

'My mother was a bit like that, too.' She said it almost without thinking. She was conscious of a kaleidoscope of shifting image, but there it was, the memory of her mother arriving back, late and dishevelled, having been out for the afternoon with her sketchbook. She'd forgotten an important dinner she and her father were due to go to. He'd been furious with her, she remembered, though they'd laughed about it together afterwards.

'Your mother was an artist too, then?' Steve asked, shifting his position slightly, pushing his long legs out straight in front of him. 'I think I remember Phil telling me that.'

'Amateur one, yes,' Leone said. 'Pen and ink sketches, *watercolours*.' She paused to smile at him. 'That sort of thing.'

'Still life or landscapes?'

'Landscapes mostly. I have some lovely watercolours of hers that she did just before she died. Wonderful sketches of moody East Anglian skies. They're really very good.'

He glanced down at his coffee mug, both hands encompassing it as if he were warming himself.

'Do you remember her much?' he asked, without looking up at her.

'A bit.' Leone paused for a moment. She straightened up and withdrew the brush from the canvas. 'Little things, insignificant moments…' She didn't feel ready to give him more than that.

He didn't push her. 'I'm the same,' he said. 'Little things. But you cling on to them, don't you?'

'You do, yes.' She gazed out of the window. It was getting dark. She stretched up and switched on the spotlight, adjusting it a little so that it shone directly on to the section of the canvas she was retouching.

There was a silence.

After a moment, Steve stirred. 'Do you mind if I make myself another coffee?' he asked.

'Help yourself.'

'Want some?'

'No, thanks. Haven't finished this yet.'

Steve went over to the table in the corner of the room and plugged in the kettle. He placed his hands on the worktop, lowering his head, poised like an athlete before a race, concentrating his thoughts. She sensed he was thinking about his father again.

After a moment he straightened up and turned back to her.

'Little things,' he repeated softly. 'Strange what you can remember, isn't it? Unimportant scenes, trivial conversations.' Behind him the kettle boiled and clicked itself off. 'You know, there is a theory that every sound ever made, every word ever spoken, still exists somewhere in space and time and may one day be recalled. I like to think that's true. Brings me closer to them to think that those conversations between us were never lost.' He spooned some coffee into his mug and poured in the boiling water. 'Do you miss her?'

'I do, yes. But in truth I hardly knew her. I was only six when she died, you see. Can't remember her very much, really.'

'But your father must talk about her.'

'Not really, no.'

'Doesn't he?' He seemed surprised. But there was no criticism in his voice.

She watched him stir his coffee vigorously and put the spoon in the sink.

'He took it pretty badly when she died,' she explained. 'When my Aunt Mary came to stay with us she told me all about my mother,' Leone said. 'But not my father. It was far too painful for him to talk about her when it first happened and now…Well, you set up a pattern, don't you? Sacred ground, I suppose. I've just got used to not asking questions.' She paused for a moment to look up at him. 'How about you?'

'No one *to* ask. My aunt died several years ago. And there's no one else really.'

'What about your uncle?'

'He died several years before that. Not that I'd have asked him anything anyway…'

Steve became visibly distressed. She'd forgotten how much he'd detested his uncle. She watched him take a deep breath to release the tension in his body.

After a moment, he said, 'Strange, isn't it? I put my parents out of my head when I was younger, trained myself not to think of them. But lately—perhaps it's the exhibition, thinking how proud Dad would have been, wondering what he'd think of the paintings.' His hands closed stiffly around the mug. 'You know, I'd give anything just to be able to talk to someone who really knew them. Someone who'd say, "God, you're so like your father," or "that's exactly what your mother used to do." Sometimes…' He hesitated, raising his head slightly to look at her, 'sometimes I can't remember what's real and what I've simply imagined about them. It's all become intertwined. Silly, isn't it?'

'Not at all.' She thought of her dream. Her own confusion.

Leone stared down at the painting. She didn't want to admit to Steve quite how ill-informed she was about her mother as well. To do so seemed a sort of denunciation of her father. They'd drawn a magic circle about themselves as protection, she could see that now. Perhaps they'd both been afraid to step outside it, not being able to ask, 'Do you remember. . .?'

For no reason she found herself remembering the trip they'd made to West Wittering when she was five. She was up on her father's shoulders, bending down so that her cheek pressed against the top of his head. She could feel the low vibrations against her skin as he sang out in that rich baritone voice of his, while her mother walked barefoot along the stretch of white beach beside them, shoes and sketchbook in hand, the sun casting long shadows across the wet sand and shimmering pools of water. Her mother's long, auburn hair was blowing across her face and she kept pushing it back and laughing up at Leone as the wind whipped it across her face again. A perfect day made all the more so because they'd endured a hot steamy week in London beforehand when tempers had been short and everyone had been grumpy and on edge.

Leone looked up. Steve was standing there watching her.

He mistook her silence. 'Sorry, have I trodden on hallowed ground?'

'Not at all, no.'

'I don't often talk about it, either,' he said. He sounded faintly apologetic. 'But somehow I sense we're alike in many ways, you and I.' He pressed his hands together, the long fingers intertwining. He drew a deep breath. 'Been through the same, haven't we?'

'Except I wasn't quite as alone as you were. I had my father, remember.'

'As you say, you had your father.' He looked as if he were about to say something more. But then he moved away from her. He crossed over to the worktop and idly picked up some brushes and then stuffed them back into their pots.

After a while, he said, 'I don't think Phil's coming back tonight, do you?'

Leone glanced at her watch. 'No, not now.' It was after five o'clock.

'Will she ring through?'

'Probably.'

'Tell her I called round then, will you?'

'Sure.'

'And tell her I'll try and reach her tonight at home.'

He moved across to the sink then and started to wash out his cup. He was very neat and meticulous, Leone thought as she watched him. Careful, controlled. So unlike his paintings. He dried the cup and placed it alongside the others on the worktop.

'I'll let myself out,' he said, picking up his leather jacket. 'Thanks for listening.'

'My pleasure.'

Leone watched Steve slip on his jacket and turn up the collar. She wondered if he knew how his gentle probing had punched holes in her own carefully erected barriers. Over the past few weeks she'd felt the layers of her past slowly being peeled away one strip at a time. She wasn't sure what was about to be revealed.

All she knew was that the images were becoming clearer, the voices more distinct.

Perhaps Steve was right. Every past action, every past sound, was held between time and space. It was just a question of reaching out beyond the tight confines she had set up. Perhaps everything was coming full circle for her.

All she had to do was wait.

～

It was very quiet after Steve had gone. Leone found it difficult to concentrate, to sit still and work. She crossed over to the banisters and peered out through the fading light. She didn't really like being alone in the gallery, despite having the radio receiver her father had insisted the police issue her with.

Leone went back to the easel and sat down, picking up her brush. She willed herself to paint on, forcing herself to ignore the silence which seemed to envelop the gallery, concentrating instead on the small incidental sounds from outside, the low hum of a car passing, the sharp click of heels on pavements, the burst of laughter from a group of schoolgirls as they passed by, the low roar of a plane overhead.

She fixed her mind on the landscape painting in front of her, bending forward to apply the paint in careful, meticulous strokes on to the canvas. It was coming together well; the colour and texture of the paint were perfect. Sometimes it could take hours before she could obtain such an exact match.

Outside the shadows were deepening. A group of boys was crossing the road on their way to the pub in the next street, shouting obscenities at each other. They were making such a noise she nearly missed the shrill peal of the doorbell ringing downstairs.

Leone hesitated—she was at a crucial point with the picture. She was tempted to ignore whoever it was, but relented and put down her brush. It could be a potential client. She stood up, slipping the front door keys into her pocket, then went across to the stairs.

She peered out over the top of the banister. It was too dark to see out into the street with the lights of the gallery on. Coming down into the gallery, Leone walked over to the door and cupped her face with her hands, pressing her cheek up close against the glass. But still she could see no one. Typical, she thought. It had probably been one of the boys ringing the bell for a joke as they passed the gallery. Morons.

Leone turned to go back up to the studio, but even as she did she became conscious of a sound out in the courtyard behind the gallery—a faint scrabbling. Cats?

She froze, listening intently, holding her breath. She was sure she could hear the rattle of the door handle as if someone were trying to open the back door. She felt a terrible dryness in her mouth, a sick feeling of panic beginning to surge through her.

Think, she told herself. Keep calm and think.

The radio receiver was upstairs, but if she went up to get it she risked being trapped up there by whoever was trying to get in. Wiser, surely, just to try to make a run for it. They were round at the back and if she moved quickly, she could be out of the gallery and across to the wine bar on the corner in a few seconds flat.

Leone took the keys out of her pocket, her fingers fumbling as she tried frantically to unlock the door. Then she was out in the street. She gave a quick glance back into the gallery. No one had come through the back door, no one had followed her. She let out a breath of relief. But as she turned to run across the street, Leone sensed someone in the dark shadows to her left, then heard the swift sound of footsteps on the pavement.

The air seemed to turn into something solid. God, he'd been quick! His strong hands were on her shoulders, catching hold of her. She screamed, pushing against him wildly, lashing out with her arms and legs.

'Jesus H. Christ, Leone.'

She stopped mid-kick, and swivelled round towards her attacker, focusing on the face just above hers. It was not the Mad Axeman from Hell. It was, in fact, horribly familiar to her.

'Jack?'

'Jesus, Leone, what was all that about?'

She caught her breath, quickly recovering. 'Just what the hell are you doing here?'

'Nice welcome, I must say. What do you think? I came to make sure you were all right.'

Now she was safe she could afford to feel anger. 'Well, I was all right until you nearly frightened the life out of me, you stupid bastard,' she shouted at him. 'What the hell were you doing coming after me like that for?'

'After you?'

'Don't look so bloody innocent. After me, as if lurking in the shadows and then grabbing hold of me without warning…'

'Actually, if I recall correctly, I rang the doorbell first. Seemed a fairly conventional approach to me,' Jack said stiffly. 'When you didn't answer I stepped out into the road to see if I could see you up in the studio or not. Next thing I know you're coming out of the gallery like a bat out of hell. Sure, I put out an arm to stop you. I wanted to know what was wrong, for God's sake…'

'Nothing *was* wrong until you arrived, Jack.'

The irony of her words made him smile.

'Listen, I'm sorry I scared you. Truly I am.' He put both hands up to her shoulders. This time she didn't brush them off. 'It never occurred to me that you'd be here alone. I should have thought. I should have rung from the airport first.'

She was not used to apologies from Jack. She eyed him suspiciously. All the same she felt her anger begin to crumble away.

'Are you all right now?' He touched her cheek with the back of his hand.

Leone steadied her breath. 'More or less.'

'Ready to go back in or do you want a stiff drink first?'

'Back in,' she told him. 'If I have a drink I won't be able to hold the paint-brush straight.'

'You're not intending to go back to work, are you?'

'I've got a deadline…'

'Sod the deadline.'

'Jack I can't afford to get a reputation for being unreliable,' she pointed out. And the landscape was needed for an exhibition. The gallery had been quite insistent about when it must be ready.

Jack pushed his dark hair back from his face. He was tempted to tell her that being thought unreliable was preferable to pushing herself over the limit like this. But he knew she'd never listen. He wondered if she knew how white her face still was, or how clammy and cold her hands felt in his.

'Honestly, Leone,' he half-protested. 'can't I persuade you to give yourself a break for once?'

'I was never one for easy options, Jack.'

'Nor was Cardigan at Balaclava. And look where it got him and his precious Light Brigade.'

All the same, he swept up his battered leather briefcase and followed her into the gallery. They went up to the studio. Leone watched him perch on the stool and spread out his papers on the work table opposite her. He didn't announce he was intending to stay, he just spread out his papers and began to work.

They worked together in companionable silence. It always surprised her how Jack could settle down and concentrate when he set his mind to it; she'd thought he'd be too restless a soul for that. But he could shut himself off from the world when he chose to. She could hear the steady scratch of his pen as he scribbled notes on to his jotter pad; he seemed almost oblivious to her presence.

It took her about an hour to finish the section of landscape she was working on. Leone painted quickly, her movements swift and precise. Some days it all fell together, flowing as easily as a choreographed dance.

She was feeling relaxed. With a bit of luck, she could apply the final varnish layer tomorrow afternoon and deliver the picture more or less on time. Honour intact.

Putting down the brush, Leone straightened up and stretched her hands over her head in an arc.

From across the room Jack heard the soft rustle of her movements and glanced up from his papers. 'Finished?'

She nodded.

'Feel like a drink?'

She'd intended to go straight home, but the truth was she felt like something to give her a lift.

'That would be great—thanks.'

They began to tidy up, Leone carefully locking the landscape away. The security of the place now rivalled the Bank of England, being part of the revised practice the insurance company had insisted on.

It took Leone a while to set up the new alarm system. It was unbelievably complicated after their old simple affair. Foolproof, though, so the chap from Banhams had said.

They drove to a wine bar in Kensington Park Road. It was packed but they managed to find a place at one of the small tables tucked away in a corner.

Jack went up to the bar. He came back balancing a bottle of claret, two glasses and an aubergine and tomato concoction perched precariously on top of a basket of bread.

'Thought you might be hungry,' he said, putting the plate down in front of her. 'Bet you didn't have time to grab any lunch.'

She smiled. 'Didn't, actually.'

'Thought as much.' He settled himself down beside her. 'If you ask me, women aren't half as efficient at looking after themselves as they make out.' He poured out two glasses of wine and handed her one.

He gave her a wide easy smile. She'd forgotten the power of that smile. Leone concentrated hard on tearing off a piece of crusty olive bread.

'So, what's happening about the investigation?' Jack asked, picking up his glass of wine. 'Andrew tells me the police now think your friend Piers may not be involved after all. He said they have another suspect. Some ex-con or other, who means to get even with your father and may be stirring things up with you and the gallery just to make his point.'

'That's one of the theories, certainly.'

'So, the other night, was that Carlton following us or this ex-con?'

'I think *that* was Carlton. But the police believe the first break-in and this attack to be the work of this fellow Morenzo.'

'Nasty piece of work, I gather.'

'Not very pleasant.' By all accounts, Carlton was a veritable choirboy compared to Morenzo but she had no intention of telling Jack that.

She started to spread the vegetable pâté on to her bread. 'Tell me about your trip, Jack. Much more interesting.' She took a bite of pâté. It was delicious, wonderfully creamy and spicy. Was it cardamom or coriander which gave it that pungent flavour?

Jack leaned back in his chair, linking his hands behind his head. She knew the trip must have gone well. He often sat like that when he was pleased with events.

'Did you manage to secure that Piero della Francesca you were so keen on?'

'Still got some loose ends to tie up but I think so, yes. I'm going back next week to finalise the sale.'

'What a coup.' Leone loved Piero della Francesca's work. She'd always admired his masterly brushstrokes—fluid almost abstract at times—the delicate harmony of the colours, his wonderful way with light. She could well understand why the Impressionists admired him so much. He was one of the first painters to understand perspectives correctly. 'Didn't you say it was in a private collection?'

'It was, yes.'

'Goodness, Jack, a triumph, no less. You had doubts whether or not you'd be able to persuade them to sell when I saw you last.'

'I must have underestimated my charm.'

'Or perhaps your bank balance?'

He laughed. 'What a little cynic you've become! It wasn't just the money, you know, it's the kudos. Owners like the glory of knowing that their prized paintings are going to a prestigious home.'

Which Mr Chiang can offer?'

'Unquestionably. Mr Chiang has every intention of building up the most estimable collection in the Far East.'

She thought about those other fabulously wealthy Chinese businessmen who'd already built up collections. If Mr Chiang hoped to rival those he must be very wealthy indeed. Jack seemed to have fallen on his feet. She told him as much.

'Don't I know it. An opportunity of a lifetime.'

She finished off her pâté and picked up her glass, holding it between her two hands as if she were warming a brandy glass. 'So will you continue working for Chiang when you come back to England?' she asked.

'Who told you I might be coming back?' He looked surprised, like a child caught with his hand in the cookie jar.

'Andrew,' she returned steadily. She heard the faint rattle of spilling beans. Andrew obviously had been sworn to secrecy. Hopeless, of course. Secrets stayed with Andrew about as long as a full glass of whisky had stayed with Dylan Thomas.

'Oh.' Jack ran the tip of his finger along the rim of his glass. She couldn't tell what he was thinking. 'Nothing's settled yet,' he said, after a while. 'Isabel wants to come back, certainly. But there are a few things to sort out before we come to a final decision.'

He didn't want to come back, she could hear it in his voice. She glanced across at him, saw the slight tightening of his jaw.

'Jack, you'd be a fool to give this job up. It's tailor-made for you.'

'But there's not just me to consider, is there?' he returned pointedly. He picked up his glass and began to twirl the long stem backwards and forwards between his strong, competent fingers. 'There's Isabel. And I can't go on being a selfish bugger all my life. I thought you of all people would agree with that.'

'I know.' But the truth was she didn't. Ironic wasn't it, when she'd tried so hard to keep him in England all those years ago? But now she could see how sound his decision to leave had been. Jack was happier away from the constraints and conformities of

England. And he would never be able to repeat the opportunities his job offered him back in London.

Did Isabel not recognise that? Or was she simply weaving her own tapestry with a different thread? Leone sensed that was the case—that Isabel was young and determined.

Isabel would try to change him, mould him into her own shape gradually, layer by layer. Andrew said he'd been house-hunting in Hampshire. God, she could see it all. The English gentleman. First the country house, with the black labrador retrievers, the Range Rover, the children packed off to some suitable prep school. That wasn't Jack.

'Jack, don't…' Leone stopped herself mid-sentence, turning her face slightly away from him. It wasn't up to her how Jack and Isabel decided to live their lives. She had no rights here, none at all.

He looked up at her, his grey eyes searching her face. 'Don't what?' he asked.

She gave a small shrug of the shoulders. 'Oh, nothing. Just don't rush into making a decision.'

Leone picked up her glass, and consciously examined the colour of the wine. She couldn't meet his eye.

There was a silence.

'You've changed, Leone,' he said quietly.

For better or worse? She couldn't tell.

She drained her glass. 'It's called getting older, Jack,' she said.

He sat there, watching her, saying nothing. Then he smiled.

'What?'

He stretched, arcing his arms upward. 'Oh, nothing. Just thinking about the last trip we made together to Paris. Do you remember the exhibition we went to at that little gallery in Rue de Pompe? How determined you were to get one of those Dufy prints.'

'Was I?'

'Don't you remember?'

'Not really, no,' she lied. She determinedly fought back the wave of powerful feelings and memories rushing over her. It was dangerous to remember her time in Paris. Their long walks along the Seine under a brilliant blue sky, the little café they'd made their own in the Rue Fosses-St-Bernard, lazy afternoons spent at the Musée d'Orsay. It had all been too perfect. She would not let him do this to her. Remind her.

Leone made a great play of looking at her watch.

'God! Is that the time? I've got to fly. I've got a pile of things to do still.'

She reached behind her and started to ease her woollen coat off the back of the chair. 'Jack, thanks for the drink. It was really great to catch up.'

'Have you really got to go?'

''Fraid so.'

'Can't tempt you to come for dinner? I'm on expenses. We can have the run of London. Vong's, Le Caprice, Sugar Club…'

'Jack, I really can't.' His offer of dinner meant nothing, she knew that. Jack cast his charm effortlessly to the wind. He had no idea of its effect.

Leone picked up her bag, pushed back her chair and stood up. She saw Jack run his hand through his dark hair, the movement achingly familiar.

She took a deep breath, struggling to keep her voice business-like.

'Can I offer you a lift somewhere, Jack? Notting Hill Gate?' He was staying with Andrew, she knew.

He looked at her steadily for a moment and she thought he was about to try to persuade her to join him for dinner again. Instead he said: 'Notting Hill would be perfect.'

Leone twined her scarf round her neck, glad of its warmth against her skin. Pull yourself together, she told herself as they pushed their way out into the street. If Jack can make the transition back from lover to friend as easily as this, then so can you. So *must* she.

What was he, for God's sake, anyway? She'd been out with better looking men, richer men, men who were less bolshie and argumentative. Jack was nothing special. *Nothing*…except he'd had a way of looking at her, of touching her, which had made her feel sensual and beautiful and alive. *That* was what she missed.

When she got home after dropping Jack off at the tube station Leone decided to pop upstairs to see her father, but Fernanda greeted her with the news that he'd rung earlier to say he wouldn't be back for dinner. Leone felt strangely thwarted. She'd wanted to speak to him tonight. Her talk with Steve Ross had stirred up a host of memories. Leone wanted to try to break through that circle of protection, to ask him about her mother and her accident. Now she'd have to wait for another time.

She went down the steps and along the paved path to her flat. She took off her coat, dropped it over the small two-seater sofa in the middle of the room, and walked over to the kitchen. It seemed strangely cold and silent after the wine bar. She pulled open the fridge door and looked inside. It was empty, save for a limp lettuce, a tub of dubious-looking cottage cheese and a carton of eggs so old it would have given Edwina Curry apoplexy. She picked up the lot and threw it resignedly into the rubbish bin.

Somehow it seemed to sum up the day.

In another part of town Richard Fleming sat in the panelled diningroom of his club enjoying a meal of an infinitely superior nature.

Opposite him, Ted Barnes paused between mouthfuls of sirloin of beef to take a sip of claret. He saw Richard looking at him, and gave him a silent appreciative nod. Conversation had been slim since the main course had arrived. Give the man his due, thought Richard, he'd not seen anyone tuck into a slab of beef with such unfettered enthusiasm since the BSE crisis began.

He watched him now, the loose skin around Ted's eyes making him look more like a basset hound than ever, head bent down over his plate as he polished off the last of his sauté potatoes. Richard was relieved they'd come here rather than to his other club. Boodles was no place for Ted. He looked as if he'd bought his suit from Oxfam, for heaven's sake. How on earth was it possible for anyone's clothes to fit so appallingly?

Still, it was only one meal, Richard told himself, and he owed Ted this. He had pulled out all the stops over this Morenzo business and on the night of Ronnie's attack had even come all the way up from Blackheath in person to sort out the débâcle. Had to leave a dinner party at home, so he'd said. Brave man indeed. Marian was renowned for her temper.

So, debts were being repaid. And Richard had always made a point of rewarding loyalty.

He took a sip of wine. It was very good Château Margaux, 1985. One of the best. Wasted on Ted, of course. He leaned forward, putting his elbows on the table and pressed his fingertips together. 'So,' he said, watching Ted finish the last of his beef, 'you really think this Morenzo business will be tied up soon?'

Ted wiped his mouth with his white linen napkin and then leaned back, folding his plump hands over his stomach. 'I do, Richard, yes. He's going to make a false move soon enough and when he does my lads will be there.'

'But what about this attack at Leone's gallery? Can't you haul him in over that?'

'We've brought him in for questioning as you know. But at the moment he's got himself a watertight alibi. His girlfriend swears he was at his flat with her all that evening.'

'The stripper, you mean?'

Ted nodded. He watched the waiter refilling his glass.

'And you can't "break her story"?' For God's sake, thought Richard, she's only a bloody stripper.

'Not yet, no. But give us time.'

'Time is of the essence, Ted.'

Ted bowed his head with slow gravity. 'I'm well aware of that, Richard. But we've got to play it by the book. Morenzo has got his smart-arse lawyers crawling all over us. But we'll get him. We've got enough men on his tail to sink the bloody *Bismarck*. One step out of line and we'll haul him in.'

'We can't afford mistakes, Ted.'

'There won't be any mistakes.'

Richard didn't miss the stiffness in Ted's voice. He paused to light a cigarette. 'And this business you were mentioning earlier?'

'About a contract being put out?'

'Yes.'

'That seems to have no foundation.'

'You're sure of that?'

'Yes.' That wasn't entirely the truth. But he was as sure as he could be. Trouble was, who could say how Morenzo might react if he found himself being forced into a corner?

Richard picked up his cigarette lighter and began to tap and turn it against the starched white tablecloth. 'I need to be sure of that, Ted,' he said. 'Not for myself, you understand. It's Leone I worry about.'

'I understand, Richard. Really I do. Got to look after our own, haven't we?'—Ted moved his arm slightly as a waiter cleared away his plate. 'And I appreciate how distressing this must be for you. Especially after losing Julia as you did.'

The words hung between them for a moment. Richard stared out of the window, past the street lamp to the building beyond. All the old emotions stirred within him, making his chest tighten. What on earth had possessed Ted to refer to Julia? he wondered. He hadn't mentioned her for years.

'That day…I couldn't believe it…'

Richard felt Ted staring at him, waiting for him to say something. For Christ's sake, couldn't the man sense he didn't want to talk about her? *Especially* with him?

Richard stubbed out his cigarette, shifting his eyes from Ted's gaze as he did so. Poor Ted. He'd never been able to hide his feelings, had he? He might only have met Julia once—and briefly at that—but it had been enough. Lovestruck—wasn't that the word?

Not that Richard blamed him. Julia had always had a way with her, a gift of being able to put people at their ease. Of making them feel special. And she'd been so achingly beautiful; she must have seemed like a goddess to Ted beside the squat and unlovely Marian.

'Senseless waste of life, it was.' The words were said on a sigh. Ted looked up and registered the look on Richard's face. It seemed to pull him back from his reverie. 'Sorry,' he said hurriedly. 'Tactless of me to open old wounds…'

Richard cleared his throat. 'That's all right, Ted.' He became aware of the waiter standing beside him with the menus and took one. After a moment he spoke, forcing some sort of normality back to his voice. 'So, what will you have, Ted? They do a very fine apple charlotte here.'

'I'll have that then.'

Ted put down the menu. He hadn't been able to read it anyway. He let out a little wistful breath, trying to chase Julia from his mind. Lovely, beguiling Julia, who so long ago had seen him at a reception, taken pity on him and had taken him under her wing. So rarely did beauty and compassion mix. No wonder it had taken Richard so long to get over her. To lose her so suddenly, so *dreadfully*, it would shatter any man.

'You'll let me know if there are any developments?'

Ted looked up. 'Of course.' He folded his thoughts away.

'And you think Leone is adequately protected by the radio link?'

'I do, yes.'

'I feel wretched she's been involved in this. Morenzo's grievance is against me, not her.'

'Sins of the father and all that…'

'What?'

'Nothing, Richard.' The apple charlotte had arrived. Ted moved slightly so that the waiter could place the plate in front of him. 'Just relax,' he said. 'We'll nail the bastard. One false move, that's all we need.'

⟶

They thought they had him, didn't they? Pathetic sods.

Vic Morenzo stood by the window of his flat and jerked the curtain back an inch, staring down into the dimly lit street below. I know you're there, you bastards, he muttered. The unmarked police car, parked at the corner opposite, stood out like a polar bear in the Sahara. Still, it made his job of evading them easy. You didn't exactly have to be Houdini to slip out across the roofs to the next building and out by the fire escape, did you? And while he made his exit they'd still be there playing at bloody Z Cars, guarding the main entrance at the front of the apartments. Sad, really.

He let the curtain fall back into place and moved back across the room to the leather sofa. He had no intention of going out tonight. They could wait, sweat a bit.

Running a hand over his face, Vic's fingers brushed against his dry lips. Denise should have been here by now, he thought to himself. Stupid cow. She seemed to be staying at the club later and later these days. He'd have to teach her a lesson. She had it coming to her. She'd pissed him off once too often. See how full of bravado she'd be when he took a knife to that perfect skin of hers.

He sank down into the deep folds of the sofa, shifting his position slightly to lean forward and flick open the lid of an ornate wooden box on the low polished table in front of him. His fingers tightened around a small cellophane bag tucked under the cigarettes at the bottom. So Denise hadn't finished it off last night. He was surprised. The bitch would steal anything she could lay her hands on.

Vic cleared the magazines off the top of the table with a single sweep of his hand and shook the white powder out on to the table. He wasn't worried about the police. They wouldn't waste time busting him for this. Any half-way decent lawyer would be able to get him off anyway.

No, he knew what they were waiting for. And they weren't exactly subtle about it, were they?

He stretched forward, cutting the coke into four narrow lines. What was it Denise had said? Coke for parties, heroin for oblivion. Well, he wasn't quite ready for oblivion yet. He pulled a twenty-pound note from his wallet, rolled it deftly up and snorted up the lines one after the other, feeling the familiar rush. He couldn't understand why Tony wouldn't touch the stuff. He didn't know what he was missing. There, at least, he and Denise were in agreement.

He shook his head, sniffed again, then licking his index finger flattened it against the few white grains which still lay on the surface of the table.

He pushed the finger into his mouth, running it rapidly across his gums, then sank back, closing his eyes for a moment. God, that felt good. The voluptuous tide swept throughout his body. He felt brilliant, powerful—he could take on the world. The police were nothing, *nothing*, against him. He could outwit them any time he wished. He smiled. He felt like a leopard in the night, the same strength, the same cunning.

No one could stop him now.

Chapter Fourteen

'Lady Carlton rang while you were out.'

'Did she?' Leone slipped off her coat and flung it over the wooden coat rack behind the reception desk. Across the gallery from her Phil was sitting cross-legged on the floor, busily trying to package up one of Pablo's exhibits. 'Did she leave a message?'

'Yes. I've scribbled it down. It's on Janie's desk. Something about lunch on Thursday,' Phil said, putting down the melinex bubble wrapping which she was attempting to pack around one of the more delicate and awkwardly shaped sculptures. 'Confirmed that would be fine by her.'

'I haven't suggested any lunch.'

'Well, she seems to think you have. Said something about your having spoken to her daughter about it.'

'Nonsense.' Leone felt a wave of exasperation. 'The old girl's going senile, if you ask me.'

'Very probably,' said Phil, matter-of-factly. 'Anyway, you have a word with her. I said you'd ring back when you got in.'

'Oh, *thanks*.'

Leone wasn't sure why she felt so rankled. She felt she'd been railroaded. In truth Thursday was probably as good a day as any to go up to Suffolk to see Lady Carlton but it was just the principle of the matter. Besides, she still had slight misgivings about going despite the fact the police seemed convinced Piers hadn't been involved in Ronnie's attack. She'd have cancelled the trip straight away if they'd had even the slightest doubt regarding Piers' involvement.

Leone went across to Janie's desk, picked up her messages, then started to sort through the pile of mail which lay bundled together with a thick elastic band. There were two invitations for later that month, but little else of interest. At least there weren't any bills. There'd been rather a lot of those recently. She placed Phil's post into a separate pile, kept out the two invitations and binned the rest.

'When do you need the studio upstairs by?' she asked Phil, pushing herself away from the desk and standing up.

'I was hoping to bring some of Steve's paintings in at the weekend,' Phil replied. She tore off a strip of sellotape and secured the end of the wrapping.

Leone did a quick calculation. 'So if I sorted things out by Friday would that give you time enough?'

'Perfect.' Phil placed the wrapped sculpture into a square cardboard box and sealed the top with some more tape. 'We've got masses of time now that we're dismantling Pablo's exhibition early, don't forget.'

'And Pablo didn't mind?' Artists could be terribly touchy about their exhibitions, Leone knew.

Phil shook her head. 'Didn't seem to. I suppose we've sold all his pieces so it didn't exactly come as a blow to him.'

The telephone rang. Leone stretched across and picked it up. It was Steve Ross.

'Phil, for you,' she said. 'Steve.'

'Just the man I want to talk to,' said Phil, scrambling to her feet. She took the receiver from Leone, sinking down into the chair. 'Steve? Hi…'

It was going to be a long conversation, Leone could tell. Phil was leaning back, one leg tucked under her, her head tilted sideways to cradle the receiver against her ear. She gave the appearance of someone who'd settled in for the rest of the morning.

Leone picked up the invitations and went upstairs to her studio. The greyness of the morning's sky was reflected in the muted colours of the room. Great caverns of darkness filled its corners. She switched on the lights. The room still seemed gloomy. The curse of winter, Leone thought as she went over to the walk-in safe and drew out the landscape she'd been working on the night before.

She brought the picture out into the open, angling it slightly to catch the light. Leone rang her finger gently over its surface. She ought to be able to varnish it later that afternoon.

She began to ferret around in the cupboard by the sink for the varnish that she'd need.

'Listen, Steve wants to know if you'd like to come out to supper with us tonight,' said Phil, her head appearing at the top of the stairs.

Leone withdrew from the depths of the cupboard. 'I'd love to, but I can't,' she said. 'I'm going to the theatre with Father tonight. Belated birthday treat.' He'd particularly wanted to see David Hare's latest at the National and tickets had been almost impossible to get. She hoped it would be as good as the reviewers claimed it to be.

'Not something you can change, then. That's a shame.' Steve had suggested a Burmese restaurant in west London that sounded great fun. 'Oh, well,' Phil shrugged. 'Another time, perhaps.'

'Love to.' Leone smiled. She felt touched she'd been invited. Phil had always said how awkward Steve could be with people. She'd obviously passed the 'presents no danger' test.

Phil disappeared down the stairs again. Leone could hear the low burble of laughter as she continued her conversation with Steve. Returning to the cupboard Leone knelt down and began to pick through the clutter.

She'd just found the bottles she needed when the telephone began to ring. She waited, hoping that Phil might break off to answer it but it went on ringing. She should have known. It would need something of the loaves-and-fishes variety to get Phil to interrupt a good conversation.

Leone stood up and crossed over to the scrubbed pine table in the middle of the studio and picked up the receiver. Lady

Carlton's assured voice came down the line.

'Miss Fleming? I thought I ought to ring you again as I'm going out in a few minutes. Didn't want us to miss each other. Thursday would be fine, my dear. Shall we expect you for lunch?'

'Lady Carlton, I think there's been some mistake,' Leone protested bluntly. She was being slightly churlish she knew but she couldn't help herself. 'I'm not quite sure why you thought I was coming up on Thursday. I certainly didn't ring and suggest that day.'

'Didn't you? Margaret said you had.' There was a slight pause, while Lady Carlton digested this new information with obvious confusion. 'Oh, dear,' she said. 'The silly girl. She must have got her wires crossed. Is Thursday not suitable for you then? Please say. We'll fit in with you, of course. Would Friday be more appropriate?'

Leone heard the tenacity in Lady Carlton's voice. She was the sort of woman, she realised, who would hang on grimly until she finally achieved what she wanted. She would quietly and relentlessly pursue until Leone eventually caved in. Perhaps it would be sensible to get the whole wretched business over and done with as soon as possible.

She did a quick mental calculation as to how long it would take her to re-organise her studio for Phil. 'I think Friday would suit me better, actually.'

'Good. That's settled then.'

Leone could hear the sound of a book being snapped shut. She could imagine Lady Carlton sitting there in her wheelchair closing her diary with a small sigh of relief.

'There is one last thing, Lady Carlton,' she added quickly. She had to make sure that Piers would not be involved in this meeting. 'I do have your assurance that your son still has no idea of our arrangement, don't I?'

'Absolutely. As it happens, he's in Frankfurt at a conference for the rest of the week.'

'I see.' Leone felt a surge of relief. Frankfurt seemed a suitably long distance away. 'Well then, Friday would be fine. I can get myself as far as Woodbridge. Can you give me directions from there?'

Lady Carlton did so. 'We'll see you at about twelve thirty, shall we say?' she said. Leone could hear a dog barking somewhere in the background, and a woman's voice, presumably Margaret's, telling it to pipe down.

'Twelve thirty, give or take half an hour or so,' she said. She couldn't be more precise than that: it depended on the traffic. The road up to Suffolk could be hellish. The reason, she supposed, why it had remained so totally unspoiled.

'And thank you again for agreeing to come, my dear.'

Leone wondered if she'd thank her after her pronouncement on the pictures. She had a terrible feeling that the majority would go the way of the Devis portrait. Still, for Lady Carlton's sake, she hoped she was wrong.

She put down the receiver and went over to the walk-in safe where she kept the pictures she was working on. The Devis painting was propped up against the wall. It looked so innocuous leaning there, it was hard to credit the trouble it had caused. She drew it out; its restoration was finished. Lady Carlton had requested her to do so, even though she knew it was a fraud. Perhaps some sentimental streak in her meant she would re-hang it in its former place of glory over their fireplace in the drawing-room in Hatherington Hall. Leave it there to be admired by those who knew no better.

Leone slipped it back into place, closed the security gates and the cupboard door. Phil had evidently finished on the telephone.

She could hear her footsteps on the stairs.

'Everything all right?' Phil asked, coming up the last of the steps.

'Fine. That was Lady Carlton.'

'Thought as much. All sorted out?'

'Pretty much so.'

'And you don't think you're tempting Fate by going up to Suffolk?' Phil leaned back, elbows against the top of the banisters. It was an attempt at casualness which didn't fool Leone. For all Phil's nonchalant pose she could see the watchfulness in her eyes.

'Because of Piers, you mean?' she queried.

'Well, he's not exactly known for his sanguine temperament, is he?'

'He isn't, no,' agreed Leone. Phil's words served to stir up all her earlier misgivings. Had she been mad to agree to go to Hatherington? Ted Barnes, at least, seemed to think that Piers had been in no way responsible for Ronnie's attack, but could she be sure of that? He'd been to the gallery that night, certainly—he'd admitted as much to the police—though they seemed satisfied he'd left as soon as he'd discovered the place deserted and had returned home to his girlfriend. But had they really any proof of his version of events?

She felt anxiety stir within her but determinedly pushed it down. Ted Barnes knew of her intended trip to Suffolk and surely he'd have tried to dissuade her from going if he had the least suspicion of Carlton's guilt.

'Anyway, Piers is away this week,' she told Phil. 'And I have Lady Carlton's assurance that he won't know of my visit.' She tried not to speculate as to whether today's little episode with the mix-up of dates was any indication of Lady Carlton's—or of Margaret's, for that matter—mental competence. 'Besides, she knows I'm not in a position to give an expert opinion on the pictures. I've told her categorically if she wishes to pursue it further she'll have to take the lot to the Courtauld Institute. My guess is she won't want to pursue it. She just wants to know if they're frauds or not for her own peace of mind.'

That was why Leone was going, at any rate. To help clarify things one way or another for Lady Carlton, an old lady with an unscrupulous son and a very persuasive manner.

'Well, I wish you were shot of the Carltons, but it's your decision,' said Phil. She pushed herself upright and stretched. 'Listen, what I really came up for was to ask if I can pinch your camera for the afternoon? I want to take some shots of a few of Steve's pictures we're not running in the exhibition. Thought it would be good to have them on record to show prospective buyers.'

'Sure,' said Leone, glad that the conversation had veered away from Piers and Lady Carlton. 'Help yourself. It's in the darkroom.' The camera was her pride and joy; a gift from her father for her birthday last year.

'Thanks.' Phil went over and switched on the kettle. 'Steve was very taken with you, by the way. Said you had a long talk together last night and you were very *sympathique*.'

'We both have a lot in common, I suppose.' Leone wondered how much he had told her.

'Well, whatever. Big compliment. He doesn't open himself up to just anybody you know. Anyway, he was very put out you couldn't join us tonight. I told him you had a far more exciting invitation which you couldn't *possibly* break. Told him he'd have to make do with us all going out together to celebrate his opening night next week.'

'Great. I'd like that.'

'Good, that's settled then.' Phil turned around at the sound of the kettle switching itself off. 'Want one?' she asked, holding up her coffee mug.

'I've just had some mineral water, thanks.' Phil's capacity for coffee always amazed her. She watched as Phil poured the boiling water into her mug. As always she failed to switch the kettle off at the mains. Leone had ceased nagging her about it, but found Phil's cavalier attitude of 'if you're going to go, you're going to go' not in the least bit comforting. Phil had only laughed when she'd photocopied the page in the *First Aid Manual* which dealt with the hazards of electrocution and had stuck it up on the kitchen cupboard door. Well, Phil had every right to laugh, she supposed. She wasn't going to be the one fiddling around with wooden broom handles or rolled-up pieces of newspaper trying to disengage the electric current, was she?

'Is Janie coming in, do we know?' Phil asked.

'Later this morning, I think,' said Leone. 'All being well at the hospital.'

'Great. I could do with her help packing up Pablo's stuff. It's so bloody intricate, each one's taking an age.' She was heaping the sugar into her coffee by the teaspoonful, Leone noticed. A sure sign she was tired. 'Have we heard any more about Ronnie, by the way?'

'Not yet, no. But I'm taking it as a good sign that Janie hasn't rung.'

'Sure. Probably right.' Phil started across the studio towards the stairs. 'Well, it's back to the salt mines for me, I guess. I'll pop up later for the camera.'

'Fine.' Leone slid off the table on which she'd been sitting. 'And thanks again for the invite.'

'No problem. Sorry you couldn't make it, that's all.' Phil bent down to tie her shoelace which had come undone. 'Anyway,' she said, straightening and pushing her straight blonde hair back from her face with a sweep of her hand, 'I know you'll have a great time at the National. Antony Sher is my absolute favourite and he's said to be a genius in this.'

'Rave reviews all round,' agreed Leone. She was warming to the thought of the play again. It would be lovely to get away from the events of the past twenty-four hours. To escape, just for the evening, into a world which had nothing whatsoever to do with either Carlton or Morenzo.

~

Leone wasn't quite sure what had gone wrong. The play had been superb, Antony Sher as brilliant as Phil had suggested, and yet here they were on their way back to Kensington driving along in strained silence.

She gave a quick glance at her father, her long-fingered hands tightening on the steering wheel. It was the music which had started it, of course. The Mozart piano piece which had threaded its way through the second act. What on earth had prompted her to remark that she could remember her mother playing that piece in the drawing-room of their old house in north London? She had caught the look in his eyes half-way through her sentence, but had blundered on, hoping...

Hoping for what? For him to say, yes, he remembered it too? For him to start talking about her mother? But it hadn't happened like that, had it? Instead she'd felt the old familiar shutters closing. She'd felt him withdraw behind his 'No Trespassing' sign, felt his leaving her, and he'd been silent and detached for the rest of the play.

Now, here in the car, she wished she could tell what he was thinking, but he sat, his broad shoulders pressed rigidly into the seat, staring out at the red tail lights of the car ahead. She did not challenge his silence. He had always guarded his emotions with the fierceness of Cerberus, closing up when people got too near. She understood that. It was a trait of hers, too. One that Jack had hated.

For once, however, she saw Jack's point. She felt excluded and wished he would talk to her. Wished she could say to him, 'Daddy, this is foolish. We *must* talk about her sometimes.' But she didn't, of course. Her previous attempts had always met with icy rebuttals. Now she was too conditioned to try to seek answers. Too conscious of stirring dark waters.

So instead she flipped on the radio and drove past the high dome of the Albert Hall towards Kensington High Street in silence.

Richard sat at his mahogany desk in his library, his large capable hands resting on the unopened file in front of him, staring out across the coal-black treeline of the garden below.

Julia. Everything seemed to be conspiring to remind him of her recently. First Ted, then that wretched piece of music which Leone had remembered.

He lit his cigarette, drawing on it hungrily. Leone's comment had startled him. She remembered Julia playing that piece, she'd said. On a summer's afternoon with the sun slowly creating shadows across the drawing-room and the air heavy with the scent of lilies. And if she remembered that, what else did she recall?

It was happening. The thing he dreaded most was finally happening.

He lifted the cigarette to his dry lips again, the tip flaring as he took another deep breath. He'd have to talk to her sometime, he supposed. But after all these years the cloak of secrecy born of a survival strategy was hard to discard. How would he begin? What should he say to her?

Simple, his sister Mary would have said. Tell her the truth. But that was easy for her to say, wasn't it? Besides, what exactly was the truth? Even now he wasn't sure.

He leaned back, drawing heavily on his cigarette again. The smoke from it reflected the light from the small brass lamp on his desk. It created the sensation of an undulating veil of gauze dissecting the room.

Screens. Façades. That was what it came down to, of course.

And now it seemed that the screen he'd erected was about to be torn down. Silence did not protect him. It only created more problems. But it had served him well, hadn't it? Had helped Leone and himself to survive. Would it really be so wise to break that illusion?

He stretched out and picked up his tumbler of whisky, swirling it meditatively for a few moments before lifting it to his lips.

Do you swear to tell the truth, the whole truth and nothing but the truth?

The sentence, unbidden, came to him. Despite himself, he smiled. The whole truth? For years he'd been listening to that question being asked in court.

Only now did he realise the impossible irony of it all.

Chapter Fifteen

As she drove past the gorse and heather of the heathlands towards the sea Leone felt her spirits rise. She'd always loved this part of Suffolk. There was something about this bleak coastline which was unlike anywhere else in East Anglia; remote, windswept and unpretentious.

Not that she claimed to know it well. She and Phil had stayed two or three times with a schoolfriend who lived near Framlingham and had made the inevitable pilgrimage to the seaside on the few days that were almost hot enough to pass as summer.

God, what a shock that had been! Leone smiled as she recalled their first visit; how they'd climbed out of the car and run towards the beach with such childish eagerness, only to stop dead in their tracks when confronted by rough, uncompromising stones rather than the sweep of sand which they'd expected after visits to Cornwall and West Wittering. She remembered how dismayed they'd been, how gingerly they'd picked their way over the sharp stones down to the edge of the cold grey sea. Yet, even then, faced with the austere bleakness of the place, she'd felt its powerful charm.

Leone changed down a gear as she came to the familiar sight of the golf course. What had been Lady Carlton's instructions? Left at the next turning, or the one after that? She quickly scanned the scribbled sheet of directions propped up in front of the gear stick—second left.

A few minutes later she was turning off into a narrow, gorse-flanked lane. The wind was stronger now, and she could feel the gusts buffeting the car. Ducking her head slightly, Leone looked out at the sky. A line of ominous dark clouds were gathering to the east. Just what she needed. The return journey would be exhausting enough without having to cope with torrential rain as well.

The road curved round to the right. Just beyond the line of wind-battered trees she could see the outline of a house. She slowed down, consulting her instructions again. This was it then. Hatherington Hall.

As soon as she turned into the unkempt driveway she knew why Piers Carlton was so desperate for money. This house was too big, too unlovely, too much in need of obvious repairs. Certainly not the place, she thought, swerving to avoid yet another pothole, to win the most romantic spot for newlyweds.

She drew to a halt in front of the porticoed front entrance. As she stepped out of her car she immediately recognised the unmistakable salty tang of the sea. She hadn't realised they were quite so close.

Crossing the sparsely gravelled pathway to the studded oak door Leone rang the doorbell. A dog began to bark from the hallway within. She heard the sharp click of footsteps on flagstones, a voice telling the dog to be quiet, and then the sound of the door being opened.

A dark-haired woman stood in the doorway. She was in her late forties, tall, with a wide-browed face and pale blue eyes. She was wearing a navy cardigan buttoned to the neck with a single string of pearls showing. On her feet were the kind of flat-soled, black lace-ups Leone hadn't seen since her schooldays. The sort Matron would have described as sensible and of which she'd have thoroughly approved.

'You must be Leone Fleming.' Margaret Carlton held out her hand in greeting. 'How was the journey? I hope you didn't get caught in those wretched roadworks just outside Ipswich. It can be insufferable if you do.'

'Wasn't too bad, actually.'

'Mother's so grateful you could come,' Margaret told her, bending down to catch hold of a passing golden retriever which was trying to escape into the garden. 'I can't tell you how worried she's been.' She pushed the dog back into the hallway, and moved slightly aside to make way for Leone. 'Come along in anyway. You must be freezing.'

'I'll just collect the picture first, shall I?'

Leone went back to the car and opened the hatchback. The Devis lay swaddled in melinex wrapping and was covered with a tartan wool rug. She lifted it out and slammed the boot closed. Margaret, she noticed, had not moved from the doorway.

The contrast between the exterior of the house and the interior could not have been more pronounced. Here was none of the grey starkness. Instead there was a noticeable warmth to the place, a jumble of personal possessions and treasures were strewn around, together with a smattering of Persian rugs—worn but of the highest quality—and a miscellany of equally fine, mostly late Georgian furniture.

'You've brought back the Devis, I see. How very kind of you, my dear.' Lady Carlton turned from her place in front of the fire to greet Leone as she stepped into the drawing-room.

She was exactly as Leone had imagined she would be—thin, aristocratic-looking with a small beaked nose and steel-grey hair pulled back into a chignon, she exuded an elegant grace which the confines of the wheelchair couldn't constrain. Her eyes were piercingly blue and Leone guessed that in her youth she would have been much admired and courted.

'Now, can we persuade you to join us in a glass of sherry?' Lady Carlton asked. She stirred slightly, nodding to the silver drinks tray on top of the walnut table in the far corner. 'Or perhaps a gin and tonic?'

It was years since Leone had had a sherry. There wasn't much call for it in the fast-moving world of London. But she could see here, in this bastion of old-world manners and charm, it would be entirely appropriate.

'Sherry would be perfect, thank you.'

Margaret uncorked a bottle of Amontillado and poured out three small measures.

'I'm glad we've had a chance to meet at last,' Lady Carlton said, indicating to Leone to come and sit beside her. 'You come very highly recommended, you know.'

'Do I?' Leone tried not to sound too surprised.

'Oh, yes. We had someone from Christie's down here about six months ago who gave us your name and you are also in that pamphlet that *Antique Collector*—or is it that other magazine, I can never remember?—sends out from time to time. You know, the one that gives names and addresses of what they call the "Pick of the Bunch". You were their choice for picture restoration. Actually, I think they said "best value for money".' She paused as Margaret handed her her sherry. 'Weren't you aware they'd selected you, my dear?'

'I wasn't, actually,' Leone confessed. She made a mental note to try to get a copy of the booklet sent to her. It would be useful publicity.

'It was part of the reason we chose you,' Lady Carlton admitted, taking a sip of sherry. Leone noticed that Lady Carlton had to concentrate to stop her hands from shaking. 'So, tell me,' she went on after lowering her glass on to the table beside her, 'how does one become a picture restorer? What made you decide to pursue that as a career? I know so little about it.'

They fell into easy conversation. Lady Carlton was a lively companion. Margaret sat quietly opposite her. She obviously had none of her mother's vivacity, nor her good looks, for that matter. Leone assumed she'd taken after her father. Margaret looked faintly dowdy sitting there in her heavy tweed skirt. The typical spinster daughter, Leone thought, obliged to look after her elderly invalid mother, with no visible means of deliverance. She wondered if Margaret resented Piers' escape to London; wondered how she viewed his high-style living, which had ultimately brought them close to the edge of ruin.

There was a resonant chime from the hallway. Lady Carlton glanced at her wristwatch.

'Goodness, is that the time already?' she said. 'I'd rather hoped we might have had a chance to inspect the other pictures before lunch. Would you mind waiting until we've seen them or are you quite famished, my dear?'

'Let's go and look at them first, shall we?' Leone wasn't one to put off unpleasantries. She didn't think she could bear to sit through lunch knowing all the while that Lady Carlton was waiting for her verdict.

Leone went out to the car to collect the equipment she'd need. By the time she returned Margaret had brought out two paintings for her to examine.

Leone felt her heart sink. At first glance they appeared to be a Gainsborough portrait and a Stubbs, worth a fortune if they were genuine.

She glanced quickly at Lady Carlton, hesitating.

'Go on, my dear.' Lady Carlton regarded her with the steely gaze of one about to face the firing squad. 'We're prepared for the worst, Margaret and I.'

'Do you mind if I start by removing the frames?' Leone asked. She'd brought all her paraphernalia with her, but first she wanted to inspect the canvas. If the paintings were frauds and had, as she suspected, been painted by the same artist who'd copied the Devis, then it would be evident that the canvas had been cut down from a much larger one. She had a hunch that at least one of these canvases would match up.

'Do whatever you wish.' Lady Carlton's voice was resigned, emotionless. She'd developed a dispassionate disposition when she'd discovered her all-too-charming husband was, in fact, an inveterate gambler and drunkard. Now she had to face the probable fact that he'd been little more than a thief as well. Oh, the mistakes one makes, she thought sadly.

She pressed her thin hands together tightly, the knuckles gleaming white against the folds of her dark woollen skirt. Dignity, that was what was important at this stage.

Leone, watching her, held back for the briefest second then bent down to pick up the Stubbs. There was no point putting off the moment any longer. She sat down, turning the painting outwards, and wedged it tightly against her as she gently began to lever back the nails from the frame.

As she started to removed the last one she could almost hear the silent prayers. She added one of her own.

'My dear, it isn't your fault.'

Leone glanced up to see Lady Carlton regarding her calmly across the kitchen table. It was silly to feel guilty, she knew that. But she did. She felt as if she'd heard a cock crow three times.

'I just wish…' She stopped. What on earth was there to say? That she wished she hadn't been the one to destroy a lifetime's hopes in less than ten minutes? That's all it had taken, after all.

Leone told them to secure a second opinion, of course, but in truth she knew there was little point. The evidence was pretty conclusive. So much so, that when Lady Carlton had listened to Leone's verdict she'd told her not to waste time looking at the other pictures she'd originally asked her to examine. There was no need, she said.

So it was over then. The last act in a lamentable little play. *Fin.*

Leone swallowed the last of her coffee and turned to look out of the kitchen window. Even in its winter shrouds the garden looked surprisingly well maintained. With its carefully dug beds and tended shrubs Leone could see that this was the one part of the estate which had not been allowed to suffer. Past the rose beds, the lawn stretched down to a small copse, with a thick dark line of rhododendrons before it. She imagined in spring and summer the garden would be lush, colourful and heavily scented.

'We have some quite unusual trees and shrubs here at Hatherington,' said Lady Carlton, seeing her interest. 'Before you leave, if you've time, perhaps you'd care for a tour?'

'I should, very much,' Leone replied. A walk would lighten the atmosphere. It seemed to offer a kinder note on which to part.

'Well, then…'

A few minutes later Leone found herself striding beside Margaret as she pushed Lady Carlton towards the far end of the garden. The wind was bitterly cold after the warmth of the

Aga-snug kitchen and the icy chill reminded Leone why she so loved being in London in winter.

She heard Lady Carlton say something and bent her head slightly to catch her words.

'Gets rid of the cobwebs, doesn't it, my dear? I love it,' she was saying. 'We've only got a few acres now but originally we had the farm, too. Most of that's gone now, the cottages too. We used to let those, you know. Just short summer lets usually—mostly to artists and birdwatchers. They all adored being here. Everyone does.'

'I'm sure they do.' Leone caught hold of the collar of her coat and pulled it more tightly around her neck.

'It's the skies, you see.'

She was talking about the artists, of course. And looking up, Leone knew instantly what she meant. Wide, dramatic skies, like no other in the world. Constantly changing skies of the sort that had intoxicated Constable and had driven other painters to distraction.

They followed the path round to the right through the copse. Here the bare branches of the trees intermingled, thrusting upwards to form a dark archway overhead. Lady Carlton made Margaret stop once or twice so that she could point out trees of special interest to Leone. They walked through the wood to a further expanse of lawn which led down to a huge reed-bordered lake.

'Piers and Margaret used to swim out to that island when they were young,' Lady Carlton said, pointing out a small islet in the middle of the lake. 'Hard to believe now. It's quite a way. . .'

But Leone wasn't listening. She was staring at the vista before her. At the lake and the weather-beaten mill at its edge. She knew that scene.

'How extraordinary.'

'What is it?' It was Margaret who spoke.

'It's just…' Leone hesitated. She *must* be mistaken, surely. And yet, there was the oak tree. She took a deep breath to steady herself. She knew she was not wrong.

This was the same scene her mother had painted all those years ago. The one in her sketchbook The dark wind-ruffled lake, the mill, the towering oak.

She threaded her fingers tightly together and brought her hands up to her mouth, pressing them hard against her lips. Myriad emotions rushed through her. She felt totally overwhelmed by her discovery.

Her mother had been here. Her mother had placed her easel in almost this exact spot one summer's day virtually twenty years before and had sat down to paint this very view.

'Are you all right?' Lady Carlton had sensed Leone's surprise.

She nodded, not trusting herself to speak for the moment.

'You've gone frightfully pale,' Margaret said, peering closely at her.

'No, I'm fine,' Leone insisted. 'Really. It's just…well, it's all rather bizarre.'

'What is?'

She pushed her hands through her hair, shaking with emotion. 'It's just…I think my mother must have come here once, that's all. You see, I have one of her watercolour sketches at home which shows virtually this exact scene.'

'Good lord, isn't that interesting?' Lady Carlton exclaimed, obviously amused by the coincidence. 'You'll have to ring her when you get home, won't you, to see if she remembers the place.'

There was the briefest pause. Leone looked out across the dark expanse of water. The golden retriever was running along its edge, flushing out the mallard ducks.

'Actually,' she said quietly, 'she was killed in a car crash a few months after she must have come up here.'

'Oh, I *am* sorry. How perfectly clumsy of me.'

'You weren't to know. Anyway it was ages ago.'

Behind them Margaret started to call and whistle for the dog who had decided to wade into the lake after a line of retreating ducks.

'I suppose your mother must have stayed in one of our cottages,' Lady Carlton mused, ignoring her daughter's shouts and whistles. 'How utterly extraordinary.'

'Isn't it?' Leone agreed. She watched Margaret head off in exasperation after her recalcitrant canine. 'I don't suppose you remember her at all, do you?'

'Probably not, I'm afraid.' Lady Carlton gave an apologetic smile. 'How long ago was it, do you know?'

'The summer of 1978,' said Leone. 'June.' That was what it had said on the sketch anyway.

'That was the first year we let the cottages,' returned Lady Carlton thoughtfully. 'Then I might. We weren't so inundated with people then. What was she like, your mother? Describe her to me.'

What to say? Leone drew a deep breath, closing her eyes for a moment, trying to bring her mother's image to mind. 'Well, she was tall. Slim, very beautiful. And she had long auburn hair. Very thick and wavy. My aunt used to say she looked like someone out of a Pre-Raphaelite painting…'

Lady Carlton lifted her head at that.

'Do you know, I think I *do* remember her. Good heavens, so that was your mother. It's all coming back to me now. Such a striking gel. I remember them both…'

'Both?'

'Your father was here, too, of course. Handsome couple they made.'

'I imagine they did, yes.' Leone struggled to keep the tightness out of her voice, to hide the nub of resentment she felt growing inside her. Her father had known she was coming to Suffolk, to Hatherington, and yet he'd said nothing to her about having been here all those years ago with her mother. He kept everything to himself. Everything.

'Oh, lord! Look at Margaret and that wretched dog of her!' Lady Carlton's attention was momentarily distracted by the sight of her daughter struggling to bring to heel one very wet retriever. 'He'll stink to high heaven now he's been into the lake. A perfect nuisance he is.'

Silence fell between them. Leone looked down at her hands.

'Margaret, hurry do!' The cold was making Lady Carlton fretful. She made an impatient gesture towards her daughter.

'Shall I start pushing you back to the house?' asked Leone. 'Margaret will be able to catch up with us.'

'That would be kind. I fear my old bones feel the cold rather these days.'

They started up the stony path towards the copse again. It was harder to manoeuvre the wheelchair smoothly over the dips and bumps than Leone had imagined. Margaret must be much stronger than she looked, she thought to herself.

Lady Carlton gave a quick glance back towards Leone. 'Managing all right, my dear?'

'Not quite up to the advanced driving test yet,' Leone admitted with a smile, 'but coping pretty well.'

'That's the spirit. Now, where was I?' The thick woollen rug covering her had worked its way loose. Lady Carlton began to tuck it around her more tightly. 'Oh, yes, I was telling you about your parents, wasn't I?' she said. 'They came up in June, you're quite right. They stayed at the cottage for about ten days, I think. Margaret and I used to watch them set off together, either to walk, birdwatch or paint. I seem to remember we thought it all rather romantic. The old couple who'd taken the cottage before them had done nothing but row. But not your parents. Very much in love they were…'

'Yes, I think they were rather.' It was gratifying to hear, though. 'Talented, too.'

'Yes, my mother was very gifted. I've several paintings of hers which are really delightful.'

Lady Carlton swung round in her wheelchair, her eyes intense. 'Oh, your mother's paintings were pretty enough, of course,' she said. 'But it was your father who was the real genius, wasn't it? I seem to remember I tried to persuade him to sell me one of his paintings but he wouldn't hear of it. Wouldn't part with any of them.'

'Oh, but...' Leone stopped in mid-sentence. She felt a tide of confusion wash over her.

There was some mistake, surely? Her father had never painted in his life. In fact, his ineptitude was a standing joke between them. Lady Carlton must be muddling them with another couple.

She was aware that Lady Carlton was waiting for her to speak. But she knew she couldn't do so. Not yet.

The truth, cold and unpalatable, stared her in the face.

Lady Carlton had not been mistaken. Her mother *had* come up to Hatherington in that summer of 1978.

But Leone knew with a deep and terrible certainty that the man who'd been with her, the man she'd so adored, had not been her father.

Chapter Sixteen

Leone leaned heavily against the glass door of the telephone kiosk, taking a long deep gasp. It had taken all of her willpower to extricate herself from the Carltons without giving in to her emotions. Now, standing in the kiosk outside the village post office, she felt she was poised at the edge of an abyss.

She heard the phone click.

'Phil?' But it was only the answerphone and Phil's disembodied voice instructing her to leave a message.

'Phil. It's Leone,' she said hurriedly. 'I'm in Suffolk on my way back to London. Look, if you've got time when you get in, give me a ring, will you? Need to talk, that's all…'

That's all! Who was she fooling? The need to talk was so fierce she thought she'd break with the pain of it.

She closed her eyes, pressing her face against the misty pane of the kiosk, feeling the glass cold as a sheet of ice against her skin.

It was the shock, of course. The shock of watching her mother tumble from the pedestal on which she'd so carefully placed her.

That was the problem with idols. They inevitably crashed to earth.

Jack had warned her about that. What was it he'd said once? *Illusions are dangerous—they have no faults.* But she'd refused to listen, hadn't she? And now she'd paid the price. It was as if she'd walked into a familiar much-loved room and found it ransacked.

She put a hand under her hair and rubbed the muscles at the base of her skull. They were bunched into knots, like a tangle of tight wires.

The trouble was, she wasn't sure what to do next.

Should she telephone her father or not? If she rang now she might just catch him before he left to stay with the Cunningham-Reids in Wiltshire for the weekend. She could ask him to wait so that they could talk. And he *would* wait. He'd always done that for her.

But what would she say to him? What if he knew nothing about her mother's affair? It was more than a possibility.

She put out her hand towards the receiver, hesitating for a moment, then picked it up and dialled her father's number.

He answered at the first ring. He must have been sitting at his desk. 'Leone? You sound miles away, darling.'

'I'm still up in Suffolk.'

'Still? What's wrong? You haven't had an accident, have you?'

'No, nothing like that. The thing is…'

She couldn't do it. She couldn't bring herself to tell him. Not on the telephone. Not like this.

'Darling, are you all right?' His voice was threaded with concern. 'You didn't have trouble with the Carltons, did you?'

'No, nothing like that. They were actually very sweet.' She felt herself draw back from the water's edge. It could wait. *She* could wait. This was something that could only be dealt with face to face. 'I just…just wanted to catch you before you left for Wiltshire, that's all. Wish you a good weekend.'

She heard the click of his cigarette lighter and the sharp intake of breath as he lit his cigarette.

'So, nothing's the matter?'

'No.' Oh, God, she hoped she sounded convincing. 'Everything's fine.'

'Good. Listen, I should get on. I told the Cunningham-Reids I'd be down with them just after seven. You know what a stickler Caroline is for punctuality.'

'Of course.'

'Thoughtful of you to ring, though, darling. Careful how you drive back.'

'I will be. Bye.'

She put the receiver back on its hook and then rubbed her hands slowly up the sides of her arms. She felt the weariness of the day's events wrap itself around her like a too-heavy coat. Ironic, wasn't it? All these years she'd been desperate to find out more about her mother and now this. What was the saying? 'Be careful what you wish for, the gods might grant it.'

She pushed open the kiosk door and stepped outside. The temperature was falling. She buttoned her coat beneath her chin, her breath steaming on to her hands.

The last of the light was beginning to fade. Leone stood for a moment looking back across the fields and the darkening line of trees. Darkness altered the atmosphere of the countryside, giving it alien shapes and sinister edges. It was no longer the innocent, benign place of her childhood memories. It had irrevocably changed.

She pushed her hands deep into her coat pockets and walked back towards her car.

It was time to be leaving.

⌒

At the intersection with the AI2, a red sports car passed Leone travelling fast in the opposite direction.

Piers Carlton, at the wheel of his Porsche, put his foot down on the accelerator, and sped on. He was in a foul temper. The last few days in Frankfurt had been hideous. The conference had been a waste of time, the speakers tedious, and the walls of the hotel so paper-thin he hadn't slept a wink. And now this. An urgent, garbled message from Margaret summoning him to Hatherington. Don't tell Mother you're coming, she'd said. Can't discuss it on the phone.

What the hell was she playing at? Well, it had better be important, Piers thought irritably. Cressida had been as sulky as a starlet forced to share a dressing-room when he'd told her he was going up to Suffolk for the night. He'd had to placate her by promising to take her to that new little restaurant in Flood Street she'd been on about for weeks.

He'd hoped to avoid that. His bank manager was acting like a little Hitler at the moment. Jesus! He hated a man like that having power over him. A tight-arsed, bespeckled grammar-school boy, who'd enough dandruff on his shoulders to ski on.

A slow-moving car was blocking the road ahead. Piers blasted his horn violently, swearing under his breath. He pushed his foot down and swerved past, his headlights piercing the winter's mist that lay across the road.

What on earth was he doing making this journey instead of being tucked up with Cressida, anyway?

But he knew the answer.

'It's about the pictures,' Margaret had said in her message. Pictures. Not Picture. Not just the Devis then. Then she'd mentioned a name. 'Leone Fleming.'

He gritted his teeth together. As if she hadn't done enough damage to him already, for God's sake. A few days ago the bloody police had turned up on his doorstep, asking difficult questions. Just what he needed. He could imagine what rumours were already circulating round the market. And now this.

Piers slammed his hand hard against the dashboard and swore again.

What had his mother done now with her bloody meddling, the silly bitch?

He just hoped to God he wasn't too late. He was beginning to feel like Prometheus holding up the world. And his shoulders were definitely shuddering under the weight of it all. He was aware that any minute now it might all come toppling down.

～

The morning light spread across Leone's bedroom, inching its way over the cream-coloured carpet like a silent predator. Leone watched as it filtered across the dressing-table by the far wall, snaking a path through the jumble of articles on its polished surface: her make-up, silver hair-brushes, hair-dryer, and a black leather jewellery-box.

She ought to get up, she knew, but just to lie here in the warmth was a sort of comfort in itself. An escape. To get up meant facing the day. And that meant acknowledging all sort of truths.

She lay for a while, putting off the moment. Then she pushed herself up to a sitting position and swung her legs over the side of the bed. A brief dizziness took her by surprise when she stood up and she pressed the heels of her hands against her temples to relieve the pressure. This morning it wasn't a question of just waking up—more of regaining consciousness. Her fault of course. She'd tossed back the drinks at the party last night as if Prohibition were about to come back into fashion.

She closed her eyes, trying to ignore the thumping in her head. She hadn't really intended to go to the party, but on arriving back from Suffolk her flat had been so overwhelmingly depressing and gloomy she just couldn't face the thought of staying there alone. So she'd gone out and got thoroughly tight.

Leone flicked on the radio and padded across to the kitchen. In the background she could hear the too-cheery DJ trying to convince his listeners that London was waiting for them out there. She filled up the kettle, switched it on and then went through to the bathroom to shower.

Fifteen minutes later she re-emerged, dressed in blue jeans and sweatshirt, her newly-washed hair tied up in a towel. The Alka-Seltzers were already doing their stuff and she was beginning to feel half-way human again.

She poured herself out a much-needed cup of Earl Grey and was just about to sit down at the kitchen table when she heard the front doorbell ringing. 'Who in their right minds called on anybody on a Saturday morning before nine o'clock? she wondered, going over to the door and peering through the security peephole.

It was Jack. Looking disgustingly bright eyed and bushy tailed.

'What brings you here at this hour, Jack?' she said, pulling open the door. 'Not like you to be up with the larks.'

He looked slightly nonplussed. 'I thought you spoke to Phil last night,' he said. 'She told you we were coming over, didn't she?'

Had she? Leone couldn't remember much of her conversation with Phil last night. It had been very late and post-party by the time she'd got through to her. She knew she'd told her about her mother because she vaguely recalled Phil offering to come round—and remembered Phil telling her she'd patched things up with Steve after their argument that morning about her photographing everything she could lay her hands on—but that was about it.

She saw Jack looking down at her expectantly.

'The car?' he prompted.

'The car! Of course.' How could she have forgotten she'd promised Phil she could take it for transporting Steve's pictures?

'Phil and Andrew are just at the gallery sorting out a few things,' Jack went on, stepping into the sitting-room. 'They should be here in a few minutes.'

'Andrew as well! Phil's browbeaten the whole gang then?' Leone tucked her thumbs into her jeans pockets and smiled. She wasn't surprised. Phil had perfected the art of persuasion. She was the only person Leone knew who could successfully cajole a traffic warden into tearing up her parking ticket.

Leone went through into the kitchen. 'Do you want a cup of tea while you're waiting?' she asked Jack. 'I've just made a pot.'

'Wouldn't say no.' He trailed through after her. 'Are you all right?' he asked, leaning his shoulder against the door jamb. 'You look dreadful, you know.'

'Thanks a lot, Jack.' She stretched up and took out another mug from the kitchen cupboard. 'Whichever charm school you went to, I should get them to give you your money back.'

'Sorry.' Jack lifted both hands up, palms forward, in a conciliatory gesture. He was aware of how carefully he must tread. 'Not exactly the most tactful statement that, was it?' He peered at her closely, head tilted slightly. 'So? *Are* you all right?'

Leone filled up the mug and handed it to him in silence. He knew. She could tell by the way he was looking at her. She sat down at the kitchen table, suddenly feeling very weak and vulnerable.

'Phil told you then?' she asked simply.

He nodded. 'On the way here this morning.'

'I should have known she would.' Share a secret with Phil and you might as well as have given it to the tabloids.

'She was worried about you, that's all.'

Jack lifted his hand, grazing it gently along the length of her hair, following its curve to her shoulder. She did not pull away from his touch. She knew now he had come out of concern especially to see her before Phil and Andrew arrived.

'How much do you know?' she asked. She looked down and began tracing an imaginary line on the table. She couldn't quite bring herself to look at him.

'That you found out yesterday your mother was having an affair just before she died.'

There was a silence. She tensed, waiting for him to say that he'd warned her about the dangers of idolising someone. But he didn't. Instead he said, with great gentleness, 'You must be devastated.'

She picked a white chrysanthemum out of the small glass vase in the centre of the table and began to twirl it backwards and forwards in her fingers.

'Yes,' she said, her voice tight. She cleared her throat. 'And do you know what the worst of it is, Jack? When I think of my mother now, when I remember our happy moments together— our time at West Wittering or just at home in the garden—I find myself wondering if she really were happy or was she just thinking of *him*.'

He covered her hand with his. 'You mustn't let yourself think like that, Leone.'

'It's hard not to.'

'She loved you. You know that.'

'And did she love my father as well? Were they ever happy together, do you suppose?' Leone asked bitterly.

'I'm sure of it. Listen, every marriage hits rock bottom at one stage or another. Lots of people fall by the wayside and climb back up again. Who knows what would have happened if she'd lived? Who knows even if the affair wasn't just a summer fling? Your father was working hard. She was bored…'

He was being terribly kind. Not one pointed remark about her father being the manipulative old sod he thought him to be.

'I'm not even sure he knows.'

'Your father?'

She nodded. 'I tried to talk to him about it last night on the telephone, but what could I say? "By the way, Father dearest, did you know that the wife you so adored was all the while busy being screwed by someone else?"'

He could hear the pain in her voice. The sound of betrayal. 'Don't,' he entreated softly.

'But it's true,' she said. 'She was. And I want to talk about it, but I'm afraid to. I'm caught between Scylla and Charybdis, aren't I? How do I find out if he knows without confronting him about it?'

She lifted the mug to her lips, her eyes silently challenging Jack to come up with an answer. Her alcohol-induced sleep had provided little comfort. She was too exhausted to think any more.

Closing her eyes, Leone tilted her head forward and covered her face with her hands.

Outside in the communal garden a burst of children's noisy laughter broke the silence. She lifted her head slightly. The Davidson tribe was on the rampage again. Their parents always turfed them out early on a Saturday morning so that they could enjoy a leisurely breakfast in peace together. She heard the children's heavy-booted footsteps on the gravel path as they thundered past. Carefree, they sounded. Assured of their parents' love of themselves and of each other.

As she had once been.

'What?' She was aware she'd just missed what Jack was saying.

'I said, there's always your aunt. Couldn't you try her? You always said she was the only one who'd talk to you about your mother.'

'But Aunt Mary would hardly know whether or not my father knew, would she?'

'She might. She was certainly there immediately after your mother died, after all. And she was close to your father in those days, wasn't she? He might have confided in her.' He lifted his shoulders slightly. 'Hell, I don't know, Leone. I'm clutching at straws here, like you. But it's worth a try, isn't it?' He saw her hesitate. 'Ring her, for heaven's sake. Find out what she knows. Or doesn't. At least it won't matter if you let slip to her about your mother's affair. She's hardly likely to go gossiping to your father about it, is she?'

'No, probably not.' The chrysanthemum lay limply on the table. Leone picked it up. Wasn't it Freud who said nothing happened by accident? Was she forcing this, driving it to her own conclusion? She could stop now. Pretend it had never happened.

'What are you frightened of?' Jack asked tentatively.

'I'm not certain,' she admitted.

'But you want to know the truth, don't you?'

Did she? She wasn't sure any more. Truth had seemed such a pure and simple commodity a short time ago. Now she was aware of its dangers, of its power to hurt and destroy.

'Ring her,' Jack urged gently.

She hesitated for only a moment more, then pushing back her chair stood up and went through to the sitting-room.

⌒

'Is this it?'

Jack brought the car to a halt. Before them a pair of white painted gates marked the entrance to a narrow driveway.

'Yes.' Leone pushed open the car door and climbed out to open the gates. She was glad of something to do, anything to stop the cold feeling of panic which was spreading through her.

What was it her aunt had said? 'I suppose you ought to hear the rest of it, now you've come this far. You'd better come down, my dear…'

The rest? She had the sense she'd grasped a snake by its tail. She shot a quick glance at Jack, grateful now that he'd insisted on coming with her. Whatever her aunt's revelations she had the suspicion that, like the twin-headed beast, they should not be faced alone.

They drove up the gravelled driveway and parked in front of the old wisteria-clad farmhouse. Mary must have been listening for them because almost before they'd drawn to a halt she was out of the doorway to greet them.

'Thank you for coming down, my darling,' she said, giving Leone a hug. 'It's been far too long.'

She linked arms with Leone and led them into the house, ushering them through the dark hallway slung with old coats and boots into the large untidy sitting-room beyond.

'Sit down, do,' she said, moving several gardening books from the peach-coloured sofa and chairs to accommodate them.

Leone watched her aunt settle herself down in the wing chair opposite. She was rather like the room in which they now were, Leone thought—spacious, homely and without pretension. She was in her early sixties, a few years older than Leone's father, grey-haired with the same heavy jawline and features. She'd put on weight since Leone had last seen her, but was still a handsome woman, well turned out in an ancient grey knitted two-piece which Leone remembered from the days she'd lived with them in London. Mary had always placed comfort above chic.

Thinking of those days Leone felt a pang of guilt. She hadn't done enough for Mary of late. She rang her from time to time, of course, but the regular visits which had once been her habit had dwindled over the past few years and had finally stopped completely over the last fifteen months or so. She wasn't sure why.

'So,' Mary stretched forward to put another log on the fire, then glanced up at Leone. 'Before we begin I suppose I should check that you're quite happy for all this to be discussed in front of Jack.'

'I think it's time it all came out into the open,' said Leone, her eyes flicking over to Jack who gave her a little nod of encouragement.

'Very wise, dear,' Mary agreed, smoothing out the soft folds of her skirt. 'Secrets have a way of destroying those who hold on to them for too long.' There was a long silence, then she said in a quiet, controlled voice, 'I'm glad you found out, Leone. If I'm honest, I've been expecting it for a long time now. I warned Richard you would.'

'But why did no one tell me?' Leone asked. Despite herself she felt the old stirrings of resentment.

'I wanted to, believe me.'

There was something in her voice which encouraged Leone to go on. 'Is that why you and Father fell out?'

'Richard felt it inappropriate to discuss the matter with you. He forbade me to talk about it. I know he felt he was protecting you, that it was all too terrible for you to take in, but all the same I thought you should be told the truth about what really happened to your mother that night.'

She felt her heart start to hammer in her chest.

'What do you mean "what really happened"? I know what happened. She died in a car crash.'

The room was suddenly very still.

Leone's stomach tightened. 'Didn't she?'

'Oh dear, this is so difficult.'

Mary stood up. She walked over to the French windows and stared out past the carefully tended rose garden to the ornamental pond beyond. She pressed her hands together tightly. Richard would be furious with her, of course. But Leone had a right to know the facts, however unpalatable. She took a deep breath. There was no painless way of telling her niece the truth.

'No,' she said. 'The car accident was simply something your father invented to shield you.'

'Then how? I mean…' Leone stopped. 'She *is* dead, isn't she? She didn't just up and leave with her lover?'

'No, she's dead.'

'Then how did it happen?' Outside on the patio a thrush was trying to break open a snail. Leone could hear its steady tap-tap as it strove to crack open the shell against the stone slabs.

For a moment her aunt didn't move. Then she turned slowly back from the window. Her face was pinched and there was no colour left in her cheeks.

'There's no easy way to break this to you, Leone,' she said.

Leone sensed impending disaster like a miner detecting that minutest change in air pressure which warns of an imminent cave-in.

The silence was overbearing.

'She was murdered, Leone. Along with her lover, Simon Rhodes.' Her eyes came up sharply to meet Leone's. 'Now perhaps you can understand why your father was so determined to protect you from the truth.'

Chapter Seventeen

Jack turned off Shepherd's Bush roundabout and drove up Holland Park Avenue. It was after eight but the tree-lined pavements were still crowded with late-night shoppers struggling home with their trophies and families with hordes of young children out for their Saturday-night treat to the local hamburger café.

He ran a hand wearily across his face. God! What an afternoon of revelations. Julia Fleming *murdered*. Killed by Rhodes' jealous wife at his hideaway studio. He still couldn't take it in. That sort of thing didn't happen to the mothers of people you knew, people you cared for.

What was it Mary had said? 'Diminished responsibility.' According to her, Margaret Rhodes had had a long history of mental illness and depression though no one had foreseen that she would react with such violence when she found out about the affair. She'd got hold of a gun and gone to Rhodes' studio and shot them both dead in cold blood. Then she'd gone home and slit her wrists. It had never come to trial. That had been the one and only thing Richard Fleming had to be thankful for.

Ahead at the pedestrian crossing a young couple out jogging together were waiting to cross and he slowed down, casting a quick glance at Leone in the seat beside him. She was asleep, huddled up against the car door with his coat tucked around her. She looked worn-out but at least she had some colour back in her cheeks. She'd looked like death for most of the journey and just outside Brighton he'd had to pull over to the verge for her to get out to be sick. Delayed reaction, he supposed. Hardly surprising. It had been a cataclysmic afternoon.

And yet, how much it explained.

Richard Fleming's relationship with his daughter, for one.

Now he could understand Richard's over-protectiveness, his almost obsessive secrecy, his need to erect a brick wall around them both. He could see that Richard's seeming coolness, his inability to sustain any long-term relationships were because of his fear that one day they might betray him as Julia had done. And how he must have suffered, the tangle of lies and half-truths threatening to suffocate him as the years went by.

How easy it is to condemn, Jack thought. He'd misjudged the man, he accepted that now. He'd been too quick to castigate. He still might consider him cold and manipulative—some things did not change but at least he understood more clearly the reasons for so many of his actions.

He even understood why Richard Fleming had opposed his relationship with Leone so vehemently. He'd always thought it was simply because Richard was such a god-awful snob. But it had been more than that, hadn't it?

He leant his head back, recalling Richard Fleming sitting there that first evening they'd met, cigarette in one hand, glass of whisky in the other, staring into the darkness. He must have sensed that Leone and he were already lovers. How uneasy it must have made him feel. Another quasi-artist entering their world. An intruder ready to jeopardise the calm tranquillity he'd fought so hard to create, threatening to take away the one person he loved. Casting shadows of the past.

No wonder Richard's welcome had been less than enthusiastic.

Up ahead the traffic lights had turned red. Jack jammed on the brakes. On the pavement outside the corner pub a mass of young people were congregating, ready for amusement and fun. He could see the steam from their breath on the cold night air as they chatted in their small groups, their loud laughter echoing down the avenue as they made their noisy arrangements for the evening. Re-grouping their molecules for night-running.

Leone stirred a little. A wisp of blonde hair had fallen across her face and without thinking Jack brushed it gently back. She slowly opened her eyes.

'How are you feeling?' he asked.

'Like I've done ten rounds with Mike Tyson, if you want the truth.'

'Only ten, huh?'

She smiled. At least she could still do that.

He stretched over and touched her shoulder. 'Listen, what about a film later on this evening? Ralph Fiennes' latest is on at the Coronet.' He knew she loved Fiennes and couldn't bear to think of her returning to an empty flat to brood alone.

She turned her head away from him, closing her eyes. 'To be honest, Jack, I don't think I could face going out. I think I'd rather just curl up at home. Do you mind?'

''Course not. All the same to me.' His voice was casual but he was staying with her, whether she wanted him to or not. 'I'll pick up a couple of videos, then.' Anything to take her mind off the past twenty-four hours.

He drove up to Notting Hill Gate. The video shop was on the right and he pulled into the kerb opposite.

'Want to come in?' he asked.

She shook her head. 'You go ahead, Jack. I'll trust your judgement.'

'Silly child. You're talking to the only man who actually enjoys obscure Japanese period films.'

'Just be discerning,' she said. 'Anyway, you know the sort of thing I like.'

'Nothing too bizarre, nothing too violent and *nothing* with Clint Eastwood in it,' he recited with a grin.

'You remember!'

'Of course I remember.'

He got out of the car and crossed over the road, dodging the traffic. The shop was packed with people. So much for the traditional Saturday night out, he thought. He thumbed his way through the line of videos trying to decide whether he should go for a couple of bright and breezy comedies, or settle for the classic all-time weepies. In the end he picked out a hodge-podge collection. *Waterloo Bridge* was a sure-fire recipe for tears, he knew, but that might be no bad thing. He could sense Leone was still holding on tight to her emotions. She'd shown shock, yes, but not grief. Not yet.

He paid for the videos at the desk, taking a chance and giving Leone's name as a member—which she was. She'd always been a film buff. That was one thing they'd had in common.

'Trying for your own private film festival, I see,' remarked the bearded man behind the desk as he handed the stack of videos back across the counter.

The cases Jack noticed were emblazoned with the words, 'Please rewind the tape after use or we might have to take your first-born.' Sense of humour—he liked that. Made a change. The British still had a tendency to be so bloody dismal about everything. Go to America or the Far East and at least they made a show of looking enthusiastic about taking your money off you. In fact 'Enjoy' was a typical American phrase. All right, so it was all obviously insincere, but frankly he preferred being told to 'have a nice day' by someone who didn't mean it, than to be told to 'sod off' by someone who did.

He came out of the shop and turned left. There was a wine shop a few yards on. He bought a couple of bottles of wine and then crossed over to the all-night supermarket for some provisions. Leone, he knew, never had anything much in her fridge.

After a quick ferret through the supermarket he returned to the car. Leone was still curled up on the front seat, head against the window. She opened her eyes as he pulled open the car door.

'All right?' he asked, climbing in.

'Fine.' She sat up giving him a quick half-smile. He could guess at the effort it took.

Jack started up the car, did a quick U-turn and drove back towards Ladbroke Grove. Ahead of him the traffic was heavy, the night air thick with exhaust fumes. He stole a quick glance at Leone. He knew her too well not to be feeling the strained tension despite her effort to appear calm and in control. Little tell-tale signs: the set of her mouth, the way she unconsciously pressed the thumb of her right hand against the palm of the other, up and down like the pulsating wings of a butterfly. It was that small movement he now remembered most from the day they'd finally agreed to go their separate ways. Not the anger, not the recriminations. Just that small, vulnerable gesture.

He turned off by the church and stopped the car a few hundred yards down the tree-lined street in front of the white stuccoed house. He pushed open the door, collected the miscellany of plastic bags from the back seat and stepped out on to the pavement.

Outside it was one of those wonderfully clear winter nights—so rare in London—when the heavens seemed almost within reach. Orion's Belt, Canis Major and the Dog Star Sirius, the planet Venus, he could easily pinpoint them all. As a child he'd spent long hours with his father in their small garden in Oxfordshire studying the skies. It was a bond between them, his normally shy, uncommunicative father opening up as he revealed the secret mysteries of the planets and the stars to him.

He remembered the thrill of being allowed to use his father's telescope for the first time, the excitement he'd felt when his father had pointed out to him the middle star of Orion's dagger, telling him that in reality it was a glowing mass of gas from which you could actually see new stars being born. To be able to stand in a small cold corner of a suburban garden and watch the universe still being created had seemed to him as a seven-year-old boy nothing short of a miracle. It had made him feel very insignificant and humble. And over the years neither age nor the edge of sophistication had ever quite managed to erase that same sense of wonder whenever he glanced up at the heavens.

Of course, the creation of those stars had taken place tens of thousands of years before in truth, he knew that. It was only now that the effects of that occurrence were being seen. But wasn't life a little bit like that, too? Full of events, the repercussions of which weren't felt for years.

Julia Fleming's death, for instance. Time had obscured the truth of that just as surely as clouds of dust in the galaxy hid a million unseen stars. Only now was it being revealed.

He turned his head at the sound of the car door slamming. Leone was standing out in the street, the collar of her coat turned up sharply against the wind. The moonlight made her hair silvery white and her eyes seemed huge and dark against the pallor of her skin. He crossed over to her and took her arm and felt her body momentarily lean against his. She was exhausted.

'Come on, let's go inside,' he said gently, leading her down the stone pathway to the flat.

Once inside he settled her down on the sofa in the sitting-room and went into the kitchen to unpack the provisions. He found an unopened bottle of Polish vodka in the fridge. Kolewska. The best vodka he had ever tasted. Forget the wine, he thought, this was a much faster route to oblivion. And that's what Leone needed tonight, wasn't it? The waters of Lethe? He broke the seal and poured out two small shots, then after a moment's pause, doubled the measure.

Leone was playing back her answerphone messages when he came through. He handed her the vodka and sank down into the highbacked armchair opposite. Phil was in mid-flow on the machine, describing the ghastliness of heaving pictures all day and saying she was about to pack up after one last trip to double-check on the gallery, and perhaps might call in on Leone on the way back to have a chat. There was a noticeable edge to her voice and Jack guessed moving Steve's pictures had taken its toll. Certainly, it sounded as if she'd worked non-stop all day hoisting heavy canvases across London.

There were three other messages. Two from men Jack hadn't heard of asking Leone to call back in response to various invitations and the last from Steve saying he'd temporarily lost track of Phil and if she turned up at Leone's could she get her to ring him.

Jack smiled. That was typical of Phil, impossible to pin down. She was just like her brother, Andrew—enchanting to know, infuriating to try to make plans with.

He glanced across at Leone. She was sitting, both hands cupped around the small glass, staring across the room at some distant, unseen object.

He wished she could trust him enough to talk to him. But then she'd never been one for opening up, had she? That had been part of their problem. Secrets had been her way of life, he saw that now.

He stood up and went across to draw the dark blue curtains. 'Do you want me to make some supper?' he asked. 'I'm a pretty dab hand at scrambled eggs and smoked salmon.'

'Actually, this is doing me pretty well at the moment,' Leone said, holding up her vodka glass.

'It's good, isn't it?' Jack agreed. It had an intense clean flavour, slightly sweet with a vanilla nose to it. 'When I was on a trip to Poland a couple of years back I was introduced to the home-brew variety. God! Talk about powerful stuff. Nearly blew off the top of my head.'

Leone took another sip, leaning her head back as she brought the ice-cold glass to her lips. 'What were you doing in Poland?'

'Oh, the usual. On the hunt for a picture.'

'Is that how it works? You're given a mandate to try to find a certain picture?'

He linked his hands behind his head. 'Sometimes. Or perhaps, more simply, to find something by a certain artist. Then it's my task to track down the best picture available and negotiate the sale. Can take months, years even.'

'You've changed. You didn't used to be such a patient man.'

He smiled. What had she once called him—restless, reckless and impatient? The Far East, he supposed, had mellowed him.

'I'm learning,' he said. 'You know what they say: "Patience, time and money bring all things to pass".'

'An old Chinese proverb?'

'Herbert actually, English seventeenth century.' He grinned, then seeing she'd finished her drink picked up the vodka bottle from the oblong glass-topped table in front of her and refilled both of their glasses.

'And do you deal mostly in Eastern Europe?' she asked, taking the glass from him.

'I go anywhere. There was a time when I used to fly out to America quite a lot. And then Russia. That was a productive source.'

'Tapping into the chunk of paintings taken out of Berlin at the end of the war, I suppose?'

'Exactly.'

'And do you mostly strike private deals?'

'Not always. Sometimes I buy at auctions.' He looked over his glass at her. She was leaning forward slightly, her chin resting lightly against her hand. She looked more relaxed; her green eyes were brighter now. 'Do you know where the best place is to look through auction catalogues? The windowseat of an aeroplane.'

'Why? Because that's the only free time you get, you mean?'

'No. Because the light's so bright and pure up there. Ethereal, even. You can see every precise little detail. Found that out on one of my trips to Paris for an auction.'

She finished her drink and put the glass back down on the table. 'Do you often go over to Paris?'

He shook his head. 'Too expensive usually. But I come over for the occasional exhibition.' It was a good way to discover who were the big private owners. 'The last exhibition I saw was Picasso.'

'I went to that.' Leone kicked off her shoes and tucked one leg up under her. She looked like a cat curling up for the night. 'I don't usually like him much but that was wonderful. I always forget what a brilliant artist he was when he was young.'

'He was brilliant when he was older too,' Jack said. 'You can't deny that. You may not *like* what he did, but you can't ignore his influence on modern art. You know what Braque said about his paintings?'

'Something like looking at his paintings was a bit like swallowing turpentine, wasn't it?'

'No!' He caught her eye and they laughed together. They'd had long debates in the past over Picasso. He stretched out and refilled their glasses.

They chatted on. She was relaxing now, the tensions of the day slipping away from her. He'd forgotten how easy it was to talk to her about art, as well as it being informative and challenging. That had been the core of their mutual attraction from the beginning.

He remembered when they'd first met that night at Andrew's, how they'd clicked instantly. No preamble. Straight into the merits of the Fauvists. It was only later when he'd locked horns with her father that the trouble had begun, though he viewed those problems in a different light now.

He picked up his vodka glass and tossed it back, feeling the liquid scorch his throat. So, what might have happened if he'd not thrown down the gauntlet that day? If he'd given in to her wishes and abandoned the idea of moving to the Far East and stayed on in London? Would he and Leone have carried on happily ever after?

He thought not. He'd been fed up with the limitations of his job, tired of the way his days had become indistinguishable from each other, stacking up against each other like discarded bills. The steady drip of disillusionment and frustration would have got to him in the end.

Besides, the rot had set in by then, hadn't it? She'd known what he thought about her father and he couldn't hide it. Nothing could change that. He simply wasn't one to walk the delicate paths between diplomacy and politeness—whatever the cost.

He was aware of her head falling forward, like a flower on a thin stem. She'd covered her face with her hands. He heard a muffled sob. He'd been so busy with his own thoughts, he hadn't seen her change of mood. Finally, the traumas of the day had overwhelmed her.

'Don't,' he said gently. 'Don't cry, Leone.' He came across to the sofa, crouching down before her, stroking her hair, waiting while she wept. After a while he heard her take in a long unsteady breath and he drew back from her, enclosing her hands in his.

She took a hankie from her jacket pocket and blew her nose vigorously. 'I'm sorry, I don't know what came over me…'

'No good bottling it up, you know.'

She pushed her lips together tightly, as if to stop any further flow of tears. She was looking at him a little uncertainly. 'Jack?'

'What is it?'

'Would you do me a great, great favour?'

'Ask away.'

'Would you stay tonight? If I made up the sofa bed. Just for tonight? I can't bear the thought of being here alone. I know it's silly but…'

'I had no intention of leaving you,' he interrupted her in a quiet voice. Had she really thought he would? Had she really forgotten so much about him?

She looked down at him, her eyes pools of liquid green. She leaned forward and put her palm against his face and then kissed him gently. 'Thank you for that, Jack.'

He breathed in the familiar scent of her skin. He reached out and softly touched her hair, lifting it back and away from her face. He could feel the warmth of her body. Tiny memories rose to the surface of his mind. Stop it, he told himself. No more of this.

He dropped his hand from her neck and stood up. He did not need complications; not now.

Without looking at her he crossed over to the video recorder and started to rummage through the stack of films on the floor.

For a long time after she'd gone to bed Leone lay awake listening to the muffled sounds of Jack's movements next door. A band of light still shone beneath her bedroom door and she knew he'd be reading. He always did, if only for a few minutes, before he went to sleep.

She pictured him stretched out on his back on the sofa bed, one arm tucked behind his head, the other holding the book propped up against his knee. She wasn't sure what he'd chosen—probably Diane Thomas's book, certainly he'd flicked through that with enough interest—but whichever one it was it seemed to have captured his imagination, because he still hadn't turned off the light. Or was he simply putting off the moment of sleep, just as she was doing?

She turned on to her side, trying to steady the thoughts swirling round in her mind like a carousel. Images converged, merged. Aunt Mary, Jack, her father. And lastly, her mother.

She tried not to think about the studio in which her mother had died. Tried not to deliberate whom Simon Rhodes' wife had killed first. But the question hung over her like a suffocating mist. Had her mother suffered or had her death been mercifully quick? She would have liked to believe she'd been killed first and had died instantly, but reality was seldom as simple as that, was it?

She closed her eyes. Outside the street was quiet. She steadied her breathing, concentrating on making each breath as slow and deep as possible, feeling her mind begin to freefall.

When sleep finally came, it was fitful and insubstantial. She dreamed she was with Jack, driving down a narrow country lane. It was summer. She could feel the sun warm on her face, the wind catching at her hair.

And then, quite suddenly she was aware of light and time changing and she was back in a familiar world. The old dream. The scent of lilies.

'Love you, little bear.'

Her mother was hurrying down the path, her high heels clicking against the stone path. Hurrying to be with her lover. This time Leone did not run after her. Nothing could change what was about to happen, she knew that now.

In her dream, time condensed. It was night and she saw her father in the drawing-room, hunched over the piano, playing that one mournful note over and over again.

'She should have stopped,' he was saying. He didn't look across at Leone. 'It would have been all right if only she'd stopped. I warned her…'

The jumble of words took on new meaning. She understood now. Her father was talking about her mother's affair with Simon Rhodes.

She heard the harsh snap of animosity in his voice.

'I told her…' He turned his head away slightly, so that those words following were lost to her once more.

She put her hand against the door jamb, leaning forward slightly. What had he told her mother? Those lost words were the last piece of the jigsaw, she knew. The last key that had to be turned.

Her father looked up from the piano then. The heavy features of his face were twisted with bitterness. She had never seen him look like that. That raw anger in his eyes frightened her. It was not his face any more.

She took a step back, shocked. A choking cry rose in her throat. This was not her father before her now but a stranger.

He was beckoning her forward, calling out her name.

'*Leone…*'

'No!' She would not go to him.

'*Leone…*'

'No!'

'*Leone, wake up!*'

She forced her eyes open, trembling. Jack was sitting on the edge of her bed. He bent over her and took her in his arms.

'You were having a bad dream,' he said gently. 'You cried out…'

She remembered now. The stranger. She shivered and pressed herself closer against Jack, feeling the warmth of his body pass to hers. His breath was a ghost kiss against her skin.

She closed her eyes. The familiarity of his body, of his touch, tugged at her heart. She felt the unequivocal rightness of him, as if they fitted together, mind to mind, limb to limb.

Without thinking, she slipped her hands beneath his shirt, feeling the corded muscles that sculpted his skin. Small circles of desire fanned out through her body. It was no good. She couldn't fight it any more. Nothing had changed for her. She wanted him. She wanted to feel him deep inside her, wanted him to fill her every sense so that everything else would be wiped from her mind. She needed that. Death by drowning. Infinite sweetness.

She lifted her hands to his head, drawing him slowly down towards her. She felt him tense slightly, resist.

'Don't leave me, Jack. Not tonight. Please, not tonight...'

She moved her mouth up to his, stretched up so that her small firm breasts brushed against his skin. She heard him catch his breath. She thought he might pull away. Then he caught her to him and began to kiss her face, her hair, her mouth.

His tongue moved softly, insistently, against hers. Gently he pushed her back against the bed. A shiver ran through her body as his lips traced the line of her breasts. She wouldn't let herself think about anything beyond this moment. She knew the dangers of retracing pathways but she couldn't stop herself. All she knew was that she wanted Jack, to have his flesh bury itself into hers. To feel part of him again.

To have his breath on her shoulder while she slept.

Just for tonight.

Chapter Eighteen

Phil picked up the telephone and dialled Leone's number. There was no reply, only the answerphone's monosyllabic tones instructing the caller to leave a message.

'Hi, Leone. It's Phil. Just wanted a chat. A couple of things have cropped up I wanted your advice about but I guess you're not there so they'll have to wait. Not to worry. Nothing that won't keep. So speak to you in the morning…'

She dropped the receiver back into its cradle feeling a nub of irritation. She'd wanted to talk to Leone about a niggling worry she had, a concern. Leone's careful, considered judgements were always a foil to her own rapid-fire decisions. Not that she always followed Leone's advice, of course, but that was a different matter. She would simply have to wait.

She drained the last of her coffee and swivelled round in her leather chair. Steve's pictures now adorned the walls—at least those in the main gallery—and looking around at them she had to admit they looked stunning. More dramatic, even, than she'd dared hope.

There were still a few more to pick up from his studio but those would have to wait. All she wanted to do now was go home and take a long, hot bath. It had been a hell of a day. She collected together the photographs she'd spread out on her desk and tucked them back into their folder. Tomorrow she'd sort everything out. She'd talk it over with Leone. Tonight she was so tired she couldn't even think straight.

Phil leaned across and switched off her desk lamp. Bone-white shafts of moonlight fell across the glass frontage of the gallery, creating bizarre shadows across the floorboards. Light and dark, sharp contrasts, just like something Cézanne might have painted. Or Steve.

She stretched and stood up. Outside came the clatter of a dustbin lid. Wretched cats on the prowl again, Phil thought. They were forever using the courtyard as a shortcut to their various feline gathering points. It was the yowling she objected to most of all, Tonight, though, there were no such disturbances. They were obviously on a peaceful patrol, maintaining radio silence.

She picked up her coat from the back of her chair and made her way over to the back door. Giving one last glance round the gallery, she set the alarm, then slipped out into the paved courtyard to where she'd parked the car.

It was as she was double locking the back door that she heard the sound. Not a cat. Definitely not a cat.

Footsteps.

Someone was with her in the courtyard.

Shit!

She froze, the hairs on the back of her neck bristling. Instinctively she knew she was in danger.

Her heart started to slam against her ribs. She half-turned and caught a quick flash of a hooded man in a dark-coloured tracksuit. Then a hand came down over her mouth and nose with such speed and force, she thought she heard the cartilage crack. She felt her head being pulled sharply back. She couldn't breathe or move. Something cold pressed against her skin then something tightened across her windpipe. A cord. He was twisting a cord round her neck.

Oh, God. Panic flooded through her. She could feel her breath being cut off as the cord tightened. *Oh, God*, she thought, *I'm going to die and I don't even know why.*

She struggled to concentrate her mind. She had to focus all her energy on what to do next. On how to escape. *Think*, she told herself. *Think.*

She tried to twist away, to get her fingers between the cord and her throat. There was no space. She tried to swallow. She saw his hands move in front of her as he pulled the cord tighter. They were sheathed in thin, translucent rubber gloves. This was a planned attack then, not random.

Morenzo? She knew all about him. Had he mistaken her for Leone?

What hope did she have if it were Morenzo?

She felt the cord tighten. She was gulping and gagging, clawing at his hands with her own. Her vision started to go black, her legs buckle beneath her.

She felt herself losing consciousness, her body starting to go limp. She was choking, dying. Every cell in her body screamed for air.

I don't want to die.

She couldn't let this happen to her. Somehow she'd find a way to beat him—if she could just make it to the car…

In one last desperate bid she focused every drop of strength and kicked out at him, legs flailing, fighting for that final breath. She felt her foot make contact with his knee. He staggered back, relaxing his steel-like grip on the cord.

She felt the merest sliver of hope. He was not infallible. There was still a chance.

'Oh, please…oh, please…'

She had to believe there was still a chance.

Chapter Nineteen

The sound of church bells awoke Leone. She stretched and turned over, glancing to Jack's side of the bed. It was empty. She felt vaguely relieved. She wasn't sure how she'd have reacted to waking up to him nose-to-nose in the cold light of day. Not that she was about to regret what had happened. It had been her choice to loop her life into an extra twist. Her choice entirely.

Grey morning light filtered through the curtains and she could hear the soft pattering of rain beating down against the flagstones of the patio outside her bedroom window. So much for the fine weekend forecast by the weathermen, she thought, tossing back the duvet.

Leone got out of bed and pulled on her jeans and sweatshirt. When she came out into the living-room she saw Jack in the kitchen. He was standing with his back towards her, grinding coffee beans. She could hear the faint hum of machinery.

He turned round as she came into the room. He gave no hint of awkwardness. She felt herself relax a little.

'Want some coffee?' he asked, holding up a mug. 'It's nearly ready.'

'Wouldn't say no.' She pushed her hair back from her face, watching him as he poured the boiling water into the glass cylinder and set the plunger on top.

In the corner of the room she could see the light on the answerphone flashing. She'd unplugged the phone in her room last night and must have missed the call. She went over and hit the replay button. It was Phil, saying she'd ring again later. Hers was the only message.

When she looked up Jack was coming through, carrying two mugs. He handed her one, watching her for a moment, assessing her expression, before taking a sip from his own.

'Listen, Leone,' he said. 'About last night…'

She'd known they had to talk about it, of course, but she'd wanted it to be in her own time. She ought to have remembered Jack was never one to sit and wait.

'Jack, let's not make a big deal about it, all right?' she said. 'It was a one-off, we both know that.' She kept her voice steady, not giving the least hint of what she truly felt. She didn't want him to feel responsible for her. She'd been the one to instigate the situation after all. 'I was feeling low, we'd both had too much vodka…'

'That was my fault,' he cut in. 'Bloody stupid of me to keep on pouring them out like that.'

'It was nobody's *fault* Jack,' she said. She didn't want him to feel guilty. Apologies and regrets were more than she could bear. She was to blame, if anyone was. 'Look, it wasn't any big deal,' she said, keeping her voice light. 'It didn't mean anything, we both know that. We're both grown-ups. These things happen…'

The phone started to ring. Leone picked it up, glad of the distraction. She wasn't sure how she'd stand up to Jack delving too deeply into her feelings about last night.

It was Steve, still on the trail of Phil. She was supposed to be at the studio to help with the last of the pictures and hadn't turned up.

'She's probably still fast asleep,' Leone informed him when he told her he'd rung her flat and got no reply. At school, Phil had always been the one to sleep through the bells and fire alarms. It had driven the teachers to distraction. 'She sounded awfully whacked last night, you know.'

'You spoke to her then?'

'No, she left a message on the answerphone,' Leone said. 'And there was another one this morning.'

There was an infinitesimal pause. 'This morning?' Steve seemed momentarily confused. 'Where was she ringing from?'

'Well, late last night, actually,' Leone corrected herself. 'I only picked it up this morning. She didn't ring you then?'

'No, but then I was out for some of the night. Went to the party up the road. She may have rung but I don't have an answerphone.'

'I see.' There was always a chance, Leone supposed, that Phil had met up with Susie in the basement flat below hers and gone on to some wild party. Susie always had a string of parties to go to and Phil had often, against all better judgement, gone along with her, eventually crashing out at someone else's flat. 'Try Susie,' Leone suggested. 'She might know where she is. And failing that she could always go and bang on Phil's door to see if she can get her to stir.'

'No, it's all right, 'Steve said. He sounded weary. He'd obviously had a late night, too. 'I'll go round myself. If she phones you, could you let her know what I'm up to?'

'No problem. Anything else I can do?'

There was a silence. She could hear Steve tapping the receiver with his fingers. She could sense his uneasiness.

'What about the gallery?' he suggested after a moment. 'I've rung, of course, but I suppose there's just a chance she might have flaked out there.'

More than likely, Leone thought, remembering how tired she'd sounded. 'I can go round and check for you, if you like,' she volunteered. It seemed foolish for Steve to drive all that way when she was so close.

'Wouldn't that be a bore?'

'It's only five minutes' drive away.'

'Well, if you're sure. Thanks.' He sounded terribly appreciative. 'That would be a great help.'

They arranged to speak again in half an hour or so. As Leone put down the receiver she saw that Jack was watching her across the room.

'No sign of Phil yet, I take it?' he said.

Leone shook her head. 'Steve's in a bit of a flap. She was supposed to be helping with the last of his pictures this morning and it seems she's gone AWOL.'

'With your car, I suppose?'

Leone grimaced. She'd forgotten Phil was in charge of that. 'With my car,' she affirmed. Honestly, sometimes Phil was the limit.

Jack downed the last of his coffee. 'So, do you want a lift to the gallery?'

'What about your trip to France? Haven't you got to get ready for that?'

'That won't take long.' He put down his coffee mug on the table and stood up. 'Besides, I wouldn't mind having a quick look at Steve's paintings. It'll be my last chance.'

'What about after your trip to Paris?'

'I don't come back to London.'

'Oh.'

Leone looked down at her hands. He was flying back to Hong Kong direct then. She hadn't considered that, she'd thought... Hell, what did it matter *what* she'd thought. He was going back to Isabel, as she'd known he would. It was as simple as that. There was no point in discussing their situation any further.

'Then of course you've got to come and see them now,' she said, quickly recovering. She forced herself to look him straight in the eyes and smile, 'Phil would never forgive you if you missed them.'

He laughed. 'Don't I know it. More than my life's worth.'

Leone stood up, collecting up the coffee mugs, and went through to the kitchen. Jack didn't follow her. He'd settled down on the sofa with the book he'd been reading last night. He was purposefully shutting her out. After all, Diane Thomas's book on art psychotherapy couldn't be *that* engrossing, could it?

She pushed the mugs noisily into the dishwasher, then told him she'd be ready to leave in about five minutes.

He didn't say anything, just nodded. She could sense he was slowly withdrawing from her, distancing himself from last night, from their shared thoughts and the whispered breath of passion.

And in her heart of hearts, she couldn't blame him.

⁓

Jack let out a low whistle and swivelled round the gallery.

'These are really something, aren't they?' he said, allowing his gaze to skim appreciatively over the huge, vibrant canvases that covered the gallery walls. 'This boy's good…'

Leone followed the sweep of Jack's hand. She had to admit that Steve's paintings looked terrific. The photographs she'd seen hadn't really done them justice. She hadn't expected to be quite so moved by them, but the brushwork was wonderful and each canvas had such depth of emotion. She began to understand Phil's enthusiasm.

'There are more upstairs,' she said, crossing over to switch on the lights to the upstairs studio.

'Are there?' Jack glanced back at her. She could tell how impressed he was. 'Prolific as well as talented? What a combination.'

'I know.' Leone thrust her hands deep into her jacket pockets and cast a look around the gallery. 'No sign of Phil though,' she observed. She wasn't entirely surprised. The car hadn't been in the courtyard.

She crossed over to Phil's desk and picked up a pile of papers, sifting slowly through them. There was nothing to indicate where Phil might have gone. One of the newly printed exhibition catalogues lay amongst the jumble and she picked it up. Phil had obviously spent last night doing the final proof check because she'd pencilled in a few comments on the top copy.

So, what had she done after that?

Leone went over to the front desk and pressed the replay button on the answerphone. There were three business calls and one, the last, from Steve earlier that morning. Nothing from Phil, though.

'Heavens, is this more of Steve's stuff?' asked Jack. He was standing by Phil's desk, holding up a folder full of photographs. She couldn't properly see them but assumed they were the prints Phil had taken of Steve's earlier work.

'More than likely,' she said. She watched as Jack slowly thumbed his way through the folder. 'They were done some time ago, I think.'

'They're certainly a different style,' Jack said. He took one last look at the photographs and then stuffed them back into the folder. 'Just as powerful, though.'

The telephone started to ring. Leone picked it up. It was Steve, sounding more than a little frantic. There was no sign of Phil at her flat, he said, and Susie had told him she hadn't come home that night.

Leone's heart sank. For the first time, she began to feel afraid for Phil's safety.

'Come on, enough of this pussy-footing around,' said Jack, recognising the anxiety on her face as she put down the receiver. 'Do you know the number for your tame policeman?'

'Ted Barnes? I think I've got his contact number somewhere, yes.'

'Then I think it's time we told him what's happened. We can get him to run a check on the hospitals for us.'

'Hell.' She took a deep breath and turned away from him. It was what she'd known they must do, of course, but suddenly, putting her worst fears into words made the possibility of an accident seem more real.

She ran her hands over her face. When she looked up she saw Jack was watching her, the lines of his face pinched and sharp.

'What is it?' she asked quietly, feeling his tension.

'Nothing.'

'Don't hold out on me, Jack. Please.'

'I was thinking of Ronnie, that's all. Of the night he was attacked here.'

'Oh, shit.' Surely the two weren't connected? It was more likely to be some sort of road accident, wasn't it? And yet, if there'd been a serious crash they'd have heard something by now, wouldn't they? London wasn't like the country, cars didn't sit upside-down in ditches for half the night without somebody noticing.

She felt her stomach contract as other possibilities rose like demon shadows in her mind.

'Jack, no one would want to harm Phil,' she said. Her voice was tense, up half an octave.

He was watching her, the tips of his fingers pressed together, prayer-like. 'What about Morenzo?' he asked quietly.

'He's not after Phil.'

There was a silence. Jack didn't say anything. He didn't need to. She instantly recognised his train of thought.

Leone felt her heart begin to thump.

'She was driving my car, wasn't she?' she asked, almost inaudibly.

And they looked so alike. Identical height, identical hair and colouring.

'Oh, Jesus. It was me he was after, wasn't it? Not Phil at all.' She sank down on to the chair, taking small, quick breaths.

Whatever had happened to Phil was her fault. All of it was her fault.

Please let her be safe.

She closed her eyes, willing it to be true with every grain of her body. She told herself firmly that Phil was capable of fighting her way out of any tight corner. Phil was wily and streetwise. She'd done self-defence. She'd have found some way to escape...

But even as she heard Jack pick up the telephone and begin to punch in Ted Barnes' number she felt all the old fears start to circle again in her mind like hungry hyenas in the midday sun.

She dropped her head between her hands, taking a deep breath.

Dear God, just let her be safe.

Chapter Twenty

The rain was gathering force. Richard Fleming lifted his head, listening to the wind as it waded through the bare-branched trees in the garden beyond. He hated that sound; it always reminded him too much of the night his father had broken the news to him that his mother had left them.

'All women are devious,' he had told Richard. 'All women keep secrets and all women smile when they lie.'

All of it true.

He stared into the fire, watching the red-tongued flames lick steadily against the throat of the grate.

'Didn't you notice anything?' his father had asked him that night, as if it were the fault of his thirteen-year-old son that his wife's affair had gone undetected. 'Nothing,' Richard had replied. But later, when he'd thought about it more deeply, he'd realised that the signs had, of course, been there but he hadn't been perceptive enough to recognise them. It had been the same with Julia.

He leant back in his chair and crossed his legs, glancing across at Leone, whose face was pale and drawn. It had been an horrendous evening so far. He'd only been back from the country a few minutes when a white-faced Leone had burst in on him. He'd thought Phil's disappearance had been the cause of her agitation, but that had only been part of it, hadn't it?

He'd just handed her a drink and was settling himself down on the sofa opposite, when she'd looked up at him and asked, coldly, quite without warning:

'Why didn't you tell me the truth about mother?'

'The truth?' He kept his voice steady, careful to hide the ripple of shock that ran through him, not sure of how much she knew even then.

'I've found out, you see. Found out about her affair. Found out about how she really died. You should have told me. You had no right to keep it from me.'

The bitterness in her voice shocked him.

'Leone…' He stopped to adjust his voice, swallowing to modulate his tone. 'I thought it was the only way to protect you. I would have told you in time…'

'When exactly?'

He was struck by the awful flatness of her voice. He'd never seen her like this before, so angry and implacable.

'There never seemed to be quite the right moment,' he admitted quietly. 'Darling, it's a shock, I know, and I can understand why you're angry and confused. But you've got to believe me, I was only thinking of you. Of the need to shield you. She died so violently, so horribly, I just didn't feel it was the sort of thing a young child should have to face. You can see that, can't you?'

'I just wish you'd told me, that's all.'

'Perhaps if you'd asked I would have done. But you never seemed to want to talk much about her, you know.'

Her head came up at that. 'I did try to. But I always felt I was treading on hallowed ground. You always seemed so upset whenever I started to talk about her. You closed up. I thought it was all too painful for you, that's why I stopped asking…'

'I was trying to protect you, that's all. I wasn't sure how you'd handle it.'

Richard watched Leone hunch forward, sinking her head against her hands. She pressed the palms hard against her eyes for a moment, then straightened up. She seemed calmer now, less angry.

He held on to the silence for a while.

Leone lifted her drink from the small table beside her, rolling the glass between her long fingers. She had thin, beautiful hands. Her mother's hands.

'Well, you haven't got to hide anything from me any more, have you?' she said, leaning back against the chair. There was still a flatness to her voice but the bitterness had gone. 'So, tell me, when did you find out about mother's affair? Was it that trip to Suffolk?'

He stared down at his whisky. 'I didn't know about Suffolk,' he said quietly.

She hesitated. 'But you knew about the affair?'

'Not really. Not until the very end.'

Richard closed his eyes and took another sip of whisky. That wasn't entirely true, was it? The suspicion had been there, like a small cancerous growth nudging against the organs: the secretive phone calls, the sudden preoccupation with her appearance, the frequent outings to see 'old schoolfriends' whom he was never permitted to meet—but most of all the unexpected end to their arguments, to her bitter grievances about his preoccupation with his job, to her accusations of his coldness, of his lack of interest in art. He should have realised what it all had pointed to, having listened to his mother's lies and being wise in the art of deceit, but he'd ignored all the signs.

It had taken that phone call to shatter his illusions and make him acknowledge the painful, terrible truth.

Margaret bloody Rhodes and her phone call.

'What phone call? When did Margaret Rhodes ring you?'

He looked up. He hadn't realised he'd spoken out loud. Leone was watching him from across the room, waiting for him to answer,

'The night your mother died,' he admitted after a while. He took out a cigarette and lit it, taking a long draw.

Leone leaned forward slightly, brushing a strand of blonde hair back from her face. 'And she told you about the affair?'

'Yes.'

Only she hadn't called it that, had she? Richard could still hear that odious woman's high-pitched, common little voice shouting down the phone at him, telling him about her husband and Julia. He'd told her to pull herself together and put the phone down on her. He'd no time for hysterical women. Besides, he'd wanted time to think, to recover from the shock.

'Did you know then what she intended to do?'

He stood up and went over to the drinks cabinet and drew out the whisky bottle. 'Kill them, you mean?' There, he'd said it. After all these years, he'd finally uttered those words. Not so earth-shatteringly difficult when it came down to it, was it? He poured the whisky into his glass and added a splash of water. 'Not the first time she rang, no. Not a hint.'

'She rang you again?'

His smile was bitter.

'More than once, yes.'

After that first call, she'd rung back almost immediately, more hysterical than ever. She'd told him she'd found out that Julia and her husband were planning to leave them. To run away together. She threatened to shoot herself with some hand pistol of Simon's she'd found. Pull the blasted trigger then, he felt like saying to her. But then she'd started to whisper down the phone at him, reading out the letters she'd found from Julia to her husband, every sordid little detail.

'Don't you want to know what they've been doing? Don't you want to know how that slut of a wife of yours has been cheating on you?'

He'd started to put the phone down on her. But something had made him stop, some base instinct had made him listen all the same. Some ghastly dark fascination.

He'd paid for his ignoble deed, though, hadn't he? For interwoven with the details of their erotic intimacies were little mocking quips about Richard, trenchant remarks about how much she detested him touching her, how she shuddered at the thought of his coming near her. He'd felt burning anger go through him like a red-hot shaft. The bitch. With every word she'd humiliated him. With every deed betrayed him.

Even now he could feel rage curl its fingers around him, squeezing the breath slowly out of him.

'Are you all right?' Leone was watching him anxiously.

He sat there, fighting to steady his breathing. He hadn't realised how much the thought of Julia's perfidy would affect him still.

'Perfectly,' he forced himself to say. He knew what she'd think, that his heart was playing up again. The terrible red, purplish colour of his face, his laboured breathing...Well, it was his heart. But not in the way she supposed.

'Shall I get you one of your pills?'

'I'll be fine. Really.'

'Are you sure?'

The telephone started to ring. Richard pushed himself up from his chair and went across to answer it. It was Ted Barnes, telling him that they'd picked up Vic Morenzo for questioning. They'd decided not to pursue Piers Carlton, he said. According to all reports Carlton had been up in Scotland stalking all weekend. Had a dozen alibis to prove it, too. Waste of time bringing him in just yet.

Richard stubbed out his cigarette and returned to his chair. It was what he'd expected, if the truth be known. To his mind, Carlton had never been a contender. He was a sadistic bully boy, nothing more. Not like Morenzo.

'That was Ted,' he told Leone, sitting down again and picking up his whisky glass. 'Seems that they've picked up Morenzo.' Nail him, he'd told Ted. Throw the bloody book at him.

Leone looked up at him. 'What about Carlton?'

'No, they haven't brought him in,' Richard said, and explained why.

'So that let's him off the hook, I suppose,' Leone said, fiddling with the band of her watch. 'It's strange, though, isn't it, how he just turned up into our lives like that...?'

He could see how much she disliked the fellow. How, even now, she wasn't quite ready to put away her suspicions.

'I thought you explained that to me. Didn't you say someone from Christie's came up to visit the old girl and recommended you to her?' he said.

'Something like that,' she agreed. She picked up her glass and finished the rest of her whisky. 'That's what she told me, anyway. I suppose it was sheer coincidence that...' she paused a little awkwardly, 'that that's where mother had been with Simon Rhodes.'

'A bloody awful one,' Richard commented, with feeling.

There was a silence. He saw her glance up at the carriage clock on the mantelpiece. He knew she was thinking of Phil. It was nearly ten o'clock and still there was no word. He realised now that when the phone had rung a few minutes earlier she'd expected it would be Andrew giving her the latest update on his sister.

He looked at her tight, tense face, aware of how on edge she must be. He knew what it was to wait for news.

'Listen, now that they've got Morenzo, I'm sure they'll get to the bottom of where Phil is in no time.' He tried to make his voice sound as light as possible but he was careful not to talk about hope. He knew it would have a hollow ring to it. He put down his drink. 'Come on,' he said, standing up. 'Why don't you turn in? You look positively done-in, child. You've had a simply ghastly weekend.'

'I'd rather wait up. Just in case.'

'Ted might not be able to get a thing out of Morenzo tonight. It would be more sensible to try to get a bit of sleep.'

'I wouldn't be able to...'

'You can't wait up all night, you know. Besides, there's nothing we can do. Ted said he'd ring us as soon as there's news.'

'Just another hour.' She gave him a plaintive look. 'Please.'

'All right.' He had a feeling unless he bullied her terribly it would turn to two. 'I'll sit up with you then.'

'There's no need. I'll be fine. Really.'

'I'd like to.' He touched her shoulder lightly with his hand then let it slip to his side. He was not one for emotional displays. It was the best he could do.

He returned to his chair, picking up his whisky glass. 'Tell you what Leone,' he said, nursing the glass against his chest, 'what d'you say to a game of backgammon? We used to play a lot when you were younger. Do you remember?'

'Of course I do.' It was when they'd lived in Queensdale Place, the house they'd moved to from north London soon after Julia's death.

'Go and get the board then.'

He pulled the glass-topped table into position between the two armchairs while Leone retrieved the backgammon set from the serpentine chest of drawers in the corner of the room.

She carefully opened up the case and set out the counters. They started to play. He'd forgotten how good a player she was. An instinctive player. In half an hour she'd wiped the board with him.

They'd just started the second game when the telephone began to ring. They glanced at each other. Richard put down the shaker and went over and picked up the receiver.

It was Jack, asking to speak to Leone. He knew without asking what he'd rung to say.

They'd found Phil's body.

Chapter Twenty-one

Jack downed his third black coffee of the morning and stood up. A feeling of infinite tiredness permeated every bone in his body. God! What a night. Dante in his darkest moment couldn't have known worse.

He bent down and picked up his battered leather briefcase and began to walk towards the departure gate. It was his own fault he felt so exhausted, he knew that. It was he who'd insisted on going down to the police station with Andrew once the phone call had come through, but then he could hardly have left him to go by himself to that depressing place knowing the task he had to perform, could he? No brother should be asked to look upon the dead body of his sister alone like that. Especially not one as sensitive and loving as Andrew.

He took a long, deep breath. It had been an ordeal he hoped never to have to repeat. It had taken every shred of self-control not to break down when he'd stood there by that glass window and watched the crisp sheet drawn back to reveal Phil lying there, waxy-skinned and still. And it wasn't just the sight of her pale, lifeless form which had distressed him so. It was the knowledge that she would suffer the indignity of post-mortem. That every inch of her would be turned inside out, every part measured and photographed so that the police and the experts could pick over the details like carrion crows.

He'd known it had to be done. That they had to ascertain the exact cause and time of her death. But mutilation, whether scientific or not, was too horrible to contemplate. She would have no secrets now. No privacy, The violation was only just about to begin. Morenzo with his mad, aberrant desire for revenge had seen to that…

He slowed his pace slightly, pushing a hand wearily across the rugged lines of his face. He wished he'd been able to get out of this trip to France. He didn't feel in the mood for swift footwork and hard bargaining. Most of all, though, he didn't want to desert Andrew in his hour of need. Or Leone, for that matter. He felt he should be with them both.

At least he'd managed to postpone his flight back to Hong Kong for a few days and now had time to return to London first. Isabel hadn't been too thrilled by the delay. They were supposed to be spending the following weekend with the Tang family on their estate on the mainland and as it was something of a coup to have been invited, Isabel was loath to miss the chance. 'It's not as if you can do anything by staying, is it?' she'd said, a tinge of irritation to her voice. 'I mean, they can't have the funeral for a while, after all. They need to keep the body as evidence for a while, don't they?'

To the point, Isabel,

Someone jostled past him, running for a plane long-since called. He glanced at his watch. It was just before eight. He was tempted to ring Leone to check whether she was bearing up, but he didn't want to risk waking her. He'd wait until he got to Paris and then call her from the hotel. He was grateful, for once, that she had her father with her. The old fool might be a pain in the proverbial but he knew the workings of grief, at least.

Ahead a knot of passengers were slowly edging forward through the boarding gate, The stewardess collected their cards with a mechanical nod, barely glancing up as they filed through, but when Jack reached her she found time to look up and flash him a smile. Devastating-looking men were few and far between on this early run to Paris and even grey-skinned and exhausted Jack stood out by a mile.

Oblivious to her interest, Jack walked on to the plane. He was fighting to keep his mind off the image of Phil in that cold, cheerless room.

He knew she had not died quickly, whatever the police might say. Her face had been bruised and swollen. She had struggled against Morenzo, long and hard, fought with every last breath of her body. She had known she was going to die. He couldn't bear that. *The bastard.*

He ran his hand quickly across his face, forcing his thoughts back to the safety of Paris and the two pieces he was hoping to acquire.

The Piero della Francesca he was certain he'd be able to secure. But the Cézanne, he wasn't so sure about. A lot of the groundwork had been done by his Paris contact already, but people were fickle about selling modern paintings. There'd been so much press about the inflated prices being achieved, it was hard not only to value them sensibly, but also to dissuade the owners from taking any picture which could even vaguely be labelled as an Impressionist painting to an auction house instead.

He cushioned the back of his neck with his hands and leaned back in his seat. At least his mandate to build up a comprehensive collection was infinitely preferable to that of trying to outguess the market, which was what some of the art dealers he knew were having to do. What a ticklish task that was. How could anyone accurately forecast which section of the market would take the buyers' imagination next? Who knew whether the Old Masters would see a resurgence—and to his mind they seemed ludicrously undervalued at the moment—or whether the trend would stay with the Impressionists or follow the new breed of experimental artists like the Hirsts of this world?

Perhaps it might even swing round to embrace other new artists. Like Steve Ross.

Poor Steve. Jack felt real sympathy for him. Phil's death had been a double blow to him, hadn't it? There he was on the verge of being discovered—and having seen his work Jack knew that Phil's faith in his talent was wholly justified—and it had all been snatched away from him.

Some other gallery would pick him up, of course. But being the sensitive soul that he obviously was, Jack wondered if Steve would ever fully recover from this tragedy. He felt relieved that Andrew had said he'd try to visit him later on to discuss what to do about the exhibition. It would keep them busy, distract them.

He clicked open his briefcase and took out the Cézanne notes which Jean-Paul had faxed him over the weekend. He'd read the report once already but he knew where his mind would go if he didn't try to divert it.

There was a low rumbling roar as the engines started up. Determinedly Jack smoothed out the pages and began to read.

⌒

'Take a left here.'

'Left? Are you sure?'

'Certain.'

Leone gave Andrew a quick glance just to double-check he really did mean her to turn into what looked remarkably like a one-way street. Andrew's sense of direction had always been a little suspect. He'd have been right there with Columbus pitching up in the West Indies thinking he'd got to India. Normally she would have teased him about it. But not today, not in her present numbed state of shock, where tears were still so close to the surface.

She slowed and turned into the street he was indicating. There was no ensuing wail of sirens. She began to relax.

'Steve's block's just up ahead on the right,' Andrew said, giving a general wave of his hand. His voice was steady, but his eyes were red-raw from lack of sleep.

'I thought Steve lived off the Prince of Wales Drive,' she said, turning to look at him. She seemed to remember Phil telling her once that the flat was close to the park. Phil had said…

Leone caught herself mid-flow, determinedly shutting the lid on the memory, afraid of where her thoughts were taking her. She swallowed hard, forcing herself to concentrate on the road ahead. She had to hang on. She had to force herself to keep going.

'Yes, but his studio's here,' Andrew replied, pointing out a modern red-brick budding just ahead.

Leone glanced out of the window. It didn't seem the place for a studio of a penniless artist somehow. 'Looks terribly smart,' she said.

'Belongs to some artist friend of Steve's, apparently. An American. He loaned it to Steve because he's away in Florence for a year. Won a scholarship to study there.'

'That was rather generous of him.'

'Well, I gather Steve's friend wasn't too keen on having to pack up all his paintings and put them into storage somewhere. Made much more sense to let Steve take over the place instead.' Andrew's voice was determinedly light. She could tell how hard he was trying to keep his emotions in check.

'Lucky Steve. Landed on his feet.'

'Deserves a bit of luck, though, don't you think?'

'More than anybody,' Leone agreed, pulling into a parking spot opposite the porticoed entrance to the flats.

They quickly reached Steve's place on the sixth floor and Leone rang the doorbell. There was no immediate reply.

'You did tell him we were coming, didn't you?' she asked Andrew. Like Phil, he tended to be slightly chaotic.

''Course I did,' Andrew assured her. 'Try again. Press harder this time.'

She did so and this time heard the sound of movement inside the flat. There was the soft pad of footsteps and the rattle of a chain being removed. Then the door swung open.

Steve stood in the doorway. Leone was shocked at the sight of him. His cheeks were sunken and unshaven, his eyes puffy and red. He looked thinner, if that were possible, than ever. His jeans and T-shirt seemed to hang off his bones as if from a wire hanger.

She drew in a short, sharp breath, instantly concerned.

'Hell, Steve, you look like death. Are you all right?' she asked. She and Andrew might look the worse for wear but surely they didn't look as haggard as this? In a few short hours it seemed that

Steve's body had just given up, caved in. He gave a small shrug of his shoulders, turning to double-lock the front door.

'Not the best, if you want the truth. Well, you know…' He stepped aside to let them in. 'Still can't truly believe it.'

'None of us can,' Leone said quietly. Even now she felt it must all be a mistake. Phil could not be dead. Not Phil. Not vital, vibrant Phil who'd loved life so much. How could it have happened? How? Leone fought back tears as she and Andrew turned to follow Steve through a dark passageway into what had originally been the sitting-room but had now been converted into the studio. It was a large, wonderfully light room, dominated by two huge French windows leading out on to a small balcony. It was possible from here to see out across the rooftops of London as far as the Thames. Leone could understand why Phil had called it inspirational. North light as well—every artist's dream.

She crossed over to the open window. The balcony was small with a few rather neglected evergreen plants pushed up against its edge.

'Don't go out there,' Steve called out in warning, seeing she was about to step outside. 'It's not very safe. Railings need to be looked at.'

'Oh? All right.' Leone stepped obediently back.

She glanced around her. The room was almost bare of furniture except for a small paint-splattered table, with two squat-legged kitchen chairs tucked under it. There were few home comforts: it was definitely a working pad. A 'Do Not Disturb' sign strung across the ceiling could not have proclaimed it any more effectively.

'Do you want some coffee?' Steve was standing in the small galley of a kitchen, holding up a kettle.

'If you're making one, then yes, please.'

'There's no milk, I'm afraid,' he said apologetically. 'Haven't been out this morning.'

He'd been here all night then. Painting or just pacing?

'Black's fine,' she said.

'Andrew? What about you?'

'Black, two sugars. Thanks.'

Andrew was standing in, the centre of the room, looking down at the massive canvas propped up against the easel. Leone couldn't see it from were she was standing. She crossed over to his side, slipping her arm through his.

The painting was unlike anything of Steve's she'd seen before. No splashes of bold vigorous colour, just black with shades of browns and beiges. Thick daubs of paint in great clusters and trails seemed to tumble in slow motion down the canvas like falling water. It was faintly reminiscent of a picture she'd seen by Thérèse Oulton—the same interwoven layers of paint—though this one had none of Oulton's delicate serenity. It was dark and oppressive. Steve's depression was so tangible in the painting that it almost seemed to envelop it in thick folds of despair.

He must have started this last night, she supposed, after Andrew's phone call about Phil. He must have worked through the night, applying layer upon layer. She glanced at Andrew. She could see the picture had affected him as forcefully as it had her. His face was gaunt. Picasso had used that particular shade of faecal brown, Leone thought, when he'd painted his friend Casagamus from memory after the poet committed suicide.

She turned to see Steve watching them from the gallery.

'It's very powerful,' she said, stepping back from the easel.

'That's how felt I suppose…'

Still feel, Leone thought. How we *all* feel. She watched him pull open a cupboard door and take out three mugs. His movements were slow and unsteady, his eyes glazed over. She wondered if they'd done the right thing to come and see him today after all. Andrew and she had strengthened each other by coming together and sharing their loss but it seemed their presence had only accentuated Steve's sense of pain.

She saw Andrew felt it too. 'Look, Steve,' he said. 'If you'd rather we left…'

'No, of course I wouldn't.' He wiped the back of his hand across his eyes in one quick movement, struggling to regain his composure. 'I'm sorry.'

'Don't apologise, for Christ's sake,' said Andrew quietly. 'None of us are feeling particularly brave right now...' His voice trailed. Leone squeezed his arm.

'It's just I keep on thinking it's all a mistake.' Steve's whippet-thin body seemed to tense even more as he spoke. 'That any minute now she'll just walk through that door.'

'I know,' Leone agreed. She swallowed hard, forcing herself to concentrate on a small splodge of paint on the polished surface of the floor.

Steve took a long, slow breath. It seemed to steady him.

'I keep on feeling it's my fault somehow.'

'Don't be silly.'

'If I'd been there with her...'

'Don't you think I don't feel like that, too?' Andrew broke in. The muscle in his jaw tightened, showing his internal conflict. 'If only I'd stayed with her to do the last of those pictures. But no, I had to hurry home because we were due at some bloody drinks party...'

'And I'll never forgive myself for lending Phil the car in the first place,' said Leone.

Steve looked up at her. His eyes seemed darker than ever. 'Why the car? I don't understand. Why should you feel guilty about lending her the car?'

He didn't know about Morenzo. She hadn't even considered that.

She paused a second, wondering how best to explain.

'The police are pretty sure that someone called Vic Morenzo is responsible for killing Phil, you see,' she said. 'He had some sort of grudge against my father. And when Morenzo went for Phil, he made a mistake. It was me he meant to kill, not Phil.'

'Shit! I didn't realise that.' Steve ran the top of his index finger across the smooth surface of the white formica, momentarily lost for words. After a moment he said, 'So if the police know about this Morenzo fellow, what have they done about him? Have they arrested him yet?'

'Late last night, yes.'

'They've brought him in for questioning, at any rate,' interjected Andrew.

Steve began to spoon out the coffee. He seemed to be trying to bring his emotions under control. 'And they think they'll be able to make the charges stick?'

'Yes.'

Andrew sounded more confident than he felt. All the police had said was that they were fairly confident of being able to formally charge him. *Fairly*. He had felt vaguely suspicious of that word. The trouble was, they had little concrete evidence at this stage and Morenzo wasn't your usual ordinary boy-off-the-block, was he? His brother had influence and power and could whistle up a top-class lawyer who could twist a judicial arm or two.

Leone looked across at Steve. She could see that her revelations had thrown him a little.

'Anyway,' she said, deciding it would be wiser to change tack for Steve's sake as well as for her own, 'do you feel up to discussing the exhibition? I think we should try to sort out as soon as possible what we intend to do. Time isn't on our side on this one.'

Steve handed out the coffee.

'What are the choices?' he asked.

'More or less what I told you this morning. Call it off or press ahead,' Andrew told him simply.

'I see.' Steve took a sip of his coffee. He stood for a moment staring out of the window at some distant object on the skyline.

'You seemed keen to let the whole thing go this morning,' said Andrew gently.

'I know.' Steve enclosed the coffee cup with both hands. 'I was. That was my first reaction, at least. But now…now I'm not so sure. I feel I might be letting Phil down by pulling out. The exhibition was her dream, you see. However painful it is for me to go ahead with it, I think…' his voice caught slightly, but he forced himself on, 'I think, for her sake, we should. As a tribute to her, if nothing else.' He looked up at them. 'Listen that's only my gut reaction. If either of you feels differently then, of course, we should cancel it.'

There was a silence. His answer caught them off guard. Leone had been almost sure Steve would say he wanted to call everything off, but he'd shown his inner strength, shown he was made of sterner stuff than she supposed. She felt a wave of respect for him. He'd put Phil first, not himself.

She glanced at Andrew.

'Well, what do you think?' she asked him.

She knew how much he'd adored his sister, knew what an immense strain it would be for him to help organise the exhibition so soon after her death. But she sensed Steve was right, that for Phil's sake it should go ahead as planned.

Andrew stood staring out across the balcony for a moment without speaking. Leone waited quietly. Andrew was not someone to prompt.

'I don't want it turning into some sort of freak show, that's all,' he said after a while, his voice grimly determined. 'But I know how important this exhibition was to her. She worked very hard on this one.' He looked across at Leone as if to judge her reaction. 'And I somehow feel it's quite fitting for Phil to be remembered at something like this rather than at a bloody wake.' He gave Leone a ghost of a smile. 'She'd have liked that idea, don't you think?'

'I'm certain of it,' agreed Leone. She remembered Phil saying more than once that she thought the English could learn a thing or two from the Irish about funerals. Phil had been too vital in life for a lachrymose send-off.

'Then we're agreed?'

'Yes.' Leone looked over at Steve.

He gave a sharp single nod. 'Agreed.'

'Well, then,' said Andrew perching himself on the edge of the table, 'we'd better sort out the details, hadn't we? Apart from having to hang those last few pictures in the upstairs studio, what else is there left to do?'

Leone pulled out a chair and sat down beside him. She noticed that Steve hadn't moved from his spot in the kitchen.

'Coming to join us?' she asked.

'Sure.'

But still he didn't move.

'Are you OK?'

'Yeah, sorry. I was just thinking about this Morenzo guy, that's all. The police are sure he did it then?'

'Pretty much, yes,' Leone said. Carlton had his set of alibis after all, hadn't he? 'They haven't got a great deal they can pin on him at the moment, but they know he had a clear motive…'

Steve stopped fiddling with his coffee mug and stared at Leone. 'Did he?'

'He wanted to get back at my father for his time in prison. Apparently his mother died when he was in there and he holds Father to blame for that.'

'I see.'

Andrew spoke up. 'Revenge. A sentiment as old as the hills. It was a by-word of the Celts, did I ever tell you that?'

'Numerous times.'

One of Andrew's passions was the mystic Celts. Once he started on the subject he'd never stop. He'd had a blazing row with her father once about how he believed the English would be an infinitely more interesting race now if only they'd merged with the Celts rather than letting themselves be taken over by the practical, logical, down-to-earth Romans. She could have told him to have saved his breath, though, her father would never have succumbed to his argument. He possessed all the Roman characteristics himself, didn't he?

She saw Steve give a wintry smile. 'Bacon called it a kind of wild justice,' he said.

'What? Revenge?'

'Yes. He thought the law ought to weed it out. He thought it dangerous.'

She looked across at him. He met her gaze, his eyes very dark and intense. She didn't need to ask him if he agreed with Bacon, she could tell by his voice that he did not. That surprised her a little. She'd have thought Steve such a gentle soul that he wouldn't advocate violence. Yet Phil's death had affected him greatly, she could see that. She hadn't realised quite how much he'd cared for her.

For a second it seemed she had a lightning glimpse into that opaque enigmatic mind of his. There was anger there and a touch of ruthlessness which she hadn't seen before. He was thinking about Morenzo, she knew. Of what he'd done to Phil.

And she hoped to hell he wasn't about to do anything stupid.

～

Jack walked through the marble-floored lobby of die Plaza-Athenée Hotel towards the elevator. Behind him, out in the Avenue de Montaigne, the evening traffic was just beginning to build up, Parisians pushing their way home through the black, wet night.

The elevator came and Jack got in, pressing the button for the third floor. He leaned his head back against the cold glass of the mirrored wall, closing his eyes for a moment. It had been a long day and the lack of sleep was just beginning to tell. At least he'd managed to finalise the deal with the Comte de Lauvelle over the Piero della Francesca and a second meeting had been fixed with the owners of the Cézanne for tomorrow lunchtime. Jean-Paul was very optimistic about the outcome, but then Jean-Paul was paid to be.

He walked into his room, chucked his coat over the back of the gilt chair and loosened his tie. Kicking off his shoes he flopped down on to the bed, stretching his arms out above his head. He closed his eyes for a moment, grateful for the silence of the room.

Jean-Paul's driving had been terrible, even for a Frenchman. He went at breakneck speed, hugging the bumper of the car in front, one hand permanently on the horn. And worse still he'd insisted on talking throughout the entire three-hour journey to Comte de Lauvelle's in Dijon and back. All through Nemours and Courtenay, gesticulating wildly to illustrate his point, turning his head to look it Jack with frightening regularity, seemingly oblivious to the oncoming juggernauts. Only in Brazil had Jack encountered such an equally appalling driver—and he'd been minus an arm and high on coke at the time.

From down below in the tree-lined avenue, he heard the wail of a siren as a police car went by. He wondered how long it would take him to disassociate that sound from Phil and last night's events. A lifetime probably. These things did not just go away.

He opened his eyes and glanced at his watch, just after six o'clock. Too late to telephone Isabel now. He'd been too busy, that was the problem, barely having time to draw breath.

He pushed a hand through his thick unruly hair, and stared up at the ceiling, noticing the leaf moulding which curled its way round the edges. It was no good, was it? He knew he was fooling himself. Time hadn't come into the equation. Phil wasn't the only person on his mind.

Without thinking his hand went out and trailed the edges of the Diane Thomas book Leone had given him as a leaving present. Hell. The truth was he hadn't particularly wanted to speak to Isabel, had he? It was almost a relief to admit it.

He stood up and went over to the mini-bar and helped himself to a drink. So what now? he thought. He couldn't go on pretending that everything was all right. He prided himself too much on honesty for that.

Isabel had known, of course; he saw that now. She had sensed the danger of the past slipping back into the present right from the beginning. That was why she had become more demanding, more irritable and insistent that he should spend his time looking for country houses for them. Trying to tighten her hold on him, fearful of the threads of the past weaving him back into its fabric.

He'd been blind to it. Isabel, with her woman's intuition, had not. She'd seen only too clearly what the outcome might be and had tried to circle the wagons. Too late, of course. Too late.

When he looked back now, he understood that the moment he'd seen Leone again at that exhibition in Albemarle Street, the rest had been inevitable. That the thread that had bound them together all those years ago had never been properly severed. And once he'd held her in his arms again, caution, credo, intentions, had been lost to him. He had not meant to betray Isabel. He did love her. But in the end, it was not enough.

Whatever happened between Leone and himself, he knew that he couldn't mislead Isabel any more. He had to let her go. He couldn't pretend. She would always stand in Leone's shadow. And she had too much to offer to be condemned to that.

All in all, he hadn't handled it very well, had he? And now he was about to risk everything on an uncertainty.

Which left Leone and himself.

Where did they go from here?

A dozen admonitions rang out in his head. Even if she still cared for him—and he had no guarantee of that, did he?—a mound of complications were still left to surmount. Her father, for one. Leone had learnt to stand up to him over the past few years, it was true, but it seemed to Jack that the balance between them would always be problematic. And how would these latest revelations about her mother affect Leone? Would the truth finally free her or merely bind her more firmly to her father?

He wasn't sure. But whatever he believed, he had to take the first step. It wasn't in his nature to let things drift. He knew he must pursue this to its bitter end, whatever the outcome. So, wise or not, he'd ring Leone and arrange to meet her tomorrow. Just the two of them. No Andrew, no Steve, no evasion.

The decision made, he reached for the telephone and dialled her number. He let it ring for a long time but she didn't pick up. Typical, he thought wryly. Now he'd have to phone her when he returned from having drinks with Xavier la Bosse, which was precisely what he'd hoped to avoid. Her father would be home by then and he didn't relish the thought of trying to persuade her to have dinner with him with the old man breathing down her neck. When he'd rung to speak to Leone last night, he'd given Jack a reception cold enough to freeze the balls off an Eskimo.

At least, Jack conceded, there'd been no pretence. None of the Greeks-bearing-gifts nonsense.

The old man had always behaved like that: uptight and possessive. He hadn't changed. And perhaps that was indicative in itself. Surely he wouldn't have treated him with such hostility last night unless he still saw him as some kind of potential threat, would he?

Jack smiled as he picked up Leone's book from the bedside table. He knew he might be fooling himself but he couldn't help but feel mildly encouraged by that thought.

~~

Ted Barnes, sitting behind his paper-strewn desk, felt anything but encouraged.

The more he thought about the Morenzo case the more disquietened he felt. He'd been so sure he'd got the bastard, especially when that stripper girlfriend of his had caved in under questioning and had admitted Morenzo hadn't been with her the night of the murder. But despite the collapse of Morenzo's alibi, the whole piece hung together as awkwardly as a grandma at a tart's tea-party.

Ted took a breath and swore softly. The powers-that-be were after a speedy conviction on this one but he refused to be pushed. He'd always been a slow, methodical worker and he wasn't about to be forced into making snap judgements. Besides, he couldn't afford to make mistakes. Morenzo's Rottweiler of a solicitor was watching his every move, waiting for him to make an error so that he could go for the jugular. Everything had to be done by the book and that took time.

He took off his glasses and began to polish the lenses on the dark lining of his woollen suit. So, what exactly had they got on Morenzo so far? Beyond the fact that his whereabouts for that night could not be substantiated, too bloody little, if the truth be known. Silent threats against Fleming and his family. Morenzo's history of violent reprisals, not much more. Nothing that could be linked to the Hope-Brown girl or the cause of death, not even one fibre matching those discovered by forensics in Fleming's Mercedes which the police had eventually found in a road off Hammers Lane.

Ted leaned back in his chair, pushing his hand through his thinning hair. So here was the first of the teasers. Why the hell would Morenzo risk driving all the way to Mill Hill to dump the body? Had he realised he'd made a mistake and killed the wrong girl? But if so, why dispose of her on an empty building site where someone would be sure to find her, when Morenzo had a dozen lock-ups throughout London where he could leave both the car and the corpse without fear of discovery?

Ted leaned over and picked up the autopsy report from the top of his papers, and began thumbing his way through the typed papers. Now here was another puzzle: the body itself. It stated here that the hyoid bone had been fractured, so according to the pathologist the girl had almost certainly died of strangulation. But then the killer had slit her wrists. After she had died. After he'd moved her body. Why in God's name would Morenzo do that? It just wasn't his *modus operandi* at all. It was as if the killer had been trying to make some kind of statement. And why choose Mill Hill? He knew that area. He'd lived there as a kid, done his first rounds as a copper there, and he could think of a dozen areas more suited to the disposal of a body.

Ted frowned and put down the report. Out of the corner of his eye he saw a slip of paper propped up against his half-empty coffee cup reminding him to buy some wine on his way home. Malcolm was down from Newcastle and was calling in for supper with his new girlfriend. Marian was all of a twitch. Last night she'd had recipe books strewn all over the kitchen and this morning still hadn't decided whether or not to make a vegetable lasagne to go with the chicken dish. She'd brushed aside Ted's recommendation not to fuss. Apparently Kelly, Malcolm's latest, was doing environmental studies so Marian seemed to think she'd be vegetarian. Probably was, too. All the young seemed to be these days. Fastidiously careful about what they ate and then rocked all night stuffing themselves full of lager and Ecstasy tablets and God alone knew what else. Honestly, it made him laugh, the hypocrisy of their behaviour.

He placed the post-mortem report back on to the pile and then leaned back in his chair, folding his hands across the soft ridges of his stomach.

He could see where they'd gone wrong with Morenzo. They'd made too many early assumptions. Morenzo seemed the perfect suspect so they'd tried to fit him to the crime rather than let the crime speak for itself. What was it that Edmond Locard said? 'Every contact leaves a trace.' They just had to find those fragments, that was all. Somewhere out there were physical and biological traces. Giveaways.

He leaned forward, rubbing a freckled hand over his tired features with a sigh. So, it was back to the beginning again. Maybe they'd find something to nail Morenzo, maybe not. He'd missed something that was all, some small, seemingly insignificant clue.

On an impulse he walked over to the door and called to Sergeant Willis to bring through the report which the Inverness police had sent down to them.

Perhaps he shouldn't have dismissed Piers Carlton quite as easily as he had done, he thought. After all, he'd rung Leone on several occasions and threatened her, once before the attack on Ronnie Jacks and the last after her visit to Lady Carlton in Suffolk.

And as Morenzo himself had proven, alibis weren't always watertight, were they?

Piers Carlton sat at the interview room's single table, glaring at Sergeant Willis sitting opposite him.

'This is getting beyond a joke, you know. It's verging on harassment.' His voice held the faint hint of threat. He slicked back his hair and then folded his arms across the dark fabric of his Hugo Boss suit with an air of studied defiance.

His gaze didn't waver from Willis's. He was not going to let the bastards intimidate him. They had nothing on him. And if he held firm and didn't lose his nerve, that's the way it would continue.

Piers glanced across to the other officer in the room. The grey-haired man was leaning up against the far wall, taking an occasional sip from the cup in his hand. A vague scent of chicken broth hung in the air. He looked mildly bored by the whole procedure but Piers suspected it might all be an act. You never quite knew with the old Bill.

'Look, I've told you all I know,' Piers said, turning back to Willis after a moment. 'I was nowhere near London on the night of the murder. For God's sake, check it out. I've already given a statement to the Inverness police. What the hell else do you need to know?'

'But you admit making threats against Miss Hope-Brown's partner?'

Piers felt his solicitor's warning hand on his arm.

'They weren't threats,' he said carefully. 'I was merely asking her to return a picture belonging to my family that she had in her possession. She wasn't being very co-operative about it.'

'So you threatened her?'

'No, I wouldn't say that. It was my bloody picture, for God's sake. All I wanted her to do was return it.'

Willis looked down at the report he held, slowly flicking through the last few pages. 'But you admit you went to the gallery on the day that Ronnie Jacks was attacked. That's correct, isn't it, sir?'

'My client has already given you a statement about that evening, Sergeant.' Carlton smiled as his solicitor jumped into the foray: Jefferson enjoyed a spat. 'Is it really necessary to go over this again? Mr Carlton has got nothing to hide. He's already told you what happened that night. He arrived at the gallery, no one was there, so he left immediately. It's as simple as that. His girlfriend, Cressida Warrington, can support his statement that he was back at their flat just after eight that night.'

'I appreciate that, sir. But we are involved in a murder inquiry here and I'm sure Mr Carlton will want to help all he can...'

'Of course I do,' interrupted Piers. This constant probing was sorely trying his temper, but he didn't want to lose it in front of Willis. Might give credence to that Fleming girl's complaints about intimidation. 'But we've been going over the same ground for the past half an hour. Do we really need to do this all over again?'

'If you wouldn't mind, sir.' Willis's voice was studiously polite. 'We just want to make sure we've got the record absolutely straight. Perhaps we can begin with the day of that first break-in. Let me just check the exact date of that…'

Piers stared down at the coffee stain on the metal-legged table, concentrating hard. God! That bloody picture. It had caused him nothing but aggravation. And now it was tying him in to a murder, for crying out loud. Just what he needed.

He felt a little uneasy. He'd had nothing to do with the murder, or the attack on that West Indian guy, but if they discovered he'd carried out that first break-in they'd never believe that, would they? He'd be stitched up faster than a suit in a Hong Kong tailor's.

So he had to keep his cool. After all, the police weren't really interested in a petty break-in, nothing had been taken. He felt his exasperation grow. It had all been such a bloody waste of time anyway; the Devis picture hadn't even *been* there.

He dropped his hands to his lap, his fingers running over the oval shape of his gold cufflinks: They'd been a present from Cressida last Christmas. He dreaded to think what this year's joyous season had in store for him. Ford bloody prison if he didn't keep on his toes.

He looked up to see Willis regarding him speculatively. How much did the bastard know? he wondered. Not a lot, he was sure of it. And he was going to keep it that way.

He leaned back in his chair again. 'The eighth, you say, Sergeant?' He gave a side glance at Jefferson who gave him a little nod. 'Of course. What is it exactly you want to know.…?'

⌒

'He's involved in some way.' Willis sat in Ted Barnes' office, carefully sorting through the interview notes in his lap. 'I've got a nose for these things. But could I get him to budge one inch from his story.'

'Clever bugger, I give him that,' said Ted. 'But he's got a temper. Crack that and you'll crack him.'

Willis smiled. He'd enjoy rattling the cage on this one. The arrogant little sod had got right up his nose. 'I'll call him back for questioning tomorrow then, shall I, guv? Put the pressure on.'

'His solicitor won't like that much. Probably try to make a three-act play out of it.'

'Just as long as it's a tragedy as far as Carlton's concerned, I couldn't give a toss,' said Willis. 'I want a result on this one.'

'So do I, Willis,' said Ted, loosening his tie and leaning back in his chair. He closed his eyes wearily. 'So do I.'

Chapter Twenty-two

Leone finished chopping the tomatoes and scraped them off the board on to the chicken browning in the saucepan. The smell of onions and garlic wafted through the kitchen. Chicken *Cacciatore* was one of her father's favourites and this version of Fernanda's was outstanding.

From the room above she could hear the sound of Puccini's *Madame Butterfly*. Maria Callas in full burst. *Un bel di vedremo*. Her father had been closeted in his study since he'd got in just after seven having arrived back with his briefcase bursting with papers. Whatever case he was presiding over this week was obviously going to be a long and tricky one, more than the usual procession of petty criminals and sorry-looking teenagers he'd been dealing with over the past month or so.

She picked up a sprig of basil and began to pull off the leaves, slowly, mechanically. She wanted to sleep, to close her eyes and ears and possibly never wake up. But she couldn't do that. She knew she had to keep going. If she stopped now she'd break down, drown in her own tears like Alice. She'd never known despair like this, not vicious and hard, but slow-seeping, like a thin cold liquid flowing into every crevice of her body.

She forced herself to gather up the parsley and began chopping it finely with the basil, holding the tip of the knife and moving the base across the herbs in quick, sharp cuts. Then she rinsed her hands and gave the chicken a swift stir. She supposed she ought to warn her father that it would all be ready in about fifteen minutes. There was only the pasta to cook.

She turned the hot-plate down a notch and started up the stairs. The study door was open. She could see her father at his desk, sitting, head resting in hands, not moving. She felt a nub of alarm, thinking he was ill, but at the sound of her footsteps, he lifted his head and started to shuffle through the top pile of papers. She wasn't fooled.

'Are you all right?' she asked, coming into the room. She stood in front of his desk, looking down at him. His face was drawn and drained of colour.

He peered over the top of his glasses at her. 'Fine. Why?'

It was typical of a lawyer to throw a question at a question she thought. 'Because you look absolutely whacked, that's why.'

'It's been a long day.' He stretched out and drew a cigarette out of the slim silver case which lay open on the desk top. 'You must be feeling pretty washed out yourself. Have you decided what to do about Steve's exhibition yet?'

She sat herself down in the comfy chair opposite him, legs straight out and drew in a short, sharp breath. 'We're going ahead with it.'

He picked up his lighter and clicked it open. 'Brave of you.'

'We decided that was what Phil would have wanted.'

'Still brave of you. It'll be a hell of an emotional drain. But then you probably know that.' He lit his cigarette, watching the thin smoke rise in wisps past the pool of pale saffron light thrown out by the desk lamp. 'Trying to carry on as normal is the most difficult part of losing someone you care for.'

'There's nothing else you can do, really, is there?'

He gave a half-smile. 'There speaks a strong woman.'

Was she strong? She didn't exactly feel so at this moment.

'You didn't give up after mother. You carried on.'

'As you say, you don't have much choice.'

She watched him tilt back his head and close his eyes. She knew Phil's death was reviving all the memories he had of her mother's death.

'I'm sorry. This probably brings it all back to you, doesn't it?'

'It does rather.' He took a long draw on his cigarette. 'At least you were spared all that,' he said, watching her through the wraiths of smoke. 'You were too young to be aware of any of it, weren't you?'

She could have left it at that, but some inner voice urged her not to hide the truth from him any longer. She needed to be able to share with him some of her fears and doubts. Last night when they'd spoken together about her mother for the first time, she'd felt an enormous sense of release, a lifting of a huge burden from her shoulders. She didn't want to draw back again, to revert to the pattern of secrets, withdrawals and silences.

'Actually, I do remember some things,' she said quietly. 'And sometimes I dream about her leaving that day. She was wearing a blue silk dress…' She hesitated. In her mind's eye she saw that scene again, saw herself standing in the hallway waving her mother goodbye. 'It's odd but I always felt I should have been able to stop her. And that because I didn't I was to blame for her death in some way.'

'You? Why on earth should you believe that?'

'I don't know. Because I have such confused feelings about that night, I presume.' She gave a light shrug. 'Probably nothing more than a child's silliness that just grew out of proportion, I suppose. You see, I always believed she'd died in a car accident. That if only I'd stopped her leaving, delayed her even for five minutes, she would have been in a different place at a different time and wouldn't have died…' Her voice trailed slightly. She looked up. Her father was fiddling with his cigarette lighter in his right hand, tapping and turning it against the polished-wood surface of his desk. His face was rigid, every muscle tight. She knew how difficult this was for him but she couldn't stop. 'Now I know that wasn't true,' she went on quietly. 'There wasn't anything I could have done which would have stopped her leaving that day, was there?'

'No.'

She looked down at her hands. All these years, all that self-destroying guilt. Nothing would have prevented her mother from leaving to meet her lover that afternoon. Nor Margaret Rhodes from seeking her revenge.

People make their own destiny, she saw that now.

Her father took a deep breath, straightening himself in his chair. 'We all felt culpable one way or another, Leone,' he said. He didn't look up. 'You can't imagine what it was like for me at the beginning.'

'I know a little of what you went through. You used to pace,' she said. 'At night. I used to listen to you.'

He gave her a wintry smile. 'Did I? Probably. Those first few days were not easy.'

Leone didn't speak for a moment. She was remembering little things about that evening. Things that she'd pushed from her mind. She felt the old anxieties stir again.

'That first night...' Leone hesitated. 'The night that Mother died, I came downstairs. You were in the sitting-room. Do you remember?'

He stretched out to stub out his cigarette. 'I can't recall very much about that night, I'm afraid. Except that after the police left I drowned my sorrows in a bottle of whisky. The rest is all rather a blur, if the truth be known.'

Leone fingered the material of her jumper. She could feel the tension in her hands. Fragments from the dream flickered through her mind. She knew she couldn't pull back now.

'You were sitting by the piano,' she said, forcing herself to look her father in the eye. 'I stood in the hallway watching you. You were so very, very angry. I remember being rather frightened. I couldn't ever remember your being angry before. You never lost your temper. Ever.'

She paused. He did not respond.

'You were mumbling to yourself,' she went on. 'Saying how you'd warned her. Told her to stop. All the time I thought you were talking about the car accident, that she'd been going too fast, but it wasn't that, was it? You were talking about her affair with Simon Rhodes.'

She watched as her father stood up and went across to the window, edging back the curtain to stare out across the blackness.

'I can't remember,' he replied softly. 'Probably. I warned her not to do something silly. I wasn't sure she was involved with Rhodes, though. Not before Margaret Rhodes rang me to tell me about Julia and her husband. Then everything fell into place.'

'And then you said…' She stopped, feeling all the old tensions returning. She picked at the rose pattern on the arm of the chair. The sound of her fingers scratching at the upholstery was the only noise in the room. The dream seemed to be filling the space around her.

'Go on.'

She stared past the light on the desk to the darkness beyond. She was back in the hallway of their house in north London. She could see her father, sitting on the piano stool, whisky bottle in hand. The bleak, blunt features of his face no longer seemed able to hide the violent rage that burned within him. She heard him say…

She stopped, pushing her hands over her face. She drew in an small unsteady breath and let it out slowly. She had to finish it. Finish it for once and for all.

'And then you called her a whore and said you were glad she was dead. I was so frightened of you. You were raging. You were like a stranger from another world.' She could see him there, weeping into his nicotine-stained hands, an awful harsh, violent sound, his veins swollen and blue at his temples, as if he were suffocating.

Her voice caught a little. Her mouth felt bone dry. 'You said…' She forced herself on. 'You said you were glad she was dead and if Margaret Rhodes hadn't shot them both you would have done it yourself.'

Her father swung back from the window. His face was ashen, but his voice was calm.

'Good God, Leone, why haven't you told me this before?'

She noticed that he didn't deny it. 'Because I buried it,' she said. 'I didn't know how to deal with it.'

Emotional block, Jack had called it. It had been the easiest way to escape, hadn't it? Damage limitation. Yet she hadn't escaped—it had always been there, haunting her, in her dreams.

Her father took a step towards her. 'I had no idea you were aware of anything about that night,' he said. 'You have to understand, Leone, whatever happened that night, I was confused. I didn't know what I was saying. I loved your mother, can't you see? That was why I found her betrayal so difficult to accept.'

She was silent. When parents fought against each other, the only prisoners they took were their children.

'I was so angry with her. So hurt…' He bent down to pick up one of the chess pieces from the board set up on the walnut table by the window, turning it restlessly over in his hand.

But she was no longer listening to his words. Out of the shadows of her mind one last image was emerging. One almost more frightening than any of the others. The last piece of her nightmare.

'You saw me.' Her voice was little more than a whisper.

'What?' He replaced the knight on to the board and looked up at her.

'You saw me standing in the doorway.'

The image became clearer. Her hands were shaking. She pressed them hard together as she felt the panic of old rise up like a shard within her.

'You came across to me and took me by my shoulders. I thought you were coming to comfort me but you didn't. You took me by the shoulders and shook me and shook me. And you told me…'

She couldn't go on. 'Don't you turn out like that fucking bitch of your mother, d'you hear, Leone? Or you'll end up just like her, laid out on some marble slab in a morgue. That's what happens to whores…' She heard again those blurred consonants, heard the drunken poison of his words.

Leone bunched her fingers and pushed them hard against her mouth. Oh God, the terror of it. And all the time he was shaking her, shaking her. She could remember pulling away from him and running up the stairs so fast, afraid he'd come after her. But he didn't. And the next morning when he'd come to her room he was just as he'd always been. Calm and controlled. As if nothing had ever happened, as if it had all been a bad dream, an illusion. She'd convinced herself she'd imagined it. That it had been a terrible dream, nothing more.

'Leone, I can't believe any of this,' her father blurted out. She'd shocked him to the core, she could see that. 'You're confused.'

She gave a violent shake of her head.

She realised now she'd carried the scar of it with her all these years. That her desperate need to please him was borne partially out of that moment too.

Her father was still. His tired face seemed to have aged before her eyes.

'For heaven's sake, child, whatever I thought about your mother, I wouldn't…couldn't have treated you in that way.'

She heard the desperation in his voice. She returned his intense stare. 'You were under terrible strain that night.' she said. 'I do understand that now.'

'But even so…'

He came to her side and stood before her, arms limply by his side. Misery radiated from him, creating an aura of shame and despair. For the first time she saw beyond his immaculate self-control. He had never seemed more vulnerable to her.

'I wouldn't hurt you for the world, Leone, you know that.'

He hesitated for a moment and then he slowly opened his arms and drew her to him.

She couldn't remember the last time he'd held her like this. She knew it was his ultimate plea for forgiveness. She laid her cheek against the curve of his chest, feeling the comfort of his arms around her and gradually all the bewilderment and pain of the past began to fade. Only the love remained.

'Whatever happened that night, it's over and done with. Finished,' she said and was surprised at how calm she felt.

It was as if a great suffocating weight had been lifted from her. She was free now. The dream would never haunt her again.

She'd faced the demons and survived. Her father was no monster, merely a man who had crumbled under the strain and pressure of one terrible night. She could forgive him that small human weakness.

Leone felt him straighten slightly, his arms dropping away from her, the steely self-control coming back into place.

'Finished; I agree. Let's leave it like that, shall we?' There was the merest hint of relief to his voice. 'We can do no good picking over the bones.'

'No.'

He touched her arm briefly, lightly, and then made his way back to his desk.

She watched him settle back down into his chair. He picked up his glasses from where they lay on top of his papers and put them on, back in command of himself.

She walked over to the doorway about to leave him in peace, then hesitated a moment.

'Daddy?' There was just one last thing she needed to know.

He looked up at her questioningly. 'Yes?'

'When Margaret Rhodes rang you, did you have any hint of what she might do?'

He looked surprised at her question but didn't falter, 'I knew she had a gun,' he said. He stretched out and took a cigarette out of its case. 'If that's what you mean.'

'I just wondered if she said something to you, that's all. And if so…'

'Whether I could have stopped her?'

Her father never ducked a point, she had to give him that. She nodded.

He didn't answer at once. He lit his cigarette and took a long, hungry draw at it. Then he looked up at her.

'No,' he said, and his gaze was unflinching. 'Once she'd got it into her head to kill them, I don't believe anyone could have prevented her, least of all me.' He gave her an apology of a smile. 'Does that answer your question?'

'It does, yes.'

So it was over. As her father had said, they'd picked over the bones long enough. It was time to bury the skeletons and move on.

~

Richard crossed to the window and stared unseeingly at the gardens below.

He'd lied, of course. But what else could he have done?

He had to protect Leone from the truth, even now. Besides, he'd only lied by omission, hadn't he? He had said: once Margaret Rhodes had got the idea into her head, no one could have stopped her. And that much had been accurate at least.

He took off his spectacles and began to polish them carefully with his handkerchief. He saw his hands were shaking slightly but he wasn't surprised. If Leone had had her nightmares, so had he. But while she'd been able to exorcise hers, he had not, and they had remained caught like arrows still beneath his flesh. They'd always be there. Just to remind him. His penance.

From downstairs he heard Leone calling out that supper was ready. He folded his handkerchief neatly back into its square and slid it into his pocket.

Sartre had once written a play about hell. Three totally incompatible people being shut in the same room together forever. But he'd got it wrong, hadn't he?

Hell was not about living with other people. It was about living with yourself.

He clicked off the desk lamp, then made his way out of the study.

He wondered why it had taken him years to work that one out.

~

He stood by the window watching the squares of butter yellow light come on in the block of apartments across the road. The flat was very quiet. Still. He liked it that way. Silence had been his friend. As a child he'd learnt that silence was stronger than words. It could insinuate anything. And everything. It had given him power.

He felt a soft brushing movement against his leg and stretched down to stroke the black cat at his feet, feeling its warm softness beneath his fingers. Nearly time now. A few more hours, that was all.

There was a smear of brown paint on the back of his hand and he gave it a swift sharp rub. It looked almost like a birth mark against the whiteness of his skin. How apt, he thought. The mark of his birth. The painter's mark. His father's.

What was it Shylock had said in the *Merchant of Venice*? "And if you wrong us, shall we not revenge?" He'd always liked that part.

He smiled. Time to collect his own debts then. To destroy what Richard Fleming cared for most.

His daughter.

Chapter Twenty-three

The telephone was ringing. Leone finished the last piece of her toast and marmalade and swivelled round to pick up the receiver from the kitchen worktop behind her.

'Leone? It's Steve.'

'Hi.' Leone rested herself against the edge of the table, adjusting the receiver under her chin. 'Everything all right?'

'Slowly getting myself sorted, I guess.'

'Glad to hear it.' He certainly sounded more together, she thought. Both she and Andrew had been more than a little worried about him yesterday.

At the other end of the line, Steve took a deep breath and went on quickly. 'Listen, I've got a favour to ask. I wondered if you were free sometime this morning? I'd really like you to call round at the studio if you've time. I've just got one last picture I want you to look at.'

She picked up her mug and took a sip of Earl Grey. Did he really think it would be possible to squeeze in another picture at this late stage? He must be mad.

'Steve, I hate to tell you this, but you haven't the remotest chance of being able to include anything more into the exhibition now.'

'This isn't a picture for sale.'

'What?' She didn't quite understand. 'Why include it then?'

'It's of Phil.' She heard him take a deep breath. 'It's just...Well, I thought maybe we could have it in the window or in the centre of the room. A sort of tribute. Of course, you may think the idea stinks…'

'No, I don't. I think it's a wonderful idea.'

'Really? You're not just saying that?' She could hear the fragility in his voice.

'Of course not.'

'Then you'll come?'

She was tempted to tell him they'd include the portrait and save herself the journey, but she had a sudden, worrying thought that Steve might have executed the painting in the same oppressive vein as the one she'd seen in his studio with Andrew. She positively refused to have Phil depicted in faecal brown and black.

He must have sensed her hesitation, because he said, 'I know you're busy and it's a lot to ask, but I'd really appreciate your coming.'

Leone pushed a hand through her tangle of hair. Hell, as if she didn't have enough on her plate already. But she could hardly turn him down, could she? Especially if the picture was of Phil. If he'd planned a more emotive pull he couldn't have managed it.

'Look, I'm not sure I can make it this morning, Steve,' she said, trying mentally to juggle her day. 'But I can probably come later on this afternoon. Between five and six?' She was due to meet Jack at seven back at the house but could put him off for an hour or so. She'd have to leave a message for him with Andrew and hope to hell he got it. 'Say six to be on the safe side?'

'Six?' There was the merest hint of hesitation. 'OK. Sure. But I'll be here all afternoon if you find you can come earlier. Just ring.'

'I will.'

'You won't let me down?'

She could hear the tension in his tone. He sounded more like the Steve of yesterday. Balancing on the edge. She hoped to high heaven he'd hold out until the exhibition.

'I'll be there. Promise.'

She made her voice as positive and reassuring as possible. He seemed to be up one minute, down the next. She was willing to bet he hadn't slept a wink for the last two nights. She certainly hadn't.

Phil's death had sparked off a host of memories for Andrew and herself. Leone wasn't sure how she'd cope with going back to the gallery without Phil being there. It seemed impossible to believe that she'd never hear her outrageous stories again, or her deep-throated irrepressible laughter. She knew what Steve must be feeling.

'Listen, Steve,' she said gently. 'Just remember I'm around if you need me, all right?'

She heard him clear his throat. 'Thanks, Leone. I appreciate that. And thanks for agreeing to come.'

'No problem.'

'See you at six, then.'

Leone put down the receiver and glanced at her watch. It was just after eight thirty. If she were going to fit in everything she'd planned to, she'd have to hurry. She was just on her way out of the kitchen when the telephone rang again.

She swore softly, darting back to pick it up, thinking it might be Andrew telling her when he was coming to set out the last part of the gallery with her. But it wasn't—it was Ted Barnes asking for her father. He sounded terribly distracted.

She didn't need to ask him how the inquiry was going.

She could tell by his voice that they'd hit problems.

⌒

'Guv?'

Ted Barnes put down his pen and looked up. DS Varton stood in the doorway, one hand out against the door jamb. He was a thin, wiry fellow who reminded Ted of John Cleese with a greater allowance of hair.

'What can I do for you, then?' he asked. He liked Varton. A bit over-obsessed with paperwork but a no-nonsense sort of fellow. One of those lads who put his head down and got on with a job.

'I thought you ought to see this, sir,' Varton said, as he stepped into Ted's office and handed him a file.

More paperwork Ted thought, but smiled as he took the file from him. He loosened his tie and leant back in his chair. 'Did you do that follow-up I asked for?'

'On Carlton? Yes, guv. I'm afraid his alibis look pretty watertight.' Tighter than a duck's arse, were the exact words of the Inverness police.

'Right.' It was what Ted had expected in truth. But in this game it didn't do to ignore the obvious. Double check and check again, that was his motto. 'And Morenzo?' he asked.

'Nothing, guv. Except…' Warton paused, then stepped forward and with a slight gesture of his head indicated the report he'd just handed Ted. 'I came across that incident report. Might be no connection, of course…'

Ted glanced down at the report.

'Third name.'

Ted ran his finger down the page. One name stood out like a neon light. Mickey Hunt. Ted glanced up.

'Presumably it's the same Mickey Hunt who was involved in the Morenzo case?'

'Yes, sir.'

Ted let out a low whistle. Mickey had been the insider who'd grassed on Morenzo and whose evidence had helped put him behind bars. Morenzo hadn't been able to discover who'd been responsible before he'd been sent down, but he'd always sworn he'd find out and even the score.

And now Mickey Hunt was in hospital in intensive care. Been left for dead, shot apparently, but not before he'd had his feet removed with a chain saw. That sounded more like Morenzo's style.

'When was Hunt taken into Guy's, Varton?' Ted asked, looking up.

'Early Sunday morning, guv. But the attack took place on Saturday night.' Varton shifted his feet. 'He's not talking yet and it's touch and go if he'll pull through. But we have two young homeless lads who were living rough in the warehouse when the attack took place. They were witnesses to the crime.'

'And?'

'Two men seemed to have been involved according to them, sir. And one of the descriptions fits Morenzo almost to a tee.'

'Hell! That changes things.' Ted raised his eyebrows. He'd thought Morenzo had been too clever to become personally involved in reprisals, but he supposed the thug in him had won through in the end. It had always been there, just below the surface, waiting to burst through the thin veneer of sophistication. Ted glanced down at the report again. If Morenzo had been over in Wapping between ten and eleven o'clock on Saturday night, he couldn't have been at the gallery in Portobello. Impossible to make it across London in time. 'Get on to Wapping police straight away, Varton. See if you can interview those two boys.'

'Yes, sir.'

Ted began to feel the adrenaline pump round his body. Thank God they hadn't formally arrested Morenzo for the Hope-Brown murder. They'd been so close to it. He'd have taken them to the cleaners for wrongful arrest and harassment and whatever else his snake-like solicitor could dream up. The only trouble was, if Morenzo and Carlton were both out of the running, where did the investigation go from here?

He had the niggling suspicion that they'd been on a wild goose chase these past few days. The murderer might simply be someone who'd had a grudge against the gallery and the Hope-Brown girl all along rather than a person seeking revenge against Richard Fleming. And yet, there'd been those threatening phone calls to Leone. Was that a separate issue or was everything in some way interlinked?

Go through this step by step, he told himself. 'Who were Richard Fleming's other enemies? Who else had threatened him in the past? Off the top of his head he could think of half a dozen—Joan Catherston and her women's lib supporters for a start—who else?

He shifted his weight a little in his chair and frowned. Only connect. That's what his old boss used to say to him. Only connect.

He closed the file on his desk and stood up, crossing over to the window to stare out across the car park. He felt like Theseus in the labyrinth, boxed in all round with no way out.

But the thread which could lead him out of the maze was there somewhere he knew.

And all he had to do was to find that first thin strand.

～

Leone glanced at her watch. It was only three o'clock and she'd already finished organising the gallery with Janie and was now on her way round London to deliver back the pictures she'd finished restoring. First stop was the Rilkington Gallery to return a Gainsborough portrait.

She'd loved working on that picture. It was one that Gainsborough had done at the start of his career. Even then he'd handled his paint in a confident and fluent way, his paint mixtures highly distinctive. He was so different from his old rival, Reynolds, who concentrated on mass and solid textures: Gainsborough was all evanescence, the flickering light and shadow on a dress. And yet in the end, it was Gainsborough who'd been the one to take such care with his pigments, and Reynolds who'd been notorious for using fugitive colours, some of which—like the organic lake colour—had begun to fade in his paintings during his own lifetime. Hellish to restore, those. Give her a Gainsborough any day.

She turned into one of the narrow streets which ran off Bond Street. Up ahead there was a tangle of cars as a chauffeur-driven Bentley double-parked to let an Armani-suited businessman slip out into one of the galleries. It seemed the art world was ready to take off again, if the latest buzz were anything to go by. Maybe it wouldn't quite reach the dizzy heights of the eighties, but there was the distinct scent of money in the air again. She could almost feel the galleries quivering with excitement. Just ahead of her she saw a parking spot and ignoring the hoots from the cars behind, pulled in and started to turn into the space. With two other pictures still to deliver in the back of the car, she didn't want to park too far away from Rilkington's. Even with a car alarm. She was conscious that there were a good many opportunist thieves out there who wouldn't hesitate to grab what they could.

Rilkington's was just on her right, nestled between a long line of expensive art galleries. She pushed open the heavy glass door and went in. It was a minimalist gallery, very white and empty but dramatic and expertly lit. Only one or two paintings hung on the wall. The Gainsborough seemed terribly out of place. But then, as John Rilkington, the gallery owner, had carefully reiterated several times when he'd handed over the Gainsborough to her, it was a family piece, his father's, not his own. He'd seemed mildly embarrassed about being in possession of such a painting. Not exactly his image.

She wanted to think he had more affection for the piece than he let on, and certainly when she was shown through to his office at the back of the gallery he seemed genuinely pleased to have it back.

He removed it from its bubble-wrapping and held it up to the light. 'Come up well,' he admitted with a grudging smile. 'Background's cleaned up a treat, hasn't it? I'll say this for the fellow, he certainly had a rare feel for the English countryside.'

'One of the best,' Leone agreed, with a quick nod.

She thought it wiser not to tell him that the landscapes he'd so admired were mostly of Gainsborough's own formulation, copied from little models he'd made up himself of moss and pebbles and which he'd set up in his studio. She had the feeling it would only lower him further in Rilkington's eyes and she didn't want that.

She looked up from the painting. Rilkington was saying something about the possibility of several other pictures of his father's which might need restoring. Perhaps he could give her a ring later in the week to have a chat about them?

'Of course.' Leone picked up her keys and bags. 'You've got my number. It's on the invoice.'

She thought she'd get that one in. She had a feeling that smooth talking Rilkington would be one of the slow-paying sort. He looked one of those cheques-in-the-post types.

He held out his hand to her. 'I'll be in touch over the next few days then,' he said. His handshake was soft and squashy—just the sort she'd expected from him.

Leone left him sitting at his large glass and steel desk and came back out into the gallery. The glacially elegant woman at the front desk didn't even lift her head as she passed by. Acknowledgement, she guessed, was reserved for the fat-cat buyers with large chequebooks. The galleries were getting cocky again. A year or so ago they'd been falling over themselves to fawn over anyone who set so much as a toe inside their four walls.

Leone made her way back to her car, checked the pictures in the back and climbed in. It was as she was pulling out that she noticed the blue car behind her. She glanced in the rear-view mirror and frowned: she was sure that the same car had pulled into the side a few paces behind her just after she'd parked by Rilkington's. Now it was with her again, keeping its distance but trailing her all the same. She felt her hands clamp rigidly on to the steering wheel. She must be mistaken. No one would be fool enough to shadow her in broad daylight. They must know she'd spot them. All she had to do was stop the car, get out and confront him.

That's all she had to do.

She found her breath was coming in short sharp breaths.

Do it. Just stop the car and get out.

But even as she started to put her foot down on the brake she saw the blue car swing away from her down Grosvenor Street. She took a deep breath, feeling the clamminess of her hands. She hadn't realised until this moment how frightened she'd been.

She drove slowly off, glancing in the mirror again. Not a sign of the car now. And there was still no sign of it by the time she'd arrived at the Hampstead Gallery half-an-hour later.

She began to wonder if perhaps she'd been mistaken. Perhaps it hadn't been following her at all and she was just being oversensitive and jumpy?

All the same, as she got out of the car and made her way to the Paul Weldon Gallery, she couldn't help wishing Jack was with her.

～

Jack threw the last of his clothes into his bag and glanced quickly round the hotel room. He'd got everything. Just the two books on the bedside table to pack, then he was all set.

He was running late. He'd hoped to be out of the meeting by three o'clock but it had dragged on and he hadn't wanted to rush things. Negotiations were delicate at the best of times. Anyway, he thought, zipping up his bag, he could relax now. The deal was all sewn up and Mr Chiang was now the proud owner of what Jack considered to be one of the finest examples of Cézanne's later works. He might have paid slightly over the odds for it, but what the hell. He couldn't have risked it going to auction, he might never have managed to secure it then, and Chiang had been insistent that he wanted a painting by Cézanne. Jack hadn't argued with him. Cézanne was an important link between the Impressionists and the Cubists—his hard-won innovations, his new way of seeing and recording the world, had prepared the way for painting in the twentieth century—and Jack believed the newly acquired Cézanne would be an invaluable addition to Chiang's collection.

Jack picked his coat up and made his way out to the elevator. Jean-Paul was waiting outside the hotel, ready to give him a lift to the airport. He'd tried to dissuade him, not entirely certain he felt up to another of his hair-raising rides, but Jean-Paul had been insistent and Jack hadn't wished to offend him. After all, he'd done a brilliant job of tracking down such a high-quality Cézanne in the first place. Besides, if anyone could get him to the airport in time for his plane, Jean-Paul would do so. Nothing would deter him.

The elevator arrived and Jack climbed in. There was a gaggle of middle-aged English women jammed inside, obviously on some sort of cultural outing. They were all clutching the same art-information pack and were busily discussing the merits of the Musée d'Orsay in Rue de Lille.

Jack smiled as he listened to their comments. He liked the Musée d'Orsay; in fact, Leone and he had spent several pleasurable hours there on their last visit to Paris. Leone had had very strong ideas about some of the paintings there and wouldn't be swayed.

He pushed his lips tightly together. That was the trouble with Leone. She was pretty intransigent. He wondered how their meeting would go this evening. He felt vaguely apprehensive about it. He supposed he wasn't at all sure what the outcome would be.

What was it the Chinese said? Nothing was certain except uncertainty. He smiled. At least it made life interesting.

⌒

Jack arrived at the check-in desk only to discover that the plane had been delayed by half an hour. He settled himself down in the departure lounge to wait, having sent Jean-Paul on his way. He was now rather glad he was flying into City Airport and not Heathrow. Just half an hour's difference and it would be hell getting into London via the A4 and Hammersmith.

He sat for a moment watching the crowd bustling past, then opened his briefcase and drew out his paperback. It was a thriller set in South America, the latest by Graham Hudson. He usually liked Hudson's novels but the plot on this one was rather thin. He'd already worked out who the mystery blackmailer was, which spoilt the whole intrigue of the book.

He hesitated a moment, then stuffed the Hudson back amongst his papers and took out the Thomas book instead. He'd found it riveting stuff. He'd just reached the section Diane Thomas had contributed, mostly based on case histories. It was fascinating, if a little grim, reading. He could see how art psychotherapy could help the emotionally damaged. Thomas maintained that it was a unique way of approaching the emotionally and mentally disturbed, and was particularly effective in cases where the patient had shown resistance to normal clinical therapy.

To Jack that made immediate sense. To his mind, imagery formed a base experience in personality development. Man thought in images before he had words. The case history Jack was reading now was of a young boy of six who'd been both physically and emotionally abused by his alcoholic mother. He'd sat silently through all other therapy sessions refusing to cooperate but Thomas had managed to encourage him to open up and express his feelings through the use of colour, prompting him to explore the different moods his paintings represented to him.

Jack turned the pages. The drawings the child had done—very Penck-like—were fascinating. As indeed were all those done by Thomas's other patients. Jack flicked through to the next four or five pages, then stopped and turned back a page. There was something awfully familiar about that last one.

He knew that picture. He'd seen it somewhere during the last month or so. The image flickered through his mind, but he couldn't place it.

Jack heard his flight being called and slipped the book back into his briefcase.

No doubt he'd remember where he'd seen it later.

⌒

Ted Barnes picked up the forensics report from the folder on his desk and started to leaf his way through the pages.

It was here somewhere, that thread he was looking for. A murderer always left something of himself behind at the scene of crime. Or took away something. Dust, minute specks of skin, a hair, a fibre of clothing—any of these would help pinpoint the killer.

He clicked open his pen. Go through it again. Check and double-check.

He drew out the pages of the pathologist's statement. Two lines of abrasion and bruising were apparently clearly visible on the Hope-Brown girl's neck. The pattern was consistent with trauma caused by a cord being tied around her neck and seemed to indicate that at some point the girl had managed to break away from her killer before being overpowered again and the cord tightened around her a second time. Which meant what? That the killer was inexperienced in the art of strangulation, or nervous, or maybe not as powerfully built as they had first thought?

Then there was the angle of the ligature marks. They indicated that the killer was four or five inches taller than his victim, say perhaps five foot eleven or so. Good, That tallied with the statement they'd obtained from Ronnie Jacks—except he'd described his attacker as muscular and athletic.

Ted closed his eyes and leaned back in his chair. Read that as young and fit, he thought. Mid-twenties, perhaps. A man whose reflexes were still fast. Maybe works out somewhere. He sat up again and scribbled down a couple of pointers, reminding him to get Varton to check out a few health clubs.

He flicked over a few more pages. Now, place of murder.

Crime squad were pretty certain she'd been killed in the area behind the gallery. There were signs of a scuffle there and one of her earrings had been found behind the dustbins by the back door. But then, as her brother had pointed out, Phil had been carrying in pictures through that way all that day with both Steve and himself, so the earring could possibly have been dislodged at some other time. Ted thought not. A girl would notice a thing like that, wouldn't she?

Of course, it didn't help that they'd been blundering in and out of the gallery with paintings all day. The whole of the courtyard area had been churned over, and worse, the car had been full of particles from the pictures, as well as being covered in dusty footprints and a whole host of different fingerprints. Not just those of Richard Fleming and his daughter, but, thanks to that little removal episode, from Phil, Steve and Andrew, too. It was a forensic nightmare.

He paused for a moment, smoothing out the page before him. Touching on fingerprints, here was something interesting. The killer had not made any attempt to wipe the vehicle clear of prints. Strange that. Sure, he'd worn gloves, but one would have thought he might at least have attempted to wipe down the steering wheel, or the door handle.

So had he had to leave the car quickly? And if so, might someone have seen him abandoning the car? Or had he been so confident he wouldn't leave prints of any kind? Assured that he'd carried out the crime according to plan.

And he had planned it carefully, Ted had to give him that. He'd worn gloves and he'd covered his feet with plastic so he wouldn't leave prints. He'd worn a tracksuit of that bloody awful shiny material which was such hell for the forensics to get fibres from. He knew what he was doing. Methodical, careful and clever, The worst sort of killer to try to catch.

Ted pushed the palm of his hands across his eyes and took a deep breath.

He was tired tonight. Too tired to try to unravel the killer's psyche. Marian had kept him awake all last night worrying about Malcolm. She hadn't liked Kelly, that was the trouble. Too forthright and opinionated, she'd said.

He hadn't minded the girl himself, apart from the appalling short cropped henna-dyed hair and the line of earrings she seemed to have everywhere. And he suspected it was everywhere too. Body piercing, she'd called it, symbolic, she'd said. Of what, he hadn't really been able to gather.

The trouble was he knew Marian still saw Malcolm as her little boy. He was nineteen, for Christ's sake. And yes, he would make mistakes—and possibly Kelly was one of them—but he had to be allowed to make them. What Marian didn't seem to realise was that by trying to throw a protective net around him she only made him all the more determined to struggle free. Into the arms of the likes of Kelly.

Give the lad some space, that's what he said.

There was a tap at his door. He looked up. It was Sergeant Willis after one of his reports. Ted found it in the pile of folders in his in-tray and handed it over. He didn't like to confess that he hadn't really had much of a chance to look at it properly yet. Willis was like Varton, keen as mustard.

Ted lifted his shoulders and stretched. Half an hour more, that's all he'd give himself, he decided, then he'd pack it in for the day. He'd take Marian out to that new Mel Gibson film she was on about seeing and take her mind off Malcolm.

He stood up and made his way out to the coffee machine at the end of the hallway. It smelled of cigarettes and stale pizza but he was past noticing. After years in the force he was immune to such things. He came back into his office and closed the door, shutting off the din of the ringing phones. He took a sip of coffee, his mind drifting back to the Hope-Brown case.

Whoever had murdered the girl was a careful planner, left little to chance. So, more likely than not he'd made a couple of trips down to the gallery to stake out his patch. Probably been inside the gallery, too, if only to get a look at the alarm which he would need to disable. Someone must have seen him, remembered him. He might even have spoken to Phil.

Killers enjoyed taking risks like that. It made it all the more exciting for them. Maybe Janie or Leone would remember something. He'd get Varton on to it in the morning.

Ted yawned wearily, wrote himself a couple of reminders, then started to pack up his desk. There was nothing more he could do tonight. Time to go home.

~

It was as the plane was coming in to land at City Airport that it came to Jack where he'd seen that picture before.

A photograph of it had been in the folder on Phil's desk. He'd seen it on the day she'd disappeared.

Jack had been confused because the reprint in the book had been in black and white and the photograph he'd seen was in its original vibrant colours. He'd missed the connection at first. Now he knew he wasn't mistaken.

He sat very still, momentarily confused. It made no sense. Leone had said that the folder was of Steve Ross's early works. What the hell was Steve doing copying something like that? He must have got it wrong. And yet...

Jack picked up his briefcase from beneath his feet and hastily drew out the book, flicking over the pages until he came to the picture again. No, he was certain it was the same.

He'd only had a brief glimpse at the photos on Phil's desk it was true, but the picture was so distinctive he was positive he was right. He hesitated a moment, then turned over a few pages to the case history of Patient S which tied in with the photograph.

Slowly, he began to scan through the facts. He felt his heart start to slam against his ribs.

It all seemed so chillingly familiar. Lost both parents at the age of ten and had gone to live with a family where he had suffered chronic abuse. Schizophrenic, prone to violent outbursts.

Now *that* he hadn't expected.

He paused, looking down at the picture in front of him. Was it possible Steve Ross and Patient S were one and the same? He couldn't believe it. It could just be some wild coincidence.

He took a deep breath. There was only one way to find out. Somehow he'd have to speak to Diane Thomas. Andrew would have her number. He glanced at his watch. He hoped to God she hadn't left her office yet.

Even before the plane had shuddered to a halt, Jack was out of his seat and shouldering his way towards the exit. Instinct told him there was some connection between Steve and what had happened at the gallery.

And his intuition was seldom wrong.

⌒

Leone came out of the Commerzbank and made her way through the narrow winding lanes. She loved this part of the City. Austin Friars was one of the few small pockets which hadn't been ripped apart.

She went to the underground car park. By coming this late in the day she'd been able to find herself a space. Parking in the City was hell, especially now they had the double police cordon spread round almost as far as St Paul's. If she'd thought about it, she'd have been wiser just to jump in a taxi. But then, of course she'd have been stuck trying to get across to the river in time to get to Steve's.

She glanced at her watch. Nearly half past five. She should be on time for him as long as the traffic didn't build up. She wondered if she should quickly try to ring Andrew to check whether Jack had got her message about running late and then decided against it. She wasn't going to stay long with Steve. A quick look at the picture then away.

It should all run like clockwork.

⌒

Jack shifted his position slightly, still holding on the line for Diane Thomas. He'd used every last ounce of charm and persistence to persuade the secretary of the necessity of his speaking to her boss. 'Strictly not allowed' and 'breaking the rules' had been batted his way several times, but she'd known Phil and that was what had swung it. Eventually, she'd agreed to see if she could catch Mrs Thomas before she left. He didn't dare ring off. He knew if he did, it would be sod's law and he'd miss her.

At last there was a click on the line and he heard the secretary's voice telling him she was about to transfer him.

Jack didn't waste time on preliminaries. He was quick and to the point. He explained about Phil, Ronnie and Leone. And about the picture.

There was a silence. Jack felt his stomach tighten. Silences usually did not bode well in these sort of situations. She was about to dismiss him, politely and firmly. Didn't she realise the seriousness of the situation?

'I'd like to help you, of course,' Diane Thomas was saying in a soothing voice Jack guessed she saved for her more unmanageable patients, 'but you've got to understand the tricky situation I'm in. I must be very careful what I say. Patient confidentiality is vital if we are to build up a patient's trust.'

'I realise that.'

She hesitated slightly, then went on: 'But I can at least tell you two things. Firstly, that the patient mentioned in the book made sufficient progress with me to be able to be referred to a clinical psychologist several years ago. I haven't seen him myself for some time but as of a year ago my records show that he was continuing to make good progress with the help of certain medications.'

'But could something have happened to start him off again?'

'It's a possibility, of course. But doubtful. Anyway, from your point of view the more important issue is that I can assure you that the name of the patient referred to in the book is not Steve Ross.'

'You're not mistaken about that?' Jack spoke before he could stop himself. He'd felt so sure he was right.

'Of course not.' Diane Thomas sounded faintly indignant.

'But the pictures…they were so similar.'

'I have several patients who paint in comparable styles,' Mrs Thomas said. 'Besides, from what you've told me, you only had a quick glance at those photographs.'

'I know I did. But I'm still convinced they're one and the same.'

'Well you're wrong on this one, Mr Thursley. I can assure you my patient is not called Stephen Ross. Although…'

Her voice trailed slightly. He heard the faint whisper of uncertainty.

'Although what?' he prompted cautiously.

There was a slight hesitation. Jack felt his heart begin to race. He had the sense that something had momentarily thrown Diane Thomas. He could hear her flipping through the pages of a file.

'Although, when it comes down to it, I suppose their names are vaguely similar,' she admitted quietly. 'Are you sure you heard his name correctly?'

He chose to ignore that one. 'How similar?' He tried not to push her too hard. He didn't want her closing up on him. 'Mrs Thomas, I *have* to know. You must see how desperate the situation is.'

There was a silence. He thought for a moment she was going to hold out on him, that she was about to give him a long speech about moral obligation, but she didn't. Instead, he heard her take in a deep, long breath.

'This is highly irregular, Mr Thursley.' He knew she was thinking of Phil. Of what had happened to her. He could tell she was weighing up the odds of whether it would weigh more heavily on her conscience to reveal the truth or to withhold it.

'I realise that,' he coaxed, 'but we live in irregular times. I wouldn't ask but I'm absolutely positive there's a connection between the two.'

She hesitated only a second more. When she spoke it was quickly as if by doing so it would lessen her sense of betrayal.

'The name of the patient is not Steve Ross,' she said. 'It's Stephen Rhodes...'

For a moment he nearly missed it.

Then suddenly the full implication of her words hit him.

'Say that again, Mrs Thomas,' he said quietly. 'Slowly.'

And as she repeated the name, a dozen pieces fell into place. Stephen Rhodes. *Rhodes*. It was too much of a coincidence. He had to be connected to Simon and Margaret Rhodes in some way. Their son?

Jack felt his calm start to fragment. He tried to concentrate on all he knew about Steve, all that Leone had told him, but all he could think about was of Margaret Rhodes shooting down her husband and Julia Fleming in cold blood. 'Mentally unstable.' That's how Mary had described her. 'Manic.' And with a terrible gathering sense of fear he knew that Steve was as unbalanced as his mother had been.

He could see now that for some mad, obscure reason of his own, Steve blamed Richard Fleming for the tragedy that had befallen his family, and Hamlet-like was out for revenge.

And somehow Phil must have got in his way.

Steve was dangerous, Jack knew that now. His fingers tightened around the receiver, his mouth suddenly bone dry.

Andrew had said Leone had rung to say she was going to Steve's flat before she came on to meet him later.

And in that moment he knew then that she was in terrible danger.

Chapter Twenty-four

He sat in darkness. He liked the dark: he felt safe in it. When he'd been living with his aunt the only way he'd ever been able to escape the brutality of his uncle was to hide in the cupboard under the stairs. His place of sanctuary. Small, dark, safe. And he'd sat there, hunched up on the floor amongst all the clutter, thin arms wrapped tightly around his knees, head down, hardly daring to breathe while listening to the bastard's stumbling footsteps as he staggered drunkenly through the house shouting for him to come and take his punishment like a man.

Like a man. Oh, God, the irony of it.

Like an animal more like. The savage beatings, the kickings, and the other crimes, that were far, far worse.

But he'd got his revenge in the end, hadn't he?

And now he was about to even the score against the man who'd been responsible for all that had happened.

He pushed his head back against the grey wall behind him, closing his eyes.

Six o'clock and she'd be here.

The curtain was about to go up on the final act. He smiled.

Snip. Snip. Snip.

Leone climbed out of the elevator and walked down the corridor towards Steve's flat. Everything seemed to be going her way tonight. The roads had been clear all the way from the City and she was here with five minutes or so to spare.

She pressed Steve's doorbell and waited. He took a while to answer. When the door swung open he looked faintly dishevelled as if he'd slept all last night in the clothes he stood up in. He looked exhausted. There were great hollows beneath his eyes and his skin was pale and drawn.

And yet, despite that, she noticed that there was an almost tangible air of energy to him. Of anticipation.

The picture, of course. Hell, she hoped she liked it. He didn't look in a strong enough mood to take a rejection.

She followed him through into the studio, expecting to see the portrait of Phil propped up on the easel—pride of place and all that. But she could see at once that the easel was empty. Even the painting he'd been working on yesterday had been removed. She was pleased about that. As far as she'd been concerned it had cast an unbelievably gloomy atmosphere across the place.

She glanced round the room. There was a stack of unfamiliar pictures propped up in several orderly rows against the wall. Presumably Steve had moved them through from the spare room. They looked so carefully arranged, it almost looked like a stage set.

She walked over to them. 'This some of your earlier work?' she asked, bending forward to examine the canvas in front of her.

'My father's, actually,'

'You've kept them all? How fantastic.'

'Some of them.' He stood there looking across at her, hands plunged into the pockets of his jeans. 'There're one or two that I think might interest you. Watercolours.'

'Ah, watercolours.' She smiled, remembering the conversation that they'd had that day at the gallery.

'Take a look. No, not that pile. The one next to it.'

She crouched down so that she could be on an eye-level with the pictures and started to flip through the stack one by one. She was aware of Steve standing behind her, waiting, she supposed, for her comments.

It was strange to think that these delicate sensitive watercolours had been painted by Steve's father. They were so different from Steve's own startling work. He was talented, she would say that for him. He had somehow managed to capture that elusive East Anglian light to perfection.

'They're lovely,' she said, turning her head to look back at Steve. 'He was terribly good, wasn't he?'

He gave her a bleak smile. She couldn't tell exactly what he was thinking. 'I thought so, yes.'

She was almost to the back of the pile when she saw it. She stopped. For a moment she was sure she must be mistaken. But when she drew it out of the stack to examine it more closely, she knew she wasn't. It was a picture of the watermill in Suffolk.

'You're never going to believe this, but I have a sketch my mother did of almost the very same spot,' she said. Lady Carlton had said her cottages were very popular with London artists but she hadn't realised just how much. 'Extraordinary, isn't it?'

She glanced back at him. There was a stillness to him she found a little unnerving. He didn't seem to find the coincidence as fantastic as she did.

'You still haven't fathomed the truth, have you, Leone?' he said.

The edge to his voice unsettled her.

She straightened, the picture still in her hand. Its wooden frame seemed hard and cold against her fingers.

'What do you mean?' she asked. 'I don't understand.'

There was a flicker of bitterness in his dark eyes. 'Turn the picture over, Leone. Tell me what you see.'

She did so. There was some writing on the brown paper which backed the picture, some pencilled initials and a date. June 1978. She looked closer, startled.

She felt her stomach knot into a tight, hard ball as the full realisation hit her. She turned the picture back, glancing down at the right hand corner. *SR.* The initials were thin and faint but still discernible.

'Oh, God.' There could be no mistake.

'You've got there at last, then?' There was a malicious note to Steve's voice. 'Phil was there much quicker than you.'

'Phil? What do you mean?' An icy coldness began to spread through her body.

He ignored her question. 'She nosed around, of course. Took those photos of my early paintings and then when she saw them in that stupid book she'd bought started to ask too many awkward questions.'

'What book? I don't understand?'

'The one by Diane Thomas. You haven't looked at it then?'

'No.'

'Well, Phil did. That was her misfortune. And then she started to dig around in my studio and came across these pictures by my father. She recognised the mill. I suppose you'd shown her the one your mother did.'

'It's on the wall of my sitting-room.'

'Ah yes, you told me that, I seem to remember. Anyway, Phil started to put two and two together. She was too inquisitive by far. She nearly spoiled my plans you know. I had to put a stop to that.'

She felt a crawling sensation on her skin. 'My God! You killed her, didn't you?' The realisation hit her like a punch to the stomach. 'You bastard! You bloody bastard!' Her voice caught in a sob. 'Why, for God's sake? What had she done to deserve that? She loved you.'

'Love!' He gave a hollow laugh. 'She didn't love me. I amused her, that was all.'

'Believe me, she cared for you a great deal.'

'She lied to me, like all the rest. I found her out.' His mouth twisted into a tight, bitter smile. 'Last week when she was supposed to be working late at the gallery, when she'd told me oh-so-innocently that she couldn't see me because she was getting my exhibition ready, I came down to the gallery to surprise her, take her out for a quick drink. But the bitch wasn't there, was she? Off gallivanting at some party or other. She'd lied. I meant nothing to her...*Nothing.*'

The Diane Thomas book launch. The duty call.

'She was at a book launch of a friend of her mother's, for God's sake. The Diane Thomas book, if you really want to know. It had slipped her mind.' So that was why he'd destroyed the picture he'd given her. Slashed it into threads. Because he'd thought she'd betrayed him. 'Whatever you may think, Steve, Phil loved you. And you killed her, you bastard. Murdered her in cold blood.'

'I told you. She got in the way of my plans.'

'And what plans are those?' Though her heart was racing she tried to keep her voice quiet and calm.

'You'll see.'

He stood there, his lips drawn back into a harsh thin line. He radiated a peculiar tension, as if he might be high on something, but she knew he wasn't. He was wrapped up in his own power, his own cleverness.

She gave a quick glance round the room, trying to assess her chances of escaping him. Her bag with the police alarm in it was on top of the kitchen worktop, too far away to get to now. And she'd heard him lock the front door as she'd come in, seen him return the keys to his pocket, so there was little chance of using that route. But what about the balcony? How close were the other flats? Might she be able to scramble across?

She saw he was watching her, his eyes narrowing. 'Look all you want, Leone. There's no way out for you. We're six floors up, in case you've forgotten.' He hooked his foot around the leg of the chair by the table and jerked it towards her. 'So take a pew, why don't you? I have a little story you might want to listen to.'

'I'd rather stand.'

He hit her then. Hard, moving with lightning speed. She hadn't realised how fast he could be. Or how strong. She felt her head snap back with the force of the blow, felt the pain of it spread through her body.

'I told you to bloody sit.'

She sank down on to the chair. It was cold and hard against her spine.

'Put your hands behind your back.'

He yanked her arms violently together behind the back of the chair and then quickly started to tie her wrists. He was pulling the cord so tight it was cutting into her skin.

She winced in pain but didn't dare cry out. She could tell by the look in his eyes that if she did, he'd hit her again.

He fixed his gaze on her. 'Can't have you running off at half-time, can we? Not after all the trouble I went to. It was me, you know, who contacted Lady Carlton about picture conservation. Went to see her and said I was from Christie's. And I sent her a little booklet I'd copied out—"Pick of the Bunch", I think it was called, just to prod her memory. She'd told me about putting the Devis into the exhibition, and it was I who told her it should be cleaned first, just to show it off at its best. I put the idea into her head. I knew she'd contact you. I wanted you to go up there, to start asking questions. I knew your mother had painted the same landscapes as my father. He always marked the paintings on the back—S.R. x 1, J.F. x 1. Rather romantic that, don't you think? You failed to see that, you know, when you looked at the back of the picture. But it was there. A little sign. I didn't miss it. I knew at once what it meant. Julia. I knew that was her name. The Fleming part I found out later.'

She wondered how he had discovered her mother's name was Julia. Had he heard it from his mother or even his father, perhaps? He'd tucked it away like a child with a precious toy, saving it, preserving it.

He had started to pace. She turned her head slightly so that she could watch him. She didn't like it when he went out of her line of vision. It frightened her. She wasn't sure what he might do.

They had fallen into silence. Silence, she sensed, was dangerous.

'So you got me up to Suffolk, Steve,' she said, forcing herself to speak, to re-connect to him in some way. 'You trusted an awful lot to luck though, didn't you? How could you be sure I'd see one of the scenes my mother had painted while she was there with your father? What if I hadn't seen the mill? What if it had been raining and we hadn't walked around the grounds?'

A cold smile sketched his lips. 'Oh, that wasn't my only plan, Leone. I'd set a dozen traps for you. It just so happened this was the first one you fell into. You were so easy to outmanoeuvre. So trusting…'

'And what was supposed to happen up at Suffolk? Was I supposed to find out about my mother's affair with your father?'

'That was a bonus. I just wanted you to see the place. I wanted you to start asking questions.'

'But why?'

'It'll all become clear in a moment.' He crouched down and loosely hobbled her feet together. 'Now, where was I? Oh, yes. As I was saying, I have a little story to tell you. It's about love, betrayal and perfidy.' He was watching her, eyes glittering.

'Go on.'

'It's about a man. An-oh-so-upright man. A pillar of society.' His voice was raw, and she could sense the anger and contempt beneath the calm veneer. 'At least, that's the image he presents to the world. But in reality, he's not this paragon of virtue. He's a cold man. A ruthless man. A man who doesn't like to be crossed.'

'You're talking about my father, I presume?'

'How very perceptive of you.'

'And somehow you blame him for your parents' death, is that it?' She tried to move her position. Her shoulders were stiffening. 'I don't see why. It was your mother who pulled the trigger, after all. Your mother who committed the crime. My father had nothing to do with it.'

'How little you know, Leone.' His face was full of contempt. 'Even as a child, I always believed Henry II was responsible for Beckett's murder despite the fact he didn't bloody his own fingers committing the crime. The same with Queen Elizabeth. The executioner might have wielded the axe but she was the person really to blame for Mary Queen of Scots' death, don't you think? Of course, they were guilty: they instigated the deeds. Simply because you don't strike the mortal blow, doesn't mean you're not responsible for it, you know.'

'You're not making much sense, Steve.'

'It will all become clear in a while.' He sat himself down on the edge of the table, folding his arms across his chest. 'You know, I've enjoyed this little game of cat and mouse. Wasn't expecting to.'

'Gave you power, that's why. Following me. Presumably it was you following me all the while?'

The smile he gave didn't reach his eyes. 'Oh, yes.'

'And today, that was you as well?'

'One last scare. Rather good, wasn't it?'

'But an awful risk. After all that planning, to have been caught at the last minute? It was broad daylight. I nearly stopped the car, you know. I was all ready to confront you.'

'I guessed as much. But think about it, Leone. You viewed me as a friend. If you'd found out it was me sitting in that car, you still wouldn't have seen me as a threat, would you? You didn't perceive me as the enemy you see, did you? Not like your *bête noire*, Piers Carlton. From the beginning you saw him as the villain. So when everything started to go wrong at the gallery you believed he was involved in some way. In fact, you *wanted* it to be him. Just like your father and that Barnes fellow wanted it to be Morenzo. It's all to do with images. False images, of course. And there it seems we've come back to the beginning again. No one is exactly what they appear to be, are they?'

'Probably not.'

He turned away from her and picked up something from the kitchen top behind him. It was a roll of thick black tape.

'Now I think it's time for this, don't you? We've done our chatting after all, haven't we?'

He moved quickly to tape her mouth. There was no hesitation. Every action had been planned, every move deliberate.

She felt herself begin to panic. She could hardly breathe. She tried to tell him the tape was too tight but couldn't move her lips even the minutest fraction. It frightened her. Her mind was telling her mouth to move but it couldn't obey. She felt like a paraplegic telling her limbs to move but getting no response.

It made her chillingly aware of how helpless she was. Of how much she was under his control.

Think, she told herself. Just calm down and think.

There had to be a way out of this. There had to be a chink in Steve's carefully prepared armour somewhere. Know your enemy's weaknesses, her father had always said. What was Steve's?

She watched him as he began to move restlessly about the studio. He seemed more on edge than ever. He went over to the kitchen area again and pulled something out of one of the drawers. She saw its faint but unmistakable glimmer as he drew it out into the light.

A knife.

Oh, Jesus, it was all about to begin.

He was smiling as he came towards her. She tried to wriggle back in her chair, tried to move away from him, but she knew it was hopeless.

'There's no way to escape, Leone,' he said. He held the point of the knife against the flat of his palm as if testing its blade. 'Just as there was no escape for me from my uncle. Do you know what he did to me, day after day . . ?'

He stopped mid-sentence, turning his head slightly away from her, instantly alert. His whole body was rigid, taut as an animal's when it senses danger. He'd heard something, but what? Had by some miracle Jack come? Or Andrew?

There was a silence, then the shrill sound of the doorbell shattered the stillness. Leone felt her heart begin to race as the first stirrings of hope flooded through her. No mistake then. Someone was here. Someone who could help her. She glanced quickly at Steve. He seemed quite untroubled. Did he think he could bluff his way out of this one, too?

But as she watched him make his way towards the front door she suddenly understood why he was so calm. He'd set this up. He'd been expecting someone else to join them from the very first moment.

And she knew who it was, even before she heard Steve open the door and politely welcome her father into the flat.

~

Ted Barnes was just about to drive out of the carpark when he saw Willis, red-faced and out of breath, racing across the tarmac towards him.

'Hold up a minute, guv,' Willis called out. He was gesticulating wildly, looking for all the world as if he were trying to guide a jumbo jet in to land.

Ted wound down the window with a sigh of exasperation. He was running behind schedule as it was. The last thing he wanted was another delay. Marian would never forgive him if he were late and they missed the film.

'We've got a lead on the Hope-Brown case, guv.'

'Serious one?'

'It's a fellow called Jack Thursley, sir. He's a friend of Fleming's daughter. He's pretty sure she's in some sort of danger, sir.'

Ted unbuckled his seat belt. 'And why does he think that?'

'Because he has proof Steve Ross was responsible for the Hope-Brown murder, sir. And Leone Fleming is on her way to Ross's flat right now…'

Ted pushed open his car door, listening as Willis went on: 'Thursley says Ross's real name is Stephen Rhodes, sir. Apparently Rhodes' mother was involved in some double murder case several years back, and there's some connection between those murders and Fleming. Couldn't quite make sense of that bit, sir…'

But Ted Barnes could. The spectre of Margaret Rhodes came back to haunt him again. He'd never forget the appallingness of that night. The shock of finding Julia Fleming's body at Rhodes' studio: bloodstained, naked, half-her head blown away. Oh, the appalling waste of it.

He shook his mind back to the present, to what Willis was saying.

'And that's why Thursley's concerned for her safety, sir.'

'Hell.' Willis's words were like an electric shock jolting him back from a flat-liner. 'Just what we need. Get the fire-arms team on to it straight away, Willis. And you'll need to get hold of Davies, that psychiatrist fellow.'

Ted got out of the car and slammed the door. It was no good. He'd have to stay. No chance of making the Mel Gibson film now. He had a feeling it would be the spare room for him tonight.

He followed Willis back into the building. 'Did Thursley know when Fleming's daughter was due at Ross's flat?' he asked as they took to the stairs.

'Six o'clock, sir.'

Ted glanced at his watch. There might still be time.

∽

It was very quiet in the flat. In the silence Leone could hear every incidental sound, every intake of breath, every soft rustle of clothing, almost every heartbeat. She turned to look at her father. He was sitting across the table from her, slumped in his chair. She could see the beads of perspiration above his lips and there was blood oozing from the corner of his mouth.

She knew he was in pain. Steve had slammed into him hard when he'd tried to struggle with him the moment he'd entered the studio and realised the danger. He hadn't stood a chance, of course. Steve was far too fast and strong for him. He'd overpowered him with very little effort, driving his fists into him, one after another, into the solar plexus, the kidneys, the face.

The violence had seemed to excite him. He was on the alert now, on his toes, as if the savagery had drip-fed him with adrenaline.

She watched him as he paced restlessly in front of them, moving the knife from hand to hand. Backwards and forwards. He was talking again now, very rapidly. Going over the events of the night his parents had died. Accusing her father once more of hypocrisy and sham.

'She wouldn't have done it without you putting her up to do it,' he was saying. 'You were like the bloody serpent ensnaring Eve…'

'You're wrong. I had nothing to do with it,' her father insisted, just as he'd done the first time Steve had thrown his accusations at him. He sat, head in hands, but his voice was very calm, insistent.

'Do you expect me to believe that? I *know* you did. I listened in, for Christ's sake. Don't you understand? I heard it all. I picked up the extension thinking it was my father she was talking to and then I heard you with your silver-tongued lies, on and on at her not to let him get away with it. Why should you be the one to suffer? you said. Why not make him pay for it? He deserves to. Both of them deserve to. If you're going to kill anyone, kill them, not yourself. On and on. You knew just how to pull her into your scheme. Knew just what to say. But then that's your job, isn't it? Persuading people to see things your way, to make certain choices. Doesn't matter what the consequences are, just so long as the results suit you.'

'For heaven's sake, face facts. Your mother was a manic depressive. She snapped. That's all that happened. Your father was leaving her and she couldn't take it. Caved in. Simple.'

'You wanted everyone to believe that, didn't you? So convenient for you. My God! You really don't care for anyone but yourself, do you? No compassion. Were you always as cold as that or have years of dealing with people at their ugliest made you that way? No, you were always like that, weren't you? That's why Julia was leaving you. Couldn't stand it any more…'

He stopped pacing and leant down, pushing his face inches from her father's. His eyes glittered bright and feverish.

'That was it, wasn't it? And your pride couldn't bloody take it. You hated her that night, didn't you? She'd lied to you, she'd betrayed you. And you wanted to destroy her for it. You talk about my mother snapping. But that wasn't it, was it?' He stretched out his hand and jabbed at Fleming with an outstretched finger. 'It was you who snapped that day. You.' Another jab, more forceful this time. 'And you bloody used my mother to do your dirty work for you.'

Steve straightened up and turned to look at Leone. She didn't want to meet his eye. She knew what her face must be showing. The recognition that there amongst all his ranting was a sliver of truth. She'd seen her father that night, witnessed his blind rage. She tried to push her doubts away, but they were gathering, like armed horsemen on the horizon. A threat to her father's version of the past.

She saw Steve's expression change, gradually, as he realised she'd seen a measure of truth in his words. He smiled, the skin drawn tight as a drum across the sharp bones.

'You know, don't you? You know it's not lies…'

She shook her head, violently. But their eyes met and locked.

'You're sick, Stephen.' Her father's harsh voice cut across the stillness like a whiplash. 'You need help.'

'Help?'

'Yes. Just like your mother did.'

'What the hell do you know about it?' Steve swung round.

'You're out of control. You know that. Leone knows that. You've been in and out of psychoanalysis for years. You're delusional. Hysterical. Just like your wretched mother.'

'Shut up, why don't you?' Steve waved the knife in front of her father's face. 'Just shut the fuck up!'

Leone looked at her father. What the hell was he up to? Why was he trying to provoke Steve? Why was he taking that risk?

Then suddenly she understood. He'd done it in court a thousand times. It was an old barrister's trick. Discredit the witness. Make him appear a crackpot and no one will believe his tale.

She felt a sudden chill. There was only one reason he'd need to employ such a ruse. The realisation hit like a sword's swath down Leone's spine.

Oh, God. The thin veneer was being torn apart. It was true, then. Steve's accusations were true.

She could see her father looking at her, pleading with her with his eyes not to believe Steve. But it was too late. She knew. She could feel his guilt like glass shards piercing her skin.

Steve stood there, slowly moving the knife from one hand to the other. His eyes were like black holes.

'So now it's retribution time,' he said. She could sense the violent anger imprisoned behind the hard features of his face. 'I've been planning this moment for a long time. Do you know that?'

Her father said nothing.

'Ever since I heard you on *Question Time* a year ago. Do you know, I'd almost convinced myself I'd imagined that phone call? Or at least my analyst had convinced me. I'd pushed that part of the night out of my mind. Blanked it out. But then, by one of those most extraordinary chances, there I was driving along the M4 flipping my way through the radio stations and suddenly I hear this silver-tongued voice. And I know this voice. It's been there all the time at the back of my mind, hidden. And I had to pull off on to the side of the motorway, I was shaking so hard. There you were, up on your legal high horse about some-thing—capital punishment, I think—and it's like all the years have fallen away in that one split second. And when I get back to London I ring my analyst and try and tell him I've remembered that night. Finally. I have recovered this memory. I tell him about you, and what you did, and he doesn't believe me. Not really. He thinks I'm confused. And I know then that I'm not ever going to convince anyone of your guilt. Who'd believe someone like me? You're an eminent, esteemed judge, for God's sake. And I know you're going to walk away scot-free. Doesn't seem right when you took away my childhood, does it? And I decided there and then that if no one else is going to demand justice, then I shall. I broke with my analyst and started to plan. I didn't care how long it would take me, a year, two years, a life-time, but I knew eventually I'd get even with you...An eye for an eye, that's what this is all about. You took away all those I loved. It seems only fair I should do the same, doesn't it?'

He swung round and caught hold of Leone, gripping his fingers into the long strands of her hair, jerking her head back. She felt fear pushing her to the brink of panic as he pressed the knife to her throat, the blade sharp and cold against her skin.

'Retribution.'

'For God's sake, Steve...' She could hear the anguish in her father's voice, the fear. 'Let her go.'

Steve shot him a last smile. 'You'll have to do better than that. Hardly the magniloquence I was expecting. Try and persuade me not to slit her throat, Fleming. It should be easy. You managed to convince my mother to do your killings for you that night, after all. Can it really be more difficult to do the reverse?'

'Listen to me, please. You'll gain nothing from this.'

'Revenge is sweet. You must have heard that before. And I've had very few things that have been sweet in my life.'

'But why kill her?'

'You mean I should just maim her instead?'

'No!'

The thought seemed to excite him. She could feel the faint quiver of his hands against her skin.

'Now, there's an idea.' Steve moved the knife blade up to Leone's face, tracing it across her cheekbones to her eyes. 'Shall I start here, do you think? An eye? So every time you look upon her and see her blindness you'll think of me and remember? It's a thought, isn't it?' He moved the line of the blade around the edge of the eye and then back to her throat. 'No, maybe not the eye. So where shall the first cut be then? Here?'

He pressed the knife deeper into the soft flesh of her collar-bone. Leone struggled to pull away but he only tightened his grip on her. She felt a sharp rod of pain as the blade pierced her skin, felt the blood starting to ooze.

'Or here?' He jerked her head round holding the knife point against the other side of her neck but this time he didn't puncture the skin. He relaxed his hold a little, lifting his head to look up at Leone's father. 'Tell you what, Fleming. You choose where. That's fair, isn't it? Not her wrists, though. I'm saving those until last. That's how my mother died, you know. After she'd done your dirty work she came back and slit her wrists. But you didn't know that, did you? Bet you didn't even care enough to find out.'

'Listen, Steve, you'll gain nothing by this. Let her go.'

'Oh, no. I can't do that. Vengeance doesn't work that way.' He moved his fingers closer together, tightening his grip on the knife. 'An eye for an eye. Remember?'

Ahead the whole street seemed to have been cordoned off. Blue and white tape was everywhere. Jack got out of the taxi, his heart pounding.

'Mind how you go now,' said the driver, taking the hand-ful of money Jack had thrust towards him. 'Looks like a bomb scare ahead.'

But it wasn't. Jack knew that. He glanced at his watch. Twenty minutes since his phone call to Ted Barnes. The police already seemed to be in position, at least that was something. He pushed his way through the gaggle of onlookers crowding about the blue and white tape. He could see a group of policemen gathered just in front of the entrance to the building.

Just let her be safe.

On the way here he'd made a pact with himself. Just let her be safe and I'll not interfere with the way she wants to run her life. I'll even put up with her sod of a father. He didn't want to lose her, he wanted to be with her whatever the price. He knew now he was prepared to accept her on her terms, not his, and if that meant having to return to England then he would. For God's sake, he'd been prepared to do that for Isabel and he'd never felt anything like this for her; hadn't felt this intense love, this desperate longing beyond explanation.

Ahead he could see the stocky frame of Ted Barnes in the centre of the group of police. He ducked under the line of tape, ignoring the shouts from the young fresh-faced policeman sta-tioned fifty yards down the street.

He couldn't wait. He had to know what was happening.

Ted saw him through the crowd and came across to his side. He tried to reassure him that everything was under control but Jack knew that until he saw that Leone was out of the flat and safe nothing would placate him. It was then that Ted told him that Leone wasn't alone in the flat with Steve.

'Her father joined her just after six,' he said. They'd found Fleming's driver waiting for him outside the flats. He had no idea that his employer had walked into a trap. He'd been under the impression Fleming was merely meeting up with his daughter. Fleming had had a message, apparently from Leone, to meet him at the flats. Another trick of Ross's, he supposed. 'Our main hope now is that he might be able to calm Steve Ross down in some way. Persuade him to give himself up,' Ted said.

'And do you think he will?'

'Hard to know what's going on up there,' Ted admitted. 'But yes, sometimes they can be persuaded to see sense.' Anyway, at least the fire-arms team were in position and the police psychological negotiator, Davies, was expected to arrive at any moment.

Jack glanced around. Through the darkness up on the roof of the building opposite, he could see the silhouette of a marksman. There was one on this building as well.

'How long will that take?' Jack asked. Every minute counted. He felt he'd been handed a grenade with the pin out.

'Depends on how easy it is to gain access,' said Ted. He broke off to turn to a young policeman who'd appeared by at his side.

'There's been a development, guv,' said the constable with a quick nod towards Steve's building.

'What?'

'Movement inside the flat.' There was a burbled message on his personal radio. He picked it up and answered it, said a few words and turned back to Ted. 'Steve Ross appears to have come out on to the balcony, sir.'

'Can the marksman take him out?'

'No, sir. They haven't got a clear line of vision. He has someone with him.'

'Fleming?'

'No, sir.' The policeman didn't look at Jack. 'The girl.'

⌒

It was very cold out on the balcony. Leone felt the wind biting into her cheeks. She could feel the warmth from Steve's body, as he pulled her tight against him, holding the knife against her throat. She could hear his breathing. It seemed to have synchronised with her own.

Her body was shaking, but not with the cold. She was terribly afraid. Because of the tape across her mouth she couldn't even try to reason with Steve, to plead, or beg. Her father had only seemed to antagonise him still further. The police sirens hadn't helped.

Steve had become very agitated when he'd heard them. He'd gone to look out of the window, peering down into the courtyard below. The police had kept well away from view, of course, but Steve knew they were there because of the knot of onlookers beginning to gather in the street. He'd paced back and forth for several minutes, like a restless caged panther, and then quite suddenly he'd told her to stand up, dragging her arms over the back of the chair, and had hauled her out on to the balcony.

She had remembered him saying when she'd last been here with Andrew—God, was that really only twenty-four hours ago?—that it wasn't terribly safe out there, and she'd tried to struggle against him. But he'd been too strong for her, hampered as she was with her feet and hands tied. The only thing she felt grateful for was the fact that heights had never worried her. She had a feeling they disturbed Steve far more.

He'd stood in the doorway that led to the balcony and had said, 'Do you want me to let her go, Fleming? Do you? Then all you have to do is to tell the truth for once in your life. Tell the truth about that night.'

'I have only told the truth...'

'Shit! Don't you ever learn?' Steve had yanked Leone back by her hair, pulling her another step towards the edge of the balcony. 'Do you really care so little about your daughter's life?'

'I know you're convinced I drove your mother to commit those murders, but I assure you, you're wrong. What you heard must have been out of context...'

'Don't give me that crap!' Steve shouted. 'I told you, Fleming, I want the truth. I want to hear you admit responsibility for my father's death—for Leone's mother's death too—and then I'll let her go.'

'How do I know you will?'

'You have to trust me.'

'So all I have to do is say that it was my fault and you'll let her go?'

'Something like that.'

'All right then. It was my fault.'

'Not like that. I want you to look into your daughter's eyes and tell her you wanted her mother dead that day. That you were too much of a fucking coward to kill her yourself so you used my mother, my poor, bloody, mentally unstable mother, to do your dirty work for you.'

'For God's sake, Steve.'

Leone felt Steve stiffen. He pulled her back another step on to the balcony.

'I'm warning you, Fleming. She'll go over the edge of the parapet.'

'All right. All right.'

'Say it, you shit.'

'It was my fault.'

'Look at Leone, damn you. Tell her you killed her mother.'

'I…'

'Say it.'

'I killed your mother.'

'Again! Louder!'

'I killed your mother.' His voice was choking, he could hardly speak.

Leone swallowed hard and closed her eyes. She couldn't look at him. This deep, desperate feeling of betrayal was tearing her apart. She couldn't bear it. The lies. The secrets. All stripped bare.

She saw now the wall of silence he'd set up had not been for her protection at all, but for *his*. To prevent any chance of his contemptible part in her mother's death being revealed. And he'd never once tried to ease her feeling of guilt about her mother's death. He'd known about it, she knew that now. He'd known how it burdened her and he'd played on it, used it to his advantage. He was a cold, manipulating puppet master. And she'd been too blind to see that he had used the past to keep control over her, to keep her with him.

She felt Steve relax his grip on her slightly, as if his arms were leaden now. He was like a long-distance runner coming up to the final marker. He'd achieved part of what he'd been aiming for, that confession squeezed out of her father.

Steve straightened a little, looking past her to where her father sat in the half-light.

'Strange. I thought that would be enough. But it isn't. Not for all those years of torture I had to suffer with my bloody uncle.'

'I'll do anything you want. Name it. Anything. But let Leone go.'

'No.'

They were at the very edge now. Leone could feel the gust of wind in her hair. She could feel Steve shaking, feel the tense undercurrent of pent-up energy.

'The police have the building surrounded. You won't get away with it.'

'Like you did, you mean? That's was all you were worried about, wasn't it? And you managed it. Even kept your wife's name out of the, public eye when the murder first hit the papers, didn't you? And who organised that for you? Ted Barnes? See, I know all about that. The collusion. A favour for a favour. What did you tell him? That it was to protect Julia's reputation or to shield your poor young child?' His voice was harsh, his mouth drawn back into a sneer. 'And by the time he couldn't keep it from the press any longer it was old news and didn't matter so much, did it? A couple of lines lost at the back of the paper. Didn't you wonder why I dumped Phil's body in Mill Hill? Didn't you decipher my message? It was as close to the spot where my father died as possible. Close to where it all began. But you missed that, didn't you? So now…' He put his hand down to the low balcony and gave the railing a shake. 'See how flimsy this is…'

He reached over and ripped off the tape across Leone's mouth.

'Do you want to say farewell to your father? Any last words? No?'

She swallowed hard, struggling to find her voice. 'Only to you, Steve. Tell me, has it really been worth it?' she said at last. 'Phil loved you, you know. You might have made something of it together. But you killed her just for this one moment of revenge. I want to know if it was really worth destroying everything for *this*? Is that your kind of justice?'

His fox-like eyes were bright with feverish intensity. 'I had no choice,' he insisted quietly. 'I didn't care what it cost. I couldn't let his actions go unpunished. He should have died that day with the others.'

She took a long, unsteady breath. 'Sometimes,' she said, 'the worst that can happen to a man isn't to die but to live with the consequences of what he's done. Natural justice, Steve. Far more terrible than that meted out by man.'

He was holding her very close. His extreme stillness made her scalp prickle. She could feel his heartbeat. She tensed every muscle, expecting him to make a sudden rush at her.

But instead she heard his voice instructing her to turn round.

'Look at me, Leone,' he said, his voice little more than a whisper.

She turned then, her mouth bone dry. There was a finality to his words which made her skin feel numb. His eyes met hers, dark and intense. She saw that his expression had changed, that the anger seemed to have drained out of his face. His sculptured features seemed almost angelic.

'You do know I was speaking the truth, don't you? I can see it in your eyes,' he said softly, insistently. His hands dropped to his side. He smiled. 'A kind of justice in itself, that. He'll have to live with the knowledge of that forever, won't he? No lies will save him this time. *You know.* He can't escape that, can he? How ironic. It's not killing you that will cause him the most pain, is it? It's allowing you to live…'

There was a breath of movement on the adjacent balcony, a shifting of the shadows. Leone could just make out dim outlines of two police marksmen crouching down in the semi-darkness against the railings. She saw Steve's head jerk round. She knew he'd seen that movement too, knew he realised he was in their sights and that there was no way out for him, no escape. She stumbled back from him, tensing herself, knowing that he would make a grab for her, bring her in front of him to act as a shield. But he didn't. There was a silent message in his bone-white features. He had extracted his revenge. He knew he had annihilated Leone's unquestioning love for her father. And he knew that by destroying that he had struck a mortal blow against the man himself.

He stood for a long moment looking straight into Leone's eyes and then slowly, deliberately, he took a step back. He didn't struggle. He didn't fight. He just stepped over the low balcony into space.

The last thing she saw was his smile. It looked almost peaceful.

And then there was nothing. Just a huge chasm of space and silence.

⌒

'Darling, you must believe me, what I told Steve Ross was a lie. I only said it to save you from him. You can see that, can't you?'

Leone was sitting on the cold concrete base of the balcony with her back against the exterior wall of the flat. She'd heard her father edging his way across the studio towards her, but she made no move to go back in. She didn't want to be near him just yet. She needed time to think. She felt so tired, so desperately tired.

'It wasn't true, any of it. Leone, believe me...'

'Don't, Father. You and I both know what happened that night.'

He'd distorted the truth, bent it with his lies.

'Darling, you surely can't believe Ross's word against mine. He was sick, very sick, you know that.'

'Just leave me alone for a moment or two. Please.'

She could hear his breathing as he stood just the other side of the French windows. It was heavy and laboured. But she didn't attempt to go to him. He had laid waste so many lives. She didn't feel ready to cope with the terrible wreckage he'd left behind.

She craved for peace. She wanted to get away. Far, far away.

There was a confusion of noise as the police ran up the flat stairs, the splintering sound of wood as they broke into the flat, the sound of heavy boots running over the polished wooden floor of the studio. Someone was asking if she were all right. Someone was helping her to her feet.

And then, through all the confusion and noise, she heard Jack's voice. He was standing in the centre of the room, the light from the lamp behind him making his tense face appear white and sculptured.

'Jack!'

'Oh, God, Leone, I thought he'd kill you.' His voice was shaking with emotion. He took off his coat and wrapped it around her. 'I thought I'd lost you for good.'

She closed her eyes, resting her head against his shoulder, breathing in the smell of him, feeling the safety of his arms around her. She needed his strength at this moment, needed to know that in amongst the shattered ruins of her world there was something still that was untainted.

'I'm never going to let you out of my sight again, do you hear?' he said, pulling her more tightly into the circle of his arms. 'Nothing like this will ever harm you again.'

She looked up into his deep, serious eyes. She believed him. Jack would always be there for her; he wouldn't fail her.

He pressed the palm of his hand against her face. 'Are you all right? He didn't hurt you in any way?'

She shook her head. 'No.' At least not in the sense that Jack meant.

His fingers gently moved to the gash on her neck where Steve Ross's knife had sliced open the skin. 'I think we should get this checked over all the same. There's an ambulance on its way. You and your father…'

'I don't want to go with my father.'

She spoke more abruptly than she'd intended. She saw Jack's surprise.

'I just don't want to be with him at the moment, that's all.'

He pushed her hair gently back from her face. 'What happened back there?' he asked gently. 'What did Steve tell you?'

'Just a few home truths.'

'About your mother's death?'

'Yes.'

He didn't ask anything more. Her face told him all he needed to know.

His hands slid protectively across her shoulders. 'Shall I get you away from here then? Shall I take you home?'

'Home?' The irony of his words hit her. She let out a small, trembling laugh. 'I don't even know where home is any more, Jack.'

'It's with me, Leone. With me.'

He made it sound so simple, so effortless. She felt a nub of emotion catch in her throat and stepped back from him a little. She could see he was looking down at her, half-smiling.

'Is that what you want, Jack? Truly? It's not just because of what's happened here today?' Her face tightened a little, hope gathering fright.

'It's what I want, Leone. Only I was too bloody stubborn to see it.'

'And are we up to it, do you think?' she asked.

'We owe it to ourselves at least to try, don't we?'

She gave a quick sharp nod. This time they would nurture their love, treasure it. They knew how precarious happiness was and how suddenly it could all slip away from them; they had seen life's fragility.

She took his hand feeling his fingers curl about hers.

'Are you ready to go?' he asked quietly.

'Yes.' She lifted her eyes up to his. His gaze was very clear and steady. She knew he was willing her to have faith, to trust in him, to take a chance. 'Yes, I'm ready.'

From the little knot of people by the door a figure disentangled itself and walked slowly towards her.

'Leone, you have to listen…' Even now her father's voice had not lost its edge of insistence. 'I can explain everything…'

She kept on walking. She was not ready to forgive him. One day, perhaps, when the pain of it all had faded. But not now.

She had lost too much. She could still smell the scent of lilies, hear her mother's soft voice whispering 'Love you, Little Bear' as she bent to kiss her goodbye, feel her gentle touch.

'Leone, for God's sake stop and listen…'

There was a hint of desperation to his tone. Could he foresee the loneliness that lay ahead, the empty bleakness?

She felt Jack tighten his grip on her hand and together they walked out of the dark shadows down towards the courtyard below.

She didn't look back. Behind her was only the past.

And now she was free of that.

Free of that forever.

COMING FEBRUARY 2004

PRIMITIVE SECRETS
A HAWAIIAN MYSTERY
by Deborah Turrell Atkinson
ISBN: 0-7434-8000-7

When Storm Kayama walks into her lucrative Honolulu law firm one morning, she's shocked—and grieved—to find her adopted uncle at her desk, stiff and cold. As questions surround her uncle's death and her adopted family begins to close ranks, Storm suspects that he has been murdered.

Heading to the Big Island to relieve some of the pressure from the murder, she narrowly escapes a terrible accident and takes refuge in the home of her Aunt Maile, a traditional Hawaiian healer.

As Storm struggles to heal her own childhood wounds and bring justice to her uncle's killer, she must also come to grips with the rifts in her own life

FLASH FLOOD
THE FIRST DAN MAHONEY MYSTERY
by Susan Slater
ISBN: 0-7434-7959-9

Dan Mahoney, insurance investigator, lands in Tatum, New Mexico, where several prize cattle on the famed Double Horeshoe Ranch have mysteriously died. The claims put a lot of money at stake for Dan's company, but that just scratches the surface of the hijinks—and high stakes—afoot in Tatum. And Dan hadn't counted on witnessing a murder, falling in love, or becoming a pawn of federal agents.

It's the flash flood that changes everything, as Dan stumbles across secrets that implicate his employer, his sister, and what seems like half of southern New Mexico. Sucked into small town duplicity, he struggles with truth and learns that dead men can come back to haunt.

To receive a catalog of other Poisoned Pen Press titles,
please contact us in one of the following ways:

Phone: 1-800-421-3976
Facsimile: 1-480-949-1707
Email: info@poisonedpenpress.com
Website: www.poisonedpenpress.com

Poisoned Pen Press
6962 E. First Ave. Ste. 103
Scottsdale, AZ 85251